Carol Thurston has been a newspaper reporter, political speech writer and university professor. Born in Chicago, she has also lived in France and Germany, and now resides deep in the heart of the Texas Hill Country that she describes in *Flair*.

Carol Thurston

FLAIR

Pan Books
London, Sydney and Auckland

First published in Great Britain 1987 by Judy Piatkus Ltd
This edition published 1989 by Pan Books Ltd, Cavaye Place,
London SW10 9PG
9 8 7 6 5 4 3 2 1

ISBN 0 330 30599 9

Printed and bound in Great Britain by
Courier International Ltd, Tiptree, Essex

Chapter 1

THE SUN WAS barely clearing the horizon when she got off the train at Vernon and walked across the bridge to Vernonnet, the town's little sister on the opposite bank of the Seine. A short way into the village, she came to still another single track, this one paralleling the road to Gasny, and almost unthinkingly she turned to the right, following the road out into the country, toward Giverny. It was little more than a mile or so to where she was going, and she kept up a quick pace, glancing off in the distance to her right from time to time to reassure herself that the mist was still rising from the bed of the river. She'd never been able to get out here so early before, but this time she was determined to see it as *he* had when he'd first set out every morning.

Some Europeans were still on holiday in September, since most schools didn't begin here as early as they did back home, but at least the crowds of July and August should be gone. Only a few cars had passed her so far, and though she knew it was still too early to tell, she was hoping the place wouldn't be inundated with tourists as the day wore on. She needed the quiet of solitude if she was going to find what she'd come for.

It wasn't long until she spied the small stream that peeled away from the Seine to string along beside the meandering road, which meant she was already more than halfway there. A small branching of the Ru River, it curved around the edge of the tiny village ahead, and it was this stream that he'd diverted to flow through the lower garden to create the lily pond.

She could have found her way even in the dark, she realized, as she finally sighted the signpost at the head of the main road into Giverny, so familiar had it all become to her over the past few years. Her stride quickened, and within minutes she was there, searching eagerly between the narrow strips of wood set into the high plastered wall for a first glimpse of the patchwork of color she knew was just behind it. Rushing to a quick stop between the gateposts marking the entrance, she stood gazing down the wide gravel path toward the long two-story pink house, breathless as much from the view as from the fast walk. An entryway fit for a castle and a king, which is just what he'd become during those years here at Giverny. Framed overhead with crimson roses climbing across curving trellises, the wide path was edged down both sides with the oranges, yellows, pinks and reds of creeping nasturtiums, dahlias and delphiniums.

She drew in a deep breath, savoring the potpourri of aromas the sun was already beginning to coax from each bloom, and shivered in anticipation of the sensual fragrance she knew would saturate the air by midday. Suddenly she did an about-face and crossed over the small railroad trestle on the far side of the rue Claude Monet, sparing the serpentine lily pond only a quick glance—she would have plenty of time for that later—then jumped the brook and headed off through the meadow.

It took no more than a few minutes to reach the branch of the Epte, which emptied into the Seine, then follow it to the juncture of the two rivers. Back then, there had been several small islands here, and it was on the tiny Île aux Orties that he'd moored the larger boat. Loaded with canvases ready for the day's work, it served as a floating studio, providing the distance and perspective he needed to view the landscape under the cool morning sun as it crested the wide arc of wooded hills behind him, along the far bank of the river. Unfortunately, the islands were gone now, victims of modern dredging operations to clear and deepen the channel. Folding her legs under her, she dropped slowly to the still-moist grass covering the sloping bank, content to watch the billowing clouds of mist take one shape and then another before dispersing into nothingness. Soaking up the scene spread out before her, recording the play of light, shadow and color as surely as the sharpest camera lens, she stored it all away for future use.

A slight movement caught at the very edge of her vision, drawing her attention there, and she spied a small boat, floating so slowly it seemed hardly to be moving at all. As if arranged by some unseen hand with an eye for both contrast and balance, the scene was a natural still-life, with the white-haired old man in the boat sitting just off center. Probably out for an early morning catch, she thought idly, watching the hills behind the boat gradually change shape as it drifted with the current. Monet's boat had probably looked just about like that one, with both squared-off ends rising from the water in perfect symmetry. She turned to look back in the direction she'd come, at the meadow beginning to tip gold, and at the orchard and garden spread out under the white morning light, just as Monet must have seen them from his floating easel in the river. How she envied that old man the view he had. What a waste! Even if he *was* one of the few to whom color spoke, which she very much doubted, at his age his eyes had probably long since gone clouded and rheumy!

She spent a languid hour or more there along the bank of the river, never even thinking to glance at her watch, then wandered slowly back toward the garden of the lily pond. The rose trees and African lilies were still blooming, though the peonies and irises of spring, her favorites, were long gone, as were the blooms of the wisteria vine that almost hid the graceful lines of the Japanese footbridge. The sun was higher now, warming even this cool, green grotto framed by tall old willows weeping shamelessly into the water.

Sumacs near the edge of the pond were just beginning to get flaming red ideas, and she could hear the tall poplars rustling dryly in the gentle breeze, foreshadowing their timeless destiny. Corollas of rose, blue and yellow water lilies floated serenely on the surface of the pond, their flat, round pontoons like huge drops of dark green oil spreading out in search of some predetermined stasis.

She was at the far end of the pond when she caught another glimpse of white hair, this time moving slowly along the path toward the railroad trestle and road, and she wondered momentarily if it could be the same old man she'd seen in the boat. More likely, it was one of the five or six gardeners it took to keep the place.

At length, she worked her way back toward the house across the road, anticipating the bronzed hues of midday. She'd left the house garden till last on purpose, so the sun would be high enough to saturate the colors to an intensity so exquisite it brought something akin to pain to the fully open, vulnerable eye. She pictured the willow bench with its curving back set in the shade of the lime trees, where she planned to sit and simply "steep" herself in color. But first she would wander the paths, among the lemony snapdragons and mauve asters, the blood-red dahlias and the pinks and marigolds, the purple clematis and blue morning glories.

Nearly an hour later, sated at last, she found the willow bench just where it had been the last time she was here, and she sat down to quietly reflect on the colors and textures spread out all around her. It was almost too much, this intensity of color that was everywhere without relief, and she was beginning to yearn for the sight of something pale and quiet, something to cool—

"Il est beaucoup de . . . uh, est trop . . . trop cher, n'est-ce pas?"

The voice came from just behind her left shoulder. Startled at first to hear her own silent musings spoken aloud, especially when she hadn't seen anyone around for more than an hour, she had to squelch a threatening smile. It didn't take hearing him stumble over how to say "too much" to know he was an American—it was obvious from the moment he'd opened his mouth. She sort of absently wondered who he might be talking to, but resisted the impulse to look around.

Not to speak to the girl he'd been catching glimpses of on and off all morning was unthinkable to Ross McCutcheon. The two seemed to have the place all to themselves, a happenstance that created a sense of identity, even intimacy, as if they were co-conspirators. That she might not be French never crossed his mind, either. No matter the age, all Frenchwomen seemed to have that certain something everyone talked about but couldn't quite put a name to. He'd about decided it was in their genes, and the closest he could come to describing it was, to put it simply, a powerful sense of being female. He glanced down across her shoulder to her crossed ankles, at feet unconcernedly bare in dusty, rope-soled espadrilles, mentally confirming that whatever it was, it didn't seem to have much to do with how much money they spent on clothes. This trip had caused him some real regret over his lack of proficiency in their language, but if she was the schoolgirl she looked to be, perhaps she'd be more tolerant of his halting efforts than he'd found most of her countrywomen willing to be.

"How do you suppose he ever got up the nerve to try to compete with this?" he tried again, in the best French he could put together, giving it a helping hand by sweeping his arm out to indicate the garden. "Was it courage or arrogance, do you think, mademoiselle?"

She only realized he was speaking to her when he rounded the end of the bench, then dropped down beside her. The pleasure of knowing that here was someone else who understood the challenge the painter had faced brought a smile to her lips and eyes.

"Courage, I'd say," she began, responding almost automatically in his language as she turned to glance at him. But her smile froze in confusion as conflicting impressions buffeted her already saturated senses. *The white-haired old man!* Then she almost burst out laughing as she got a really good look at the man sitting only a few inches away. His hair might be white, all right, but everything else was all wrong.

Without warning, he stuck his hand out toward her. "Hi. I'm Ross McCutcheon." His smile hit her with the force of a bright light. Sitting slightly slouched, with his sport coat wrapped over one arm and tie pulled crookedly loose, he appeared deceptively relaxed, even as he radiated a sort of vibrant energy.

"Julia Bonner," she offered back, smiling straight into eyes level with her own. The hand that gripped hers so firmly was big and warm, and the palm was slightly rough, but the eyes were like none she'd ever seen—so light and cold a blue they made her think of ice, yet they burned with a depth and intensity that locked her gaze to his. They were like cool sapphires, set in the warm gold of his tanned, square-jawed face.

Ross stared as he clasped her hand, caught in the enigmatic smile he saw on her face. This was no damn schoolgirl, no matter the braided pigtail or how she might be dressed! Hell, he should have known that, just from the stillness, the way she was sitting when he'd come upon her. None of the school kids he'd ever been around seemed able to manage that—they were always in some kind of motion, jiggling a foot or cracking their knuckles. Then it suddenly dawned on him that she'd answered him in English! And while there was something vaguely odd-sounding about it, it was definitely American! He found himself struggling again, but this time to find some safe footing among the fragments of his shattered assumptions.

"Courage, huh?" he asked, hoping she would speak again so he could place that slightly sibilant slide into the "s" sound.

She nodded. "And dogged determination." Julia couldn't keep her eyes off him, from feeding on the color of him. She smiled, slightly embarrassed, then looked away to collect her thoughts and begin again. "I choose courage over arrogance because I think he was on the trail of something, that he had a vision in his head—at least during those last years here. It became a kind of Lorelei, a seductress, if you will."

"You mean the paintings he did as a series? The same subject over and over under different conditions of light and atmosphere?"

She looked thoughtful for a moment. "In a way."

Ross waited, somehow sure that she was simply puzzling over how to explain what she meant. His eyes roamed the lively black hair, too curly to lie smoothly no matter how hard her effort, pulled up high in the back before being plaited into a rope nearly as thick as the mooring hawser of an oceangoing ship. And the long curving line of her neck framed by delicate wisps of hair that escaped the braid.

But he was wrong. Julia was off on another track entirely, wondering how a man with such dramatic coloring could be so unconcerned about his clothes. A scruffy brown tweed sport coat that needed a good steaming. And look at that shirt, so spectacularly wrinkled, he might well have spent the night in it! The idea stirred something on the periphery of her consciousness, and suddenly she blurted out, "You *were* the one! Down there in the boat, on the river, weren't you? Early this morning?"

He grinned and nodded slowly. "I'm familiar with the paintings he did from out there. Was that why you were—you *were* the schoolgirl lolling on the bank, weren't you? The one watching the old man in the boat?"

She didn't even try to hold back the giggle that bubbled up and out, and then they were laughing together, at themselves and each other.

"What was Monet's Lorelei?" he asked when he was able to speak again. "I thought the series paintings were simply his way of enhancing reality—by showing the passing of time."

"In the beginning, perhaps, with the haystacks. Don't misunderstand me, I don't mean that the series paintings aren't beautiful in themselves. But actually I suspect that was simply his way of getting somewhere else, working with the effects of colored light. And he probably got onto that from—well, he *had* been to London, don't forget." But that was way off the track, she realized. "Where he was headed all along, I think, finally emerged in those last paintings of the lily pond, the ones where the horizon disappeared." She glanced at him. "You know the ones I mean?"

Ross nodded, not wanting to interrupt. He watched the flush of color rise in her neck and cheeks, and her face grow increasingly animated as she reached the point she was trying to make.

"He finally penetrated the picture plane, don't you see?" she went on. "The viewer enters the painting, is completely surrounded by, immersed in, color. In sensation. *Pure* sensation, like music."

"Ah-ha!" he pounced gleefully, as if he'd caught her in some childish misdemeanor. "You dare refute the wisdom of the academics, do you? Monet, of all the Impressionists, they say, never developed intellectually as an artist. Isn't that right—that he stayed stuck in the superficiality of the impression?" He leaned close and touched her arm as he spoke. It was quick and light, almost a caress, and she could tell from just that one gesture that he was a toucher. But it was natural to him, not contrived, or an attempt to "come on" to her.

"Hogwash!" she spluttered, scowling melodramatically, mostly for his benefit, while she watched his mobile face. Thoroughly bemused by this mysterious American who quite obviously understood exactly what she was trying to say, in a sudden flash of insight she recognized in him the charisma and instincts of a natural politician. What, and who, could he be? "What do those pedants know? They don't even feel color, let alone speak it!"

If her exclamation caught him by surprise, incongruous as it was to both the person and place, it was the idea of "speaking color" that held him in thrall. But before he could question her about it, she was continuing.

"They also call Manet the 'giant' of Impressionism. What's so great about making everything two-dimensional?" she asked. "He did away with chiaroscuro—but Cezanne was far bolder, treating shadows as shapes in their own right." She paused, then added, "Manet was never able to free himself from his past, and he continued to paint with a muddy palette." She threw him a mischievous glance. "Besides that, he was emotionally constipated." She grinned, almost sheepishly. "Sorry about that. I get a little carried away at times."

A loud laugh erupted from the man sitting beside her. "My God, another female rebel! Carried away, my foot!" He moved to sit halfway turned toward her now. "And who do *you* think was the 'giant,' mademoiselle?"

She caught him sneaking a quick glance down at her hands. "No one!" she shot back with more heat than she'd intended. "Van Gogh painted for only ten years—only five after he discovered color—but surely they're some of the most powerful paintings ever done. He saw an almost ecstatic movement in the landscape—his way of expressing the creative force in life. Cezanne saw stability and permanence in that same landscape, and changed our whole way of seeing. How could you choose Van Gogh and not Cezanne, or Cezanne and not Van Gogh? Anyway, Impressionism was just a kind of incubation period. Except for Manet, of course—he never hatched."

Ross laughed again. "You've got something personal against Manet. What is it? Did he do some poor woman wrong?"

"That's not fair!" she countered vehemently, but in the same bantering tone now. "Almost all of them were womanizers, or at least users. Look at Monet. He wore out, and outlived, three women—two wives and a daughter-in-law. All of them willingly gave themselves to servicing his every whim and need, from producing children and food to stretching his canvases and soothing his seething anxieties."

"You're avoiding the question, Julia Bonner. Back to Manet—what have you *really* got against him?"

Her lips curved in a sort of confessional grin. "Perhaps if he'd been a better painter, I could forgive him. He was the worst kind of bastard, you know—an opportunist—with no real loyalty to anything or anyone, let alone to his friends in the Impressionist movement. He kept a foot in both camps, playing it safe by staying in the good graces of the academy while playing at being in the forefront of this new movement—except when the occasion called for denying his friends in order to protect or promote himself."

She pulled herself up straighter on the bench. "No, I take it back. That was really the reason he *couldn't* be a better painter—he compromised even his own work!"

Ross nodded his head slowly, understandingly—seriously considering what she said while trying to hide the smile that pulled up one corner of his mouth. He still couldn't place that slightly odd quality in her speech, and after that "hogwash," she really had him curious. But he was having too much fun to interrupt with a question about where she was from. Wondering if she might catch a curve ball, he instead asked, "And Turner? What do you think about him?"

Surprise at the leap he'd taken was evident in her deep blue eyes as well as in her one arched brow as she turned toward him.

"You did say Monet had been to London, remember?" he added. "I thought perhaps you were going to claim Turner as the first of the Impressionists. He preceded them by only—what? Fifty years or so?"

"Something like that," she murmured, staring at him speculatively. Just how savvy was Ross McCutcheon about all this, anyway? Was he making the simple association he claimed, or was he baiting her? The connection with Turner, the great British colorist, could be made with either Monet or Manet, she realized now, but for very different reasons. Turner had accepted accolades from the fusty British academy and big fees from his adoring public for his darkly somber, traditional portraits and landscapes, while at the same time indulging his private visions in pure color, using watercolors and transparent tints to create "airy visions, painted with tinted steam." At least that's what Constable had called them.

"I can't help but think that, like you, Mr. McCutcheon,"

she almost drawled the words as she smiled at him sweetly, "he must have been something of a sly devil."

Ross clapped his hands together in appreciation as he broke out in a laugh, and then they were laughing together again.

"Could I persuade you to join me for a loaf of bread and a jug of wine, Julia Bonner?" he began as he rose slowly and turned to face her, bending slightly in an almost courtly bow. "Perhaps we can continue this debate while we assuage our other appetites. Certainly, mam'selle, you will not deny me the chance to defend myself?" His eyes closed to narrow crescents in the brief instant it took his brilliant smile to flash again.

He extended one hand to help her up, and Julia took it unhesitatingly, nodding her assent as she rose to join him. "Only if you promise to stop calling me that." It was a pallid condition to put on her cooperation, uttered for no reason but a weak attempt to mask her eagerness. At that particular moment she wasn't sure she wouldn't have said yes, no matter what he'd suggested.

Fifteen minutes later they were seated in a little restaurant at the far end of the village, one she'd suggested because they could walk to it. It was a family business in which the husband served as chef, a typical arrangement in hundreds of small restaurants all over France.

"You've been here before, I take it?" Ross asked as they scanned the menu. The woman who'd greeted them at the door obviously recognized Julia, and though he hadn't understood everything, she'd spoken with unmistakable warmth and friendliness.

"I've been coming to Giverny every chance I get since the garden was reopened to the public back in 1978. It's a source of inspiration, a place to learn to see again with a fresh eye, to peel away the false, the artificial. This was your first time?"

He nodded. "Yeah. I drove all night, from Munich. I've got a killer of a schedule this trip, but something was pushing me to get here. The hand of destiny, perhaps." He smiled conspiratorially and reached for one of her hands. "Don't you feel it, Julia Bonner?" Before she could respond, the brief touch was gone and he was asking, "Now, what does the chef do best? I didn't have breakfast this morning."

As if acutely sensitized to even the slightest nuance of expression in his intense eyes and mobile mouth, Julia found herself almost breathless at what she saw and felt in just those few seconds he was speaking. "What were you doing in Munich?" she asked, needing to touch ground somewhere.

"Visiting a couple of electronics companies—Siemens and Eurosil. Nothing very exciting, I'm afraid."

"What do you do, Ross? Where do you live?" She hated asking, already tasting the disappointment of finding out that he was an ordinary businessman—or ordinary anything else!

"Texas. And I suppose you might say I'm interested in languages." As if his answer was purposefully enigmatic, he grinned and added, "Not the usual ones, as you must know from my French. Now, let's get to the food. What would you suggest for wine?"

The coincidence was almost too much, coming on top of everything else Julia was feeling. Perhaps it would be better to just let the questions drop. It really didn't matter. In another hour they would be going their separate ways.

Ross finally settled on one of the specialties of the house, *entrecôte aux poivres*, a thick cut of beef with cracked peppercorns pressed into the surface before grilling, while Julia ordered a simple omelette and small green salad.

Seated directly across from her now, Ross could watch her face at will. More than the faint fan of lines at the outer corners of her dark eyes, it was what he saw in them that branded her woman instead of girl, making her infinitely more interesting to him than any schoolgirl could ever be. Bright with mischief, they were at the same time somehow vulnerable, as if some great sorrow lay somewhere in their depths. He noticed one flyaway brow lift quizzically, and quickly broke off his silent scrutiny.

"So you think Turner was such a great painter that you're

willing to excuse *his* schizophrenia?" he asked as soon as he'd tasted well of the food on his plate.

Julia had been expecting some return to their earlier exchange, but now there was no doubt in her mind that he was at the very least well-read, and that his query about Turner had been no stab in the dark. It also meant he probably wasn't the ordinary businessman his Munich contacts suggested, and she warmed to the challenge of the unknown.

"I have to confess that it never even occurred to me to put Turner and Manet together before, Ross," she answered, considering the idea. "You've given me something new to think about. But my spur-of-the-moment opinion is that Turner was different."

"How so—aside from his paintings, I mean?"

"It's as if he was playing a huge joke—on everyone. He's an enigma, but especially when it comes to color."

He waited, almost holding his breath, expecting the unexpected. What would it be this time?

"He wrote at length on color theory in his journals, everyone presumes for his own record. But it's all wrong. It's crazy, in fact, and certainly doesn't fit what he did with color—his paintings are all the proof anyone needs to see that! I haven't the slightest clue as to why, but I think he was laying a false trail." She looked up, grinning. "Like you!"

"Did you simply drop from the sky this morning, Julia Bonner? Or did you rise from the meadow mists?" Ross asked, more pleased with her, and himself, than he could have imagined possible.

She laughed softly. "How I wish it was so simple. In fact, I should have gone back to the train instead of coming here with you. I'm due in Paris at four o'clock." She consulted her watch. "About two hours from now, and I really *have* to be there."

"No problem. I'm headed there, too, and judging by the map, it's only about twenty-five miles. We should make it in plenty of time," he assured her. "Someone waiting for you there?" He asked it lightly, but she noticed that his hands went suddenly still.

"Yes, Dominique Chapotin—and a showing. She's a fashion designer." He seemed to relax again. What would his response have been if she'd mentioned a man's name? That she was supposed to meet Alex, for instance? "That's mainly what I came for, to see her collection, that and a bit of other busin—"

"You're a writer!" he guessed suddenly, glancing up as he interrupted her.

"No, though I suppose you might say that I'm interested in languages, too." She used his own words to tease him, almost intuitively understanding his delight in exploring, in uncovering information bit by bit on his own—sensing that he loved the process of discovery itself, just as she did.

"Hmmmm," he muttered thoughtfully, then refilled their glasses with the Beaujolais Villages she'd suggested.

Julia gave him her full attention as he sipped the wine and took another bite. Without being fully conscious of it, she drifted into silence, absorbing the interplay of colors he presented. Her fingers itched to reach out and feel the texture of the wiry-looking, close-cropped hair. Not silvering at the temples, not a salt-and-pepper mix, but white. Pure, shocking white. She wondered how old he really was. Forty? The sound of his voice startled her, abruptly interrupting her daydreaming.

"It's been like this since I was about twenty-two. I suppose it's genetic, but I was adopted so I don't know anything at all about my biological parents."

How long had she been staring? Her face flushed at being caught in such an adolescent breach of manners. She'd never intended to make him feel uncomfortable, but maybe he was sensitive about his hair. His earlier self-deprecating remark about the old man in the boat showed he was very much aware that people often jumped to the conclusion that he was old, or at least older than he actually was.

"Hey, it's okay," he assured her, touching her arm again

in an attempt to put her at ease. "I'm used to it. No need for that." If anything, her face grew even hotter at the realization that her embarrassment showed there. "I'm thirty-eight, in case you were wondering about that, too." He smiled, as if trying to reassure her. As if he felt that everything that was happening was so—so natural!

Again, she couldn't bring herself to look away. "I didn't mean to stare, but your wonderful coloring—do you have any idea at all how—I mean your coloring is—" She almost stuttered, then picked up her glass and took a quick sip of wine, chagrined by the realization that she was about to commit still another faux pas. But when she glanced at him again, he was wearing a smile of such pure pleasure and satisfaction that she couldn't help returning it.

"I take that as quite a compliment." He touched her arm again, but this time his hand stayed there, and she watched, fascinated, as his smile slowly turned devilish.

Chapter 2

If Ross McCutcheon had had a strong sense of being on foreign territory before, it was nothing compared to what he experienced when he walked into the ballroom of the Hotel Angleterre. He stood just inside the door for a few minutes, trying to take it all in. A fairly small room as hotel ballrooms go, it was nonetheless quite opulent, obviously a relic of that period around the turn of the century the French called the Belle Epoque. It seemed fitting, therefore, that it was packed with what the popular rags referred to as the "beautiful people." It was pure theater, he thought, and everyone here, male and female, was "on stage"—and dressed to the teeth.

Ross felt the interloper, a member of the audience, and very much alone. It went way beyond the gray business suit he was wearing. Hell, the longer he stood there, the more he felt like the third sex! Maybe he should just forget the whole thing, and slip right back out the door he'd come in. He didn't see Julia anywhere, so maybe she hadn't spotted him yet, either. Would he even recognize her? Curiosity finally got the upper hand, and he moved forward to circulate through the crowd, snagging a glass of champagne from a passing waiter. It helped to have something in his hand.

What in hell was someone like Julia doing here, anyway, among all these airheads? She didn't belong here any more than he did. Or did she? Maybe he'd been kidding himself earlier. Got carried away in that fantastically sensuous garden! When he'd asked her to dinner, she said she wouldn't be free until after this fashion thing, and he'd agreed to meet her here readily enough. But that was because of that awful sense of urgency, or whatever it was, that had gnawed at him the whole damn time they'd been driving to Paris from Giverny. It wasn't until after he'd dropped her at her hotel, in fact, that he recognized the sense of foreboding for what it really was—anxiety about losing touch with her. He experienced a feeling something like that again, here, but now it was the push-pull of the need to find her, coupled with the dread of discovering that she'd metamorphosed into one of these phony bitches who were chattering and gushing all around him.

The word "penetrate" broke on the surface of his mind, sending ripples of sensation skittering up his spine. No bubblebrain he'd ever run into spouted intellectual phrases like "penetrating the picture plane," though he had to admit that her use of the word this afternoon had set off some very "unintellectual" thoughts where she was concerned, thoughts that had absolutely nothing to do with lily ponds—or painting! A picture of her appeared in his mind's eye, on that bench in the garden, and he quickly rejected his initial fears and began searching for her in earnest, without the hesitancy he'd felt a few minutes ago.

Her voice came from behind him, soft and familiar in his ear even before she slid one hand under the bend of his right elbow. "You must have slipped in the one moment I wasn't watching the door. I spoke to the doorman—did you have any trouble getting in?"

He shook his head even as he turned toward her with the beginning of a smile, which shifted into full speed as she came into view, bathing her in the brilliant light of unadulterated pleasure, not to mention relief. The first thing he thought was that she was taller than he remembered. He stepped back, away from her, making a melodramatic show of considered appraisal, as if his face hadn't already given away his verdict.

"Yeah—well, I was looking for you, too, but maybe I just didn't recognize you. *Something* is different from the girl I met this afternoon," he drawled, pretending puzzlement, "though I can't quite put my finger on exactly what." He continued giving her the up and down once-over, deliberately, openly—struck again by that indefinable aura he'd noticed earlier, when he'd assumed she was French.

She was wearing a jet black man-tailored suit, the wide-lapelled jacket swinging casually open to reveal the knife-edged creases of straight-legged trousers. All else was in stark contrast to the severe color and cut, from the delicate apricot lace crossing itself over the base of her throat to the toes of black lace pumps. When she placed one hand in her trousers' pocket, the jacket was pulled back to reveal a gold filigree buckle that fastened a braided leather belt circling her slim waist. The buckle's three flower centers were shadowed by the darkening of time and studded with tiny pearls, echoing the long drops swinging from her ears. Though he had no way of knowing it at the time, it was his first encounter with what had long since become one of her trademarks—the unique ability to pull together disparate elements, to surprise by creating harmony from contrast and conflict.

Julia went along with the charade, turning a bit to one side to show herself to him. Her hair was smoothed back from her face, held behind each ear with a comb before falling to her shoulders in a jungle of wild curls—put there by the plaiting she'd worn earlier in the day. Her face had more color tonight, reflecting the peach-toned lace framed in black, while her lips glistened as wetly as if he'd just caught her sipping from the glass of champagne she held in one hand. Her eyes seemed darker, a sort of mid-Atlantic blue, but one birdwing brow still threatened to fly away at a moment's notice. And those quirky lips, each corner with a mind of its own! Infinitely more interesting than any classical beauty, her face betrayed both a quick intellect and strong emotions, not to mention a capricious sense of humor. And he suspected it was a face that often gave away far more than she realized—or intended.

"What happened to the medieval look?" he asked at length, taking her completely off guard. But he took pity on her and explained, "The chausses. Isn't that what you call those things you had on this morning? Like the baggy tights men wore back then—that they had to sort of tie on in order to make them stay up? I figured that was why you had your shoelaces wrapped up around your legs. I even felt sorry for you, having to hold your trousers up that way!"

She stood there, speechless for a moment, then laughed and shook her head in disbelief.

"You're full of surprises, aren't you?" she teased back at last.

"Like you," he grinned, amused, before his eyes and mouth turned serious again. "You look good enough to taste." His hand sought one of hers, wanting to touch her, wanting to get her alone, anywhere away from here. "I'm starving again. When can we get out of here?"

"Anytime, but come and meet Dominique first." She seemed as anxious as he was. "I'll tell her I'm leaving."

Ross followed as she threaded her way through the crowd, reaching out to touch her shoulder from time to time, until the crowd got so thick she extended a hand back for one of his. At last she broke through the circle of people gathered around the woman he assumed must be the designer, and the reason for all of this.

"Ah, *oui!*" She seemed to breathe out the words as her eyes fell on Ross. "So this is the flower you plucked from Monet's garden, eh, Julie?"

"Dominique Chapotin, Ross McCutcheon," Julia began, pulling him up close against her so he could hear. "Kiki and I go back a long time, as friends and conspirators, and tonight she's the toast of Paris," she explained, her tone leaving no doubt that she approved and applauded.

Tall and reed-thin, Kiki was strikingly beautiful, even though her eyes had seen too much. Framing a remarkably sculpted face, the designer's toffee blond hair was perfectly straight and cut to a blunt edge that clung to the line of her jaw, sweeping along the edge of it in fluid waves as she slowly moved her head up and down.

"Kiki," Ross mumbled, pushing out his right hand, which she clasped and jerked down in one swift motion, causing him to consciously realize for the first time that he found this curt continental handshake somewhat unpleasant. It was cold, impersonal and unfriendly. He didn't have the slightest notion of what to say to make polite conversation with a fashion designer, nor did he even feel like trying.

"And what do you do in Paris, M'sieur McCutcheon? Do you stay in our city long?" Kiki asked softly, the words English but the sound of them French.

"A couple of days," Ross told her, glancing sideways at Julia. "I'm here for a conference—a meeting."

"Ahh, I see. Is a pity, that. Well," she turned again toward Julia, "you must be off then, eh, my love. But I will come to you soon." With that, she leaned forward and gave Julia a quick kiss on the cheek, muttered "M'sieur" to Ross as she gave his hand another quick jerk, then turned away to a group of people pushing toward her. The abrupt dismissal made him bristle with sudden dislike.

They caught a taxi outside the hotel, and Ross gave the driver the name of the restaurant where he'd made reservations, wondering if he'd been wise to act on the recommendation of a hotel clerk. Les Capucines was relatively new and not well known yet. It wasn't in a fashionable part of town, the clerk had explained, though it soon would be because it had just been awarded a second Michelin star. Actually, Ross had been intrigued to happen on a restaurant named after one of the flowers he'd noticed earlier in the day along the edge of the path to Monet's house—nasturtiums—and he liked to think it might be a favorable omen.

"What do you find to talk about with people like that?" he asked, as he sat back, his shoulder pressing against hers.

"I don't understand—people like who?" Julia asked, puzzled.

"Who?" He blew the word out between his lips. "That so-called friend of yours! Where the hell does she get off, acting the queen?" His voice betrayed his still-simmering anger.

"Oh, I see. I'm sorry you took offense—that's just Kiki," she explained. "Maybe it's French. But it doesn't mean anything. Besides, she's the center of attention, trying to be available to everyone tonight, and that comes hard for her."

"So I noticed," he commented, his voice heavy with sarcasm. "But it's no excuse for rudeness."

"I suppose I learned to accept the French a long time ago, Ross, though I know a lot of Americans are offended. Maybe I don't notice because I—" The taxi stopped in front of the restaurant, interrupting what she was about to say.

"I sure hope this is all it's cracked up to be," he whispered as they were seated at a table near a window, private from the street because the glass was etched to imitate lace. A colored-glass hanging lamp enclosed them within its intimate circle of light, and Julia saw similar "Tiffany" lamps hovering over each of the other tables as well.

"So *intime,*" she commented. "However did you get onto this place? I've never even heard of it." She could hardly keep her eyes off the Mucha-type mural along one wall.

Ross ignored her question. "I'm finally catching on that you spend a lot of time in Paris, or in France. How often do you come here, Julia?" He looked up as the waiter approached. "How about an apéritif?"

Julia shook her head. "Just wine, please. With dinner will be fine."

"Bring us a bottle now, maybe this Bergerac," he ordered, pointing to the listing on the wine carte. They were silent until the obsequious young man returned, then waited for him to go through the ritual opening and pouring out of a small amount for Ross to taste and approve before filling their glasses.

"Two, maybe three times a year, but usually only for a few days at a time," she answered, then tasted the wine and glanced around at the room again. "There are two major fashion weeks, one usually in April and the other in October. We come for those, and sometimes in between on buying trips." She watched him closely now. "But I was here for over a year, just after I finished college, as an apprentice in the house of Balmain."

"That explains your French, then," Ross concluded with a slight nod of his head, as if methodically putting pieces of a puzzle in place.

She glanced away for a second, neither agreeing nor disagreeing, then went on with her story. "Kiki was a model for Balmain back in those days. We ended up sharing a little apartment. It was awful. Never enough heat or hot water. But I guess we were too young to mind. Everything seemed an adventure. Anyway, we never lost touch, even after I went back to New York. We think alike about a lot of things, Ross, in spite of the impression you got tonight."

"I find that pretty hard to believe," he injected. "Like what?"

"Oh, lots of things. How apparel ought to be marketed, and—" Her words trailed off as she smiled a secret sort of smile, almost to herself.

"And what?" he asked, impatient to know.

"Well, we, uh, one time we were trying to decide how to contribute to the cause—you know, the women's movement—because nothing much was happening here at that time." She peered at him intently. "Promise you won't ever, ever, even *think* of telling anyone about this?"

"I swear," he intoned solemnly, going along with the game.

"Well, let's see, how to explain it? The conventional wisdom is that great design—and the 'great' designers are almost always men, you'll notice—lies in the ability to translate the vision of the ideal woman into fashion reality. But the ideal woman, to a man, has always been one who is under his control, captive, restrained. The history of fashion demonstrates that over and over again."

"Oh come on, Julie, how can you say that after the miniskirt? My God, if you gave women any more freedom, they wouldn't be wearing a damn thing!"

"That freedom and exposure was quickly tempered by the introduction of tights—have you forgotten that? And what about the high platform-soled shoes that came along soon after, Ross? What woman could escape, could be free, in those ridiculous stilts? They could barely walk in them. Hordes of women suffered broken ankles and other injuries, provoking doctors to issue dire warnings about the potential dangers of wearing them. The miniskirt was lip service to liberation, Ross, not the real thing. Fashion went right on hobbling women, almost as effectively as those high-class Chinese women were hobbled with their bound, deformed, useless feet."

"Okay, I'll take your word for it. So, what did you and Kiki dream up?"

"Balmain lent us to the son of one of his dear friends for a few weeks, René St. Philippe, a young designer he thought had promise, to help him with his first showing. And the *pièce de résistance* among his designs was a black evening dress. It barely covered the nipples and was as tight as a sausage casing all the way to the knee, then belled out to the floor in a rippling black lace ruffle. See-through lace, of course. But that was just the backdrop for the shirred pink silk taffeta 'ribbon' wrapped around the really important part of the package—from the pelvis to the knee—which was tied in a huge bow across the derrière, with the loops flopping up and down, slapping the buttocks with each step the model took."

He laughed at the picture she'd conjured up. It was too preposterous to believe; she had to be exaggerating. "How could a woman take even one step tied up like that?"

"You catch on fast, McCutcheon," she muttered dryly, then continued. "Kiki minced down the runway in that rag, tight as a second skin, taking demure little steps—the only kind possible, of course. Up until then, the crowd had been no more than polite. Apparently they didn't find the virgin-whore paradox quite so profound as our pimply-faced boy wonder did. But when Kiki made her turn, they were startled into shocked silence, then burst into excited applause. They didn't quit, in fact, until René finally came out for a bow. It was a real show-stopper!"

"What happened?" he exploded. "Dammit, Bonner, out with the punch line!"

"With the help of an ancient little seamstress, who'd been around longer than all of us put together, and knew more than René St. Philippe will ever know, in spite of his big reputation today—" She saw his tanned face turn a deeper, ruddy color and decided she'd better forget the details. "The back seam opened—all the way up, or at least as far as anyone could see under that stupid bow—when she made her turn at the end of the runway."

His face lit up with understanding, and he began shaking his head from side to side as he pictured the scene in his head. "How did you manage it?" The spirit of conspiracy was contagious, causing him to whisper the question.

"We built a release into the back seam of the skirt." She barely got the words out before she broke into funny little giggles, remembering.

"Did he ever find out who did it?"

"He never even asked. Didn't want to know, I think. The press called him daring, the man to meet the challenge of profound social change that was sweeping the western world—yet still preserve the mystery that was 'woman'—and a lot of other garbage like that. I went back home soon after."

She was interrupted by their waiter, who brought a plate of pâté de foie gras and a basket of crusty, thickly sliced bread.

"Fabulous, isn't it?" Julia commented after the first bite, curious to see whether he liked it as much as she did. This particular version of the Alsatian delicacy contained tiny chips of black truffles. She waited for him to nod, then continued.

"The life span of a fashion model is short, and it was even shorter back then, so Kiki eventually went to work for *Elle*, a popular women's magazine here. Now at last, she's doing what she's wanted to from the beginning—designing. She has a boutique on the Boulevard Haussmann, with a small but faithful clientele. And her *prêt-à-porter* designs are being handled by some of the bigger stores, like Galeries Lafayette."

"Listen, Julie, I don't understand fashion jargon when you speak English, let alone French."

"Prêt-à-porter? Ready-to-wear. That's where all the action is in the fashion business today. Haute couture is just barely hanging on by the skin of its teeth. Economically, it's too—oh, I guess you might say it's too limited, not only in the number of customers or sales, but it's too elite. Maybe too conservative." Once again, her face was glowing with the heightened color he'd noticed earlier, when she was really caught up in what she was talking about. "We have problems in ready-to-wear, too, of course. Like how to shorten production time, to close the gap between the time the designs are shown and the time they're delivered to stores. And getting them into the stores at the right times—warm clothing when the weather is cool, and cool when the weather is warm. But I started out to say that by showing now, instead of during the usual couture week in July, Kiki's haute customers can buy and wear the garments almost immediately. That's one of the things we used to talk about, back then."

"You sound as ancient as that little seamstress, Julia," he kidded. "Was it really that long ago?" To his surprise, she didn't return his smile. Instead, he caught a fleeting impression of sadness, and when she looked up he saw hurt in her eyes, the deep, silent hurt of an injured animal, and he felt a wrenching in his gut.

She stared into her wineglass for what seemed endless seconds, then nodded slowly. "Yes, that is how it all seems now. So very long ago." Then she seemed to shake free of the momentary nostalgia, or whatever had struck her, and looked up with a wry smile twisting her lips. "It really was, you know—almost fifteen years."

Ross didn't attempt to hide the surprise and momentary disbelief that showed on his face as he estimated and added numbers together.

"I'm not sixteen, Ross, in spite of what you may have thought at a distance in Giverny. I'm thirty-six." She sounded her usual self again, though slightly chiding.

"Lord, girl, you don't look it," he tossed back, relieved, but still wondering what could have caused that look in her eyes.

Julia recognized the colloquialism as pure Texas, and she couldn't keep from laughing. "You do have a thing about 'girls,' don't you, Mac?" She'd never called him that before, and though he was used to it from most of his friends and colleagues, he discovered that he didn't much like it coming from her. "First you thought I was a French schoolgirl, and mademoiselled me all over the place, and tonight I look different from the 'girl' in chausses you met this afternoon. Perhaps now that you know the awful truth, you'll admit that I'm really way too old for you."

She might not look it, or at least what he usually pictured as "thirty-six," but he hadn't thought of her as a girl since the moment he'd dropped down on that bench. He looked at her now, speculatively, taking his time, not caring what his own face showed, memorizing every inch of her face, until Julia began to wonder whether he was going to respond to her remark at all. Instead, he reached across the table, to lightly stroke the back of her hand with his. Then his fingers curled around it, tightening as if he was holding on for dear life. Time simply stopped for a few seconds, locking them together in a charged silence.

He didn't release her hand even when he finally said, "You know, I have a colleague in Austin who studies birds. And she claims that color affects some birds' mating behavior. Oh, I don't mean just that brightly colored mates attract females—I guess everybody knows that's the way it is with birds. But in some species, the females have a definite preference among the various colors available in the males. Female finches prefer the males with bright red leg bands over the ones with green bands, for instance.

"Do you suppose something like that could be happening with us?"

And then the waiter was there, serving the main course.

Julia couldn't even remember what she'd ordered, and was mildly surprised to look down and find the *canard à la framboise* on her plate.

Ross spoke matter-of-factly, as if nothing unusual had just passed between them. "The season opener was already sold out. Anyway, I wasn't sure if you'd still be here. So I got tickets for the rehearsal concert tomorrow night, at the Salle Pleyel."

Julia looked at him quizzically.

"Barenboim and the Orchestre de Paris," he explained patiently, "and they're doing a cello concerto, one that isn't performed very often. I thought you might like to go."

Julia didn't know whether to believe what she was hearing or not. Was she daydreaming again? How could he possibly know? Almost immediately she realized that he didn't, that it was just another uncanny coincidence.

Ross saw the silent question in her face, and he couldn't deny himself a self-satisfied grin. "Elementary, my dear Watson. Remember the Nielsen First, this afternoon on the car radio? I figure anyone who knows a relatively obscure Danish composer well enough to hum along is bound to be an aficionado."

"You don't miss a thing, do you?" she whispered, then cleared her throat in an effort to get the world back on an even keel.

"Not where you're concerned." He spoke softly, sobering quickly when he saw how white her face had become. Then he noticed that she wasn't eating. "Let's order something else for you," he suggested.

"No. It's wonderful. Really. I've never had it fixed like

this before. The sauce is very delicate, with raspberries." She began moving food around on the plate with her fork. "I'd like to go," she said at last, "to the concert, I mean. Thank you."

"Good. That's settled, then. Now," he demanded, "tell me why you became an apprentice. To do what, and why here in Paris?"

"To learn as much as I could about the fashion business," she answered, somewhat reluctantly, "but I'd much rather hear about the meeting you came to Paris for, and what you do. I think it's my turn to—"

"Later," he assured her with a wave of one hand. "You had to come here to do that?"

"I was fresh out of school with two degrees, one in fashion design and the other in advertising, and almost no real experience. Where better than here?"

"I would think the United States, if that's where you wanted to work. I've had the impression that they're somewhat out of date here, that everything is still being done—well, more or less by hand," he answered.

She laughed. "Yes, I guess there is more of that than at home, at least in women's apparel. But the 'engineered suit' for men was developed in Europe, just a few years ago, and our manufacturers have been very slow to adopt it, even though it's far more advanced in many ways than the way we work."

"What do you mean, 'engineered'?" His ears almost visibly pricked up at the image her words provoked.

"A way to mass-produce a quality man's coat. It puts all the skill into pattern making, with predetermined amounts of fullness and compatible seams, to eliminate the shaping usually done during the sewing and pressing operations, which then can be mechanized. It cuts costs by 'de-skilling' as many operations as possible, which means eliminating people, of course. God, how I hate that kind of jargon! Sounds like government bureaucrats have gotten into it, doesn't it, or else computer nerds?"

Ross almost choked on his food, though she didn't seem to notice.

"It requires more cooperation between clothing and equipment manufacturers than we generally see at home," she continued, "and maybe the unions are part of the problem, too. But the answer to your original question is—because the French have had a hundred years of experience in the fashion business, a century of haute couture, which really blossomed during the Belle Epoque. Back then, every woman was dressed from head to toe and inside out with a custom-made precision unknown anywhere else in the world. The idea of fit wasn't applied only to dresses, you know, but to everything—from corsets and petticoats to hats and gloves. And that's what's important, no matter what process you use, don't you see? I think Paris still makes some of the most beautiful dresses in the world, even today. No one's ever quite been able to match the way they work with fluid fabrics here. Granted, we're way ahead of them when it comes to sportswear, and always have been, probably because we simply have a different way of life. A different attitude. Americans are very relaxed, aren't they? The real talent here seems to lie in their ability to create what we call the complete silhouette."

They talked lazily until their desserts were served, which turned out to be too distracting to ignore. Julia's was a thin disc of puff pastry decorated with a spiral of apple slices and a sprinkle of powdered sugar. "Is that as good as it looks?" Ross asked as she took the first bite. She obliged by pushing the apple tart toward him. "Want to trade?" He'd ordered a dense, mousse-like bittersweet chocolate cake. "How about going halves," he suggested, "so we each get to taste both?"

It wasn't until their table had been cleared and the waiter had brought tiny cups of dark steaming coffee that Ross picked up on something she'd said earlier. "And you, Julia. What about you? Are you doing what you've always wanted to do, too?" His hand reached for hers again, and she decided it was his way of constantly trying to reduce the distance between them, no matter what they might be talking about.

"Probably. I guess I don't have time to think about it anymore. It's a hectic business, always a race against time—the seasons never stop changing. Anyway, I've never really known for sure just what I most want to do. I've always been torn between several things, or at least more than one."

"Like what?"

"Well, at Ben Taggart, where I've been for six years, I'm sort of a jack-of-all-trades. I do some market research, plan merchandising strategies, and act as liaison between just about everybody—marketing and design and workroom people, and even our production supervisor. We contract out everything. Ben Taggart is a relatively young house, one of several that have become well-known in the last few years for putting the haute look into prêt-à-porter fashions. Right now, our designs are sold mostly in department stores around the country, plus small specialty shops."

"No designing?" he asked, surprised somehow.

"One collection a year, but a relatively small one—resort and holiday fashions. Ben is head designer, of course, and he does most of our women's wear. Alex Danilo, who's here in Paris with me, designs our menswear. He's one of the best in the business today, in my somewhat biased and not very humble opinion." She smiled wryly.

Ross read her smile as a kind of end sign. He'd been almost subconsciously listening and watching all day, attuned to the slightest nuance of word and expression, the unconscious movements of her slim-fingered hands, the tilt of her head and her body attitude—everything that was uniquely Julia. Now he suddenly realized that she was tired to the point of near-exhaustion. He signaled the waiter, reaching for the wallet in his hip pocket at the same time.

"I should have realized sooner, Julia, I'm sorry. I'll bet you got up before it was light this morning to catch the train to Giverny."

"What about you?" She laughed softly, almost under her breath. "You didn't sleep at all!" He dismissed her concern with a sweep of his hand and a grin. "Actually, I found the garden very restful—until I ran into you, that is."

They were comfortably silent during the drive back to her hotel on the rue de l'Université, near Saint-Germain-des-Prés. Ross dismissed the taxi as they got out, ignoring her protest that it would be difficult for him to find another one at this time of night. Just inside the hotel lobby she hesitated a moment, then inquired whether he'd like to stop for a drink at the bar. Ross quickly shook his head and steered her toward the elevator. "You need to get to bed."

They rode the slow, dignified old lift to the top floor, which had been done over into split-level suites built under the sloping rafters. "It's one of my favorite places to stay in Paris," Julia explained as they walked down the hall toward her room, "even though the rooms are small to the point of coziness. I love the view over the rooftops of the city, and there's a truly luxurious bath, complete with huge, fluffy towels that are always warm—from hanging over the exposed hot water pipes."

She slowed as they arrived at her door, then turned toward him, unsure exactly what to say, but wanting to get it over with quickly, before she said anything that might be too revealing. She was even hesitant to ask so much as how long he'd be in Paris. He'd been so vague when Kiki had asked him earlier in the evening, which in Julia's experience usually meant a man who wanted to keep all his options open—who was very wary of being "trapped" into being with someone, or doing something, he didn't want to do. At least she'd see him one more time, at the concert tomorrow night.

In fact, Ross wanted just the opposite, and he was stretching the minutes with her as far as he could. Now he took her face between his hands, turning it toward the light for one last look. "Good night, Julie," he murmured, and before he thought about what else he was going to do or say, his lips were on hers, warm and gentle. He tasted her lightly, once, twice, not pushing, giving her a choice, waiting for her to make the decision. Her lips spoke in small hesitant movements at first, then parted slightly as she felt his tongue lightly touch the corner of her mouth. His arms slid around her, pulling her closer, while hers slipped naturally under his open jacket and around to his back. All reservations suddenly gone, both explored with tongues and hands, each one breathing in the scent, the essence of the other, hearing and feeling their hearts pounding together.

His lips finally slid across her cheek to her temple, and he hugged her even closer as he whispered into her hair, "Spend the day with me tomorrow, Julie?" He pulled away a little, to search her face, one palm cupping her cheek as he waited for her answer. The thought of waiting twenty-four hours—being away from her that long—was like a weight pressing on his chest. "We can do whatever you want, go anywhere you say," he urged. "I just want to be with you." Her face was in the shadow of his shoulder, but at his unexpected confession, he saw the corner of her mouth turn up.

"I'd like that," she whispered, her mind racing through what she had to do tomorrow, "but—"

"Damn! I just remembered!" Whatever she'd been about to say was drowned in his explosive exclamation. "I'm giving a talk in the morning!" He thought for a minute, his mind working furiously on how to get around this stumbling block. "I'll be through about ten-thirty. Could you meet me somewhere, say at eleven?"

"Actually, I have something to do, too, in the afternoon, at two-thirty, but perhaps you could come with me," she suggested eagerly. "In fact, I can almost guarantee it will be a new experience, something few visitors to Paris ever see. What do you think?" She was wearing that enigmatic smile again, and he wondered what he might be walking into this time.

"I—it won't be like last night, will it? Will I need to wear armor?"

"No," she kind of giggled, knowing almost instinctively

how he'd felt in that crowd at the Angleterre. "I think your virtue will be safe, if that's what's worrying you."

It was obvious she didn't intend to tell him any more, and he guessed that might be because she enjoyed surprises herself. He gave her another quick hug and then gently sent her away.

Chapter 3

JULIA STRETCHED LANGUOROUSLY, willing her eyes to stay closed while she mentally reviewed the past few hours, savoring the touch of Ross's hand, the sparkle of humor in his icy blue eyes, and even the flash of indignation at Kiki's unintended slight. How could she feel like this about someone she'd known for less than twenty-four hours? Because he was sort of a mystery? Surely she'd managed to get beyond those adolescent games by now!

But she could remember his touch, could almost feel it now—his hand on her arm, clasping her hand, and when he pulled her against him. The chiseled lips, urging, seeking, and then the light scrape of his beard against the tender skin at her temple. Most of all, she remembered the exquisite sense of closeness. Not just a physical closeness, though there was that, too, but the indescribable, intuitive understanding that sometimes just "happens" between two people. She'd experienced it with only a few people, and never with the compelling overtones of sexual attraction she felt with Ross. Always before, it had seemed to have less to do with sex, or age, or even blood relationship, than with some intense and unique "meeting of the minds," some unexplained recognition that produced an almost manic "high." A person who believed in reincarnation probably would interpret it as a reunion with someone you'd known before, in another life, though no doubt a chemist would simply reduce the whole thing to a matter of pheromones.

It had been a long time since she'd felt more than vaguely attracted to any man, a situation that bothered her a lot more than she was ready to admit, even to herself. It was almost unnatural, the way Ross *didn't* monopolize the conversation talking about himself, which was something she couldn't say about most of the men she'd met over the past few years. At her age, the "pickings" were damned slim! So many of them were "rejects," available only because they'd already failed in one or more relationships. The divorced, disenchanted and depressed, she called them, saddled with damaged egos, guilt or child support payments—most of the time all three. And then there were the walking disasters, the psychologically hungry boys with avid eyes, peering through the window of the *boulangerie* and sniffing the aroma of freshly baked bread, without even a *centime* in their pockets and no idea where to get one. And the married men, the ones who wanted it all—the security of predictability and the excitement of the hunt.

Might Ross McCutcheon be one of those? She mentally pushed the question away. What she *did* know was that he at least seemed interested in her as more than just a potential bed partner, though she didn't doubt that he was attracted to her that way, too. She'd have to be blind, deaf and numb not to realize it. But apparently he didn't need to physically dominate in order to prove his masculinity. Look at how he'd been willing to share the decisions about what happened between them. And that gave her a glimpse of a *kind* of equality she'd never known with any man, not even with Tom. Which enticed her as much as anything about him. Except his astounding, fantastic coloring.

What else did she know about Ross McCutcheon? She snuggled down under the covers and began to list them one by one on her fingers. One, he was knowledgeable and interested enough in art, or at least painting, to drive all night to see Monet's home at Giverny. Two, he knew and liked music, the kind of music that was as natural a part of her life as breathing. Certainly it couldn't have been coincidence that the car radio was tuned to France Musique, the classical music station in Paris, when he'd turned it on yesterday. And then there was tonight's rehearsal concert.

He claimed to be from Texas—Austin, apparently—a coincidence she still found hard to believe, even though his speech gave him away as a recent arrival. But so far, she couldn't make even a wild guess about what he did, about his work. Something to do with languages, he'd said, but you could stretch that to include almost anything. Then there were the electronics companies in Munich. And a colleague who studied birds! The corners of her mouth lifted as she recalled the devilish sparkle in those unbelievably light blue eyes, and felt his hand, slightly rough and warm on hers—while he talked about what color legs female finches preferred!

Suddenly she became conscious of the light penetrating her eyelids, and she opened them to look straight up at the skylight cut into the steeply sloping ceiling. Sparing only a frantic glance at her tiny travel alarm on the table next to the bed, she threw back the covers and ran to the bathroom, mentally calculating how much time she had, even as she twisted the faucets on the big old-fashioned tub.

She was half-dressed when she heard a couple of quick taps on her door. *"Un moment, s'il vous plaît,"* she called, hastily pulling on the garments she'd laid out on the bed. Clutching the shirt together with one hand, she eased the door open a crack, then pulled it open.

"Come on in, Alex—but I'm just getting ready to leave." She continued dressing while she talked, not even conscious of what she was doing. "I've got to be across town, the other side of the Étoile, in less than thirty minutes. I'm meeting someone and I don't want to be late." She began tossing items from the dressing table into a big striped satchel with wide shoulder straps, then disappeared into the bathroom for a second, leaving the door open.

"Uh-huh, I saw him last night, at Kiki's. Can't say I blame you," Alex Danilo called after her. "You sure took off in a hurry. Weren't trying to avoid me, were you, Julia baby?"

She reappeared, searching distractedly for something on the dressing table. The innuendo was a tease, just like the trite "Julia baby." He knew damn well how much she hated it, but she had neither the time nor inclination for a snappy comeback this morning. "Look, Alex, do you mind going to the *prêt* alone?"

She'd intended to go with him to the big semiannual men's ready-to-wear trade show at the Porte de Versailles, just to see the European trends this season. But it wasn't the main reason she'd come to Paris, and it really held little interest for her, so she was just as glad to have a reason to skip it. So many menswear designers today were more businessmen than fashion innovators, like Cardin, whose primary concern was expanding his licensing empire. He might rake in millions in royalties on the thousands of items bearing his name or initials, but somewhere along the line he'd lost his inspiration, his pizzazz. He didn't seem to know when to quit, and now his stuff was not only pedestrian, but overexposed.

"I'll still be seeing Lesage, of course," she continued, corralling her wandering thoughts, "but I probably won't be back until late in the afternoon. And I'm going to a concert tonight. Okay?" They were accustomed to sharing the business chores when they came here, and clearing what they were doing with each other was a natural courtesy, not only to a colleague, but to a close friend.

"Whatever you say, Julia baby," Alex tossed back, heading for the door. As soon as he had opened it, however, he looked back and in a serious tone added, "He's probably just a businessman on holiday looking for a fling with a French doxy, so have a care, huh?"

Julia recognized the concern under his attempt to be flippant. The caring and taking-care habit was strong between them, and was the product of more years than she liked to think about. Alex was wearing white trousers and a V-necked cotton sweater in the deep black-purple he was using so much of this year, with canvas shoes to match, and she knew at a glance that he was involved with someone himself, in what he sometimes referred to as "the preliminary skirmishes."

"You, too," she murmured as she walked toward the door, then gave him a quick hug along with a kiss on the cheek.

It was a little after eleven by the time Julia got off the Metro at Porte Maillot, hurried up the stairs to street level and almost ran around the grassy circle in front of the Palais de Congrès. She'd had to change lines only once, but hadn't counted on it taking twelve stops to get here. Pushing open the door of the big convention center, she quickly scanned the crowd, mostly men. Maybe he'd given up, thought she wasn't coming, after all. Then she saw him, standing just to the side of a big message board near the registration desk, talking with another man. He was wearing a dark suit, navy or black, she couldn't be sure, and it was his white hair that stood out among all the other dark suits milling around in the reception area. Undecided about interrupting him, she hesitated, noticing for the first time the banner over the registration desk, with CAD-CAM printed across it in big red letters. Probably the name of a company, or even an organization, she thought, but it was no help at all.

Ross looked toward the door and spotted her, then was mumbling hurried apologies even as he started toward her, a big smile lighting his face.

"I was beginning to get worried. Did you have trouble getting a cab?" His hands rested lightly on her shoulders before he kissed her, taking his time. Then he reluctantly pulled away and let his eyes wander over her face. "I've been thinking about doing that for hours—could hardly concentrate on what I was supposed to be saying in there." His head vaguely indicated some place off behind him, but his eyes stayed on hers. "So I wouldn't be surprised if I have an uncontrollable urge to do it again." He was only halfway teasing. "Soon."

"I thought the Metro would be faster, but it seemed to take forever. Sorry," Julia apologized, returning his smile, talking just to be saying something, anything, while soaking up the color of him again.

Just as he'd done the night before, he took the time to look her over, to study the midnight blue trousers and silk shirt that matched her eyes, the taupe suede jacket, and the way her hair was pulled back today, twisted into a smooth knot at the back of her head and held in place by an intricately lacquered wooden stick.

"I like the chopstick!" he commented.

She smiled indulgently, sensing that he felt inadequate when it came to commenting on a woman's appearance and sought safety in humor. "What would you like to do?" she asked.

"Anything. Tell me—what would you be doing if you had no commitments, no have-tos? That's what I'd like to do—tag along with you, see Paris through your eyes."

She thought a minute. "Are you up to a long walk?"

He nodded eagerly as he steered her toward the door, then just outside he pointed toward a big building across the way. "I'm over there at the Meridien. It's convenient, though that's all I can say for it—more than a thousand rooms and absolutely no character. Would you mind if I make a quick change?"

She waited for him in the lobby. He was back in just a few minutes, wearing dark brown corduroy pants, matching shoes with thick crepe soles, and the same tweed jacket he'd had over his arm yesterday in Giverny. Outside the hotel once again, they turned the corner and started down the Avenue des Ternes, Ross eagerly following her lead. As they walked and talked, he touched her arm, or took her hand, then dropped it, only to grope for it again a little farther along.

After a couple of blocks, the activity on the street began to pick up, and when she guided them across the street and down the rue Poncelet, it grew into a bustling mélange of noises, sights and smells. As far as they could see, the street was lined with stalls, and the booming voices and shrill cries of merchants hawking their products filled the air. Fruits and vegetables were arranged in rows, with careful attention to shape, size and color. Stalks of celery framed heads of creamy white cauliflower, while the ruffled green leaves of Swiss chard were set in sharp contrast to the pointed swords of Belgian endive, and fat red peppers to thin green beans.

A merchant called out from time to time as they worked their way among the stands—*"Jetez un petit coup d'oeil"*—and Julia translated for him, "Take a quick look." A little farther along, she dug around in her shoulder bag and pulled out a *filet,* one of the knotted string nets used by French housewives to carry their purchases when they go shopping. Actually, big baskets had begun to replace filets in the last few years, but Julia still preferred the filet because it was expandable and convenient to carry in her purse when not in use.

She stopped first at a fruit stall and bought two *sanguinellie,* oranges from Italy with blood-red meat. Ross listened and watched her, bemused. She'd turned into a French housewife, rejecting the first piece of fruit in a rapid-fire exchange with the merchant. It was obvious the man wasn't going to get away with pawning off an inferior orange on her! Still farther on, she added a red pear to the filet, exclaiming over her shoulder, "You have to taste one of these." Next she stopped at a *fromagerie,* and after a lengthy discussion with the thick-bosomed woman behind the counter, she tucked three small wedges of cheese—Colummier, Vieux Pané and Chavroux—into her filet.

"It's best to come early in the morning, because everything here is intended to be eaten today, within a few hours," she explained to Ross as they meandered down the street. "That's the real secret of French cuisine, I think. Everything is ripe, the flavor of the food is perfect to begin with." She was having a terrible time concentrating on her selections for lunch, mostly because of his hand on the back of her neck. She knew it was just his way of keeping contact with her in the crowd, but—

"How about a bottle of wine?" Ross asked as they neared the end of the stalls and shops, though he could only guess at what she might be planning.

Julia nodded. "I'll get a *baguette* while you do that." When she came out of the boulangerie, Ross was waiting with a bottle under one arm, a colorful bunch of flowers in his hand and a big smile on his face. "I hope you have some place in mind to eat close by. All this fantastic food is making me crazy! Do you know we've just passed a half dozen boulangerie-patisseries, five butchers, three fromageries, four charcuteries, a coffee-tea-spice shop, three fishmongers, four poultrymen, two triperies, five flower vendors, and at least a dozen fruit and vegetable merchants."

She looked at him in amazement as he took the bulging filet from her, handing her the flowers in exchange. They walked over to the Boulevard de Courcelles, then along the few blocks it took to reach the Parc de Monceau, where Julia headed for her favorite bench. He followed without questioning, though he couldn't help wondering exactly how she intended to manage this.

She sat down at one end of the bench, opened her big shoulder satchel and laid out a small towel between them, then handed him a corkscrew to open the bottle of wine. Next she placed two small plastic glasses on the towel. "Hope you don't mind plastic," she mumbled, "it was the best I could do on short notice." She twisted the baguette in half, unwrapped the cheeses and laid them out on the towel, then dug in her bag again and withdrew a French peasant knife.

"You've got me really curious about what else you have hidden away in there," he laughed. "How did you manage all this?"

"In Paris, there's always a way when food is involved." She smiled her enigmatic smile again. It was a glorious day, sunny and warm, and she was doing one of the things she loved best, simple and uncomplicated, with someone she liked being with, and it showed.

"Aren't you missing something you shouldn't, Ross?" Julia asked while they were eating, pausing to throw out crumbs from time to time for the birds beginning to gather around them. "You came all this way for that conference, and here you are sitting on a park bench."

"I could have hung around to talk with people, which sometimes is productive, but I finished what I had to be there for. And this is more important." He glanced at her, then added, "Much more important."

"What was your talk about?" she asked. Would he tell her, finally?

"A new language I've been working on," he answered without any hesitation at all, "a language for machines to talk to machines."

Confused, she understood the words but not their meaning. "I'm not sure I know what—"

"A language that enables a computer to talk to other machines, like manufacturing equipment. Julia, I'm one of those computer nerds!"

She knew he was halfway joking, but that didn't keep her face from flushing as she recalled the disdain he must have heard in her voice when she'd uttered those very words. It was a judgment born of very little experience, though she couldn't help remembering the computer nuts she'd run across in school, first at St. Michael's and then at the university. Actually, she'd never gotten to really know them very well, and she didn't think anyone had, because they preferred machines to people. They were a bunch of cold fish as far as she was concerned, and she'd found them just as uninteresting as they had found her, with their rumpled clothes, uncombed hair and eyes red-rimmed from hours of peering at the computer screen or poring over stacks of computer printouts. That was all they ever talked about. And how they seemed to love "lording" it over anyone who didn't speak or understand their weird jargon—if they didn't just ignore them!

That Ross could be one of them was a lot more than unexpected. It just couldn't be made to fit the images in her head, and all at once she didn't know him anymore. She felt cheated somehow. Suddenly as tongue-tied as an embarrassed child, she searched frantically for something to say. "What does CAD-CAM mean?" she asked finally, seizing on the first thing that came to mind.

"Computer-aided design and computer-aided manufacturing," he answered, watching her face.

She picked up on the word design as if he'd thrown her a life ring. "What's computer-aided design?"

"Generating images with the computer. Designing equipment, machine parts, drawing or drafting with a computer. Mostly engineering stuff. A mouse or a light pen lets you draw freehand. You can touch the pen to the terminal screen, for instance. You can plug in dimensions and change the scale, assemble components, or see a drawing from different perspectives. It's quite flexible, has enormous potential. And the freehand sketching capability is a lot of fun."

It was hopeless. She would never be able to understand what he did, what drove him or how his mind worked. Where was that wonderful "meeting of the minds" now? "And the manufacturing part?" she asked, just going through the motions.

"Controlling the manufacturing process, instructing the manufacturing equipment through a computer program." Ross could tell by both the look on her face and the attitude of her body that he was losing her. He groped frantically for some way to reconnect the fragile thread that was only beginning to bind them together. "Did you know there's a historical connection between the textile industry and computers?" he asked.

She shook her head silently, not even looking at him.

"Yeah, the British inventor of the first computer got the bright idea from a Frenchman." He didn't doubt for a second that she would be familiar with the Jacquard weave. "Jacquard developed a system for controlling the patterns woven into cloth, using stiff cards with a series of holes punched into them. With each throw of the shuttle, the cards blocked some thread-carrying rods and let others slip through." He smiled engagingly. "You *have* seen a computer card, haven't you—do not fold, staple or mutilate? Those holes allow an electrical circuit to be completed."

"That's interesting." Her smile was no more than polite now, giving the lie to her words. "And your colleague who studies birds? What do birds have to do with computers?" Her question was born of a deep sense of betrayal.

"You've heard of artificial intelligence? We study all kinds of communication, trying to figure out how the process works, so we can make machines operate—think, maybe—more efficiently. Take a factory robot, for instance. Just to make an arm move out to perform one relatively simple operation calls for extremely complex thinking."

Julia nodded slightly, staring off in the distance. For god's sake, now he was even talking about robots!

Ross looked down at his feet, desperation beginning to fog his mind. Then he noticed her shoes. They were dark blue pumps with wide shirred bands crossing over the vamp, medium heels and thin crepe soles. They must be comfortable for walking, yet somehow the way she wore shoes—any shoes—just the way they fitted her foot, enticed him. Should he tell her that? "Your shoes," he started, then stopped. That wasn't it.

He started over, trying a completely different tack this time. "I notice you're pretty big on trousers, Julie." She glanced at him, puzzled and obviously wondering what he was getting at. But at least he had her attention again.

"Yesterday at Giverny, you were wearing those chausses, then last night that suit, which I must admit I liked a hell of a lot better, even though it was pretty, uh—" He hesitated again, searching for the right words. "I just realized that I've never seen your legs. You're wearing pants again today. Is that because trousers are all the rage, or—?" He stopped and grinned, and Julia heard what he didn't say, plainly.

So he thought there might be something wrong with her

legs, that she had a reason to hide her legs, did he? He had one hell of a lot of nerve, implying that she was the one with something to hide, after the way he'd played it so damned cagey about his work! A surge of adrenaline shot through her veins as she pulled herself up straight against the hard bench, then drilled him with a look so intense that he couldn't mistake the effect of his words.

"Trousers function one way, provide one kind of freedom, and skirts another. What I wear depends on how I feel, or *want* to feel. And on what I'm going to be doing."

"Really?" He almost drawled the question, in a way that made her not quite sure whether he doubted her or was just carefully considering what she'd said. "You want to know what I think?" he asked finally, then hurried on without waiting for her answer. "For a woman today, wearing pants is probably a way of sending a message, of giving an outward or visible sign of freedom and independence. They're sort of a challenge, a way for a woman to assert her freedom to move—economically, socially, geographically—you name it. Is that what you've been trying to tell me?" He chanced a quick glance at her face, wondering if he'd gone too far.

Denial was the first thing that came to mind, and it spilled from her lips. "I don't need to assert or defend my independence, Ross," she protested. "It's not up for debate. It just is." But close on the heels of her words another question surfaced inside her head, unspoken. Could he be right? Had she been trying to put him to some kind of test without even being conscious of it?

"Well, I'm pretty new at this," he continued, before she had time to think that through. "So I'm probably going to make some awful blunders. You see, Julia, up until about twenty-four hours ago, I thought the whole idea of 'fashion,' and everyone even remotely involved with it, was pretty damn boring. Frivolous, consumptive, theatrical, decadent." He took a deep breath, then confessed, "Probably even slightly dishonest."

Julia's thoughts were racing now. Could he be saying what

she thought he was, or was she reading something into his words that wasn't there? How could he possibly know the disappointment, even futility, that had nearly overwhelmed her at his revelation that his work was something she neither understood nor had ever found of any interest whatsoever? Trying to force down the rising excitement that was beginning to lift her out of desolation, she warned herself that she was probably only hearing what she wanted to. But the next thing she knew, his hand was at the back of her neck, firmly turning her head so she had to look directly at him.

"Do you understand what I'm trying to say, Julia?" He wasn't smiling now. He was waiting, silently beseeching her to understand.

He did know! He'd understood exactly what she was thinking, how she felt, she suddenly realized, because he was wrestling with the same demons! That she hadn't detected it before gave her a fleeting moment of dismay at her own blindness and insensitivity.

She nodded her head at last, but it wasn't enough. It just didn't satisfy. Reaching out a hand, she laid her palm along one side of his face, learning the texture of his warm bronzed skin before sliding her fingers through the crisply waving hair to cup his head, gently pulling him toward her—to caress his lips with hers, tenderly, longingly, saying everything she couldn't find the words for, sealing a bargain of faith. Of willingness to share, to try to learn, to understand.

When they separated, his eyes were sparkling with humor. "Damn!" The word exploded from between his lips, but softly. "What a time to be sitting in a public park!"

Julia wondered if she was tempting fate by taking Ross with her to see François Lesage, but it was too late to make other arrangements now, so when he asked about the rare glimpse of Paris she'd promised him, she determined to try to make it as interesting as possible for him.

"François Lesage is one of the famous *paruriers* of Paris, Ross. He heads a house that supplies embroidery not only to most of the haute couture houses in the world, but also to the top ready-to-wear designers," she explained as they started through the door of Lesage, "a house that's a hundred and twenty years old. Once upon a time, there were a hundred or more—paruriers, I mean—small artisans who produced accessories and trimmings. What you might call the fluff to gild the lily. Hats, bags, buttons and belts, veils and ribbons, feathers and flowers, and miles and miles of embroidery. They all produced a collection twice a year to show the leaders of Paris fashion. And there were two thousand fashion houses then, six hundred of them important ones. Worth, Poiret, Doucet." Her fascination with the past, with the history of the fashion center that was like a second home to her, was apparent in her rising enthusiasm. "But now there are only ten paruriers left, one for each specialty. So if you want embroidery, you come to François Lesage. I usually buy a season ahead, every time I come to Paris, even though he's recently started coming to New York."

The older man who rushed up to greet them was shorter than Julia, but he didn't let that stop him from greeting her with an exuberant hug and a kiss on each cheek, all the while laughing and talking in rapid-fire French. So fast, in fact, that all Ross could understand was the "Madame Bonner" when he ordered an assistant to take her jacket.

Julia hastily introduced Ross, and after that Lesage's speech was a crazy mix of English and French, since he refused to slow down even when he couldn't find the right English word. "You have come to stay in Paris now, ma chérie?" was his first question to Julia. When she shook her head and mumbled a negative response, he turned to Ross to explain.

"New York—it is too far away. Here we have everything in one place, where it should be. For the important designers, it is necessary. Many times it is the grand idea that comes on the spur of the moment—the last moment, *peut-être.* Saint Laurent calls me in the middle of the night and says 'toreador.' Two days later, I give him toreador embroidery."

Ross laughed and nodded his understanding, but a second

later his curiosity was piqued when Lesage added, "I must try always to persuade her. It is time for her to come back, to come home."

Ross tagged along happily after the two of them for the next hour, watching Julia select from the two hundred or more samples Lesage showed her, listening to her exclaim from time to time over the fragile threads in one piece, the color or design in another—an hour that changed his whole concept of "embroidery." At one point he made a comment about a piece of copper foil with stitchery inserts so delicate they looked like spider webs, and Lesage answered grandly, "Ah *oui*, m'sieur, the house of Lesage, we can do wonderful things. Once we even embroidered a lettuce that the great Schiaparelli picked up at the market to use as a hat."

Julia tried to hurry through the ordering, but even so, it was nearly five by the time they were ready to leave. She noticed that Ross had been writing on a small pad, and hoped he hadn't been too bored. "Were you—" she began, giving voice to her concern just as he caught one of her hands and swung it up to brush his lips across the back of it, turning his brilliant smile on her.

"You were so right, Julie! Damn, but that was fantastic. What an idea-mill the place turned out to be!"

"You weren't bored?" she ventured doubtfully, wondering what had excited him so.

"Bored! My God, who could be bored in there! That's some of the most intricate, complex stuff I've ever seen. And it gave me one wild idea—I don't know, it's just a glimmer right now."

"An idea about what?" She didn't have the slightest notion what he was talking about.

"How to interface, make a connection, between two completely different things. I'll tell you about it later after I work on it some. Hey, isn't it time for afternoon tea or coffee? A pastry? Something." He grinned. "No reflection on your lunch, but I'm hungry again."

They stopped at a little corner pastry shop which also

served at tiny tables lined up along one wall, and by the time they finished, it was almost dark. Fortified enough to forgo dinner until after the concert, they went their separate ways to change.

Julia needed a little extra time, anyway, and she was keeping her fingers crossed that she'd be able to reach Kiki.

Chapter 4

By the time Ross came for her Julia was more than ready for him, and at his first light tap on her door she swung away from the mirror and strode confidently across the room, relishing the thought that he would be dining on his words soon enough!

She threw open the door with a flourish, vaguely noticing his dark suit and burgundy tie before her arms slid over his shoulders and around his neck. Then she forgot everything in her joy at being with him again. She covered his face and neck with soft running kisses, then nuzzled his chin with her cheek before reaching for his slightly parted lips. This time there were no questions to ask, and he opened eagerly to her, recovering quickly from his initial surprise. Julia felt his heart racing against her own as his tongue tried to tease her lips open more. But she denied him full admittance, caressing his partially successful invader with her own, at the same time limiting his progress. It was a game, a contest, until she suddenly became conscious of his strong erection pushing against her thigh, and felt her nipples contract in response.

Not now, she admonished herself, reluctantly moving away.

"We'd better go," she whispered against the curve of his neck, "or we'll be late."

Ross stood motionless, trying to get his breath under control, scouring her face with his eyes, wondering what she was up to. She turned abruptly and walked toward the closet, then swung around without warning to catch him off guard. The expression on his face was even more rewarding than she could have imagined! Stupefied was the word! Then her delighted laugh seemed to bring him out of it, though he still wasn't able to utter a sound.

Julia was wearing one of the numbers from Kiki's fall line, one of her signature designs—a split skirt. It hung sedately straight to the ankle while she was standing, but with each long stride, one side seam in the black plissé skirt opened to reveal both calf and thigh, and occasionally even a hint of delectable derrière. She'd topped it with a cashmere twin-set banded in matching satin, and her long slim legs were encased in shadowy black hose above high-heeled black pumps.

"I believe you thought I might be hiding something, McCutcheon—wondered whether something was wrong with my legs?" she dripped sweetly, innocently batting her eyelashes at him.

He moved at last, striding toward her in mock anger, grasped her face between his hands and began to rock her head back and forth with a pretense of roughness. "You will be made to pay for that," he muttered darkly, and she pictured him twisting the tips of a handlebar moustache just before his lips butterflied across hers. "And pay." Again the soft words and lips. "And pay." Then he was kissing and hugging her all at the same time. "You're back," he whispered into her hair, relieved, as they stood holding each other for one long, timeless moment.

Finally, she swirled a below-the-knee-length cape around her shoulders, and Ross mumbled, "Thank God for small favors," took her arm and steered her out the door.

For Julia, it was an evening of discrete scenes and images—or at least that was the way she always remembered it. She recognized the Delius cello concerto, but was more aware of his hand gripping hers than of the music. Nor did she really notice where they went for dinner, or what she ate. Her eyes saw only Ross—the color of him, the intensity, the barely restrained energy, the way his smile and eyes lit his face. And all were turned on her, given to her as a gift, with loving attention.

She was alternately sipping rich dark coffee and her favorite French brandy by the time she finally asked, "What are you doing in Texas, Ross?"

His response was almost a laugh. "You mean, how did I get there, I take it?" he asked, surprising her again with his perceptiveness. "I guess I used to be just what you thought, Julia. One of those guys who sit at a terminal for hours and hours, in love with their computers, shutting everything else out. After my Ph.D. at Stanford, I stayed there and took a job designing system software for Fairchild Semiconductor."

"What does that mean," Julia interrupted, "or is it too complicated for someone like me to understand?"

Ross shook his head and smiled. "You know what software is? A program, or instructions to a computer. Well, system software is the program that translates the commands you give a machine into instructions the machine is equipped to understand. It's stored inside—but I'll explain all that to you some other time.

"Anyway, a couple of years later, six of us spun off our own company, and for the next five years, I lived and breathed computers, and almost nothing else. As it turned out, our timing was good, but the pace of work, the lifestyle—I don't know what it was, but one day I woke up and decided I had to get out, that there had to be more to living than that. So I cashed in my chips and took a job teaching, at the University of Texas." His lips twisted in a wry grin as he whispered, "I'll let you in on a secret if you promise not to even think of telling anyone else."

Julia nodded almost automatically.

"I discovered that I was in love with the idea of a university, and I suppose I still am, but I hated teaching. It was even more draining, maybe because it was depressing, than what I had been doing in California—the bureaucratic crap, the students, everything. It was like having your face rubbed in what's gone wrong in our society, what's happened to public education, every day without letup. About the time I decided I couldn't face another semester, a consortium of microelectronics companies formed a research group in Austin and started romancing me, and that got me to thinking about what I really wanted to do. And I figured, why work for someone else, jump through their hoops? So I started my own software development company. Now, I pretty much take on only what I want to, follow my nose wherever it leads." He reached out for her hand again. "A pretty dull story, I'm afraid."

"There weren't any women in your life to make it more interesting?" She simply had to know.

Now his face took on an expression of comic puzzlement. "No women? I can't even imagine it!" He grinned, and she knew he was kidding, but then he quickly turned serious again. "Sure. I guess there've been three or four really important women in my life, Julia. My mother found me in an orphanage and took me home with her. She died about five years ago. And my grandmother, who is one fantastic woman—and she is really going to like you."

He was silent for a second, reflecting. "When I was about eleven years old, she took me to a concert at Orchestra Hall, in Chicago. I grew up in a small town near there, a suburb. Anyway, the soloist was a cellist, a Frenchwoman. She came out on the stage dressed in flowing black trousers. She looked—well, French, I guess is about all I can say. I'd never run into anything quite like her before." He paused and a distant smile curved his lips and was reflected in his eyes. "Her name was Anne-Marie Lacombe. I suppose I was at an impressionable age, but I think I fell in love with her, or at least with what she represented. She was unique. Beautiful. Brave."

Julia had sucked in her breath and held it, waiting, the sense of disbelief, then of déjà vu, almost overwhelming. Now she was sure that their meeting, their coming together, was more than chance. It had to be the hand of destiny, as Ross had called it that first day. But she'd never heard the woman he was talking about described in quite that way before. Beautiful, yes; unique and special, certainly. But what did he mean by brave?

"I'm not even sure what was on the program anymore," he continued, "Bach and some other things. But she played an encore that has haunted me ever since, and I've never heard it again, never been able to find it. But I guess I'll never forget her. The picture in my head is as clear today as it was that night! She sat on the edge of a straight chair in the middle of a colorless, austere stage. All alone. No accompanist, no sheets of music on a stand, no page turner, nothing. And she filled that silent hall. There was nothing but her and the sound she created. I'm not sure I can describe it in words. She gave—she spoke to me in a language I never even knew existed up to then. It was an experience like you described at Giverny, Julia—pure sensation. So I knew exactly what you meant, you see." He sat perfectly still, remembering, staring into his coffee cup.

At last he looked up with a wry grin. "That concert is probably the reason I have such a hard time passing up a cello performance." He straightened in his chair, as if physically pulling himself free from the memory. "And what about you, Julie?"

She couldn't speak for a minute because of the tears welling in her eyes and choking her throat. She swallowed convulsively, trying to force them back, but one spilled over and started down her cheek. Quickly wiping it away with a finger, she hoped he hadn't noticed.

"Julia?" He hesitated, looking and sounding concerned.

She smiled at him and shook her head. "I'm just an easy mark for a sentimental story, McCutcheon. And you're a good storyteller." His face smoothed in relief, but she didn't plan to give him much respite. "You're not going to believe this, but I'm from Texas, too. I even went to school in Austin. At the university."

"Impossible, you don't sound—" he protested, just as she knew he would. "Where in Texas?"

"I grew up in the Texas Hill Country, about fifty miles west of Austin. LBJ country. On a ranch."

"Oh no you don't, Julie." He denied it with easy assurance this time. "You can try to pull my leg all you want, but that one just doesn't wash. The slur, the soft slide into words that start with 's,' the slightly—" That reminded him of something else. "What did François Lesage really mean when he said you should come home?"

All the little things he'd noticed were rising to the surface of his mind now, and Julia laughed with delight, listening to him piece together bits and pieces of evidence to refute her claim. It was a response she'd grown used to over the years, though she'd never enjoyed it so much as now. "He's an old friend, that's all, trying to pull the father act. He considers me French, Ross, because of the time I spent here, and the way I speak. Because my—"

"It's not a foreign language to you, is it? You fit right in here, as if you were born to it. Where—when *did* you learn French, Julia?"

She heard both suspicion and a dawning awareness in his question. "I have absolutely no recollection, Ross. My father is a Texas rancher. Pure, unadulterated Texan. I swear it. And his father before him." She was enjoying herself so much she couldn't control the mischievous grin, and Ross held his breath, waiting for the other shoe he knew was going to drop.

"But my mother is French."

It was well past midnight when Ross paid off the taxi in front of her hotel, just as she expected he would, then took her arm as they walked through the lobby. His hand slid down to hers while they were riding up in the elevator, but neither of them spoke. When they reached her door, Julia inserted the key and turned it, then pushed it open a crack before turning back to Ross. He ran both his hands up her arms to her shoulders, pausing only long enough for a light squeeze before cupping them around her neck. His eyes held hers as he rubbed his thumbs along the line of her jaw, and she wondered what he would decide. Then he kissed her, a deep searching kiss that spoke to her own yearning need, while his hands slid down her back, pulling her body against his.

She could almost taste his reluctance to let her go tonight. Then his head moved away just a fraction, and his lips were taking quick, tender nips at the corner of her mouth, up her cheek and over her closed eyelid, as if storing away the taste and shape of her. At last he buried his face in the hair curling back from her temple, and she heard his breath begin to slow again.

"Tomorrow?" he whispered, still holding her close.

She was perfectly still for as long as it took to draw a long, deep breath into her lungs, then she slowly rolled her head back and forth against his neck, caressing him with her hair while gently telling him "No" without saying the words.

But as she drew away from him, she was already pushing against the door behind her. Taking one of his hands in hers, she looked straight into his eyes and answered the puzzled look she saw there with an enticing Mona Lisa smile. And just one word.

"Tonight."

Ross followed silently, momentarily stunned, wondering if he could have misunderstood. He'd already developed a very healthy imagination where she was concerned. All his doubts disappeared, however, with the fluid sweep of her cape, tossed with careless abandon toward the bed before she turned back toward him, sliding her arms under his, capturing his body between them while quietly pushing the door closed behind him, even as she nuzzled her face into his neck.

"I wouldn't be able to sleep," she murmured, "knowing you'd never find a taxi at this time of night, worrying about who you might encounter walking the streets of Paris."

He didn't need to see or feel the smile on her lips to catch her playful mood. "My God, girl, if you only knew what's going on inside my head right now, you'd know your worries are misdirected!" He hugged her to him tightly, waiting, letting her set the pace and direction of whatever was to happen next.

Julia sighed with exaggerated resignation, keeping up the pretense. "Girl?" Her lips began to move against his neck, sending tiny shivers up his spine, then up and over his jawbone, slowly, teasingly. He turned his head, trying to catch them with his own, but she'd already eluded him. Next, she was nibbling his earlobe, even as her fingers stroked over and behind his other ear, until he grasped her head firmly between his hands. Her eyes were wide open, watching him in the dim light pouring in through the window, as he dropped his head to catch her mouth in a deep searching kiss. His hands slid slowly over her shoulders and then down her back, molding her body against his to send her still another unspoken message. He wasn't going to be able to play this game very long, and much as he wanted her, he also wanted her to be sure about where they were heading. He sure as hell didn't want anything to go wrong between them at this point.

"Julie?" His voice was barely above a whisper as he raised his head and looked directly into her eyes. "Are you sure?"

She nodded her head, slowly. "Yes. Don't you feel the hand of destiny?" She smiled teasingly again, repeating his own words spoken in the restaurant at Giverny. Then all of a sudden another thought struck her, bringing a rush of heat to her face. Had she presumed too much! Was she misreading his reluctance as willingness to let her decide or to share?

She turned away from him suddenly, forcing a casualness she didn't feel, and strolled toward the window, to stand looking down to the courtyard below. Any place to escape those all-seeing icy blue eyes. Searching frantically for a way to allow him, and her, to retreat gracefully, she pleaded silently, Why don't you just go, make it easy on both of us?

The little lamp on the table beside her bed lit the room with an orangy glow, and she glimpsed his shadow in the window, just before she felt his hands on her shoulders.

Ross felt the rigidity in her shoulders, noted the way her arms were crossed as if she were holding herself together. He wrapped one arm and then the other around her from behind, intertwining his hands with hers, pulling her back against him. Then he laid his cheek against her hair, slowly rubbing it against the mass of silky strands.

"Oh, ye of little faith," he chided. "Do you have so little confidence in yourself, Julia? In what you must know I feel? Can't you give us a chance? Don't try to tell me you don't feel it, don't hear it, can't taste it, every minute, every second we're together!" He tightened his hold, nuzzling his lips against her neck, while one hand rose to enclose her breast. "Even when we're not!"

Her last fully conscious thought was the sudden realization that this sensitive, sharing man had reached out to both her feelings and her mind, all in one engulfing sensual wave! She loved being touched by him, just as she loved touching him. Loved looking at him! She turned into his arms then, one hand reaching up to circle his neck while the other slid under his jacket and around his waist.

Ross pulled her closer, his lips at her temple, then swept feathery kisses from her hairline to her chin, stopping teasingly at the corner of her mouth. One hand massaged the back of her neck, loosening the tight muscles, while the other slid up and down alongside one breast. Then he was peeling away the clinging cashmere and letting it drop to the floor where they stood. Her skirt pooled around her ankles a second later, before he lifted her feet off the floor, leaving everything behind as they moved toward the bed. Then he stood away from her long enough to work at his shirt buttons, eyes feeding on her—her straight thighs and flat stomach, the generous breasts—even as she watched him strip off his trousers and shorts, stepping out of them to stand straight before her in the dim, shadowed light,

The tension in her body pulled tighter and tighter, and her

breath came faster. Her heartbeat was pounding in her throat, so hard she wondered if he could see it. She closed her eyes as his warm skin brought fiery shivers to hers, from breast to thigh, just before he bent to pull back the spread covering the bed. They stretched out together and she turned her mouth to his, beginning a kiss of caressing exploration, while his long fingers stroked her along the inside of her thighs, sending an icy-hot ripple up and down her back. Simultaneously receiving and giving, she explored his chest and shoulders with her hands, finally moving them down his back to grip his firmly rounded buttocks.

Her name escaped his lips, carried on one long agonizing breath as he strained against her, until she pulled away enough to make room for her hand. He quickly covered it, stopping her with a steely grip.

"I won't be able to wait if you do that." He whispered the words against her mouth. "I want you too much already."

"Me too," she mouthed against his lips, her breath coming so fast she had to speak in short bursts. "I'm not even sure I can wait! Could you hurry! Please?" She covered his face and neck with quick kisses, while he raised his body over hers.

Copying the movement of her tongue, he slid gently up and down before pushing inside, and she moaned softly with the filling pressure of his entry. Then she was holding her breath as she felt herself rising in one gigantic crescendo, before fragments of light seemed to shatter behind her eyelids and shoot out to the tips of her fingers. Almost instantly, the tight pulsing rhythm of her release triggered his, and as she felt him continuing to move deep within her, she was rocked by a second paroxysm of pleasure, this one in some hidden inner place she hadn't even known existed. And it went on and on, and on. And on.

At last they stilled, allowing the waves of pure pleasure to subside with their bodies still integrated in the most intimate way possible. Julia continued to stroke his back, while he nibbled kisses along the edge of her hair, homing back to her receptive lips from time to time.

Finally, Julia let one hand slide down the length of his back, into the dip at his waist, then rise again to stroke the curve of his buttock. "I can't seem to get enough of touching you. Especially *there,*" she teased. She could feel his head roll from side to side in mock dismay. "And I thought it was men who were hung up on T and A!" he grumbled, then rolled away from her and brought up the covers. "Come under here and get warm," he urged, gathering her into his arms again.

"But I'm not cold," she protested sleepily.

"I know," he chuckled softly as she drifted off. "Julie, my love, you put even my wildest fantasies to shame."

Consciousness came slowly to Julia, though she somehow knew the room was already flooded with light. One picture after another appeared in her mind's eye, and though it was her usual before-getting-up habit to review and evaluate yesterday, followed by planning ahead for today, this morning she seemed hung up on the review part. Reveled in it, in fact, stretching lazily, slowly, luxuriously, as her mind refused to move beyond the images of the past two days. And last night! She couldn't keep from smiling, from expressing her happiness in some overt way. Had she ever before felt so fantastically, fully satisfied, so— What was the word she was searching for? Fulfilled? She almost giggled out loud. A casualty of the women's movement, the word had become a cliché in the past decade or so.

Had she ever felt like this with Tom, or was it simply so long ago that she couldn't remember? Was this particular pleasure, like pain, quickly forgotten? It saddened her to think it might be. Then again, maybe she'd been too young with Tom—perhaps she hadn't been mature physically. Not that she didn't reach orgasm, though she was honest enough to admit she hadn't always. But she and Tom were both beginners. More often than not in the years since, however, orgasm was a purely physical sensation. And because it was, it seemed somehow incomplete. Easy enough under the right circumstances, rare as that was with some men, her "satisfaction" varied in intensity from time to time, yet was still more or less superficial. Orgasm was, after all, nothing more than a reflexive physical response, even if it was more brain-controlled in women than in men. She knew that to expect more was to buy the old romanticized myths about "ultimate ecstasy," but it was either that or accept that her own sexuality might be somehow flawed.

But last night had been so different! The attraction, the chemistry, with Ross was strong and constant. She'd never become aroused so quickly before, but she'd also never experienced nearly forty-eight hours of constant foreplay! A smile of pure satisfaction played over her lips as she took pleasure in the remembering.

At last she rolled toward her right, as naturally as a flower bending to follow the sun across the sky, no longer able to resist the desire to look at him before he woke—and opened her eyes. Instead of finding him quietly asleep, though, she met an icy blue stare so intense that it brought a flash of alarm surging through her body.

"Is something wrong?" She tried to raise herself to a sitting position, but Ross's arm slid across her ribs, holding her where she was.

"Tell me about that," he ordered, the brief dip of his eyes telling her exactly what he meant. She'd completely forgotten about it last night. And that had never happened before, either—not that she hadn't wished she could. Most men, it seemed, or at least the few she'd allowed to see it, found damaged goods more than a little difficult to deal with. Maybe because it interfered with their pleasure to be reminded of their own mortality, especially during the act that reaffirmed the very essence of life through their own virility!

"I had a biopsy. Years ago," Julia explained, keeping her voice as even and neutral as possible. "Fortunately, it was benign." She paused only a second, then plunged on. "Unfortunately, the surgeon didn't do a very neat job, did he?"

Ross made no answering comment, and in fact didn't say a word. The seconds seemed to drag into endless minutes as he stared at the scar, a nearly half-inch-wide vertical line of puckered white flesh which began at the slope of her left breast and stopped just short of the nipple.

Judging by the strip of untanned skin either side of the scar, it was partly covered by the straps of her swimsuit, or her bra, which must be why he hadn't noticed it last night. He glanced quickly at her other breast, noting the difference in size, then absently rubbed one eye. His lids were burning, and he blinked to give them ease as he swallowed, fighting the tightening in his throat. Then he leaned over her, unable to stop himself, even though he knew it might offend her.

Julia felt his lips touch the scar, gently caressing, first at the top of her breast, then lifting momentarily before butterflying again to one spot after another, until he'd kissed the entire length of what she'd tried for so long to rationalize into acceptance. Vulnerable now, with her long-held guard down—behind which she'd hidden the sense of having been violated, by a man, a faceless and impersonal surgeon—she experienced a tenderness and intimacy she'd never known before with any man.

"I'm sorry, Julie," he murmured at last, laying his head against her breast as if trying to make his peace with something. "But thank God you didn't wait. Didn't put it off!"

She wondered at the vehemence of his words. "Maybe. But I've never been convinced it really was necessary. He—the doctor—I don't think he ever found the lump himself. If it was a lump, rather than just some—oh, you wouldn't know how hard it is to examine your breasts and know for sure if something is different!"

He smiled against her breast, but didn't interrupt.

"During his examination he never even touched me here, where I thought it was." She put a forefinger to the scar, near the top of it. "When he'd finished, he asked me to show him what I'd found. Then, after he'd felt around for a while, he took a pen out of the pocket of his white coat and doodled circles on my skin."

"God! What an insensitive bastard!" Ross exclaimed, suddenly angry. He straightened, pulling her into his arms.

"It was small, he said, but it didn't pay to take chances. Too often in the past they'd waited, then discovered it was a mistake. I was young, unsure what to do, and I didn't have anyone else to talk to about it. Oh, my father was there, outside, waiting for me. But you know what I mean."

No woman to talk to, Ross thought, no one who'd already gone through this, knew all the pros and cons and had made her decision. Had learned to live with what happened to her, to accept her feelings about it.

"Not your mother?"

"No. She was—away at the time. I suppose it wouldn't have mattered, though. You don't really have a choice, do you?"

"No," he agreed softly. "Where'd you have it done?"

"In Houston." She named one of the best-known medical clinics in the country. "The doctor was supposed to be one of the best. Aren't they always? Who was I to question him? Maybe I was just looking for an excuse not to do it. That's what I finally told myself. Then, when I was in the operating room, after the nurses had scrubbed and painted my body with some foul-smelling orange stuff, he came in and discovered that his little ink squiggles had disappeared. So he asked me to show him again where it was. It was too late then to—"

Too late to start asking all the questions someone should have been asking that bastard much earlier, he finished for her, but silently. To, at the very least, help put her mind to rest, to remove the doubts. Ross held her tightly, sensing that she was reliving the fear she'd experienced back then.

"Later, after it was over, he came in and told me it was much larger than he had expected—and this was the result." Her finger followed a familiar trail, down the glassy smooth channel with puckered edges. Her voice dropped to a murmur. "But I've always thought he was a sadist, and this was one of the ways he got his jollies!"

Her bitterness had turned to anger, Ross realized, a seething fury that still burned within, marking her more deeply than any scarred flesh. He searched his mind for some way to deflect the anger and ease her deeply felt injury, to convince her that it made no difference to him—unaware that what he'd already done had accomplished that as no words ever could.

For Julia, giving voice to her thoughts and feelings was a kind of catharsis. Her anger disappeared as quickly as it had come, burned out by simply being allowed into the open.

Ross stroked her breast lightly with the tip of one finger, then leaned to tease the nipple with his lips and tongue. At her quickly indrawn breath, he raised his head enough to glance at her face, an impish grin curving the corners of his lips. "Just testing your sensitivity, Julie love. It's still intact, huh?" He was reminding her, rather than asking, as she well knew.

Disadvantaged by the emotional upheaval of the past few minutes, Julia had to work at an appropriately tart reply. But before she could think of anything, two quick raps came at the door, followed by a muffled, *"Petit déjeuner, Madame Bonner."*

Ross cast her a startled look, but Julia was already scrambling out of the bed. *"Un moment, s'il vous plaît,"* she called out, grabbing her robe from a chair and slipping her arms into it as she hurried to the door. "I completely forgot," she tossed back over her shoulder. "I always have breakfast brought to my room at eight."

Ross swung out of bed and swept his clothes up off the floor, where he'd dropped them last night, then disappeared into the bathroom, closing the door behind him. By the time he had finished and dressed, Julia had pulled a little table and two straight chairs over to the window, where the sun was streaming into the room. It was set with two plates and cups, and sported a basket of croissants and hard rolls, a small plate of foil-wrapped rectangles of butter, and a glass dish containing what looked like strawberry jam. A tray with a silver coffeepot and smaller pitcher of hot milk occupied the broad windowsill.

Julia glanced up and smiled, taking in his somewhat wrinkled trousers and shirt. Not very different from the way he'd looked after driving all night from Munich, she thought, finding it hard to believe that had been only two days ago. "Hungry?" she asked, pulling out a chair for him. "Would you mind if I brush my teeth first? I promise to hurry. Why don't you go ahead and pour yourself some coffee?"

She was quickly back, sneaking up behind him to wrap her arms around his neck before planting a minty kiss on the side of his face. Then she sat down across from him.

She'd brushed her hair, he noticed, but apparently hadn't felt the need to put on anything else, even makeup, and he liked that. He didn't require artifice in a woman, though he had to admit the way she usually looked was something special. One of these days he was going to have to stop long enough to give that some serious thought. Figure out just why—what it was about her. But he intended to make this unplanned little intermission as short as possible, because right now, he was much more interested in getting her back into bed. And that's when he thought of something else that had been bothering him.

"Julia," he began, then stopped, uncharacteristically at a loss for words. There was no other way to say it except straight out. "Are you on the pill?"

Her coffee cup stopped halfway to her mouth. "No." She shook her head to underscore her answer. "But I—"

Ross reached for her free hand, enclosing it inside his own. "I want you to know that I went into this, last night, with my eyes wide open, and I hope you did, too. I realize that you're the one who took the big risks—put your physical and emotional health on the line. But I want to share that with you, as far as that's possible. Do you understand what I'm saying? I'm in—"

"Shh," she murmured, reaching her fingers out to touch his lips before he could say more. She wasn't sure what else he'd been about to say, but she didn't want to take any chances on ruining this special whatever-it-was that was going on between them. He was concerned, and that was enough—another first in her experience. But her emotions were already too close to the surface, and if he continued, she wasn't sure she wouldn't dissolve into a heap of quivering Jell-O, right here in front of him.

"I thank you for that, Ross. But there's no reason to worry. I have a friend here I've known a long time, a doctor. I'll give him a call and pick up a four-pack later at a pharmacy."

"What in hell is a four-pack?" Ross asked, suddenly wary. "Not DES? Isn't that dangerous?"

"No, it's just four regular birth control pills, to be taken within seventy-two hours, two at a time, twelve hours apart. They haven't been approved at home yet, though any woman with access to the pill could use them that way if she really wanted to. Over here, it's widely known, and available," she explained.

"And you're very well informed." He no longer looked at her, but down at his plate, so she couldn't see his eyes. But he sounded almost cynical, or maybe angry, so his words had the effect of a dash of cold water.

"Any woman who isn't, Ross, is a gambler—and a fool."

She was right, and he damned well knew it. In fact, she was saying exactly what he'd always believed himself—all wrapped up neat and tidy in just a few words. Men and women who allowed themselves to get carried away without any thought whatever about the consequences of their sexual behavior were both irresponsible and foolhardy. They were gambling not only with their own lives, with their futures, but maybe with the futures of children, too, who had no choice about the kind of hands they were being dealt. That was probably exactly how he himself had arrived on this earth, and he'd always wondered what had happened to them—his unknown mother and father—how they'd fared, afterward.

So why should it bother him now to discover that Julia knew what she was doing, that she could and would take care of herself? Did he have some subconscious need to believe that she'd been so aroused she couldn't control herself—that he'd swept her off her feet—the oldest cliché in the world? Or was it that he was still hung up on the double standard?

Julia felt as if she'd just received a mild shock or slap, sort of like stubbing her toe. It wasn't an unknown sensation, since stumbling into unseen pitfalls always seemed to have that effect. It was just that they were so unexpected, and usually she couldn't figure out afterward how they'd come about. The silence between them grew longer and longer, and was beginning to feel uncomfortable by the time another light rap sounded on the door.

Julia rose from the table, glad for any interruption, though her mind continued to scramble for some safe way over the sudden impasse.

"Hiya, Julia baby!" It was Alex, too cheery and too loud. "What time are you going to be ready—? Oops. Sorry. Didn't know you had company!" Julia stood aside as he breezed on into her room, a huge grin on his face. He walked straight to Ross and shot out one hand. "I'm Alex Danilo."

His luxuriant curly beard, a rich dark auburn that glinted copper when he stepped into the streaming sunlight, showed off straight white teeth as he flashed him a smile. He was tall and full-bodied, dwarfing both Julia and Ross, but without an extra pound anywhere, and he radiated an exuberant energy. He looked, Ross thought, like some damned pirate standing on the deck of his ship, in full possession of everything, as far as his eyes could see.

Chapter 5

ROSS WAS MOMENTARILY taken off guard, but quickly recovered, rising to clasp Alex's hand. "Ross McCutcheon." He waited for Julia to say something, make some explanation.

"Alex is chief menswear designer for Ben Taggart, Ross. One of the best anywhere, here or there, I might add." She grinned fondly but mischievously at Alex, and he reached out a big hand to ruffle her hair playfully, then pulled her to him in a bear hug, their shared affection so obvious it was palpable.

"I suppose you finished at Lesage yesterday, huh? Is there anything I can do before the plane?" Alex asked, finally releasing Julia. He tilted his head just a fraction of an inch toward Ross, and she knew he was volunteering to complete any unfinished business she might have, so she could spend the remaining time with Ross.

"Is it time to go home already?" She laughed at herself, but without embarrassment. No reason not to admit to him that she'd lost track of time. "No, I finished, Alex. But thanks." She glanced at Ross, apologetically, it seemed to him. "We've got to—"

"Julia has decided not to go back to New York until tomorrow," Ross interrupted, surprising them all, himself included, though the baldfaced lie didn't show on his face. "We'll be on the Concorde, late tomorrow evening."

Alex peered questioningly at Julia, and she almost broke into giggles as she glanced quickly from Ross to Alex, and then back at Ross again. But she nodded, confirming with a happy smile what Ross said.

"Whatever you say," Alex responded jovially, starting toward the door. Then, as if it were an afterthought, he turned back to Ross. "I suspect I'll be seeing you again." A wide grin lit his face.

"You can count on it," Ross answered, matching Alex's grin and offering him his hand on it.

Not sure how to interpret what she'd just witnessed, Julia walked with Alex to the door. "See you bright and early Monday morning, okay?" That wasn't really what she was telling him, however, and Alex knew it. She wanted his approval.

"He's a beaut all right, babe, except for those rags." He spoke softly, hoping Ross wouldn't hear him. "But I never figured you'd go for the macho type! I don't want you getting hur—"

"He's not macho, and I don't have a type, Alex." She kissed him quickly on the cheek. "Anyway, after tomorrow, it won't make any difference! Now go," she urged, smiling, then pushed him out the door and closed it behind him.

When she returned to the table, the smile was still there. She dropped down onto Ross's lap, curling one arm around his neck, and the next thing he knew, her lips were all over his face, like a friendly puppy. "Did you mean it about going back with me tomorrow? What about your meeting? I guess I'd better call Air France and get my reservation changed first thing. And then I—what should we do first?"

"You can't stay longer?" he interrupted, as soon as he got his mouth free of her trailing hair. "I could arrange to—"

"I wish I could. Truly. But Ben is so busy. He's just starting on the new spring line. And my holiday collection is in production, so I need to have a look at how that's going, and there are all the fall trunk showings to coordinate, and—"

"Okay, okay." He held up a hand to close off the long listing of why she had to be back in New York on Monday. "We'll just have to squeeze in as much as we can today. And tonight." He stopped and pulled her closer, bringing her lips down to his for a long moment—"Or whenever." He squeezed one hand between them to loosen the tie of her robe, at the same time whispering in her ear, against the side of her neck and across her cheek—"On second thought, I don't think I want to wait even that long. You feel so good, taste so good"—until she couldn't tell where the words ended and the sensations began.

On Saturdays, the sidewalks of the Boulevard St. Germain turned into an extravaganza of sorts, colorful and entertaining. The weather continued to favor their explorations on foot, and Julia and Ross strolled along hand in hand, watching the show of brilliantly garbed shoppers. A mother and daughter in matching blue fox jackets and platinum hair, their alligator bags thrown over matching shoulders. A teenage girl in orange harem pants set off by black Adidas. An "older" woman in white mink tails and mauve leather pants. And a young man encased in trousers so tight he attracted more than one turn-around stare, when curiosity as to what he might reveal from the rear became too powerful to resist.

They browsed La Papeterie, an old-fashioned stationer's which had been operating for generations in the same location and now offered antique fountain pens, sumptuous marbled endpapers—a sampling of which Julia couldn't resist buying—and a seemingly endless selection of notebooks. Ross was bemused by the wineshop displaying a multicolored selection of candies out front, in huge covered glass jars lined up on two low red wooden benches placed on either side of the entrance. He paced back and forth along the benches, taking his time while examining the contents of each one, and Julia waited patiently while he negotiated with the clerk in French.

She refrained from offering her assistance, and he didn't ask for it.

They'd gotten a late start on the day, and the lunch hour was almost over by the time they arrived at the Brasserie Lipp on the Left Bank, a veritable institution which sported another turn-of-the-century interior, complete with mirrors, faience tiling, and bare-breasted negresses on the ceiling. And Alsatian *cuisine bourgeoise.* The proprietor, who stood at the foot of the stairs to greet and direct customers, recognized Julia immediately with an exuberant flow of French. She hastily introduced Ross, and after another short exchange with Julia in French, he showed them to a table just to the left of the door, explaining that it provided a good view of the passing scene. They ordered the plat du jour, today *jambonneau*, and a carafe of Alsatian Gewurztraminer.

As far as Ross was concerned, he'd have been content with nothing but Julia to look at. She was wearing a sort of orange-sherbet-colored long-sleeved shirt, all silky and clingy, and a straight skirt of about the same color, only darker, which at first glance was pleasing, if unexceptional except for the brilliant pink and yellow scarf at her neck—until she moved, causing the half-dozen pleats down one side to open and close in one uninterrupted fluid motion.

"Why cuisine bourgeoise, instead of regional? Isn't it all the same thing?" Ross asked after he'd tasted the steamed ham hock, which was served with tiny gherkins and horseradish, and a side dish of warm potato salad.

"Not really. *Bourgeoise* means of the common people. *Regionale* can be bourgeoise, ordinary, or haute cuisine." They were silent for several minutes, enjoying the food and wine, and glancing out the window from time to time.

Ross tried to sound nonchalant when he spoke again. "I take it you and Alex are pretty good friends."

Julia heard the unasked question under the surface of his query, but didn't really mind that he felt a twinge of jealousy. "For a long time," she agreed, nodding. "Since high school, in fact. He's from Houston, though you can't tell it from his speech anymore."

"A high school sweetheart?"

"No." Her answer seemed unequivocal enough. "You've heard of St. Michael's School, a few miles outside of Austin, in the hills?" He shook his head. "It's a college prep school, a private boarding school, though it also takes some day students from Austin. Even back then, all Alex was interested in was fashion design. After we graduated, I went to the university, but he came here. To the Beaux Arts. Then later, when I came to work at Balmain, we spent a lot of time together." She paused for a fraction of a second. "I guess I sort of leaned on him. It was a, a kind of difficult time for me, and he—"

When she looked at him, Ross found the same expression in her eyes, the silent agony, that he'd seen that first night when she was talking about the year she'd spent in Paris. What in hell could possibly have happened that still affected her so deeply, that seemed to haunt her, after fifteen years? A love affair gone awry, perhaps? He reached for her hand, the need to hold on to her too overwhelming to resist—to bring her close to him, give her a sense of connection or support, whichever she might need. "Can't you tell me about it, Julia? What was it that happened back then?" he urged.

She knew he was asking her to let him into the most private part of her life again, which he'd already succeeded in doing once this morning, without any warning at all. And though she suspected she would cherish that memory for the rest of her life, she wasn't sure that she wanted it to happen again. It was easy to get used to having someone share your thoughts, your fears and your hopes, but not at all easy to get used to being alone again. And for all she knew, these few days with him were all there would ever be. What would the cost to her be then? Besides that, though, she just couldn't bear to tear the scabs off old wounds that were still so painful, that she'd lived with for so long she didn't think they'd ever heal. And suddenly she was unable to speak, so simply shook her head, refusing to meet his eyes.

"Okay." He squeezed her hand, bringing the brief interlude out of time and place to an end, then lifted the carafe and refilled their glasses, to give both of them time to pick up the threads of ordinary conversation.

"Anyway," she continued, recovering first, "we've never been out of touch since. And for the past five years, since Ben introduced his menswear line, Alex and I've worked together a lot."

He downed half his glass in one swallow. "Okay, Julie, where to next?"

She tried to think what might be of interest nearby. There were a number of unique fashion shops in the area, but she doubted they would appeal to him at all. Not too far, along the rue Bonaparte, were some interesting antique shops. "How about antiques?"

"Take them or leave them," he answered curtly, "whatever you want. I thought you were going to continue my education about the fashion business, though it would be hard to top yesterday."

"Are you serious?" she asked, not quite believing him.

"Sure. I intend to learn—no, to try to understand—what it is that fascinates you about this business, draws you to it. Where better than in Paris?"

"You don't need to do that, Ross. I understand how you feel, about the business, I mean."

"It's not just for you, Julie honey. I hate like hell being kept in the dark about something, once I realize that's where I am. With you or without you, I'm going to have to get into it, but I'd rather it was with you."

"Then how about going to the new museum, the Musée des Arts de la Mode, just at the end of the Louvre overlooking the Tuileries Gardens? That part of the building hasn't been used for more than a hundred years, until now. It's a national museum," she went on to explain as he settled the bill, "a historical record of the people who created fashion and how they did it, from sketch to finished garment—the draping, cutting, sewing, pressing, photographing, presenting, whatever was done at a particular time. The last I heard, they had about fifteen thousand costumes, a couple of million fabric samples, and God only knows how many accessories. Plus documents, photographs and sketchbooks."

"I'm in for a crash course in fashion, huh?"

She nodded eagerly. "And it's not too far from your hotel. Maybe we could pick up your things on the way back." She glanced out the window, hoping to at least sound casual, even if that wasn't how she felt.

"If you're trying to seduce me, Julie, you managed that a long time ago—in Giverny." Their eyes met, and then they laughed, each knowing all too well that they'd both been well and truly seduced.

"I'll collect my stuff from the Meridien tomorrow, before we catch the shuttle out to de Gaulle. The Air France terminal is just across the street. No point in wasting any time today."

It was only a few minutes by Metro across the Seine to the Louvre stop, which presented a foretaste of what could be seen upstairs, inside its namesake. The platforms on either side of the tracks were lined with glass cases containing casts of Roman statuary. Unlike any other subway station Ross had ever seen, it was clean, well-lighted, colorful, and unusually quiet, since the trains on this particular line ran on rubber tires.

"Eventually the museum will occupy all nine floors of the building," Julia explained as they went through the first-floor reception area, where signs advertised the current show, *Moments de Mode*. They took the elevator to the ninth floor, to start with the eighteenth century. Julia translated most of the display legends for Ross as they went along, assuming correctly that he'd be unfamiliar with the vocabulary of fashion.

"It's amazing that any of this survived," Ross commented at one point, "after two or three hundred years of wars and fires, and moisture and moths, and who knows what else."

"I'm sure some of these pieces must have been in pretty bad shape, but the museum has a restoration lab. They hired retired seamstresses, buttonmakers, and weavers—people with unique skills and years of experience. Of course, there was nothing much to keep before about the end of the fourteenth century—people simply used up their clothing. Then during the Renaissance, man stopped thinking only about heaven and hell, began seeing himself as king of the universe, and decided his own body was worthy of celebration. So this is more a museum of history than of art, because the evolution of the human form is the story of the human condition—what we valued, how we occupied ourselves, how we tried to communicate with others," she smiled wryly, "and what we *tried* to say, often without much success, I'm afraid."

"Yeah, but fashion craziness started awfully early, it seems to me. What in hell was Louis the fourteenth and all his pals trying to communicate? That they didn't have to work, or were they just so weak that they let their women push all that lace on them? And why the lice-infested wigs?" He stopped, chagrined, and watched Julia whoop with laughter.

"For nearly two hundred years, lace was a luxury sought not by women, but by men, Ross. They just about ruined France with their ribbons, embroidery and lace, a lot of it in gold and silver. They put it on their shoes, their garters, anywhere they could think of. Trousers came to just below the knee, then were finished with lace hanging down around the calf. Apparently Louis the fourteenth had great-looking legs and liked showing them off."

Ross draped a deceptively lazy arm over her shoulder, then pulled her close for a quick hug. "But that was the Age of Enlightenment, Julie girl, the century of Newton and Descartes! There's nothing here but ostentation, a bunch of fops. Yet you claim fashion is a sign of the times."

"Yes, but rationalism—your Enlightenment—couldn't have happened until religious fanaticism no longer had a stranglehold on people, and neither could this! After thirty years of constant war, the influence and power of Spain was at a low ebb—of all of Catholic Europe, for that matter. Louis's power went unchallenged, and he dominated the aristocracy, the church, parliament and even the middle class. The result was that France reached an intellectual and cultural brilliance it hasn't known since."

Caught up in her explanations and enthusiasm, Ross became more and more engrossed in both what he was seeing and what she was telling him.

"Warmth and protection were never the only reason for covering ourselves, not once we crawled out of the cave," Julia continued. She glanced around the room. They were alone. Her arm slipped around his waist.

"Clothes very quickly came to be a mark of the social status of the wearer. And also a way of attracting the opposite sex. Louis not only had great legs, he was quite short, about five feet, five or six inches. So he needed these high-heeled shoes. After he began losing his hair, he also took to wearing a peruke, and since everyone copied him, that caught on, too."

Julia stopped suddenly, pointing to one of the mannequins. "Just look at the silhouette of that mannequin, Ross. The entire silhouette. Can't you see what it *really* represents?"

He stared appraisingly. "What?"

"Male genitals—the shoulders and arms and torso, all broad and rounded, are the testicles, and below that, the legs, always so slim and narrow, are the shaft!"

"My God, woman! We're nothing but sex symbols to you, are we?" But he couldn't keep from laughing. "Methinks you have a one-track mind."

They moved toward another eighteenth-century tableau, in which a man dressed in waistcoat, vest and knickers seemed to be beckoning across a garden path to a seated woman wearing a flowing *volante* gown of rich brocade with lace at the neck and sleeves.

"Like a Watteau painting come to life, isn't it?" Ross asked.

"So it would seem." She turned away from him, to a different display. "Then under the influence of Rousseau, helped along by a young Marie Antoinette—she hated wearing a corset—there's a return to simplicity. Hoops are gone and skirts are soft. Tight corsets and wigs and high heels disappear, and even the hair is combed into soft curls instead of stiff poufs. It's also one of the few times in history that a female dominated as a fashion designer—Rose Bertin. She was the first, in fact." She paused, obviously lost in thought.

"Come on, Julie, tell me what you're thinking," he urged, his hand sliding up to the back of her neck to turn her to face him.

"I was thinking about the 'wet look' that was a fad at one point during the eighteenth century, when Frenchwomen affected the draped look of ancient Greek and Roman statuary, wetting their gowns to get that clinging look. So many of them ended up dead of pneumonia that the government finally made it illegal. Slaves to fashion have been around for so long, Ross. But don't you think that says more about our innate need to belong than about our foolishness?"

"I guess I've never really thought about it before, Julia. Maybe. But then how do you explain those who aren't? Slaves to fashion, I mean."

"Only the need to bond with others is innate, Ross, not how we satisfy it. I meant that for some people the sense of belonging is so elusive they're willing to do all kinds of things for it, even submit to torture. And maybe women have fallen victim to fashion more often than men because we've never really managed to get the full approval of society. Our sense of belonging is incomplete."

Ross gave her all his attention now, partly because he could sense that what she'd said was not just an offhand remark. "Yeah, I see what you're saying. And maybe some of us have to constantly reaffirm that sense of acceptance. I read a book not too long ago, I forget the guy's name, but he claims that our sense of masculinity is fragile and needs constant nourishment, and that watching sports on television gives men a sense of kinship with other males, which they need in order to maintain their masculinity. We used to get this bonding through the sexual division of labor, he says, but with that breaking down, we have to get it from sports. And if you can't play the game, the next best thing is to watch it on TV. What do you think of that?"

Julia was too amazed to even try to respond. She just stared at Ross, tempted by the thoughts circling inside her head, until a smile broke out in spite of herself. She lifted their clasped hands to her mouth, to brush the back of his across her lips.

"I think any man willing to talk about even the possibility that his masculinity might be fragile and in need of constant nourishment simply doesn't have to worry about it, Ross," she whispered softly.

He leaned forward and placed a quick kiss on her cheek, then pulled her with him, tucking her hand under his arm for safekeeping. "My lesson in fashion's going to be damn short if this keeps up, Julie, so we'd better get on with it while we still can."

They went down to the eighth floor, the nineteenth century, only to discover a nude mannequin lying sprawled in the rumpled disarray of her canopied four-poster, layer upon layer of lacy Belle Epoque lingerie strewn around the room in what could only be described as a risqué manner.

"Status symbols, huh? Looks more to me like all you fashion nerds ever think about is sex!" he teased.

"Well, that's because the status thing got sidetracked by our ability to produce ready-to-wear clothes of good quality, through mass production and improving technology. Unfortunately, not much of that is going on today."

"Why not? Cost?"

"Not entirely. Even three hundred years ago, when Louis the fourteenth's finance minister tried to stop the use of gold and silver in clothes, because the country was in such bad financial shape, it wasn't only the aristocracy who threw a fit, but also the artisans who made the embroidery and lace, and who wove the gold and silver cloth. Now it's the garment workers' unions, objecting to every attempt to modernize. Sometimes I think they'd rather see the whole industry go down the drain than give up one job. The manufacturers want to restrict foreign imports, but what we really need is better equipment, some way to reduce production time and costs." She reflected a second— "And then a different marketing approach, but that's another story."

By the time they'd worked their way down to the twentieth century, Ross was beginning to appreciate clothing as a uniquely expressive human language, possessing qualities as complex as any language he'd ever encountered. And also beginning to view his own unawareness as a kind of sensory deprivation.

He saw that passengers on the Orient Express dressed for dinner in this new century, in long flowing dresses by Paul Poiret, who draped the natural female shape to reveal it as never before—until Madeleine Vionnet discovered the sensuous fluidity of the bias cut. Here also was the playfully zany Schiaparelli, Coco Chanel's black ribbon dress, and Christian Dior's New Look—one of what Julia called the "miscues" of history—along with, a decade later, Yves Saint Laurent's bare-breasted look.

"Now the power suit, like the one you had on yesterday, has been around for a long time. Too long." Julia stopped before a mannequin in a three-piece business suit. "Those suits have appeared on the streets of every city in the western world, with only slight variations, for about a hundred years."

"Why do I have the feeling I've just been set up? Okay, why power suit?"

"When I arrived at the Palais de Congrès yesterday, I didn't see you at first, in that seething mass of clones. Not until I spotted that." She gently rumpled his hair with one hand, then lovingly smoothed it back in place, seemingly unaware of what she was doing. "The corporate uniform. Everyone dresses more or less alike, showing no individual initiative, no deviation from those in power—the old men." Ross winced.

"Power and wealth in the business world have always resided in older men. Men who need to mask their bodies, to hide their waning virility. Of course, that image has its own sex appeal for many women, since it means wealth. But the three-piece suit is the old men's revenge, Ross—a way to level the competition, so to speak, by forcing younger men to conceal their natural masculine beauty."

Her expression was innocent enough, but he was on to her now and he laughed out loud, squeezing her shoulder in an affectionate hug. He couldn't help wondering about her perceptive comment about clones, however, since he hated the suits she was talking about, and wore one as little as possible. He'd never felt the need to ape older men, maybe because there'd been so few of them in his life, even in his work. Computers and young men were synonymous, or had been until recently. As for money—well, he hadn't worried very much about that, either. It was the work that he really cared about, and the money just sort of came with it. More than he knew what to do with at first, though Marilyn had sure tried her damnedest to solve that problem. So why in hell had he ever bought that navy suit?

"Why do most of us go through life so unconscious of what we're doing most of the time?" he asked quietly.

Rhetorical as it sounded, Julia chose to answer his question. "Probably because it's impossible to give our attention to everything. So we set priorities—whether we're aware of it or not. We make some choices very deliberately, and in those areas we have a lot of control. But when we don't, for whatever reason, we're still making a kind of choice. Decision by default—a decision not to decide, to let happen what will."

He looked at her appraisingly. What to her was a simple, compassionate explanation was for him a habitual way of approaching a problem. "Ah, Julie, my dear, dear girl," he breathed against her ear, "we're not so different as you would have it, after all. That was about the neatest summary of how computer programming works I've ever heard."

Now it was Julia's turn to look nonplused, but he was too quick for her. "Tell you what, Julie love. Let's make a deal. I promise to never again conceal my natural masculine beauty," he pledged with a mischievous grin, "if you agree not to hide those gorgeous legs anymore!"

She laughed her delight. "Not a chance, Ross. Don't you

see that what Saint Laurent did with those see-through blouses back in 1968 was to demolish the female breast as an erogenous zone? We women are desirable objects as a whole, of course, but the male mind is too weak to take it all in at once. He can only concentrate on one place at a time, so we have to emphasize or exaggerate that one little area. Then when he gets bored with that, we use fashion to shift his attention elsewhere. So you see, we'd both be losers if I agreed to give up any of my options!"

"Damn! Outmaneuvered again! You never quit, do you?" He settled one hand around the back of her neck, again producing that unique sensation she found so difficult to ignore. "But I can't imagine ever getting bored with any part of you."

The Chez Pierre reflected the origin of its owner—who'd come to Paris from the Béarn region in the southwest of France near the Pyrenees—in both cuisine and décor. Situated in a restored nineteenth-century house, it still retained the intimacy of a private residence, an atmosphere that was enhanced by the fact that the chef greeted them personally at the door.

"*Bonsoir, Monsieur McCutcheon. Madame.*" He extended a hand, first to Ross and then to Julia. "All is prepared, exactly as you ordered it, Monsieur." He smiled conspiratorially at Ross, then included Julia as he turned to escort them toward the stairs. They walked past a large dining room on their left, decorated entirely in shades of rose, from the floral satin chair seats and backs to the paper above the walnut wainscoting, and even the china on the tables, and were escorted to a small private dining room upstairs. Soft warm sconce lights brought out the rich colors in the paintings on the walls—all landscapes of the Béarn region—and the single table was covered with a pristine white cloth. In the center were two glowing white candles flanking a low glass bowl, almost completely hidden by the pansy blooms spilling out in a riot of blues, purples and yellows.

Julia suddenly had a vision of the Monet garden in early spring, which she'd mentioned offhandedly was her favorite time of year there, and knew without the slightest doubt that the pansies were no mere coincidence. She turned toward Ross with a quizzical lift of one eyebrow, and he smiled broadly. Apparently his clothes weren't the only "bit of business" he'd taken care of after dropping her off at the hotel late this afternoon. Their host pulled out a chair for Julia, then handed them the menus, after which he busied himself at a serving table set off to one side of the room. Julia feasted her eyes on Ross instead of the menu, until he glanced up and noticed.

"Decided already?" he asked. "Or shall I order for both of us?"

She nodded, her eyes never leaving his face. She was consciously aware that she was consigning every expression she saw there to memory, of storing away each sight, sound and feeling so it could be cherished, and relived again and again, when she was alone.

Monsieur Pierre returned with two stemmed glasses. "Is kir okay?" Ross asked, and Julia simply nodded again. Actually, she felt quite lukewarm about the apéritif that seemed so popular everywhere these days, a combination of white wine and cassis, but she wasn't about to change anything about the way Ross had this scene planned. She listened while he asked questions and then instructed the chef, partly in French and, when that failed him, in English. The restaurant was known particularly for its *poule au pot Henry IV*, apparently named in honor of the monarch born in Pau, in the center of the Béarn region, who'd vowed to put "a chicken in every pot." And that's what Ross ordered. After a few more questions, he decided on the wine, Monsieur Pierre wished them *bon appétit* and left the room. From here on, one of his waiters would take over, providing the efficient but completely unobtrusive service that marked every good restaurant in France.

Julia wasn't in the least surprised that Ross hadn't taken her to one of the more "predictable" restaurants, like Maxim's or the Tour d'Argent, but instead had chosen a new experience for her. He knew all too well how to tease and entice the senses—and he understood that was where she was most vulnerable.

"Ross, I don't mean to pry into your private life, but—" she began, then didn't know how to go on. "I guess I need to know, even if—"

"Shoot. Anything you want. If I can." Once again he reached out to touch her, across the table, covering her hand with his.

"Why are you not like all the others who are so involved in computers?" The question was constantly in the back of her mind now, and she needed to find the answer before tomorrow, before he was gone and it was too late. "And don't try to tell me you aren't. I already know you better than that."

He flashed her a brilliant smile. "Do you?" He might have known she wasn't going to ask predictable questions. "Then why don't you tell me how or why I don't fit your preconceived notions."

She thought a moment. "Not just because you drove all night to see Monet's home, though I suppose that's part of it." She hesitated a second. "No—because you were out on the river, trying to see what he saw."

Her answer was so unexpected, so different from anything he guessed she might come up with, that his eyes sparkled at her even though he didn't laugh. "And you, Julie—you're not only a delight to the eyes, though there is that, of course." He let his eyes drift, caressing first her mouth and eyes, and her hair, then her neck and shoulders, and her breasts. "But do you *always* swim upstream?"

She looked across the table, at the coppery skin and light, light blue eyes that never let her escape—so cool yet at the same time warm with life and vitality. When he'd come back to the hotel this evening, she couldn't help simply staring at first, and then wanting to constantly touch him. He'd appeared without any warning whatever, transformed by the charcoal gray flannel trousers and black leather bomber jacket, but he refused to even discuss clothes, and finally, he'd jokingly threatened to tie her hands if she didn't stop and get dressed for dinner.

And tonight he'd shed the leather jacket in favor of a Donegal tweed sport coat brightened by tiny flecks of red and turquoise and gold buried at random in the nubby surface of the fabric, worn over a knit turtleneck in a sort of deep red plum color, the supple fabric gently contouring the shape of his chest. For the first time, his clothes suited her mental image of him—the soft shoulders, the textured fabric and the mixture of colors. Julia didn't deny the intensity of the physical attraction she felt—she tried not to be dishonest with herself—but she also recognized that her response was more complex than that. This intense awareness of him was all mixed up with his curiosity about painting, and his sensitivity to color, to almost everything going on around him, in fact. And his emotional response to music. And then there was his almost intuitive insight and understanding, his sensitivity to what she was thinking and feeling. He was about as different from any computer jock, in fact, as she could imagine possible. And nothing he could say would convince her otherwise!

"Swimming upstream, huh?" she asked finally, somewhat pensively, as the waiter served their first course, a soup made from the bouillon in which the chicken had been cooked, to which very thin, delicate noodles had been added. "That's a quaint way to put what I take it is not exactly a compliment!"

"I wouldn't want you to be any other way, Julie, don't you know that? You're so special, so unique—my God, just to look at you opens new doors for me." He threw her a teasing grin. "And I can even understand most of what you say when you're speaking French. Certainly that proves something!"

"Only that I speak slower than the others. The result of my Texas upbringing, no doubt!"

Suddenly his face grew serious, and he released her hand. "I'm not refusing to answer your question, Julia. For years I guess I was pretty much like your stereotype, your computer nerd. I didn't think about much but my work. I didn't even want to. Then one day I suddenly woke up. But I have absolutely no idea why. It's a question I've asked myself a thousand times. Why didn't anything else matter to me back then? Why didn't I even *notice?*"

Julia recognized the pain in his voice, and the question with no answer was uncomfortably familiar. She wanted so badly to ask *what* it was he hadn't noticed, but she hesitated to intrude on something so private. Whatever had provoked that agonizing question, it was something terribly important to him.

Ross almost visibly climbed back out of the black hole he'd inadvertently fallen into for one inexplicable moment. "Remember the woman cellist I told you about?" he asked, pausing only long enough for Julia to acknowledge his question. "I can't explain why, but the picture of her stored away in my mind all those years came back to me, as alive and fresh as the night I heard her, just as I was beginning to realize how much I'd closed out of my life. I think it must have been through her that I got my first inkling that to really *know* something is to experience it not only with my head but with my feelings." His lips twisted in a wry grin. "But I'm still learning, Julia—in the last three days more than ever before."

Chapter 6

ORIGINALLY THE BRAINCHILD of two very different imaginations, Ben Taggart, Inc. had débuted its first collection only six years ago. In a business in which the best-known designers have always been the highest priced—the Blasses and Beenes, and the Lagerfelds and Montanas, all of them catering to an élite group of women who want and can afford innovation—Ben and Julia had launched a name and design concept built around the belief that a great many women would wear "designer" clothes all the time, if they could afford to. That it was an idea whose time had come was amply demonstrated in the phenomenal success of their three-day trunk show at Bergdorf Goodman, followed by a cross-country trek that brought in a half million dollars in orders in just two weeks.

Ben's almost intuitive feel for what Julia called a "feminine" silhouette combined with her own flair for color to create apparel that drew all manner of women to the Taggart designs—particularly women who'd entered the work force in such staggering numbers over the past decade. The way to reach these women, Julia believed, was with well-designed, quality merchandise at prices they could afford—and their response had confirmed her strong conviction that the changes she'd observed were irreversible, because they amounted to a fundamental transformation in self-perception. Even the conservative political climate of the eighties—which certainly made no apologies for elitism—rather than pushing women back toward traditional roles and values, was making it even easier for them to justify upwardly mobile attitudes and expectations. The result was that women consumers wanted and expected both more and better—a mindset that Julia considered crucial to marketing to women.

Taggart soon was joined by a rush of imitators bent on getting their piece of what now appeared to be a perfectly obvious and lucrative new market—business and professional women—and even the big names in Europe, as well as the high-priced American designers, began introducing new ready-to-wear lines aimed at these same women.

Alex Danilo had joined them two years later, when the company expanded into menswear, and then just two years ago they'd gone public, acquiring a new injection of capital that allowed the company to expand both the size of their collections and the types of retail accounts they could serve. They'd also moved from the old Flatiron district loft to a 500 address on Seventh Avenue. Though Ben had been named President, he preferred designing and already had the habit of leaving most of the business decisions to Julia, with the result that the day-to-day running of Taggart was now largely in the hands of three vice presidents.

The marketing slot had fallen to Julia in recognition of her role in formulating the company's original marketing concept. Max Starke was in charge of contracting for production, quality control and inventory management. He was still a big question mark to Julia after a couple of years of working with him, though she had reason to know he was very good at his job. What made her uneasy about him was that he seemed to either ride the fence, exhibiting a strict neutrality when it came to controversial policy issues, or to keep a safe foot on both sides. So far as she knew, he never involved himself socially with anyone on the staff, even in the most minimal way.

And then there was Tony Gianni. As Vice President and Managing Director, Tony was chief financial officer of the company, which in effect gave him veto power over the other members of the team—unless Ben really disagreed with him, and that was rare and getting rarer. The handsome, managerial whiz kid had been brought in by a Board of Directors impressed with the findings of the 1978 Delphi Survey which castigated the industry for its outmoded and "unprofessional" management—but Julia found him less than sympathetic to the company's, and her own, marketing philosophy. Though at least ten years older, Tony's fashionable façade reminded her of the male models who appeared in the pages of the slick fashion magazines, with no imperfections of skin, body or teeth, and no discernible character, either—like architectural spaces "decorated" by interior designers that lacked the most important ingredient of all, the personal imprint of the people who occupied them. Unfortunately, he was also the stereotypical macho stud, at least in Julia's book of character types, with all the outmoded assumptions and behavior that implied. Women were irrational, silly and gullible by nature, a "fact of life" that was reflected in his ideas about advertising and merchandising. And in the last few months, Julia had detected more and more little signs that Tony's views were beginning to pervade the entire Taggart operation, particularly his desire to relax the company's quality standards in order to maximize profits.

It was nine-thirty Monday morning when Julia stepped off the elevator, considerably later than her usual early start on the day, and was treated to a brilliant smile from Billie, the first line of defense at Ben Taggart, Inc.

"Morning, Ms. B." Billie dragged out the "s" in Ms. into a "z," then added, "Had a great trip, huh?" as a statement of fact.

Julia nodded almost automatically, trying to throw off her tired, dispirited mood. "But it's good to be home." She passed through the reception area and down the hall toward her workroom-office. Jet lag usually affected her more going the other way, but last night she hadn't been able to get to sleep, couldn't get her mind turned off, even with a boring book and a glass of wine. It could have been from being over-tired, except that she recognized the old familiar sense of loss—a kind of grieving that seeped into your bones and, like a dull ache, never seemed to go away entirely, no matter what you were doing or thinking. How she could possibly feel that way about someone she'd known for only three days was beyond comprehension.

Julia forced a smile as she entered her secretary's office, bracing herself for the problems and crises that always seemed to accumulate while she was away. "Morning, Connie. Sorry I'm late. Anything that can't wait, or do I have time to get a cup of coffee first?"

"Hi, Julia. I was beginning to wonder if you were going to make it in this morning." Consuelo Perez recognized the tired look on Julia's face. "I thought you were going to have some fun this time, for a change. Or was it a case of too much fun?" She smiled, rising from her chair as she reached for a folder on the corner of her desk. "I put these in the order you need to see them, but all you really have to know right away is that Tony's called a staff meeting for ten-thirty. Storm blowing up, maybe."

From the very beginning, it had been Consuelo's habit to keep Julia informed of a lot more than the obvious, and Julia always listened when she "sensed" that something unusual was afoot. "Why don't you do a quick flip-through while I get your coffee?" Connie suggested, then in spite of her words followed Julia into her office.

Though Julia's head was bent to the folder of phone messages and mail, something broke through her concentration—perhaps the faint but unusual aroma in the room. She looked up, startled into sudden immobility. Sitting on her big white worktable in the middle of the room was a graceful handblown glass pitcher, as bubbly as a glass of just-poured champagne, stuffed to overflowing with pink, red and white peonies. Julia whirled around. "When—?"

"About an hour ago," Connie answered the unfinished question. "There's a card—"

"I know who they're from," Julia murmured, almost to herself, recalling a comment she'd made back in Giverny—"I think I love the garden best in the spring, when the pansies and iris, and the peonies, are in bloom." She moved closer to her desk, a lazy smile curving the corners of her mouth.

Connie took one look at her face and without a word backed out of the room, quietly closing the door behind her.

Julia bent to breathe in the not-too-sweet perfume, picking up the small white envelope at the same time. She'd first discovered peonies that year in Paris, when she was trying to put her life back together, in the open market where she usually shopped for fruit and vegetables. They were almost unknown in Texas because of the climate, though she'd heard they grew way up in the northern part of the state.

"I miss you already." There was no name on the small white card, which didn't surprise her at all.

"Ah, you're here at last!" Alex intoned the obvious as he threw open the door without knocking, then strode across the room and enveloped her in a hug, which had long ago become his way of expressing very fond feelings where Julia was concerned. And he didn't care who knew it. He gave her a huge grin, revealing brilliant white teeth. His shirt was unbuttoned and both sleeves were rolled to the halfway point, revealing a thick covering of glistening coppery hair. "I thought you might have decided to run off with him after all, and we'd never see or hear from you again!" He pulled up short when he saw the flowers, then grinned knowingly. "That bad, huh?"

"Alex." The single word was heavy with admonition.

"Where did you leave him?" he asked, ignoring her.

"He went on to Austin last night," she explained, as neutrally as possible.

"You've got to be kidding! Austin? That's a little much, isn't it? I'm surprised you'd fall for—"

"Please don't start again, Alex! Anyway, why would he lie, especially when he didn't know I was from Texas, not at the time. I had a hard time convincing him, in fact. I don't *sound* like a Texan, he says." She grinned, remembering.

"Well, at least he's right about that. But what else do you know about him? Is he m—"

"Only that he works with computers. Moved there from California a few years ago. Has his own company."

Alex exploded. "Honestly, Julia, I just can't see you getting it on with a computer jock! What's the big attraction—aside from his looks? I'll give you that all right. He has a perfectly marvelous look about him, my dear."

"Drop it, Alex, And why in hell are you acting the heavy father bit, anyway? You of all people—"

Alex sobered immediately. "Someone needs to, you're too—" He let out his breath all at once. "Maybe you just need to take it a little slower." He seemed unwilling to say straight out whatever it was that was bothering him.

"And just how fast do you think 'it' can go, with him in Texas and me in New York? You know how I feel about that, Alex." Alex was more protective of her than her father, Julia realized, and he worried about her a lot more, too. Carey Blanton had always matter-of-factly assumed she was capable of making her own decisions, which also meant she was able to handle whatever befell her as a result of those decisions.

"Well, judging from that," he pointed to the peonies on her desk, "I wouldn't say it's slowed down much," he observed dryly, "but—" His voice changed suddenly. "You heard about the staff meeting I suppose?"

"What's he got up his sleeve now, do you know? Connie seems to think something is brewing."

"Yeah, but he's playing it cagey. His memo says seasonal planning and status reports, the usual stuff." He glanced at his watch. "I've got to go." He turned and walked toward the door, almost colliding with Elaine Mettlen and Claire Kennamer. "Oops. Come in girls, I'm just leaving." With a wave of the hand, he was gone.

Elaine watched him, mesmerized as always. "Ah, God, what a gorgeous man! Can't you just picture him with a sword in his hand, a gold hoop in one ear? I wonder why—" She turned back to Julia, catching her first sight of the flowers. "Ah, the man in Paris?" She interrupted herself to slip in a soft "Glad to have you back, sweetie," before continuing the interrogation. "Who is he—come on, give. I've never seen Alex at such a loss for words in describing a man before, Julia." When Julia didn't respond immediately, she goaded, "Keeping your little secrets to yourself, huh?"

"Between you and Alex, no 'secret' could last even two minutes around here," Julia observed, her exasperation moderated by the affection she felt for both of them. Elaine had come to Taggart back when they first started, when they couldn't afford to pay anyone a decent salary. She was thirty-four and had no formal work experience, she told them straight out, but her brain was still working in spite of the fact that she'd been a full-time wife and mother for twelve years. Her ex-husband was paying child support for their two girls, who were six and ten at the time, so she could get by on very little salary, or so she claimed. She could draw, which she'd demonstrated very well indeed, and she'd offered them a deal. "I'll trade my two most valuable assets—my hands and my brain—for the chance to learn."

"What are they?" Claire asked. "I think a man who sends unusual flowers is so—so, don't you?"

"Peonies," Julia answered shortly. Claire was Fashion Coordinator for Taggart's trunk and runway shows at their big department store accounts around the country. Elaine claimed she had just the right touch as a guest style show commentator, but Julia found her inane and effusive comments difficult to take.

"Where are we on our fall promotional materials, Elaine? Is Claire ready to go with them next week? How does the schedule look at this point?" Julia and Elaine had done a lot of learning together that first couple of years, but it was Elaine who'd created the tone as well as the distinctive visual idiom of the original Taggart ads, which had become one of the best-known and successful campaigns in the business. Now, she was the company's director of public relations, and was responsible for all their publicity, advertising and special events, and Julia didn't know anyone in the business whose opinion she valued more. She was also a good and close friend.

"How about taking a look at the new videos sometime this afternoon, Julia? You can also cast a final eye over some of our ad copy then, too, since the rest of the morning is about to go down the tubes." Reminded, she glanced at her watch, then at both Julia and the peonies one more time. "Speaking of which, I suppose we'd better get a move on."

Julia played the role of spectator while waiting for Tony to reveal the real reason for this meeting, giving only half of her attention to the eight others gathered around the big rectangular conference table. The rest of it wandered, viewing scenes from her own experience in frozen frames that she could examine one at a time.

"The October press preview is all set, Ben," Tony was saying, "for the twenty-third, just as you wanted. Everyone else," he paused to glance around the table, "please take note. How are your spring-summer numbers coming, Ben?"

Ben Taggart looked thoughtful for a couple of seconds, his dark brown spaniel eyes blinking rapidly. "On schedule, I'd say. Arlette's people"—he gestured with one hand toward the woman in charge of the Taggart workroom—"are progressing on the samples, and all the fabrics are in, so we're in good shape there. A few problems with accessories. Nothing major."

"Max?" Tony began working his way around the table.

"Fall production is slowing. The way it looks now, we should complete shipping on the fall line in another two weeks. Julia's holiday line is in full production, and we expect to begin shipping about the first week in October."

Everyone in the fashion business was ruled by the inexorable reality of changing seasons, which at times seemed as unrelenting as a ticking metronome, but Max's job was, in

Julia's opinion, the most nerve-wracking of all—always juggling two seasons, figuring costs and negotiating contracts with manufacturers for one collection, while filling orders for another.

"Julia would like to speed things up a little bit this year," Max continued, "so we're planning to complete shipping on the holiday-resort numbers by January one."

"How come, Julia?" Tony inquired, as she knew he would.

"November and December are simply our best sales months, in price and volume. After that, most of it moves as off-price merchandise, and I'd like to see if we can't change the percentages. I talked with a number of buyers about it last year, in Chicago and Dallas, before we worked out this new schedule, which I think will be better for them and for us."

"Okay, but get back to me as soon as you have figures. I want to see if you're right. Bucking the industrywide schedule just puts us out of step with what everyone else is doing, and if we get crosswise, we could find ourselves in more trouble instead of less." He stopped and looked down at the sheet of paper on the table in front of him. "You're going to the Paris Prêt as usual, right? Let's see, yeah, the first week of October. I know that's your old stomping ground, but see if you can't cut back on the social life this time, and get your tail back here quick—maybe a day or two would be enough—so you can report what you see to Ben in time for him to make whatever last-minute changes or additions are necessary before the twenty-third."

Julia nodded to show that she'd heard him, but refrained from saying anything. She could feel the sudden heat of anger in her face, and she had to work at not letting his remark, or his dictatorial style, get under her skin. How a seemingly intelligent man with several years of solid experience could be so insensitive when it came to dealing with people and still move up the managerial ladder was simply beyond her. But Tony wasn't through with her yet.

"And by the way, Julia, I want you in Dallas for the last couple of days of market week in October—that's right after we show here on the twenty-third. We're going to need to make some decisions, and I want a readout on what our orders look like across the country as soon as possible. No later than November one. Elaine, you'll take Atlanta, and Claire's going to LA. I'll probably pick up Chicago myself."

That, Julia realized with a start, meant he was sending someone to every one of the big regional merchandising marts. If it wasn't a storm blowing up, as Connie put it, at least something out of the ordinary was in the wind. She didn't have to wait long to find out what.

"As I mentioned earlier, it's absolutely crucial for us to begin planning *now* for any changes we plan to put into effect next year. Not you, Ben. I know you're busy with the spring-summer numbers. But the rest of us need to be focusing on where we're going next *as a company*—and since the fall collection is the really important one in this business, that's our target. I don't have to remind you that one of the reasons I was brought into this company was to implement long-range planning. We need to begin thinking beyond next season and next year—to look at long-term trends." He paused, taking time to glance around the table, including each and every one of them in what he was proposing.

"First, let me refresh your memory about where we've been and where it appears we are now. Then we can talk about where I believe our future lies. Ben, I want to say right off that what you've done with this company comes damned close to a miracle." Tony flashed his most ingenuous smile at Ben, who was sitting directly across the table. "And I want to remind the rest of you what I mean by miracle—an 85 percent profit hike year before last, followed by a 71 percent hike last year, when we had a little over $600 million in sales and $73 million in net profit. That simply has to qualify at the very least as spectacular, if not miraculous." He looked around the table again, gathering nodding agreement from everyone as he went.

It was an old technique, Julia thought, as she assessed his performance with cool detachment, like an outside observer rather than the emotionally and financially involved participant she actually was. But she'd had years of experience at this, watching and listening to her father's political friends. Tony was "warming up the audience" by massaging their egos, making it more difficult for them to disagree with him later on, because they'd have to mentally switch gears or change sides first. It was a strategy that worked well if you didn't overdo it, especially if your audience was naive, easily manipulated or unsuspecting. And that pretty well summed up Ben. Much as she dearly loved him, Julia also recognized his weaknesses, though to tell the truth she'd never been entirely sure that in Ben's case the adamant refusal to believe ill of anyone wasn't an endearing strength. Back when she and Ben were junior designers for Merino Mariani, she'd watched more than one young assistant "rise above" himself because of Ben's quiet encouragement. And even the Taggart organization had more than its share of hero worshipers, people who'd undergone a kind of resurrection thanks to Ben's unshakable confidence in them.

"As most of you know, we're down some from that this year, which is perfectly normal," Tony went on. "It has to happen at some point down the line in a fast-moving company as its base expands. The law of diminishing returns, you know."

Julia pulled a pen and small lined pad from her purse, and quickly jotted down the figures he'd mentioned, though she had all of them in much more detailed breakdowns in her office. But from here on, she was going to document everything he said, rather than rely on her memory.

"We have about 1,600 customers, operating 6,000 department stores and specialty shops, which I don't have to tell you is a good solid base. And though the company was organized originally to design, contract and market apparel for business and professional women, that concept has already undergone modification from time to time, as it did when Ben decided to expand into menswear, for instance."

Tony was setting the stage for something, painting a scenario, and completely ignoring both her own and Alex's contributions to the "spectacular growth" he was talking about. That meant he was counting them out as supporters for whatever he was about to propose. Julia chanced a quick glance at Alex, wondering if he was aware of where Tony was headed, but he didn't meet her eyes.

"Ben was smart enough to recognize that a business like this has to change as time goes on if it's going to remain a dynamic operation, keep up with the demographics. And it's time for us to make another bold move. We could simply try to maintain a steady though modest rate of growth from here on out, with more accounts, for instance. Though our marketing guru here," he dipped his head toward Julia, "is very much opposed to that, as you all probably recall." He was reminding them of the meeting in which he'd proposed that Taggart triple the number of accounts they were selling to. She'd pointed out other companies who'd tried that, with nearly disastrous results—Evan-Picone, for one—losing their reputation for quality merchandise, resulting in plummeting sales. Even today, 80 percent of that company's sales was still to department stores, which wasn't a very good position to be in when the sales volume was tipping toward specialty shops.

"What the entire industry has been suffering from most in the last few years," Tony continued, "is that there's so damned much stuff coming from so many different points—Japan, England, Italy—that it's almost impossible to have a new and total fashion change that makes everything else in the closet démodé."

Elaine caught Julia's eye and they exchanged a conspiratorial smirk at his clumsy attempt to sound "hip." The French word for out of fashion sounded like nothing but affectation on Tony's lips.

"How about the fact that half of all the women's dresses sold in this country go at half price," Julia injected quietly, feeling compelled to add at least one of the realities he persistently ignored, "because they're in the stores at the wrong time of year?"

He brushed her question aside as if it were only an annoying insect. "That's an entirely different problem, one of logistics, not a fundamental fact of life. What's really wrecking the industry is this anything-goes mentality—pants *and* skirts, long *and* short, wide *and* skinny, casual *and* elegant. On top of that, we're also seeing some companies move into more transitional apparel, which is exactly the wrong direction to go. You may sell more stuff off-season, but by the end of the year, the bottom line is going to be a lower total volume of sales. No, let's not kid ourselves about where the really big money is. It comes when everything in the closet is suddenly out of style and women have to go out and buy an entire new wardrobe!"

"And just how do you propose changing an industrywide problem, Tony," Alex asked finally, "by what we do here at Taggart?"

"I don't," Tony returned bluntly, "because I think we're finally getting back to a more elitist social milieu in this country. We've finally begun to shake off the impact of the 'dirty nothings' of the sixties, which is all the industry needs in order to correct itself. The mentality of this decade is expressed in just one word—upscale—and we can either grab the opportunity staring us in the face, or we can sit here with our thumbs in our mouths and watch the dollars go to someone else."

Ben spoke then, in his usual quiet way. "I suggest that we listen to the rest of what Tony has in mind, and then we can discuss it."

It was the go-ahead signal Tony was waiting for. He pulled forward a tall tripod with a large newsprint pad propped up against it, and with a flourish uncapped a broad felt-tipped pen. "It's a three-part plan, and like everything else with three points of support, is designed to provide balance as well as diversification." He scrawled a big red 1 at the top of the sheet of paper. "One, we aim at the high end of the market, and open a boutique on Fifth Avenue."

Julia watched the startled expression bloom on Ben's face, and glanced quickly toward Alex again, who looked as surprised as everyone else. She suddenly realized that Tony had timed the meeting for this morning deliberately, hoping that she'd be unprepared and disoriented after being away. Certainly he would have to be an idiot not to expect opposition from her.

"Women who buy the more expensive rags are where the big bucks are in retail sales, so we aim our merchandise at them. We do strong seasonal stuff, which means more sales because they're the ones who are most concerned about keeping up with the latest look. We build a big reputation with splashy showings, get reviewed in the *New York Times*, which in turn will up our license fees and royalty percentages. And that brings me to number two."

He scratched a big 2 on the pad, then added License Fees and Royalties. "We license to others, let them carry the burden of the manufacturing and merchandising operations—contracting, scheduling and oversight, orders and shipping. Get completely out of mass marketing, in other words, and put more of our capital into building Ben's name as a top designer, his reputation." Again he smiled indulgently at Ben. "So far, Ben's immense talent has been restrained by the limited imagination of a bunch of middle-class women trying to act like men. I for one think it's time to turn Ben's genius loose!"

Julia could feel Elaine's elbow nudge hers, and knew that after all the effort and smooth talk, Tony had just pushed every woman in the room off his team.

"That's a pretty big change you're proposing," Ben commented at last. "Have you tried the idea on Charlie, or any of the other board members?"

"I mentioned it to Harkins, but only briefly, and he thought it sounded interesting. But I wanted to put it to you first, get the group here to brainstorm the idea before we begin developing estimates for a detailed presentation to the board."

Ferret out what and where the opposition is, you mean, Julia thought, as she listened to the exchange.

"What do you think, Julia?" Ben asked.

"Well, maybe we should listen to the rest of Tony's plan.

He said this was a three-legged stool,'' she replied with a smile, turning Ben's earlier suggestion back on himself.

''Part three,'' Tony said as he wrote the number 3 on the pad with a grand flourish, ''is to eventually set up a chain of our own boutiques all across the country—high style at high prices—taking your designs directly to the women who want them, Ben. Giving them access to *all* your designs, not just the two or three some local shop owner decides to buy that season.''

Julia hadn't dreamed Tony would move so quickly to try to change both the basic design and marketing concepts on which the house had built its success, though she'd been well aware right from the beginning that she and Tony approached the business from two different points of view. Tony believed in the old trickle-down concept of fashion adoption—that fashions were picked up first by women at the top of the social pyramid, and then gradually won acceptance at progressively lower levels of society. At times, the pyramid got turned upside down, of course, as it had during the 1960s and '70s, when jeans and sweat shirts moved from the bottom to the top, from lower income groups to higher. But in his view, the big middle of society was always slow to adopt whatever was new, and never generated any fashion ideas.

Julia, on the other hand, believed that fashion flowed horizontally, so to speak, among groups of people on similar social levels, with the innovators and influential leaders of *all* social groups exposed to fashions at the same time because the population was so thoroughly inundated by information carried in the mass media. What was crucial in all this was that which view you took affected your prediction of how long any specific fashion might last. And until now, Ben had been relying almost entirely on Julia's judgment in this regard.

''Julia?'' It was Ben again, waiting for her response.

''You already know how I feel about licensing, Ben,'' she answered finally. ''It's the best way in the world to lose control of quality. I don't care how many specifications and qualifications you write into the contract. Oversight is nearly impossible, especially with so many manufacturers going outside the country for cheap labor. We could end up like Calvin Klein, having to buy out and become a manufacturer ourselves, which would greatly enlarge our capital outlay, not reduce it as Tony wants to do. Or we could end up like Pierre Cardin, with so much junk on the market carrying your name that your now very solid reputation would be diminished, too," she added.

"Junk in your opinion, Julia," Tony interrupted, "but have you looked at the latest figures on Cardin's royalty income? I hardly think we would turn our noses up at that kind of money! Nor would our board."

"Maybe not, Tony. Perhaps you're a better judge of that than I am. But is that the kind of name you want, Ben?"

Ben didn't answer her directly. "What else, Julia?" he asked instead.

"I'm not sure the profit potential in Tony's plan matches the very high risks it entails. We do need to make some changes, two in particular I think, but they're not so drastic or so risky as what he is proposing. One is to reshape our account list to reflect what we know is already happening. I'm talking about the growing customer preference for boutiques and specialty shops. That is partly due to the proliferation of shopping centers in cities all over the country, most of them with an almost identical mix of department store branches and chain apparel shops. The customer has the sense that she's seeing the same clothes everywhere. And more and more women today—certainly the business and professional women who are our customers—want to look, if not at the leading edge of fashion, not exactly like everyone else, either. So they've reacted by seeking out the small shops that carry something 'different,' which also provide a more personalized kind of service. We need to reduce the number of department store accounts and increase our specialty shop accounts. And we could also offer buyers more choice, at least in color and fabric selection, and maybe in designs too."

"That's nothing more than a band-aid, Julia," Tony snorted

derisively. "So you drop a few bucks here, pick up a few there, we're still about where we were, which doesn't look too good at the moment. We're down to about a 35 percent increase in profits this year—a pretty hefty slide from the 70 percent we racked up last year, wouldn't you say? We need to do something to stop it. Turn it around. Not just patch it up."

What he'd referred to earlier as a "perfectly normal" leveling off of the company's rate of growth had suddenly become an ominous warning of impending disaster, which couldn't be doing much for Ben's ego.

"I know our rate of growth is down over what it's been, but let's not lose sight of the fact that at 35 percent, most of our stockholders are five times as well off as they were three years ago. As you so rightly pointed out, Tony, we have an enviable record of performance—all of us." She just couldn't resist the temptation to set the record straight about that. "I'm not sure that what you're proposing isn't simply a trade-off, since higher prices mean reduced sales volume, and you haven't produced any figures to indicate that we wouldn't simply be making an even swap."

"That's because we're not at that stage in the planning yet, but we expect to be able to show that the potential in the licensing and royalties area far exceeds anything we could expect with our present mix."

"Julia," Ben injected, "I think you weren't quite finished. What did you mean, more design choice?"

"Perhaps what would have the greatest impact on our sales would be a major shift in both our design offerings and schedule. Department stores tend to reduce the diversity available to women, because they remove the boldest designs and stick with the best sellers. So do license manufacturers. I think we'd be better off introducing another line rather than licensing—and moving to a 'buy-now' regional-seasonal concept, as I've mentioned before."

"Yeah, you have, haven't you? Come on, Julia," Tony grinned, obviously more at ease now that they were back on familiar territory, "you can't still be that naive! Why is it you can't see that even the ladies in your great state of Texas aren't going to go for that 'regional' crap—they want stuff straight from the horse's mouth, from New York or Paris!"

"I'm as aware of that as you are, Tony—so I don't think Ben or anyone else here is naive enough to be deceived by that red herring! I'm not talking about designing down to our customers, with casual or folksy stuff. I mean elegant apparel with enough diversity to fit different climates and lifestyles—in color, fabric and design—delivered in season. That means apparel delivered in August that can be worn during September, October and November in Texas, for instance, when the temperature may still go to 100 degrees and doesn't drop below 70 at night. Apparel that provides a change of seasonal look, nonetheless—not the same heavy wool stuff that will sell here, or in Chicago, but layered clothing that comes off and goes on easily.

"We need to completely rethink the idea of a coat, for instance—to create something entirely new." She recognized the glimmer of interest in Ben's eyes, and she remembered how they had worked together on the first Taggart collection, bouncing ideas off each other that resulted in giant leaps of imagination. She'd missed the fun of that the last few years, because they'd never worked together in exactly that same way again. "A lot of people in Texas, and California, too, for that matter, never put on a coat, even in the winter," she finished quietly.

"Oh hell, you know that's a fucking affectation. Everybody's on to that gimmick—a bunch of have-nothings trying to act 'cool,' or imply they've got a chauffeured limousine waiting just outside!" Tony interrupted. "Listen, Julia, you go trying to fool around with the seasons and you'll lose what access to the press we do have. Do you think every paper in the country is going to send writers to New York to cover just our collection? And the same goes for buyers."

He seemed bent on purposefully misconstruing whatever she said. It wasn't the seasons she wanted to "fool around with," but what was offered and when it was delivered to the stores. If anything, she wanted to follow the seasons more closely, not less. She wanted the Taggart collection for any given season to do a better job of recognizing that there were big regional differences in climate, which she believed would mean a big boost in sales. Most of all, she wanted to match what was available inside the stores to the temperature outside.

Alex jumped in next. "You can't just close your eyes and ignore the fact that the rag trade is facing two nearly overwhelming problems—and you can't avoid them by converting to licensing, Tony. One is this out-of-phase seasonal situation Julia has been talking about, and that partly results from the other problem—our outmoded production. We need to put our energy into trying to find ways to speed and improve the production process, which in turn would cut costs."

Tony nearly hooted. "And I suppose you're expecting that to happen tomorrow, huh? What are we supposed to do in the meantime—think happy thoughts while our profits go all to hell? You're beginning to sound like a clone, Alex. We've got to deal with the real world, not this pie-in-the-sky stuff. And until something happens to bring down production costs, I think my idea is the way to go—get out from under the production and mass selling problems altogether, let the manufacturers we license take those risks, or at least bear the brunt."

"Well, I agree with Julia that we need to at least take that into consideration more in our planning," Elaine chimed in. "One of the reasons we're looking at the figures you've been citing, Tony, is what happened all over the Southwest this past winter. In January, which normally is the one cold month they can count on in that part of the country, it never dropped below freezing. Retailers not only resorted to unprecedented reductions, but most of their winter merchandise didn't move at *any* price. Our publicity went begging because there's no way you can get people into the stores to look at heavy wool clothes when it's still 102 outside. We even talked a few stores into experimenting with temperatures in the dressing room areas, keeping it cooler there than in the rest of the shop. That seems to help once people are in the store, but it won't bring them inside in the first place."

Alex agreed, nodding his head. "Besides that, thanks to Julia's insistence on a consistent quality, we've got some pretty loyal customers. And they're one helluva smart bunch of women, with their own money, and their own ideas about how they want to look. You're wrong, Tony. Most of them don't want to dress in unobtrusive little menswear suits 'feminized' with floppy bow ties—which is precisely why this company and Ben's designs are one of the big success stories of the industry. These women have acquired something, I don't care what you call it, maybe it's self-confidence, but I don't think they're ever going back to being the little *hausfrau.* Hell, even big names like Adolfo have seen the light and climbed on the bandwagon, with his new Atelier collection of short jackets, skirts and pants that can be mixed to look matched or not. Halston has Halston III and Halston, Jr. now, and Lauren has Polo. You're suggesting that we should toss our customers away for a bunch of fickle junior leaguers who'd follow their leader to the guillotine without the slightest hesitation. Personally, I think that kind of woman is a dying breed." He took a breath, then muttered, "And the sooner the better as far as I'm concerned."

"And when did you of all people become our resident expert on women, Alex?" Tony sneered. "I suggest you stay in your little boy's playground—which is much more your speed."

Chapter 7

THE MEETING RESULTED in nothing definite beyond a commitment on Ben's part to give Tony's ideas some "serious thought." Except for Max Starke, who probably stood to lose more than anyone else—maybe even his job—if Tony's scheme was adopted, the sides had been drawn early on in the debate. Max had taken his usual neutral stance, managing to find something of value in almost every idea put forward.

After lunch, Julia closed her door, with instructions to Connie that she was "out" for the next two hours, which meant no interruptions, no phone calls, no nothing unless it was an emergency. It was Julia's way of escaping the pressure and frustration that at times threatened to overwhelm her, though she hadn't expected to feel it so intensely her first day back.

Her office was simply furnished, all in white except for the plush royal blue carpet, and felt even larger than it actually was, partly because one end wall was completely mirrored. A haphazard collection of colored fabric swatches and yarns, small sketches and magazine photos tacked to the wall behind her desk formed a massive abstract collage above a row of custom-made drawer units.

The afternoon light poured in through a long wall of windows, reaching to where Julia sat staring thoughtfully at the peonies. She lost track of how many minutes passed before all of a sudden she jumped up and rushed around to the other side of her big drawing table, and slid a sheet of paper under the spring clip across the top. Then she flipped on her stereo and pushed a cassette into the slot. She filled two porcelain cylinders with water from the small lavatory built into one end of the storage wall and set them in the tray attached to the front edge of the table, which already held several bottles of opaque watercolor paint.

More than two hours passed before she straightened up and stretched, then looked around to take inventory of the sheets spread helter-skelter all along the top of the waist-high storage cabinets. It was time to get on with her other work, but at least she had some of her ideas down on paper, ideas that had been germinating since Giverny. And a sense of renewal, with even a touch of pure joy, had taken the place of frustration and discouragement.

Julia stayed late at work that evening, since she couldn't really relax until she had more or less caught up anyway, and by the time she left at nine she'd filled two tape cassettes with dictation for Connie. She called for a contract cab, as usual, and as soon as she got home, she put in a call to Austin, though not to Ross. It was her habit to touch base at home after she'd been out of town, just to make sure everyone was all right. After that, she listened to the late news on television while she fixed herself an omelette, trying not to think about how lonely her apartment felt. Seeking relief from the silence, she turned on the tape player and then headed for the shower. She had just finished and slipped on a nightgown when the phone rang—so unexpectedly shrill that she grabbed the receiver instantly to make it stop.

"Hello," she ventured tentatively. It wasn't really so late, but anytime her phone rang after ten o'clock, it set off all her mental alarms, leaving her with a pounding heart and breathless voice.

"Hi. Hope I didn't wake you. I—"

"Ross! No, I was just about to climb into bed with a book." She looked down at the paperback in her hand, one that was fast-moving enough to hold her interest but wouldn't keep her awake once she got relaxed—Robert Moss's *Moscow Rules*. "I'm so glad to hear your voice—"

"Yeah, me too. Damn it, Julia, I miss you too much!"

She laughed. "I know. I mean I miss you, too. And I love the peonies, though they haven't helped much—I've had a terrible time concentrating all day." She was looking at the four blooms she'd brought home while she spoke.

"Good. Aside from that, how did it go?"

"Pretty rotten, actually." She told him briefly about the staff meeting, going over the high points of what Tony was proposing, and the problems for the company as she saw them if the Board of Directors decided to go along with him on the licensing. "He even wants to do cigarettes, like Yves Saint Laurent—I call that a license to kill." She was still angry, and he could hear it in her voice. "I don't know what I'd do without Alex. He's my strongest supporter, he and Elaine. She's our public relations director. The trouble is, Ben is so—so, oh I don't know. He wants so much for everyone to 'get along' and work together, to keep the peace."

"None of them is on your board?" Ross asked.

"Only Ben. We went public two years ago, and he holds 20 percent of the stock."

"And the others?"

"Do they own stock, you mean? The company has a five-year incentive stock option plan, about 75,000 shares altogether I think, though I have no idea how many of them have taken advantage of it yet. Tony holds about ten percent, which he bought when he came into the company two years ago, and I own eight percent."

"You do!" He sounded surprised.

"Yes. Ben and I started the business together six years ago. He's great at designing, but when it comes to the rest of it, well— But that's enough about me. What about you?"

"Let's see. I got sort of a late start, because I have to confess I didn't sleep too well last night, and then I got carried away while I was eating breakfast, thinking about you at Giverny. The rest of the morning I spent reviewing all the places we went together in Paris, everything we did. And our last night together."

"Oh Ross, stop it!" She laughed and heard him join her. "It's bad enough as it is—"

"You asked." The smile was still in his voice. "Hey, is that a cello I hear playing? And should I read some special significance into that?"

"You have a one-track mind! It's Samuel Barber's violin concerto."

"Oh. Yeah, well, I called you earlier in the day, a couple of times. First your secretary said you were in a meeting, and then you were just 'out.' "

Julia laughed again, doubly pleased now. "I'll tell her to put you through next time. I was there, but it's the only way I can get any work done sometimes, though I admit I was hiding this afternoon. I was back in the garden at Giverny today, too, Ross—doing watercolor washes, sketching my color ideas for the fabric mill. Maybe tomorrow I can find time to start on the line drawings, for the patterns. I have to get them down before I lose them. And I'm already pretty sure about the fabrics for my next collection, which of course means I also have at least a glimmer about the designs, since it all sort of goes together. So I feel pretty good about that."

"I wish you could try out the new terminal I just got in today—an AED 1024. It's a beauty—a high-resolution screen and eight video memory planes, which means complex shading and high-quality color images. How about next weekend?"

Julia had to laugh at the devious way he'd worked around to the subject they'd had their one disagreement over, coming back on the plane yesterday. "Stop tempting me—I've already admitted that I'm not finding it very easy as it is! I can't even see past tomorrow at this point, and I have no idea how long it will take me to catch up. I can't even think about leaving town again so soon."

"Okay, but don't expect me to make it easy for you. You agreed you wouldn't close doors, remember? So when do you think you can come?"

Her mind raced. "Let me think—ummm, I'm probably going to the mill in North Carolina, so they can start on the fabrics, then there's the Paris Prêt the first part of October, and getting ready for the spring-summer showing, and—I know! Market week in Dallas is the last of October, and I need to be there for a couple of days. I could probably come on to Austin after that, for part of the weekend anyway."

"The last of October! Hell, that's almost two months from now!"

"I know, but—don't you see, Ross, that's exactly what I was trying to tell you yesterday. It's probably less painful to end it quickly, not to stand by and watch something wonderful slowly disintegrate." Her voice caught on the last word. "Time and distance have a way of subverting even the best intentions. And the strongest feelings. It just isn't going to w—"

"Don't, Julia!" he interrupted. "You said 'something wonderful.' Let's concentrate on that, okay?"

She nodded her head, smiling, then whispered, "Okay." The few seconds of silence that followed were comfortable, even warming. "Do you think you might be coming this way sometime? On business, or something."

"Maybe. I'll let you know. Get a good sleep, and I'll talk to you soon."

"Okay. Good night. And Ross—I'm glad you called." The smile was still in her voice, and she knew he would hear it.

The first thing Julia did the next morning was instruct Connie to put through any calls from Ross McCutcheon, no matter where she was or what she was doing.

"The peonies?" Connie inquired, but Julia only nodded by way of response. She spent most of the morning with Elaine, going over last-minute changes in the brochures that would be distributed during the Taggart trunk shows around the country.

"What did you think about Tony's idea, Elaine?" she asked as they were finishing up. "And don't spare my ego."

"Well, I could see the benefits in licensing, Julia, if we hadn't already gone the hardest miles. Targeting the women we design for, giving them consistent quality, and building a solid base of customers. We're already a success. We've got a proven track record when it comes to sales which, don't forget, are still going up, are not flat. I don't have to spare your ego, Julia, because you're more responsible for the policies that mean loyal accounts than anyone else around here. We guarantee buyers that all styles in the sample line will be produced, and we deliver orders on time. We give them advertising allowances and all kinds of promotional support—from ad copy to statement enclosures, in-store sales clinics and very classy videos. The preselected package deal was your idea, too, which they get at discounts while we keep our losses down. Really, we're at the point where all we have to do is stay on top of the pack, design-wise. Are you worried about that?"

"No, not really. But I thought Ben seemed pretty taken with Tony's idea. Didn't you see the visions of beaded and sequined sugar plums dancing in his eyes?"

"Maybe, but if we do anything like that, I think it should be just a glitzier line, but still affordable to our market, or maybe a line with a younger look. Then maybe I could bring home something my wild young things would deign to put on." She shook her head and grinned wryly. "Have you really looked at what the sixteen-year-olds are wearing lately, Julia? This latest friend of Tina's—I have to admit I haven't the slightest idea what might be going on inside the head of a kid who looks like that."

"Yeah, I know." Julia made the noncommittal comment, rather than speak her mind. She wondered if Elaine's oldest daughter knew how successful she was at getting her mother's attention. It was Julia's private opinion that that was the real reason for the constant confrontations Tina provoked.

"Do you have any idea what Max was really thinking yesterday, Elaine? He must have been born in neutral gear—or else he's been badly burned somewhere along the way, wouldn't you say?"

"Beats me, Julia. He keeps pretty much to himself. You want me to see what I can ferret out?" Elaine suggested. "Actually," she grinned, "he's not bad-looking, do you think? And I hear he's not married—can you believe that?"

"Yes, I can believe it. Who could possibly get interested in a man with no apparent likes or dislikes, no thoughts and no opinions of his own, no nothing that I can detect?"

"Might be a relief, actually. Maybe I should just feel him out a little." She stopped and laughed at herself. "You know what I mean. It wouldn't hurt to know what side he's going to come down on when Tony starts tightening the screws, right?"

The next day Julia, Elaine and Claire were in Julia's office reviewing the in-store videos, which had become so popular during the last couple of years and served to keep the Taggart collection in the public eye after the trunk and runway shows were over, when Connie came in with the mail.

"You might want to take a quick look at the one on top," Connie whispered on her way out. Curious, Julia went to her desk and found the unopened envelope on top of the opened and unfolded letters. Her name and address were hand printed in bold black letters. She knew instantly it was from Ross.

"Excuse me a minute," she mumbled to Elaine. "I have to see what this is." She tore open the envelope, leaving a jagged, messy edge. Inside there was only a small piece of newsprint with a brief unsigned note attached with a paper clip. "You will no doubt be glad to hear that the sisterhood is alive and well among the next generation, too."

The clipping was from the *Daily Texan*, the student newspaper at the University of Texas, and even before she finished it Julia burst out laughing. Couldn't stop, in fact. She quickly reread the first paragraph, before handing both the note and the clipping to Elaine. "Here."

Elaine's curiosity was piqued, since she rarely saw Julia laugh to the point where she had to grab a tissue and wipe her eyes. The headline read: "Student Protests Professor's Sexist Treatment."

> Professor Tom Phillipson yesterday referred to one of the female students in his undergraduate history class as a "girl," to which the student responded by walking to the front of the room and handing the professor a card, which he read aloud to the class. Much to the surprise of Phillipson, and the class, the card said: "You have just insulted a woman by calling her a girl. This card has been chemically treated, and in 24 hours your cock will fall off."

The article went on to describe the discussion that ensued—during which the meanings of not only "girl" but "lady" and several other words were debated by the class—and ended with an eloquent statement by one of the female students. "The future belongs to those of us who recognize that for too long the entire structure of our society—from the disproportionate salaries women receive in comparison to those of men to the subtler impact of our language on the way we perceive the world—has perpetuated the myth that men are a superior sex, that only they are capable of leading the society and of managing the wealth that is deservedly theirs, while women are equipped only to sit at home and be demure, pretty, ladylike."

"She sounds like a walking textbook," Elaine commented when she finished, "but would you mind if I make a copy of that? I think I'll take it home." She handed the clipping to Claire to read.

"I met him in Paris," Julia explained, "but he lives in Austin. How's that for a coincidence?"

"You mean a man sent you this," Elaine asked, astonished,

"the same one who sent those?" She dipped her head in the direction of the peony-filled pitcher. Julia nodded, still chuckling from time to time. "You know, Julia, I'll bet it's a rare man who would find that as funny as we do."

"I can't imagine a man sending anything so crude to a woman," Claire complained, her bow-shaped lips forming a moue of distaste.

"He must be—well, at least different?" Elaine suggested.

Julia thought about that for a second, then agreed. "Yes, at least."

The rest of the week went quickly, and Julia heard from Ross in one way or another almost every day. On Thursday, she went over the production and shipping schedule with Max Starke, though the main thing she wanted to talk to him about was ordering the fabrics for her next collection.

"I've already done the color samples, and I'm working on the pattern drawings right now, Max. But I have something sort of special in mind. I wanted to check with you first, because I'd like to go ahead with this, to give myself more lead time."

"You don't need my approval, Julia, you know that. And you don't have to be concerned about stepping on my toes, either, if that's what's bothering you," Max responded, his face giving nothing away at first. Then he smiled. He looked to be in his midforties, Julia thought, until he smiled. She couldn't help wishing he'd do it more often. It wasn't that he was unattractive. Just unmemorable, unknowable and distant. The opposite of Ross.

"I wasn't worried about that, Max. But it means taking delivery earlier than usual. How would you feel about getting the bills at the end of January or maybe the first of February?"

"Are you going over budget?" he asked immediately.

"I suppose I could tell you that better after I've talked with the mill. I thought I'd try Monarch."

"If you stay within budget we've got no problem. It really doesn't make all that much difference when we're billed. If you're going over budget, though, maybe you'd better ask the mill for real figures, because we'd have to go to Tony and he doesn't like working with estimates." He smiled again. "You might as well give yourself whatever benefits you can if it comes to that."

She nodded and got up, a little surprised by his last comment. "Could you tell me who would be best to talk to down there?"

"Just let me know when you want to go, Julia, and I'll see to all the arrangements for you myself."

She glanced at him quickly, surprised again, then muttered her thanks and left. As she walked back to her office, she passed Tony in the hall, talking to one of his assistants. "Hey, did you watch the game last night? See that pass Davies caught in the fourth quarter, with only thirty seconds left to play?" she heard him ask Harris Goldman. That reminded her of Ross's comment about men watching football on TV in order to replenish their fragile masculinity, and she almost giggled out loud.

Later that afternoon she received a small package by special delivery, and when she opened it she found a cassette and another brief unsigned note. "Hovhaness says he hears music in his head all the time, and always has. Thought everyone did, in fact, until way into his adult years." The recording was of the American composer's "Mysterious Mountain" and several shorter selections Julia didn't recognize. She inserted it into her player, then went back to work, now even more driven to hurry and get caught up. Somewhere in the back of her mind she was trying to figure out where she could find a couple of days to go to Austin—and much sooner than the last of October.

Sunday morning after a late breakfast, she slipped the same cassette into her tape deck at home and settled down on the couch with the *New York Times*. A piece on computer-guided tools caught her eye, about so-called FMS installations, "production systems that contain two or more machine tools served by automated materials-handling equipment and supervised by a computer." It was the most boring thing she'd ever read, but she stuck with it. A week ago, she wouldn't even have noticed the article, let alone read it from beginning to end. A little later, she found herself reading an article about the Japanese Fifth Generation Project, a ten-year, $800 million effort to produce "thinking machines," the second in a series the paper was running on advances in artificial intelligence. It was the announcement of the Japanese project in 1981, she learned, that spurred several American companies to form a joint corporate research effort. "If we don't shape up," the chairman of Control Data Corporation was quoted as saying, "we'll end up as distributors for Japanese products. The stakes are high. The first nation to develop this new generation of computers, and put them to work, will be poised to dominate the post-industrial world information economy." The American answer to the Japanese effort had been MCC, the research consortium Ross said had located in Austin. She was digging through a week of old newspapers, searching for the first article in the series, when the idea struck her.

As she listened to the phone ring, she found herself as breathless as if she'd been running. By the fifth ring, she was ready to hang up.

"McCutcheon."

"Ross?" Suddenly she couldn't think why she'd called.

"Julie! Damn, I'm glad you called!"

"I'm listening to your tape, and I thought I'd call and say thank you."

"Is something wrong?" He picked up immediately on the hesitation in her voice.

"No. Actually, I was reading the paper, and I ran across an article about artificial intelligence that mentioned MCC, and—"

"And that's what caused you to think of me," he finished for her.

"Well, no. I think it was the other way around. I suspect I was reading it because I was thinking about you."

"Oh, well, I like that better." She could hear him smile and relax.

"Did I interrupt something?"

"I was swimming a few laps in the pool."

"You have a pool? Indoors or outside?" She knew it would still be warm enough there to swim outside.

"Both. You'll have to come try it—anytime, winter or summer. And the Jacuzzi, too." She could hear the grin in his voice now. He was trying to entice her again.

"Where do you live—what part of town, I mean?"

"West of the lake, in the hills, but that's all I'm going to tell you. You'll just have to come see for yourself."

On Monday, another envelope came in the mail from Ross, this one containing still another newspaper clipping, from the *Wall Street Journal.* It was a report on the new U.S. Labor Department figures showing that white women now filled forty-eight percent of all professional positions held by white Americans, while black women accounted for sixty-six percent of all black professionals. He probably thought the information might be of interest because of what she'd told him about Taggart's target market, but what the clipping really told her was that he was reading newspapers the same way she was—he had her interests in mind.

When the flowers had come a week ago, she had been reminded again of the excitement of courtship, how wonderful it made you feel. But Ross was up to a great deal more than courtship—with the flowers, the newspaper clippings, the phone calls, and the tape cassettes. He'd initiated a dialogue, an exchange of thoughts and ideas, to refute her arguments about the effect of separation on a relationship. He was showing her, rather than telling her in words—forcing her to think about and to respond to him just as he did to her, even when they were not together.

And that was when she decided it was time to become more actively involved, that she'd add a little heat to this dialogue he'd begun. She worked at her stereo tape deck on and off for about an hour that evening, and on Monday, when she arrived at work, she dropped a small padded envelope on Connie's desk.

"Send it out with the rest of the mail," she instructed casually, though she was unable to hide a somewhat anxious, though self-satisfied, expression.

Julia didn't get home Wednesday until nearly seven o'clock, and she could hear the ringing even before she put her key in the lock. She dropped the sack of groceries on the floor just inside the door and sprinted for the phone.

"Where the hell have you been?" The words exploded from the receiver even before she had a chance to say hello. He sounded very upset—and angry.

"What's the matter? Has something happened to—?" Julia bit off the words, realizing Ross didn't even know about her, so that couldn't be what was wrong.

"Nothing's 'the matter'! I just played the tape, that's all," he said, speaking through what sounded very much like a locked jaw. "You knew I would as soon as I got it, didn't you? You must have, with her name on the label. And then you just up and disappear."

"What do you mean, disappear? I just walked in the door. You could have called the office if it was so important," she responded, more than a little irritated by his behavior. She had thought that he'd probably get the tape today, and might call tonight, but she sure as hell never expected this.

Ross didn't say anything for a minute, and neither did she. "I'm sorry, Julie, I didn't mean to come down on you like that. I guess I just let my imagination get away from me. I was worried. I did try to call earlier. Consuelo told me you'd already left, so I waited a while and then tried your apartment. After I couldn't get you there on the third try, I—"

"I stopped to get groceries." She sort of vaguely wondered when he'd begun calling Connie by her first name. And then she realized she'd succeeded in "heating up" the dialogue, all right, though this wasn't exactly the result she'd had in mind. "What did you think? Of her 'Poems,' I mean?"

She heard him drag in a ragged breath, trying to get his

voice under control. "They reach right inside and grab you by the gut. Make you want to cry—and shout with the sheer joy of living—at the same time."

How well those few words summed up the gamut of emotions Julia herself experienced whenever she listened to Anne-Marie Lacombe's "Poems." Written when the cellist was a young woman, most of them before she was thirty years old, they at the same time fascinated and repelled Julia, perhaps because they made her feel too much—joy and pain, both remembered and only imagined. They also left her feeling slightly uncomfortable, though she'd never been able to figure out exactly why.

"Yes, they do, don't they?" she answered softly.

"You knew all along, didn't you, Julia? That one of them was the piece I've been trying to find for—for twenty years!"

"No, I only thought it might be. From what you told me in Paris." She'd made an educated guess, in fact, because she knew the woman he was talking about often played one of her "Poems" as an encore, and that no commercial recording of them had ever been made, which was the reason he'd never been able to find it.

"Where did you get that tape?"

"It wasn't a commercial recording. I—I tape a lot of things when I'm listening to the radio. I just made a copy for you from mine." He was already upset, and she didn't think he'd take very kindly to hearing the truth right now. That particular music, or the woman who wrote it, had to be the symbol of something far more important than the youthful experience he'd described to her in Paris.

"Look," he suggested finally, "could we just start over, wipe the slate clean and pretend that you just picked up the phone. And that I didn't act the heavy?" he pleaded.

"If that's what you want." She sort of laughed the words.

"That wasn't what I called about, anyway, or why I called."

"No?" She didn't really believe him, but she waited, wondering what he would come up with next.

"How about dinner tomorrow night, about eight? I've got

reservations at the Arcadia." He said it with neither preamble nor explanation.

"You mean here? In New York?" She wanted so much to see him that she couldn't help wondering if she'd leaped to the wrong conclusion. Ross heard the wide smile breaking across her face as she asked, slightly disbelieving.

"Yeah, the one on East Sixty-second Street. I tried for Lutèce, but no dice. See you then."

Chapter 8

IT WAS THE great nineteenth-century architectural vistas and ornamentation, the Renaissance-style arches, carved fish and floral motifs, that had first drawn Julia to the Flatiron district in Manhattan, an area roughly bounded by Park Avenue South and Avenue of the Americas on the east and west, and Twenty-third and Fourteenth Streets to the north and south. The Flatiron Building, now little more than an architectural curiosity squeezed into the wedge-shaped piece of property created by Broadway slashing its way diagonally across Fifth Avenue, had been the tallest in the world when it was built back in 1902. At the turn of the century the district had been New York's most fashionable shopping area, then after World War I it had been invaded by men's clothing manufacturers, with the streets as choked by trucks as the Seventh Avenue garment district was today. Then during the sixties the garment makers began moving out, to the south, in search of cheap labor, setting the stage for the district's recent transformation to a mixture of residential and office space.

When Julia first moved here, now a little over six years ago, the entire area was deserted after dark and she never walked anywhere. Then grocery stores, deli's and small clothing shops followed the residents here, mostly architects, photographers and painters who were attracted to the large loft spaces where they could both live and work, and it began to feel like a neighborhood, with people everywhere both day and night. It had taken more than a year of constant tear-up, of living in one room at a time while the others were being worked on, to finally get her loft apartment exactly the way she wanted it—clean and uncluttered, with broad open spaces filled with natural light.

In spite of her determination to leave work early Friday afternoon, it was nearly six o'clock by the time Julia got home. She slammed the door closed behind her, out of breath both from hurrying and from pure unadulterated anticipation. The same questions that had kept her awake last night began bouncing around in her head again as she started the water running for her bath, hurriedly stripping off her clothes and then pulling her hair together into one hand. She gave it a twist and fastened it up on top of her head with a curving plastic clip, one of those clutching teeth things she'd picked up at Galeries Lafayette the last time she was in Paris—the day before she'd met Ross. Everything, not just Paris, seemed to be falling into before and after Ross these days, and though she wasn't sure that was such a neat idea, she couldn't seem to stop it happening.

He certainly had been anything but forthcoming on the phone— "See you then"—not even mentioning what time he'd be getting in. Was he coming to New York for her, or for business as usual, with Julia Bonner as the side dish, the frosting on the cake? How long would he be staying? Did he assume that he could just waltz into town, and her bed, whenever he damn well took the notion? That she would simply be sitting here waiting—free and available? How would he have responded if she'd said she was busy tonight?

But she was so anxious to see him again, and she couldn't help wondering if it would be the same between them now. Or would the harsh realities of this merciless city dispel the timeless magic of Paris, the city that was so much more than simply a symbol of escape from reality for Julia? If a place could nourish, then certainly Paris was mother to her, for it was there, fifteen years ago, that her torn and bleeding soul had begun to mend. During solitary walks along the banks of the Seine, in the midst of the noisy, colorful market stalls and the art and architecture that spoke so eloquently of human continuity. But why was she plagued with all these misgivings? Why couldn't she just take whatever fun and pleasure came her way and be satisfied with that, rather than be worrying over hidden motives or misplaced assumptions? Her feelings and her mind were at war again, with one insisting that Ross didn't fit any of the stereotypes that the other knew from years of experience were alive and well in the real world.

By the time she stepped out of the tub, Julia was fervently wishing he would hurry up and get here so she could finally have some answers, and that he wouldn't arrive at least until she'd had time to dress. She'd spent a lot of time thinking about what she was going to wear, and the scenario was all set in her mind. But she still had on her white velour kimono and had just slathered her face with moisturizer when the door chimes sounded.

"Oh my God, now what do I do?" she whispered out loud, grabbing for tissues and swiping at her cheeks. She looked around the room frantically, searching for something she could put on quickly, then just as quickly gave up the idea. There simply wasn't time. He'd have to take her as she was—the unadorned and unvarnished truth! She grinned in spite of herself and rushed for the door, never even noticing that her feet were still bare. All she could think about was that Ross was here!

Julia pulled open the door, and was suddenly overcome by shyness and uncertainty. He just stood there, and her face flushed with the pure pleasure she always felt just looking at him, and had from the very first time. The expression in his eyes was enough, and she indulged herself, letting the intense, almost yearning look wash over her. Then his smile broke, and he stepped through the door and enclosed her in his arms, pulling her close.

"My God, Julie, I never knew I could miss anyone so much," he murmured into her hair.

"I know. Me too." She hugged him to her, running her hands up and down his back, under his tweed sport coat, relearning the feel and scent of him.

He pulled away for a moment and searched her face, thoroughly and slowly, before reaching up to release her hair from the clip, letting it fall to her shoulders, his eyes never wavering from hers. Then he clasped her head between his long-fingered hands, gently turning it to meet the kisses he began scattering with agonizing slowness all across her cheeks, and eyelids, and nose, before finally taking pity on her, and himself.

Julia turned her mouth into his, eagerly, and there was nothing tentative about the way his lips settled on hers this time. Or the way his tongue slowly but surely searched out her own, fueling a need that suddenly threatened to overwhelm him. He massaged the muscles at the back of her neck with one hand, and a warm glowing sensation came to life somewhere inside her. And in no time at all that, too, mushroomed to an urgent intensity. Before she realized what she was doing, Julia's hands had moved together down the length of his back, into the slight indentation at his waist and then to cup the curve of his hips, stopping there, holding him still while she swayed from side to side, rubbing against him, trying to damp the fire that was burning there.

He strained against her, then moved away just enough to loosen the tie of her robe and spread it open. A warm hand spanned the suddenly sensitive bare skin over her rib cage, then moved up to surround and lift her breast, taking it to meet his descending mouth. An involuntary shudder rippled through her body. She thought her legs might collapse under her, then knew his hand and arm supported and held her securely.

Suddenly Ross straightened and pulled away, breathing hard.

"I'm sorry, Julia," he mumbled, at the same time making a somewhat inept attempt to close her robe again.

Julia's mind reeled, unable to understand what was happening for a second. He held her away from him now, his fingers digging into her shoulders to prevent her body from making any contact whatsoever with his, as if she was too hot to touch.

"I never intended—at least not the minute I walked in the damned door! My God, I just—!" He shook his head. "I don't know what came over me." One hand swept up through his hair in the timeless gesture of frustration, and she heard his deeply indrawn breath.

A wry expression pulled at the corners of Julia's mouth as she retied her robe and tried to get her own breathing under control. "Gosh, and here I was thinking I might have something to do with it." She took his hand and pulled him with her into the living room.

When she turned around, he was grinning sheepishly. "Yeah, well, maybe," he drawled, "but I was planning to be on my very best behavior, you know, to make up for the way I jumped you on the phone last night."

"Well, if it makes you feel any better, this isn't exactly the way I'd planned to greet you, either. I was going to be dressed to the teeth when you arrived, in fact, and be looking so absolutely smashing that you wouldn't be able to resist me!"

They laughed at themselves, releasing the unexpected tension that had blossomed so suddenly. Ross glanced around, taking in the room for the first time.

"What time did you get in?" Julia asked, watching his face.

"I like it, Julia. Wonderful feeling of space," he commented, "which isn't easy to come by in this city, is it?"

Julia felt inordinately pleased that he'd noticed the single most important thing of all to her.

"When? Oh, I was on the nonstop morning flight—around eleven. Actually, I'd planned to catch you at Taggart, see you in your element, but I went out to talk to a guy at Columbia and didn't even make it back to the hotel to change until almost six."

Her cheeks stung suddenly, as if she'd just been slapped. She'd wanted answers and now she had them, and without even having to ask. The reason for his little trek to New York was business, not Julia Bonner, and he hadn't assumed a damn thing—he'd checked into a hotel! Because he wanted a way out? Didn't want to be too committed?

"Make yourself at home while I get dressed, Ross. Would you like a drink?" she asked, turning quickly toward the small kitchen that was partly open to the big living room. "We don't have too much time if we're going to make your reservation at the Arcadia. I hear it's nice. Have you been there before?" She was trying to make conversation, and also reprimanding herself for being overly sensitive.

Ross followed her into the kitchen, came up behind her and nuzzled his face into the curve of her neck, pulling her back against him with one arm. "I've been acting like a kid, Julia," he confessed. "I could have taken a later flight, but I had this uncontrollable urge to hurry up and get here. As soon as I got off the plane, all I could think about was coming for you, hauling you off somewhere. I checked into Morgan's and sat around in my room for a while, trying to kill a few hours. I figured you'd be busy and wouldn't know what to do with me if I just came barging in. At least not before midafternoon. Finally I thought of a guy I know at Columbia, so I called him, just to talk. He insisted I come out to see some new equipment he'd just—" He'd begun to turn her around while he talked, but stopped when he saw the smile of pure joy spread across her face. "What—?"

Julia threw her arms around his neck and squeezed until he thought she was trying to choke him. "Oh, Ross, I'm so glad you told me," she whispered near his ear, between soft little kisses that walked along his neck, and then under the line of his jaw. "Because I thought I was the only one. Who was acting like an adolescent." She drew away a little and looked at him with a coquettish smile. "And you're going back to your hotel tonight, after dinner?" She knew the answer, but she wanted to hear him say it.

"Not if I can help it, Julie love." He reached for her lips again, but touched them playfully this time. "But first I'm taking you to dinner—come hell or high water, or even that damned robe." Her robe was plain to the point of looking unisex, but the tie had slipped loose again, threatening to reveal a great deal more than it already had. "So you'd better go get dressed," he added, dragging his eyes away from her. "But will you do something for me?"

She was already nodding. "What?"

"Remember that black dress you wore in Paris, the last night?" She nodded again. "Would you wear it again?"

She gave him a brilliant smile, then waved a hand toward the wine. "If you'll pour and bring me a glass."

He watched her float toward the bedroom on silent feet, then sauntered back into the living room for a minute, wanting to really look this time. When he was talking to her on the phone, he hadn't been able to picture her in any particular setting, here in New York, and that had sort of bothered him.

Spacious and uncluttered, even utilitarian in a way, the room emanated a warmth that made him feel good. Comfortable. The white walls, except for one that was glass from floor to ceiling, provided a stark contrast to the dark old oak floors which had been burnished to a high gloss and mostly left bare. Far from being colorless, however, the white served to background several large paintings. He walked closer, frowning slightly as he bent to read the signature on one—Danilo—then backed off and assessed it anew. It gave off an almost luminous glow, not from the dying sun shining through the windows, but because each color influenced the one next to it, giving it a life it didn't possess alone. Like the "Poems" of Anne-Marie Lacombe, the painting exuded both a rational deliberateness and an almost unbearable sensuality. It also made him feel like a novice.

A large formica-topped worktable occupied one end of the room, and big sheets of paper were scattered across its top.

He glanced through her sketches quickly, at the drafting style that was hers alone, the alternately thin and bold fluid line suggesting a dynamic exuberance. By the time he got to the last one, he thought he understood for the first time what she meant by "silhouette." Each figure was different, yet all were sufficiently similar for him to see that she was working on one specific shape or idea—developing it.

The centerpiece of the room was a lush L-shaped white leather couch and three chairs grouped around the edge of a richly patterned old kilim. Predominantly blood-red and deep rich oranges, the colors in the old rug were repeated in embroidered pillows tossed into the corners of the couch—and in the chairs, one of which was a sleek chrome Mies van der Rohe with tan cowhide seat and back. Several magazines were stacked on an antique table at one end of the couch, and under it, on the bare wood floor, were five shallow earthenware Mexican bowls stacked one inside the other. The top one was filled with red and yellow apples. A six-foot-tall pencil cactus in a big terra-cotta pot occupied the corner just beyond the fireplace, a living piece of sculpture.

Ross lost track of time as he perused the top of the long, low built-in stereo cabinet, a veritable museum of tiny bits and pieces lifted from nature, where they would have been hidden from his eyes. The lacy skeleton of a leaf. A dried milkweed pod, caught in the act of releasing its feathery white parachute seeds. A scattering of small smooth pebbles. The exquisitely delicate jawbone of some unknown small animal, complete with a perfect set of pointed white teeth. And he was filled with the sudden awareness that these little natural artifacts—of no tangible value to anyone—provided a rare glimpse into Julia's private visual world.

At last, he walked over to the sliding glass door set into the center of the window wall and looked out across the small rooftop terrace. It was almost pitch-dark now, and he stood watching the lights come and go between the buildings across the way, lost in thought. The room was like Julia, deceptively simple and straightforward on the surface, yet underneath possessing a complexity that intrigued and enticed.

"Ross? There's another bottle in the refrigerator if you're having trouble with the cork."

He started guiltily and hurried toward the kitchen. "Coming," he called as he poured out two glasses of white wine, which he'd already learned was about the only thing she ever drank.

Julia was sitting at her dressing table when he walked into the bedroom. He handed her a glass, then set his own down and lounged across the bed, propping his head on one hand. Her hair was drawn up and twisted into a high knot now, giving length to the line of her neck. She looked around at him and smiled, then turned back to finish her makeup, which she was applying as a painter might blend watercolors. Ross watched, fascinated, while she used brushes of different sizes, first adding a faint blush to her cheeks—so natural that he wouldn't have known had he not seen her put it there—and then a frosty blue to her eyelids. Her naturally long and dark lashes didn't need mascara, but she lined the edges of her lids with a darker blue pencil to bring out the color of her eyes. Then she lightly brushed her entire face, smiled at him again, this time through the mirror, and rose.

She slipped off her robe as she neared the closet wall and accordioned back one door, then stepped into the black dress he remembered so well—a shadowy organza that turned simplicity into elegance—and turned to face him. He sat up straight.

The softly rolled collar narrowed to lapels that never quite came together before reaching her waist, where all the fullness over her breasts was gathered into a hip-defining yoke, only to break free again at the top of her thighs, billowing out with every move she made. She did a short practiced runway walk, a few steps away from him, then a quick turn, and he saw her skirt flare out like a fan, then fall gently back to outline her legs from thigh to calf. His eyes were drawn down, to her smoky hose and lacy black pumps with high straight heels.

"Isn't this the one?" she asked at last, wondering why he didn't say something. "I still have to add jewelry, but—"

"Yeah, that's the one," Ross confirmed, but he was shaking his head as he rose from the bed and went to her. "Try these." His hand dipped quickly into the pocket of his jacket.

Julia looked down into his open palm. She didn't need to look twice at the diamond chandelier earrings he held out to her to know they were the real thing—and that there must be about fifty stones between the two of them. They looked French—surprise, followed by confusion, flooded her mind, and then he was reaching for her hand and she felt the warm stones touch her palm. "I'd put them on for you, Julia, but my hands aren't too steady at the moment."

"Oh, Ross, I can't—" she breathed.

He stopped her mouth with his own. "No strings attached, Julie love," he murmured against her lips. "I promise. Now put them on and let me see."

Ross stepped back and watched her insert the posts into her lobes, then look at him again. The gently swinging loops of perfectly matched stones gave off sparks of light, matching her sparkling eyes. He nodded sagely. "I knew it the instant I saw them this afternoon."

"Where?" she asked, still stunned.

Ross only reached into his pocket again, withdrew a small velvet box and handed it to her.

She opened it almost automatically, instantly recognizing the name printed on the satin lining of the lid—A La Vieille Russie. They were antiques, she realized all at once, not copies. "Oh, tell me what you know about them."

"Eighteenth century—Louis the sixteenth. I think they probably belonged to one of your ancestors. I can just picture her in them, at court, bowing before the king." He smiled indulgently, watching her turn her head back and forth, trying to see them in the mirror.

"I love them—they're so gorgeous I can hardly stand it." She bubbled with excitement, like a child.

He laughed, trying to get his breath under control. "Me

either, so maybe we better get going." He tried to make it sound light and failed. Instead, it came out sort of ragged, giving him away.

It was almost eight-thirty by the time they arrived at the Arcadia, but the restaurant was still holding his reservation, which surprised Julia. She hadn't been there before, but it was a much talked about and popular place. Considered the most elegant of several restaurants serving "American cuisine" that'd sprung up recently in Manhattan, it occupied the ground floor of an eighty-year-old townhouse. They were seated at a table in the mural room, which was already filled to capacity. Julia glanced around and quickly decided that neither the bland pastoral depiction of the four seasons, nor the reputedly "posh" patrons, were any match for Ross McCutcheon. So she settled down to fill her eyes with him.

"Not exactly an intimate little corner, is it," Ross mumbled, as if talking to himself. He indulged in one long look at Julia. "It's not that I don't want to show you off, Julie, but I did have a little more privacy in mind. There's too damned much light in here." When he glanced up from the menu and asked if she was ready to order, she simply smiled and shook her head. She hadn't even looked at the menu, and didn't intend to.

The waiter arrived to take their order, and Ross asked first about the domestic Foie Gras. It was served on Lamb's Lettuce with a Currant and Port Wine Sauce, he was told, and when he looked up and saw the dreamy smile on her face, Ross decided he might as well go ahead and order for both of them. Would she like to try the Chimney Smoked Lobster with Tarragon Butter, and Celery Root Cakes? She continued to watch him, and he ducked his head in a "yes" signal to the waiter.

But as soon as he'd finished ordering the wine and the waiter was out of earshot, Ross leaned forward. "You're going to get us both in a lot of trouble if you don't cut that out, Julie, my love," he warned in a stage whisper.

"Why did we ever come?" she whispered back, her voice

much softer than his. "We should have just stayed home and gone to bed!"

He laughed out loud, shook his head at her, then shifted forward in his chair and reached across the table, covering her hand with his own in a gesture she'd come to depend on. He gave it a quick squeeze, then asked, "Can I assume from the way you're behaving that I've succeeded in changing your mind? I knew you'd—"

"No," she interrupted abruptly, surprising even herself. "All I said was we should have gone to bed."

Ross stared disbelievingly. "And there's nothing more to it than that, huh?"

"I didn't say that, either."

"Well, maybe you should explain to me exactly what you *did* say, then. I could have sworn, earlier tonight—"

"It's simple," she said slowly, "because nothing has changed. My work is here, and I don't intend to give it up! I can't! Yours is in Austin, a thousand miles away. We do not live together, cannot live together, can't even *be* together, except once in a blue moon! Why can't we just enjoy what we *do* have, Ross, for however long it lasts, and stop talking it to death."

"How can you be so damned sure that's all there's ever going to be, Julie? Why?" He looked down at their entwined hands.

"What we're feeling right now, Ross—the excitement, the glow—just can't survive when two people are apart so much. I love how you've made me feel—more alive, happier than I've been in a long time. But what happens to us when this, this infatuation or whatever you want to call it, isn't there anymore? I simply don't believe that any relationship can be sustained over the long haul when people live two different lives, concerned about and giving their attention to entirely different things. They just grow farther and farther apart, without meaning to. Both of us would wake up one day and discover that *not* thinking about or considering the other had become a habit, simply because the 'other' wasn't there!"

Ross had ordered the foie gras because of their first dinner in Paris, but he withdrew his hand and sat back in his chair now, while the waiter served a memory that was turning bitter in his mouth before he even tasted it. Even after he left, Ross continued to watch Julia's face, making no move to eat.

"People can grow apart even when they're living together, Julia, day after day after day, and year after year. And I damn well know that's true—because it's what happened to me and my wife." He saw her eyes widen in surprise and waited.

"You're married?" She could barely get the words out, past the suffocating tightness in her throat.

"Not anymore. But I was. For eight years. Seems a long time when I think about it now. She became an alcoholic, Julia, while I was out seeking the Holy Grail—and I didn't even notice! How's that for growing apart?" He didn't expect an answer. "I was blinded by my starry-eyed vision of what could be done with a silicon chip! Or maybe I just refused to see what was going on, to admit it, even to myself. I don't know. What I do know is that I'm never going to let it happen again, Julia." He took a bite of foie gras and chewed slowly. "It wasn't exactly the best eight years of my life, but at least it woke me up, made me realize there was a whole other world out there I was letting pass me by."

"You have children?" she asked.

Ross shook his head quickly. "No," he mumbled, and then the silence descended again. Minutes dragged by, feeling more like hours. Julia wished they were somewhere else, and that they didn't have to talk about what they were talking about. But she took a deep breath and plunged in.

"I was married, too, Ross. When I was nineteen. For exactly eleven months. We were together for three months before he went to Vietnam." She looked down at her plate. "He never came back."

"Oh my God, Julia! Why didn't you tell me sooner? Is that why—?"

"No!" She almost shouted the word, then dropped her voice. "I loved him— I still love him, I always will, but—"

He could hear the anguish in her voice. "Can't we please talk about something else? How did we ever get into this?" The evening had started out so differently! Please don't let's spoil it, she pleaded silently.

Ross nodded grimly, reached for the bottle of wine to refill her glass, giving her some time. His voice seemed to shift gears as he settled back then and motioned to the waiter. "Why don't we get rid of this while you tell me about the house of Taggart." He interrupted himself to speak to the waiter, then continued as if their brief emotionally loaded exchange had never happened. "So you own eight percent of the company? I guess I didn't realize from what you told me in Paris that you were that involved."

Julia was stunned by the sudden switch, but she needed to get off the emotional roller coaster she'd been on for the past few hours, so she followed his lead and began telling him about Ben Taggart, Inc.

"Ben is a very gifted designer, because he's so sensitive to women, I think. He loves women, in fact." She saw him beginning to grin. "No, he's not a womanizer, Ross! Anything but—he's been married to the same woman for the past, oh, fifteen or so years, I guess. What I mean is that he has an almost intuitive understanding of how women feel, deep down inside somewhere. He doesn't see women as sex objects, as others want us to be, but as we are—feminine human beings."

Her hands moved to help the words, and he guessed she was having trouble explaining what she wanted to say. Or perhaps it was a carryover from her second "native" language. "But if Ben were to start designing for a different type of woman, the upper end of the scale—the woman who wants something 'unusual' simply because what she's wearing serves notice to everyone that 'I'm a member of an élite'—it would change everything! Her motivations are too mixed up with her own self-consciousness about social status, her position in society. It colors her every thought and shapes her perception of the world around her, preventing her from ever *really* knowing herself."

"But no one is very conscious of social status anymore," Ross injected. "Isn't that the real lesson in what we saw in Paris, at the museum?"

"Sure, but even though it might appear otherwise on the surface, as you go up the social ladder, the constraints become more and more inflexible when it comes to dress."

"I take it you're worried about Tony's plan, and you think the board may go along with him? What about Ben?"

"The idea tempts his ego, I think. The reputation, the fame, the status." She stopped and cast him a wry smile. "I wish I could think of some way to head it off—before the fact rather than after, I mean."

"Tell me how come you own part of the company."

"Ben put in $50,000 originally, and I put in $100,000," she explained between bites. "We figured in our ideas and expertise at another $100,000 for each of us. Ben's father-in-law was our big investor—$350,000—but he died a couple of years later, and Ben and Lucy inherited his share. When we went public two years ago, our initial offering was a million shares, at a little over three dollars a share. We agreed to sell off all but the 28 percent Ben and I were holding." She thought about that for a minute, and while she did, Ross did a little quick figuring. At sixteen dollars per, which he knew Taggart shares were worth now, that meant her eighty thousand were worth well over a million dollars.

"I suppose I could buy more stock, but it would take an awful lot to do any good, and I can't really afford it right now," Julia continued.

"Aren't you in deep enough already? What did you do, use your husband's insurance?" As soon as he asked, he wished he hadn't.

To his surprise, she laughed and shook her head. "No. Remember my telling you my father was a true Texan? A man of the land. He lives it, breathes it, eats it and sleeps it. All his life he's been buying and selling land, a section here, a couple of sections there. And a lot of it is the most worthless, sorriest ground you ever want to come across."

Ross couldn't help grinning, because whenever she talked about Texas her speech changed, in both inflection and vocabulary. It was the only time she sounded even remotely like the native she claimed to be.

Julia paused while the waiter served their lobster, then tasted it before she continued her story. "He's sold and traded a lot of land in his life, but one thing no Texan in his right mind would ever do is part with all the mineral rights. So on my sixteenth birthday, at a time when I was thinking about dresses and cars, and boys—what do you suppose I got from my father?" She paused to add a touch of suspense to her tale, and saw that she had him hanging on every word. "A deed to half the mineral rights on two sections of land in West Texas.

" 'It's time for you to learn to make money earn money, Julia,' he says, 'Petty Geophysical wants an exploration lease on that land, and they've already offered us five thousand. I told them it's up to you. You can either take it or try to up the ante. Course you understand that doesn't necessarily mean they'll ever drill?' " She cut a bite of lobster and put it in her mouth.

"And?" Ross urged, impatient to hear the end of this story.

She chewed slowly, taking her time. "I took the five thousand dollars, of course. Put it in a CD, and just let it sit there and draw interest!" She laughed at herself. "Then about 1974, after oil prices skyrocketed and everyone was so anxious to get more of the stuff out of the ground, they finally decided to drill. The rest, as they say, is history. But it helps pay the bills."

"Dare I ask where these two sections of land were?" he asked, already suspecting she'd set him up—again.

"Scurry County."

He burst out laughing and shook his head in disbelief. "One of the biggest oil fields in the state! The good old Texas myth! I don't know whether to believe you or not, Julia, which I guess is proof enough that you're just what you say you are—a true Texan!"

Chapter 9

ROSS OPENED HIS eyes slightly, slowly, caught a shadowy glimpse of the Flatiron Building silhouetted against the gray sky of breaking dawn, and wondered what had awakened him. Even with the quilt down around his waist, he felt completely relaxed and warm—like floating in a tub of warm water, he thought, before his heavy lids dropped and a kind of thick fog began to sweep over him again. But his imagination seemed to be playing tricks, painting his chest with a brush made of downy-soft feathers—back and forth, slowly, insistently—across first one nipple and then the other, drawing them into tight points as effectively as a blast of cold air, before sweeping an inexorable path down over his rib cage and across his abdomen. He felt an involuntary visceral clutch deep in his gut and a swelling surge in his loins, as if his body was responding to subconscious desires, or alien commands. What dark fantasy was this, come to torture him while he slept?

His tentatively exploring hand discovered the softly curling strands trailing across his chest—and a picture of Julia's thick dark hair, swinging free as she moved, exploded in his mind's eye. Threading his fingers through the heavy mass, he gently cupped them around the back of her head. "Julia?" He whispered her name softly, not sure if she was awake—was conscious of what she was doing to him.

"Shh—be still," she whispered, barely interrupting her caressing exploration of his body, leaving nothing untouched by the thick sweep of shiny dark hair, nimble fingers and soft, moist lips. And each time he lifted a hand to touch or caress her, she stilled it with one of her own, holding it immobile, refusing him even the tiniest distraction from the sensual feast she was preparing, until he had no will to do anything but lie there as the minutes spun out, giving himself entirely into her tender keeping.

Julia's head moved down over his stomach, blazing a trail of anticipation with her lips and darting tongue, a weapon that turned languidly gentle as it reached his turgid penis. His anxious waiting peaked into ecstasy as her mouth closed over him, and he knew himself to be nothing but a mass of pure sensation, carried along on a huge rising wave. But just as the intensity of pure pleasure flooding his entire body threatened to overtake and engulf him, Julia pulled away for one endless moment, leaving him suspended in limbo, unable to go either forward or back.

The next instant she had risen over him in one smooth swing to sit astride his thighs. Slowly she raised herself, teasing and torturing him with her soft, pouting nether lips, until finally he felt a warm wet sheath close over his entire length, ending in one still interminable moment before she began to slide up and down, all the while watching his face with a satisfied smile.

Ross's control exploded like a burst of steam, and he suddenly thrust up as she came down, his hands grasping her hips to pull her hard against him. She knew the exact instant he climaxed, sensing the muscles beginning to contract against her own, and fell forward over him, to lay her cheek against his heart, listening as the life-giving pump beat out its frantic pace, then gradually began to slow.

When Ross opened his eyes again, it was to not only near-daylight, but also to the conscious realization that Julia had focused her every move and touch on his pleasure, submerging her own in order to enhance his. He'd reached such an intense pitch of arousal, in fact, that he was still firm inside her, so he slowly and deliberately rolled her over, reversing their positions and preparing to take her with him this time. And he soon had her writhing under his hands and mouth, and then his filling thrusts, until one long loving embrace from her entire body told him what he wanted to know, at the same time triggering his own release, less intense this time, but somehow more complete. He rested on his elbows over her, trying to keep his weight from stifling her gasping breaths, and felt her go soft at last. A few minutes later he withdrew, but held her to him, nestling her head into the curve of his neck.

Julia was gone when he woke again. He glanced around the room, then lay still, listening. The shower was running, so he waited, thinking about last night. And this morning. Old memories surfaced, of the other times in his life when he'd experienced the heady euphoria of discovery, the conscious awareness of moving a giant step forward, but none of them could match the unexpected sense of revelation he'd felt this morning. A unique and immensely exhilarating discovery, though it did occur to him to wonder whether he was being naive. Did everyone but him already know about this—this whatever it was? Hell, he couldn't even put a name to it yet! But it made him want to leap out of bed and shout or laugh, loud and long, just for the pure joy of it. So he did.

Julia was so startled by the sudden burst of noise that she forgot herself and threw open the bathroom door. "Ross? What—?"

"Ah, my beautiful Julia," he breathed when he saw her, "what a sight you are!"

His words brought awareness of the picture she must present—fresh out of a steaming shower with wisps of hair falling and curling haphazardly around her face, the handle of her orange toothbrush dangling between her lips. A self-conscious blush rose in her face, which was ridiculous and she knew it, especially after last night, but she simply couldn't help it. So she slammed the door shut again, only to hear him break into laughter once again.

Damn him anyway, she thought, jerking the door open again. But he'd jumped up and was standing right there, no more than six inches away, ready and waiting. And he didn't give her a chance to speak, or anything else. He simply grabbed for her, wrapped her in a giant hug and twirled her around in circles while he went right on laughing. When finally he let her feet touch the floor again, she swayed against him dizzily.

"If you insist, Julie love, but I think I need some sustenance before we go at it again." He grinned the words. "So how about some breakfast first?"

"Damn you!" she exploded, laughing in spite of herself, then softened momentarily to rub her cheek against his chest before forcing herself to straighten. "If you'll let me out of here so I can find some clothes, I'll go fix food for the ravening beast. Talk about insatiable!" She tried to break away, but he held her fast, smoothing the hair back from her face with one hand and forcing her to look at him.

She broke away from the tenderness she saw in his eyes, unsure what to do with it. "You can have the shower now, and—oh, I put out a new razor and toothbrush for you," she tossed over her shoulder as she quickly crossed the thick carpet to her closet and pushed open two of the louvered doors that lined the entire wall, "since you make a habit of getting separated from your luggage."

The suddenness of her escape reminded Ross of their nearly disastrous confrontation in the restaurant last night, and he realized he'd have to go slower, stop pushing her. Somehow, he was going to have to wait until she was ready to confront whatever it was she was so hung up about. Which meant he'd also have to learn to live with the anxiety he'd first felt on the drive to Paris. He finished showering and while dressing browsed her bedroom, seeing it in broad daylight for the first time—the elegant ivory satin comforter on the bed, the lush cinnamon carpet and the various shades of beige throughout, from the rough-textured fabric covering the walls to the built-in closet wall and chest of drawers. All those seemingly endless days after he'd left her at the airport, when he couldn't get her out of his head, his mind's eye had been picturing her in one setting or another in Paris while his brain told him she was in New York.

On one side of the bed an extension of the headboard formed a low table, and it held a wine carafe containing four pink peonies. He grinned, liking the idea that she had wanted to bring some of them home. Next, he wandered slowly across the hall, into another bedroom, this one smaller than her own but just as warm and comfortable looking. Rather than the sterile, unused look of a guest room, it had the appearance of being lived in, from the small framed photographs lining the top of a chest of drawers, to the porcelain tray spilling over with bottles, combs and other toilet articles. He sauntered in, to take a closer look at the people in the photos. The largest one was in color. A smiling young man on a horse, maybe twenty or twenty-two, blond, well-built, fairly tall. It seemed to have been taken out in the country somewhere, in Texas probably, since the field behind him was blanketed with bluebonnets and Indian paintbrush. Next to that one was a black and white studio portrait of an older couple, about the age of Julia's parents he would guess, and then a group shot of several young girls, perhaps ten or twelve years old.

"Hi," Ross greeted Julia as he came into the kitchen, planting a quick kiss on her cheek. She had on a dusty pink knit exercise suit. The top was quilted and looked bulky, but wasn't—and it was very, very soft to the touch. She wasn't wearing any makeup again, and had allowed her hair to dry any which way it wanted to after her shower, with the result that it was even curlier than usual. She looked, in fact, a lot like the teenager he'd first taken her for, in the garden at Giverny.

"Smells fantastic in here," he added, "and so do you, but not the same fantastic. Anything I can do to help?" He watched her pour orange juice into two short, squat glasses. The counter separating the kitchen from the living room was already set, and she was flipping over bacon on the electric range built into the kitchen side of the veined brown marble slab.

"Since you're always hungry," she teased, "I fixed a regular ranch hand's breakfast, but I was waiting until you got here to start the eggs. All I need to know is how many. The biscuits are in the oven and should be about done."

"You are really unbelievable, Julie love, in bed and ou—" He was teasing, too, but stopped himself when he realized he might embarrass her.

Instead, however, Julia turned and curved her arms around his neck, pulling him to her so she could sweep her lips across his, from one corner to the other and then back again. "I've never done that before, Ross," she confessed haltingly, between soft short kisses, first on his chin, then moving up to the corner of his mouth again. "This morning I mean, but I—"

He sensed that she felt shy about what she'd done in the dreamlike world between sleeping and waking, now that they were face to face in broad daylight. But she also was struggling to say something. He wanted to help, but wasn't sure how. "I don't mind if you want to experiment with me, Julie," he offered. "You *could* tell that I sort of liked it, couldn't you!"

"Yes, but it wasn't an experiment, Ross. That's what I'm trying to tell you. It was very well practiced, in fact."

Now why the hell did she have to say that? "Yeah," he muttered, "I noticed." Didn't she have enough sense to know that no man wanted to be reminded of all the other men she'd been to bed with?

She faced him then, braving it out, eye to eye. "That particular scene has been one of my most cherished fantasies, for a long, long time. I've thought about it, planned it all out in detail in my head,'' she explained, so clearly that it took his breath away when he really understood what she was saying. ''He'd be completely under my spell, in my power.'' She grinned mischievously. ''But I've never been able to put a face on the man before—or wanted to, I guess. Until now.''

Before he had time to either recover or react, she'd stepped away and was pulling a big round pan of golden biscuits from the oven.

After breakfast they went to the greenmarket in Union Square, a farmers' market just a few blocks from Julia's apartment. It was a cool but sunny day, and she pointed out some of her favorite buildings as they walked, one of them just on the edge of Union Square at Sixteenth Street. The one-time Bank of the Metropolis was an eclectic creation, to say the least, with bowed Ionic portico at the bottom, and an enormous cornice jutting out over the slender shaft. ''Doesn't it remind you of Louis Sullivan?'' she asked, peering up at the ornamented tower.

Ross recognized the name of the pioneering Chicago architect, but the only building he knew of Sullivan's was the Carson Pirie Scott department store in Chicago. ''Sort of,'' he responded thoughtfully, ''but perhaps too cool.''

She turned. ''What do you mean?''

''Detached, I suppose. Or maybe timid. No, that's not it, either. I don't know—I'm not very good at this. You've heard music you thought at first sounded kind of like Debussy, and then a bit like Puccini, or whoever? It wanders all over the place, searching for you never know what, and in the end you feel frustrated because it all came to nothing—it never went anywhere, never developed a sound of its own.''

''Like the particular 'look'—uniquely her own—that every great painter discovers sooner or later,'' Julia agreed, understanding perfectly what he was getting at.

Ross contained his smile, knowing she'd used the female pronoun on purpose, and that it was another of the little tests she put him to from time to time, whether she was willing to admit it or not.

On the way back, they walked several blocks out of their way, just to go "building watching." In between, he asked, "What's for tonight, Julia? How about the Met—do you know what's playing? Or maybe Sam Shepard's latest play. We could have a late dinner someplace, and then—" He grabbed her hand and began swinging it, grinning, then pulled her to him and planted a loud smack on her cheek.

Julia didn't mind his public display of affection, but shook her head. "Nope, I thought I'd treat you to the Greene Street Cafe in Soho. I have a feeling you might really go for the High Heeled Women." At his quizzical expression, she added, "You haven't heard of them? Four women. They sing, dance, do satire and—" Suddenly the pitch of her voice changed. "Tarzan and I had a big fight, Cheetah. All I said was 'Tarzan, help me fix the place up, hang a few vines. You live here, too.' And he said, 'Jane better watch step. Name not on lease. Tree house going co-op.' That's New York humor, and they're crazy." She paused to catch her breath. "And this afternoon, after we take this stuff back to the apartment, you might want to try the Munch retrospective—you know, the Norwegian expressionist. Or does that sound too boring? We could—"

"Julie," he interrupted, draping an arm around her shoulder, "nothing you can suggest is going to bore me, but you don't have to entertain me, either. Do you have any more of those mysterious tapes by Anne-Marie Lacombe?" It was a subject neither of them had broached so far.

"I might be able to find one or two," she teased playfully, "if you—"

"If I what?" he urged, grinning and hoping she might confess another fantasy.

Ross was sitting on the couch later that afternoon, listening to one of her Lacombe tapes and reading the paper, when Julia came from the bedroom and snuggled up next to him, gently nudging the paper aside. She'd just bathed and put on a loose-fitting galabia that he noticed without comment, and her feet were bare, so she tucked them up under her. The soft unbleached raw silk was almost as appealing to the touch as the dusty pink outfit she'd worn at breakfast this morning.

"Listen to this, Julie," he commanded, lifting his arm to drape it around her shoulder and pull her against him. "I design for the New York woman," he began reading, "who I think is the most international of all. But today she likes a uniform, she doesn't want to hear about what's in or out this season. She has overdosed on clothes, overdosed on theater, and overdosed on food. She's jaded, is what she is. The one thing she wants to do is lay back and be taken care of right now." He looked up and smiled. "Are you jaded? Is that what you want—to be taken care of?"

"That has to be Franchina," Julia laughed.

"Yeah," Ross agreed, checking the name of the designer the article was quoting. "Can you believe a name like that? You know her, huh?"

She nodded. "She's the one who started the big shoulder look."

Ross's mouth twisted in a grimace of distaste. "You mean the Salvation Army rag-barrel look, from that old Woody Allen movie?"

"No, that's androgyny," she laughed, "oversized menswear, or haberdashery-for-her. Franchina put shoulder pads in sweat shirts."

"For the 'international New York woman'?" he injected, incredulous.

Julia nodded. "They became a sensation almost overnight. Before we knew what was happening, she'd launched a new silhouette—the inverted pyramid—very broad at the top and narrowing to the hips. We had little choice but to follow." She rose from the couch while she talked and walked into the kitchen.

"Yeah, I know the one you mean now—Amazon women."

"It had a phenomenally fast rise, and lasted longer than any of us expected. Would you like a drink? Or a coke. I'm going to make some herb tea."

"Whatever you're having." Her small kitchen was almost completely open on one side, from the marble counter up, and Ross eased down onto one of the leather-covered stools on the living room side, while Julia talked on about fashion cycles and the importance to both designers and manufacturers of correctly estimating the rise, popularization and decline of a fashion.

"Sounds something like the learning curve in the semiconductor industry," he commented, explaining that the price of a single chip decreases by 20 to 30 percent for each doubling of total production during its life cycle, which is relatively short. "As a firm learns how to produce a chip of higher and higher quality, it gets fewer defective chips and more good chips for the same cost and effort. So as learning goes up, the cost and price per chip goes down. But if you don't learn as fast as everyone else, you're soon out of business."

"You complain about fashion jargon, Ross! What about microprocessor, integrated circuits, RAM and ROM, mainframes and micros, and all that? I hate it—I suppose because it makes me feel so inadequate."

"A microprocessor is just a chip containing an electronic circuit that's the central processing unit of a computer, Julie. All the operations it's capable of doing are packed on one chip. Two memory chips are attached, one to hold data and the other to take the program that drives the central processor—that's the system software I told you about—and you have a computer than can perform all kinds of tasks, depending on the program you use to instruct it. The same microprocessor can be used to do all kinds of things. One of the new sewing machines, for instance, uses a single microprocessor to control the stitching pattern—replacing about three hundred and fifty gears, cams and other mechanical parts. It not only lowers the price of the machine but also makes it more reliable."

It sounded simple enough the way he explained it, she thought, and she was about to ask another question when Ross asked, "Are you a New York woman, Julia? Overdosed on the theater, dinner at the Russian Tea Room, stopping by The

Palladium afterward to be seen? How do you usually spend your weekends, when I'm not here?''

Julia hooted as if he'd just told a hilarious joke. "Keeping the company's name and his own in the public eye is Ben's job, not mine, thank God. Besides,'' she confessed, "I'm not very good at massaging egos or spouting phony platitudes, so nobody minds if I refuse to spend my time that way.''

"So how *do* you spend your time, on weekends, I mean?'' he prodded gently.

"Mostly work. I travel a lot and sometimes I just collapse when I get home—don't 'do' anything or go anywhere if I can help it. My family comes in from Austin fairly often. Or I go out to Elaine's place in Connecticut, help in her yard, or whatever needs doing around the place. That's what I miss the most I guess, here in the city,'' she mused dreamily, "being so cut off from the feel of grass between my toes. That and space.'' She exhaled a sigh, then added, "Sometimes my eyes ache with wanting to focus on the horizon, ten miles off in the distance, instead of just over there.'' She waved a hand toward the building just across the way.

"Certainly you have other close friends? Besides Elaine, I mean.''

She realized what he was hinting at, but did he really think she could be with him like this, and then another man tomorrow or next weekend? "Oh yes, of course,'' she answered breezily, then asked if he'd looked at her sketches, just to change the subject.

"Is that him, the picture in the other bedroom? Your husband?'' Ross asked, refusing to be distracted.

His quiet question shocked her like an unexpected stumble. "Tom? Yes.'' What else was there to say?

"Good-looking young man,'' he observed. "Were you married then—when the picture was taken, I mean?'' His eyes never left her face.

She nodded mutely. "Two days before,'' she mumbled, then turned away to pour the tea. But she was too late and he saw her eyes, already brimming with tears.

"Tell me why you're still crying, Julia. After fifteen years. I'm sorry if that sounds—I just need to know."

She shook her head this time, denying something, though he wasn't sure what. "I don't, Ross." She tried to smile, to laugh at herself for her silly, maudlin behavior, too embarrassed to do anything else. "Maybe because being with you, because what I feel with you is so—I just don't know." She gave up in defeat, then without warning covered her face with her hands and just stood there sobbing.

Ross went to her, not knowing if she wanted or would accept the comfort he wanted to give her, but she clung tightly, her arms locked around his waist. At first, he just held her, gently stroking one hand over her hair, or up and down her back. After a few seconds, he shifted enough to dig the handkerchief out of his hip pocket, then pulled one of her hands free, forcing her to take it. She sniffled, trying to stop, while he smoothed the unruly curls back away from her face. Finally, he lifted her chin, making her look at him. "It's okay, Julie. I didn't mean to—"

"It's not that, Ross. It's me," she explained hesitantly, gulping breaths every few words. "I didn't want him to go, begged him not to go. It's the one thing we disagreed about, argued about, the whole time I knew him. But it was my fault, really—if I'd just tried harder, I could have done something to keep him from going. Suggested we go to Canada. Anything! God, what an awful waste!" The tears were threatening to spill over again. "And now, no matter how hard I try, Ross, I can hardly remember what he looked like anymore." Her anguish was almost palpable. "You'd think I could do at least that much for him, wouldn't you?"

He fitted her head into the curve of his shoulder, stroking her hair, trying to comfort her. "Maybe it's better not to have pictures of the people we love in our heads, Julie. Perhaps then it would be easier to remember the other things—the important things about him, and the way you loved each other, which you haven't forgotten, and never will. Isn't that right?

And I guess sooner or later we have to find some way to live with the 'what ifs,' too."

His words sounded so sad, Julia thought, as if he knew exactly what she was feeling. But they were strangely consoling, too. She nodded and straightened, fighting the morass of self-pity into which she'd fallen. But Ross held her, forcing her to look into his sapphire blue eyes, filled with tenderness and concern for her.

"Don't you know you couldn't have made that decision for him, Julia? Stopped him from going, I mean, if that's what he believed he should do? That responsibility didn't belong to you then, and it doesn't now. If you argued, as you say, he had to be familiar with other opinions, other points of view. Maybe he just couldn't see it the way you did, couldn't be comfortable doing anything else. Lots of guys couldn't, you know—though plenty of them sure as hell went like a bunch of robots, without thinking about it one way or another. But you didn't let him do that, did you? You argued, forced him to think about it, right? And that's all you could do. In the end, it was his decision to make—his life, not yours."

They had a gay, laughing time at the Greene Street Cafe, leaving the brief tearful episode behind as if it had simply never happened. Ross discovered another, and entirely unsuspected, Julia, in her unpretentious enjoyment of the broad, often raucous humor of the four High Heeled Women. He watched her toe-tapping response to their musical antics far more than he did the performers, bemused by both the way she looked and her uninhibited behavior. It was almost as if what she wore tonight heated up the fervor of her responses and set her free—her shiny orange satin trousers, clinging gently around her hips and thighs, topped by a loosely fitting overblouse and long-sleeved smoking jacket in hot pink, with matching orange lapels. Huge clumps of flashing multicolored brilliants swung from her ears as she kept time to the music.

Julia was still "high" when they got back to her apartment, talking animatedly until Ross kissed her mouth shut and began slowly peeling off her jacket, at the same time backing her toward the bedroom. He was working at the tiny buttons closing the front of her sleeveless top, stopping from time to time to dip underneath to the warm flesh so slowly being revealed—until Julia giggled. "What?" he mouthed against her cheek.

"I was thinking of Ben," she confessed, giggling again.

"You're thinking about another man at a time like this?" he exploded, with both incredulity and wry humor.

She teased his lips with two fingers, slowly, enticingly, while she explained. "This is one of his," she glanced down at the buttons, "and you can tell how a designer feels about women—in the sexual sense, I mean—by how they fasten clothes. Small buttons and button loops are not for cloddish lovers—but, well, he likes undoing them. Says it turns up the excitement, the anticipation. Does it?"

Ross moaned in mock agony. "Julie, my love, I've got about all the anticipation I can handle, just being around you."

They made long, slow love to each other, as if trying to prolong the few remaining hours that were left to them, giving in at last to a satisfaction made even more exquisitely intense by restraint.

Sunday morning they woke to a gray and drizzling sky. Julia suggested going uptown to Zabar's, a kosher-style deli and supermarket on Broadway that had freshly baked croissants. "Besides, it's great fun. A spectacle." She didn't want him to know she felt drawn toward the noisy impersonal setting because she needed to prepare herself against his going. Ross protested that she thought about food even more than he did. "Let's just have coffee. I'll be doing double laps in the pool all week as it is."

He proceeded to devour three pieces of toast with homemade peach jam—"My mother's," Julia explained with an enigmatic smile—and then they took their coffee cups into the living room to browse through the Sunday paper in companionable silence. But Julia was restless and unable to sit still very long.

"I've been thinking about what we talked about yesterday—

you know, the computer, and the sewing machine." She twisted around on the couch to face him and he lowered the paper. "I wish—no, I think I *should,* learn more about the new production technology, whatever there is at this point. What the possibilities are. But I don't know where to start. Do you know of something I could read?" she asked with a worried frown.

"First, tell me, what is it you want to know?"

"Oh, I don't mean for you to—you wouldn't want to know how really ignorant I am, Ross," she confessed, not looking at him. "Just some basic stuff, for beginners."

"You can talk to me about anything, Julie, include me in any of your fantasies, or whatever—" He leaned across and kissed her quickly on the corner of her mouth, before she could protest, then leaned back and ordered, "Shoot."

Julia was still smiling as she began telling him about the Delphi Study, done almost a decade earlier, which had predicted the major changes likely to take place in the fashion industry through the year 2000. And one change was greatly improved productivity through the use of new technology, particularly automated cutting and sewing machines and computer-assisted pattern grading and marking.

"But about all we've seen so far is some semi-automated sewing and cutting equipment. Some of the smaller manufacturers have been consolidated into larger ones, which I suppose is necessary because only the big operators can afford the costs of new equipment, but—"

"Wait a minute! What's grading and marking?"

"Grading the pattern. That means sloping the dimensions up and down to adjust the pattern for each size. I understand that's being computerized, too, by some companies. And I've heard some real horror stories about mistakes that weren't caught until after the fabric had been cut."

"What I want to know is how you get the first pattern, the one you slope up and down from?"

"The designer, or an assistant who is skilled at patternmaking, does it, either from sketches or from a draped model—

blocking out the garment on manila paper, correcting the sketch lines and using a set of prescribed measurements for each piece. We modify the pattern during sample construction—that's the garment we make to show and take orders on—as the pieces are fitted together. That's when we test how the sample feels and looks on a model. Factory construction methods are tested at this point, too—all of which may mean more adjustments in the pattern. Costs and profit margins are figured—still another reason for changes in the pattern—and then we do a master production pattern."

Ross thought for a minute, then sat forward. "And marking?"

"The marker is the master plan for cutting the cloth. A long paper guide that shows all the pieces of the pattern as they should be laid out—on the bias or the straight of the material—to cut the cloth in the most economical way. We do the production patterns in-house, but we contract out both the marking and cutting. The number of layers that can be cut at one time varies with the thickness of the fabric, of course, but as many as six thousand garments of one style can be cut on a long table in one operation, using the new laser-beam cutting systems, which are faster and more accurate than electrically driven knives. Unfortunately, not everyone has them yet."

"Sounds like a costly waste of time and effort to me," Ross replied. "Once the marker is in the memory of the computer controlling the cutting system, the whole damned operation would be automated—you'd eliminate the paper altogether and telescope the time required. But you know what's really missing? What could change the entire picture?" His rising excitement and enthusiasm reached out to her.

"What?" she urged breathlessly.

"Tying the design process itself to the grading and marking. Designing directly on the computer! Then all the information needed to grade the patterns would already be available—in the memory of the computer. You could even input all the allowances if you could standardize them, like the engineered suit coat you were telling me about, remember? Why not do the same thing with other garments? And the graded pattern dimensions would in turn automatically produce the cutting markers—not paper markers, of course, but the machine language instructions to the cutting machines."

"Oh rats, Ross. You engineering and science types always assume you can replace the creative process with machines—"

"I'm not suggesting any such thing, Julie! Open the damned doors, woman! You've just never seen what can be done with a computer, especially with the fantastic graphics we have today. If I could just show you, there's no telling what wild ideas you might have. It's not the machine, Julie, but the mind manipulating the machine. What the machine allows *you* to do!

"Only the tools you would be using to visualize or describe your ideas would be different. A keyboard, light pen and mouse, and a lighted terminal monitor screen—not the ideas themselves. Or maybe they would." His words slowed thoughtfully. "I can't even imagine what the possibilities might be for someone like you—what might come to you if you could manipulate a figure any way you wanted to, for instance. Make it run or sit, view it from any direction, in two dimensions or three. But then, I guess you'll never know until you try it, right?" He grinned audaciously, daring her.

Julia had to grin back. "Did you make all that up just to entice me into your lair?" she teased, knowing he hadn't. "I may be able to sneak a couple of days to come to Austin after I get back from Paris. I was going to tell you anyway, even without all this—this 'persuasion.' But I'll have to wait and see. It gets really crazy just before an opening, Ross, so I can't make any promises."

"That's good enough for me, Julie love, as long as I know you want to." He twisted her around in front of him, cradling her body against his chest, hugging her and nuzzling his face into her wildly curling hair.

"But damn it—now I'll never know for sure whether you're after my body or my computer."

Chapter 10

THE NEXT TEN days seemed to fly by, partly because Julia had so much to do, but also because now she was looking toward a definite time when she would see Ross again. After Paris, as soon as she had reported to Ben on the Prêt. She didn't know exactly what day, or exactly which flight to Austin she would be on, but it was enough just to think "after Paris."

About midafternoon the day after he left, a huge bouquet of light blue irises arrived at Taggart, along with another cryptic, unsigned note—"It's not getting any easier." This time the flowers recalled his eyes to her rather than the garden at Giverny. Another day, she found a tiny clipping in her mail, which appeared to be one of those odd "facts" used as fillers in newspapers. It was about a seventeenth century mechanical doll named Franchina which had belonged to philosopher and mathematician René Descartes. "He took her on an ocean trip to see if her walking mechanisms would compensate for a slight deck roll. They did, and she ambled along just fine, until the ship's captain screamed that she was the work of the Devil, and tossed her overboard." Julia giggled when she read the attached note—"Recommended for all Franchinas"—and remembered his incredulous response to the comments of the fashion designer of the same name. And they talked almost every day, with the result that she felt a little twinge of expectation every time the phone rang, whether at home or the office.

Later in the week, at lunch with Alex and Elaine, Julia described Ross's idea about designing with a computer, and somehow tying that to the grading and cutting processes, and was more than a little taken back by Alex's enthusiasm.

"Hot damn! If you think he knows what he's talking about, Julia, why in hell haven't you dropped everything else to go after it—find out what it would take? Benetton is already using computers to do their sweater patterns, you know, and I've heard about a few offbeat designers trying it. But this sounds like a helluva lot more than that! Maybe the house of Taggart could be the one to breach the virgin's maidenhead—to finally drag this holy whore of an industry into the twentieth century, kicking and screaming all the way, of course. And not incidentally, turn back the yellow tide."

Elaine seemed unaccountably spellbound, too, then wanted to know if Julia had talked with Max about it. "He's into all that computer stuff, you know, though he hasn't had much luck convincing Tony to go along. He's already got inventory control and shipping on the computer, but he wants to go a lot further."

Julia looked at her, wonderingly, surprised. "Sounds like you have his ear, so why don't you try it out on him then, see what he thinks?"

Alex jumped on that immediately. "I smell something going on that you guys aren't telling me about!"

"All that stuff about computers bores me to death," Elaine complained dramatically, "but I guess—since he's taking me to dinner tonight—I'll make the ultimate sacrifice and give it a try!"

"You mean mummy Max has hormones under that tight wrapping, after all?" Alex joshed.

Elaine made a quick face at him. "You're just jealous! Did you think I'd sit around waiting for you forever?"

When Julia arrived at work Friday morning, Connie shoved a little white card in front of her face. "Consuelo—you may want to hide these from you know who and her insatiable appetite." The lack of signature was its own signature.

Julia laughed. "So what are you *not* hiding from me?"

"This is very definitely the right man for us, Julia," Connie concluded sagely, producing a long white box that could contain only one thing. She untied the red ribbon, lifted the cover and carefully folded back the green florist paper. There were at least a dozen, and they were long-stemmed all right, and even arranged among lacy white baby's breath. But the buds and unfolding petals were molded in dark and light chocolate. "How do you suppose he knew," Connie wondered, "or did you tell him I was an addict?"

Julia shook her head, mumbled something about Ross being sort of intuitive and went on into her office, as pleased as if the chocolate roses had been sent to her, maybe more so.

The following Monday she and Max flew to Raleigh, then rented a car and drove to King's Cove. She'd been surprised when Max first volunteered to go with her, but after they'd talked a while, she could see he was trying to help, not intrude or try to hinder what she wanted to do.

"Monarch is still relatively small, and willing to work with a designer on something new, even when it doesn't look like orders are going into a hundred thousand yards or more," he'd explained when she told him what she was looking for. "They look on it as an investment in future business. You remember that angora-cotton combination Ben wanted a couple of years ago for his fall line? He's used that same fabric for I don't know how many numbers since then, and now Alex is using it in menswear, too. Monarch is the only one making it, so it was a smart investment, I'd say."

"That's exactly what I want, Max, not just good color saturation in the dyeing and printing, but I'd like to find out if they have any ideas about how we might open up the weave.

We need to find some way to develop fabrics with bulk but not too much warmth, texture without weight—goods that look like fall and winter, but will function in warm climates better than wool. I keep thinking about thermal blankets, and letting air in—not to keep warm, so we don't want to trap it—but to provide circulation and cooling. Or maybe both, I don't know. I need someone who does—know a lot more about the technical possibilities, I mean."

"You've got more in mind than your resort collection then, right?" he'd suggested softly.

"Maybe," she admitted. "It's a general problem, certainly, and it's time we did something about it. Why wait to see what the fiber producers give us, or what the mills do with new fiber developments? I think we ought to get into the process earlier, work closer with the producers so they know what we need or want."

That was when he'd volunteered to go with her, since he'd worked out the deal on Ben's angora-cotton goods and thought maybe he could help. And he'd been even more enthusiastic on the flight down, when she showed him the color washes and pattern drawings she'd finished up over the weekend.

"I've never done a collection completely from scratch before, Max, including every piece of goods. I'm pretty sure about the colors, but textures contribute their own design to the cloth, so my pattern sketches are vague, just possibilities."

By the time they got back to New York, late Monday night, Julia's opinion of Max had undergone a drastic change. Not only was he far more knowledgeable about textile production than she had any idea he might be, but he was creative in the most fundamental way—always able to view a problem with a fresh eye, never taking anything for granted. Often that meant no more than asking questions, but they were questions that had never even occurred to any of the rest of them, even the mill foreman. Looking back on it, Julia realized it was Max's questions that had always seemed to start the ball rolling, to provoke a host of innovative ideas from the others. In the end, they'd all come away from the long brainstorming sessions with a sense of excitement and expectation.

Three days later, Julia was getting ready to go to Paris—she was leaving from JFK on the Air France flight that evening—when Tony came into her office, complaining about a "lack of innovation in the organization."

"I've just been talking to the people at Synectics, Julia—they're creativity consultants—about putting our personnel through some of their exercises, especially their new product sessions. Those guys are astute enough to appreciate that corporate meetings are hostile environments for new ideas. Everyone is so damned defensive, the only thing that ever comes out of them is opposition—why something *won't* work." He thrust a clutch of slick-looking brochures across the desk at her. "Take a look for yourself—GE's self-diagnostic appliances, dial-your-own-octane gas pumps, Gillette's new shampoo—those are just a few of the new products the Synectics boys had a hand in. I think we could use them on a continuing basis, the way Wang Labs and Chase Manhattan do, for instance, to goose everyone from our secretaries on up. And your marketing staff sure as hell could use a poke in the ass about now. Take a look at these and let me know what you think."

Julia recognized Tony's standard operating procedure, which was to go through the motions of consulting and listening, then do what he wanted to in the first place. If he could get away with it. Obviously he'd been stung by her comments about his licensing idea, and this was his ploy to try to sidetrack her. If he could somehow make it look as though Julia herself agreed with his broad indictment—that there was a lack of innovation in the organization, as he put it—he would stand a better chance of getting Ben on his side when he took his licensing idea to the board.

"Our marketing department uses some of the most sophisticated research instruments in the survey business, Tony, giving Taggart access to the kind of information no one else has." Julia intended to leave no doubt whatsoever that she not only disagreed with his assessment, but that she wouldn't stand idly by while he maligned the entire Taggart staff. "We've done some in-depth studies of socio-economic factors, and we've also used psychographics to develop attitude and value profiles. We probably have as much information about women today as any market research outfit in the country. Yet Taggart continues to ignore a great deal of it, and instead continues to rake over the coals of the same limited demographic data everyone else is using, which I don't call exactly innovative."

Instead of looking at him, she glanced through one of the brochures while she talked. "Why should we spend money to enhance our 'creativity' when we aren't using what we have? Our ads have won awards for three years running. We're putting out some of the most imaginative videos in the business, though I know they have a limited audience—" She broke off suddenly and burst out laughing. "Is this what you mean, Tony? 'Synectics gets groups of employees together and has them play with crayons, daydream, tell stories about dragons and play word games,' " she read aloud. " 'It was during one of these sessions that Gillette's Silkience developer pretended she was a human hair!' " She chuckled derisively, knowing it was probably the worst thing she could do.

"Laugh all you want, Julia, but that doesn't change the fact that George de Mestral, the guy who invented Velcro, got the idea from wondering why he and his dog were covered with burrs after a walk in the woods. And today, he's the one who's laughing, all the way to the bank!"

"That's not what I'm laughing at, Tony—it's not the same thing. Open-ended play with crayons, or stories or whatever, is thinking in a vacuum. Creativity is making new connections, and using everything and anything to do it—your sensory apparatus, imagination, intuition, logic or whatever. It's also unique flashes of insight that seem to come out of nowhere. But I don't intend to argue the definition with you. I'm only saying that I don't think it's very smart to insult some of the best people in the business, whom we're very lucky to have working with us. Not to mention the wisdom of spending money to do it." She pointed to a column of figures on the back of one of the brochures. "I'd say a hundred thousand to a half million or more is pretty steep—and a very frivolous expenditure of company working capital!"

Tony had begun pacing back and forth in front of her worktable, sort of like a caged tiger, which gave him an air of barely controlled energy. That was probably part of his sex appeal, Julia thought as she watched him, though she herself rarely thought of him as sexual at all, which he probably was able to detect, and resented. He'd had a constant stream of successful career-women companions since coming to Taggart, which had to be paradoxical in a man who believed women didn't belong in the upper echelons of business, and who made no bones about letting everyone know it. But a lot of women apparently were attracted to the overbearing, macho type.

"So now you're not only the resident expert on creativity, but the financial expert, too, right?" he snarled, turning on her suddenly. "You've just got to have your little finger in everybody's pie, don't you?"

They'd been at unspoken swords' points almost from the day Tony had come to Taggart, largely because he resented her history with Ben, but Julia was unprepared for such a vitriolic response. Usually he jabbed at her through implication and innuendo, which went right over Ben's trusting head. Both she and Tony were well aware that, except for her influence with Ben, any number of decisions at Taggart might have gone differently.

Connie interrupted them at that moment, using the arrival of Julia's mail as an excuse, which relieved Julia of the need to respond to his last remark. Julia suspected her secretary listened in whenever Tony was around, and then found some reason to intrude if she thought things were getting too heated. "The little package on top came next-day mail," Connie pointed out, making sure Julia would at least glance at it before she left to go home and pack. But Julia didn't have any intention of putting off finding out what Ross had sent this time. She ripped back the tab along one edge of the padded mailer, and a tape cassette fell out, this time without either label or enigmatic note.

When Julia looked up again, Tony was already halfway to the door.

"Ben likes the Synectics idea, Julia," he observed dryly, "so you may want to read that stuff over anyway, just so you'll know what to expect when the sessions begin." He turned and simply walked out then.

By the time he was halfway through Connie's office, the strains of Doug Kershaw fiddling and singing "Louisiana Man" caught up with him, and Connie began laughing, even before she saw the startled look blossom on Tony's face.

The French Chambre Syndicale du Prêt-à-Porter, des Couturiers et des Createurs de Mode didn't even begin organizing ready-to-wear fashion shows in Paris until 1974. Now, little more than a decade later, "The Paris Collections" attracted about six hundred buyers from nearly forty countries, as well as a couple of thousand journalists and photographers, to view the new seasonal lines of more than seventy designers—including Azzedine Alaia, Issey Miyake, Karl Lagerfeld and Claude Montana—in three canvas tents set up in the courtyard of the Louvre or the Tuileries Gardens. Though representatives from the big American department stores might not buy entire lines from the big name designers, they always took home a few samples, so their other buyers would be ready to "buy the best" when they went to New York or to one of the regional fashion marts. Others used their Paris buys to test the market for a month or so, then had quick copies of the best-selling numbers made locally. No matter the considerable influence and success of American designers these days, there was no denying the Paris mystique—whether it was used for adaptations, inspiration, or simply to generate a little excitement. Even the store reps who had no intention of buying soaked up the flavor and enthusiasm of a few showings, and then spent the rest of the time sampling the boutiques and soaking up street scenes, just to get the "feel" of what was going on in Paris.

For at least a decade before this circus of international stars had stolen the spotlight, however, the Salon du Prêt-à-Porter Féminin had been holding forth in the big trade-fair building near the Porte de Versailles, where fifteen hundred exhibitors of more moderate-priced apparel and accessories showed their wares. Though the noise and press of bodies was exhausting—to say nothing of the days spent tramping the aisles of the Parc des Exhibitions building, which was larger than the New York Coliseum—it was this show that Julia usually found most interesting. Because it was here in the less expensive setting that the new, and often most innovative, designers showed their work.

Alex followed Julia into her hotel room, where she pushed off her shoes just inside the door. They'd just had dinner at a little restaurant only a block from the hotel, and all she could think of was getting off her feet and climbing into bed. She'd pushed herself hard for the past three days with a purpose—she intended to catch the afternoon flight back to New York tomorrow. Tony wanted fast, she'd give him fast, she thought smugly, and then she'd have maybe three whole days in Austin.

"You've got to come with me in the morning, Julia! You're wasting your time at the salon when you could be seeing this stuff." Alex had decided to come along at the last minute, for the *Semaine de Cuir,* and he was still all wound up about a collection of leather jackets by a new British designer he'd seen earlier that day.

"No one I talked to has even heard of this guy before, but he must have worked with someone to be that good. Wait till you see the way he's using color." He flopped down in the overstuffed chair near her bed. "My God, this time change is a bitch! I never get used to it."

"Alex, all I can get excited about right now is a hot bath," Julia responded, starting toward the bathroom. "Back in a second—I'm going to start the water." She nudged the door halfway closed behind her and began peeling off her pantyhose while she waited for the water to run hot. What a relief just to get her toes free! When she walked back into the bedroom only a couple of minutes later, Alex was on the phone. As soon as he saw her, he mumbled hastily, "Here she is now," and extended the receiver toward her, grinning, with one eyebrow lifted.

"Hello."

"Julia? How's everything going?"

"Oh Ross, it's so good to hear your voice! We just got back. I'm absolutely exhausted, but almost finished. I'll be leaving here tomorrow afternoon."

Alex walked to the door, opened it, and mouthed, "See you in the morning," blew her a kiss and then left, closing the door quietly behind him.

"The shows run this late?" Ross inquired, a little incredulous. He'd figured the time difference exactly, thinking she'd surely be in her room before now.

"No. We went to dinner. Alex and I."

"Yeah, hearing his voice was quite the little surprise. Somehow you failed to mention that he would be going with you." His own voice sounded flat, without its usual energy and bounce.

"It was a last-minute decision. He came for the Semaine de Cuir."

"Whatever the hell that is! A convenient excuse, at least, I guess."

Exactly what did he mean by that, she wondered, too tired for guessing games. "I'm not sure I understand, Ross. Excuse?" she queried through lips that suddenly felt stiff.

"He's never very far away, is he? Your 'good friend' Alex?"

"Yes, he *is* a good friend, Ross, but you've known that from the beginning."

He waited. "Is that all you're going to say?" If anything, he sounded even more incredulous now.

"What's wrong, Ross? Has something happened?" She had

a growing sense of uneasiness, of dread, and had to fight the urge to hang up.

"Maybe *you* should tell me—I seem to be the one who doesn't know what's going on." He paused and waited several seconds for her to respond. "It's sort of late there, isn't it?" he asked finally. "I cut my dinner short and rushed back to call you because I had the crazy idea it might mean something to you, that it might matter. Instead, I get Alex. In your room. Oh hell, let's just forget it!"

"No, let's not!" Her anger flared white hot all of a sudden, the adrenaline pumping through her veins heating her face, making her breath come in short bursts, and her head pound. "I understand perfectly! So what do you want from me, Ross?" she asked quietly, ominously.

Still he waited, hoping she would deny what he was thinking, reassure him somehow or other, without being prompted. "If you don't know, I guess it doesn't really matter," he muttered finally. "Let's talk about something else. How long do you think you'll have to stay in New York, before you can come to Austin, I mean?"

Now Julia was the one who was incredulous. How could he switch just like that, with the snap of a finger, from acting the jealous, suspicious lover speaking with barely contained fury, to wondering when she would come to him? She had an almost overpowering urge to scream at him—"When hell freezes over, that's when!"—but instead took refuge in a little white lie, the coward's way out.

"I don't know yet. I'll—I'll have to let you know sometime after I get back." Her throat was tight even before she got all the words out, and tears were beginning to make everything go blurry. She blinked frantically, trying to force them back, and failed. Instead, like water going over a dam, they spilled and ran down her cheeks in silent rivulets.

The silence that followed was nearly unbearable. Neither of them knew what to say to change what had already been said, or even how to end the uncommunicative yet somehow devastating conversation.

"Okay," Ross mumbled finally, "I'll be waiting to hear from you, then." Silence again. "Is there anything else, Julia?" It was a final plea for her to say something to ease the pain eating at his gut.

"No," she whispered, trying to keep him from hearing the tears in her voice. "Good night, Ross. Good-bye." She dropped the receiver onto its cradle, stumbled to her bed and fell across it.

L'Aquitaine was only a ten-minute walk from the Parc des Expositions trade-fair center, and Julia particularly liked the restaurant in warm weather because it had a first-floor terrace that overlooked La Ruche, the *cité des artistes* where Soutine, Chagall and Modigliani had worked. The owner-chef, Christiane Massia, was living proof that nouvelle chef Paul Bocuse didn't know what he was talking about when he claimed that women show no imagination as cooks. She was, in addition, a quiet feminist who employed only female assistant cooks.

It must have been sometime after four before Julia finally had dropped off into a restless, superficial sort of sleep, only to be awakened even before her alarm went off by the sound of rain on the skylight over her bed. The day was a perfect match for how she felt—cold, empty and gray—condensing into a slow drizzle from time to time without the slightest warning. She sat alone in the restaurant, at a table directly under one of the skylights that usually lit the spacious interior, waiting for Alex and wondering whether her flight might be delayed by the weather.

One minute she wanted to cancel it and stay here, simply never go back home again, and the next she felt an almost overwhelming need to run home and hide, close herself up somewhere and not come out until she stopped hurting. She didn't want to speak to anyone, or have to wear a false face. She'd survived this kind of grief and anger before—and would again—but she was absolutely furious. Not with Ross, but herself. Because she'd allowed herself to believe he was different from the others. In the end, though, Ross too had to play the watchdog. Because, well, we all know a woman's not to be trusted, right? If you don't watch her, tell her what to do or not do, who knows what mischief she might get into—who she might sleep with. You say she has male friends? That's a laugh, man!

"Here you are!" Alex touched her shoulder with a gentle hand, then bent quickly to brush her cheek with his lips and soft beard before he sat down. "Sorry I'm late, but—" He stopped suddenly when he caught a glimpse of her face. "You look like holy hell, Julia! What happened, are you sick?"

"Thanks, I really needed that," she muttered dryly. "No, just didn't sleep well, that's all. I'll make it up on the plane home."

"You know better than to try that with me, Julia," he admonished gently. She'd never been able to sleep on transatlantic flights, and he knew it. Her eyes were swollen and puffy, from a helluva lot more than lack of sleep. So either she was ill, or she'd been crying.

"What happened, last night after I left? Come on, give!"

"Nothing much. We didn't talk very long."

"I could tell he wasn't exactly happy at hearing my voice, but—he doesn't know about us, does he, Julia?"

"What's to know? That Ross feels the need to put a chastity belt on me? That he doesn't trust what I thought was happening between us?" She laughed quietly, but without humor. "The only thing I can't figure out is why I set myself up for this again. Do you suppose I'm a latent masochist, have some subconscious need to punish myself?"

"Cut out the crap, Julia! For God's sake, why not tell him? You have a screwy sense of—sense of privacy, or whatever the hell it is!"

"I shouldn't *have* to tell him, Alex. Maybe it's asking too much, but that's not the kind of relationship I want. Anyway, it wouldn't last. Sure, I admit I want to share my life with someone so bad I can almost taste it at times. But that doesn't mean I want to be jerked around on the end of a string, like some damned puppet, hopping to someone else's tune! Is that asking so much? He'd be happy for me to be his little girl, no doubt, so he could take care of me, make himself feel like a big, grown-up daddy! Even my own father never treated me like that." She looked down at her hands, then added, "What happened last night is only a symptom of the muck hidden somewhere under the surface. If it wasn't you, it would have been something or someone else, sooner or later. I was wrong, that's all. It's no big deal."

"No? That's funny! Somehow I got the weird idea it might be. Maybe you shouldn't start thinking in the past tense so goddamn fast, Julia. How much does he really know about you—what have you *let* him know? How far have you opened that big thick door you keep yourself hidden behind? Does he know about Tom?"

Julia nodded. "Yes. I told him, and then he saw his picture, at my apartment."

"I can just imagine how much you told him. What else? What about Beth?"

Julia just shook her head.

"And you call that giving him a fair shake? Much as I love you, Julia, and I probably will no matter how pigheaded you get, I have to tell you that sometimes you just expect too damned much of us—the people who love you. You need to let us be human once in a while, you know." He tried a smile on her, but to no avail.

"Who said anything about love, Alex? Ross never even mentioned the word."

"Maybe he didn't think he needed to—maybe he thought you would know."

"Maybe," Julia agreed sadly, "but he was wrong then, wasn't he?" She drew in a deep breath and straightened her shoulders, as if determined to throw off the weight pressing her down. "Anyway, it doesn't matter now."

A fresh bouquet of orange and yellow lilies was sitting on her desk when Julia arrived at the office the following morning, but she only glanced at them briefly and then began pulling papers out of her briefcase.

"I simply cannot understand why you refuse to stay home and rest instead of pushing yourself till you're sick," Connie began as soon as she saw Julia's face. She followed Julia into her office, hovering over her like a mother hen, then bustling around the room opening blinds to let in more light, the way she knew Julia liked it. "Did you think we couldn't make it one more day without you?"

"Don't start on me, Connie," Julia warned quietly. "Just leave me alone so I can get to work."

As soon as Connie had gone, Julia sat down and stared out the window, lost in thought. After a few minutes, she sighed, picked up the phone and quickly dialed Ross's home number. It was an hour earlier in Texas, so he'd probably still be there.

He answered on the third ring. "McCutcheon."

Would she ever get over the ridiculous little lift she felt whenever she heard him say that, knowing he was there, that she could connect with him this way no matter how far apart they might be?

"It's Julia," she said. "I just called to tell you that I can't make it, Ross."

He didn't say anything immediately. "Not at all, or not for a few more days?" he asked finally.

"Our spring-summer preview is the twenty-third, and there's just too much going on around here for me to get away. I should have known better than to think I could."

"You couldn't have any more than just walked into the office. Maybe things will look different after a day or so."

"No, I don't think so. Sorry."

The silence lasted even longer this time, and Julia was about to end it when she heard Ross speak again. "I didn't know you could be like this, Julia. I guess I just didn't expect you—"

"Yes, well, I guess we're both finding out some things we didn't know about each other, aren't we? Better now than later."

"Spare me the platitudes, damn it," he interrupted suddenly, trying to forestall the kind of ending he could feel coming. "It's not going to work, so forget it. I'll give you some time, Julia, if that's what you have to have." She heard him draw in his breath, then let it out again. "But I'm not about to let what's between you and me go down the tubes. Or let you toss it away, just because you—because I—" It was the first time she'd ever heard him inarticulate. "I'll call you in a couple of days, okay? Just let it simmer. And Julia?"

"Yes?"

"I miss you like hell." She heard a soft click and then she was holding a dead line.

Connie sat behind her desk, frozen by surprise for a minute, then followed Julia down the hall to the workroom, where she handed the vase of lilies to Arlette Kovacs, Taggart's *chef d' atelier.* "Enjoy," Julia instructed breezily, then backed out and quickly returned to her office, closing the door behind her.

Connie waited fifteen minutes, then went to the coffee urn down the hall to fill a cup for Julia. It had taken that long to get over the shock of what she'd just witnessed. And then to decide what to do. Everything as usual was the way she intended to play it, so she tapped lightly on the door and then simply walked into Julia's office.

"Here's your coffee. Anything you want me to do about phone calls?"

Julia was caught off guard. She hadn't even opened the folder of messages and letters that had accumulated while she was gone. "Was there anything particularly important?" she asked Connie without looking up.

"One from a Podge Slocum, at the Dallas Apparel Mart. Don't know if that's male or female. Voice sounded female, but she could have been some male's secretary, I suppose. He/she wants to talk to you right away, wouldn't talk with anyone else, didn't say what about. And your mother called. Said for you to call when you get caught up, so I guess that wasn't about anything special."

Connie hesitated, still unsure about what was going on, and whether she was doing the right thing. "I had lunch with him while you were gone." She let it just hang there.

"Who?" Julia asked absently, leafing through the phone messages.

"Ross."

"Ross was here, in New York?" Connie had Julia's full attention now. "You mean you had lunch with Ross?"

Connie nodded. "He came here, to Taggart. I suspected who he was right away, then he called me Consuelo, like he always does, the minute he walked in the door, just as if he recognized me. Said he was in town on business, knew you were gone, but wanted to come by anyway, meet me, maybe take me to lunch—if I could spare the time." She moved her head slowly from side to side, as if still unable to believe it. "He looked through the open door there, asked if that was your office, said it looked like you. Said he'd never seen where you worked. I showed him around a little. He seemed really interested in what the sample hands were doing."

"And I suppose during lunch he pumped you with questions, and you obligingly spilled your guts about my private life!" It must have felt like a slap in the face to Connie, and Julia was instantly sorry. She also was furious at the thought of Ross sneaking around behind her back.

"No," Connie answered quietly. "I'd never do that, Julia, and I sort of thought maybe you knew him better than that, too." She remembered how he'd refused to even set foot in Julia's office when she wasn't there.

"No," she repeated, "he gave an awfully good imitation of being really interested in me—Consuelo Perez. Can you imagine that? In fact, he never even mentioned your name during lunch. And neither did I." Then, without another word, she turned and left Julia's office.

Chapter 11

THE HOUSE OF Taggart was, as Elaine put it, a "lunatic asylum" for the next two weeks—and this was just for the spring-summer opening. It would be even more frantic before the fall-winter show, since that was the most important collection of the year in terms both of new designs and volume of orders. Sometimes they introduced seasonal lines in Dallas prior to the New York preview, just to "feel out" the buyers, but this show consisted for the most part of minor variations in well-established silhouettes from the previous season. At this point, Julia considered the collections being offered by most of the big names in the ready-to-wear business a case of arrested development in fashion cycle terms. The only surprise was how long this particular "look" was continuing to be pumped up by the fashion press and to sell. Clearly, the time was ripe for new ideas, perhaps even an entirely different silhouette.

The Taggart workroom hands were putting in long hours to complete duplicate samples, since the opening on the twenty-third marked the beginning of showroom selling not only in New York, but also at the major apparel marts around the country. The press kits were almost ready to go out, and Claire was helping Ben run the models through their paces. Julia worked twelve- to fourteen-hour days herself, and even then usually carried work home at night.

A pot of big red tulips had arrived only two days after Julia had taken the lilies to the atelier, almost as if Ross knew what she'd done. He could have talked with Connie, she supposed—but then new flowers began arriving every few days after that, and she had to conclude that it was Ross's way of showing support during a stressful and busy time. There were no more newspaper clippings or tape cassettes, but after that first week, he called every few days, always after she got home from work at night. Julia wondered if he knew that was the time she thought about him the most, that even when he didn't phone, she spent the evening wondering if he would.

She went out to dinner one night with Len Everitt, Taggart's legal counsel, whom she hadn't seen for the past two months, except briefly in the office one day when he'd come on company business. Before she'd met Ross, her relationship with Len—neither platonic nor overtly sexual—had been wandering aimlessly in a no man's land of indecision. Actually, she realized now, they had little in common beyond the business, though he sometimes sought her advice in his continuing battle with his ex-wife over their two sons. He was a pleasant enough though ordinary-looking man, but he had none of Ross's charisma, or vitality—or color. And now that she really thought about it, she knew she didn't much like his hands, either. They were too white, and the fingers narrowed too much at the ends. Or was it just something about the way he used them? Whatever it was, she felt no desire to have him touch her.

As Julia was reading the *Times* one night while eating a late supper, she came across a piece about a female psychologist who claimed that men's voices reflected how they behaved in bed. "A soft-voiced man is usually an unselfish and tender lover," according to the psychologist, "while the loudmouth is energetic and frequently brutal." Julia thought about some of the men she knew, trying to make them fit one description or another. Ben definitely had a soft voice, and she didn't have any trouble imagining him as an unselfish and tender lover. Max's voice didn't fit any of the descriptions, and Alex alternated between boisterous and melancholy. Only the latter was described in the article—a melancholy voice meant a lover who was potent, imaginative and flexible in bed. She laughed out loud when she came to the glib fast-talker. He was "the worst of the lot—hasty, selfish and premature, substituting talk for action, the sound of his voice for fore- and afterplay." That had to be Tony!

Ross's voice didn't really fit any of the described "types" either, since he somehow managed to sound both soft and energetic at the same time. Not melancholy, though on one or two occasions he'd sounded quite sad. That was when she first admitted to herself that she'd been wrong in thinking for even one minute that Ross *wasn't* different. How she wished she could turn the clock back to that night in Paris, relive those few minutes in order to do and say everything differently. He'd taken her by surprise with his unreasoning jealousy, when she was too tired to think straight, when her mind tended to follow well-worn pathways to old assumptions and conclusions. What was it Alex had said? "You need to allow us to be human once in a while."

Ross just didn't fit into neat categories, whether it was his voice or what she'd expected of a computer "jock." Quite often, in fact, he'd behaved in entirely unpredictable ways. She thought about the morning he'd yelled out of sheer happiness, frightening her while she was brushing her teeth! And never, as long as she lived, would she be able to forget the feel of his lips against her scarred breast. Most of the men she'd known felt so uncomfortable around a tearful woman they had to either hush her up or make a quick exit. Instead, rather than try to cajole her, even though she was crying about another man, Ross had silently held her in his arms and let her sob.

And now he was trying to continue their relationship as if

nothing had happened—except that now he never allowed anything personal to slip in when they talked. He never mentioned that he'd been in New York while she was gone, and she didn't ask about it. Instead, he inquired about what was going on at Taggart, and he sounded genuinely interested. He was giving her the time he sensed she needed, and he didn't press her about coming to Austin. He also began telling her about what he was doing, which more and more came to sound like progress reports on something he was doing specifically for her—developing a computer program that not only would have fashion-designing capability, but also would incorporate pattern grading and the markers for cutting the cloth.

"I talked to a guy in the art department at the university today, Julie," he told her one night, "and then went down to visit his life drawing class. I've got an idea, but I need to know what you think about it."

"Sure," she responded readily enough, "though I doubt I can help, I know so little about computer stuff, Ross."

"We're changing that, remember?" He stated it as a foregone conclusion, and didn't give her time to either deny or confirm it. "All you have to do right now is listen—and think about it. What if I get this student I talked to today to use my computer to draw figures—several basic body types, both male and female. Then we could include them in the data base so the designer could call them up at will. That doesn't mean you wouldn't be able to do freehand drawing with the light pen or a mouse, directly on the screen."

"What's this mouse you keep mentioning?" she asked.

"Oh—well, that's just a little ball you can roll around on the desk to move the cursor—the pointer—on the screen. Think of it as an interface between your hand and the screen, as just another way of drawing on the screen." Again he didn't wait for a response but picked up where he'd been interrupted. "One of the reasons for having access to these basic body sizes and shapes, though, is to see how any particular design you do freehand might look on different types—short, tall, Amazon shoulders, or whatever." Julia smiled at the "Amazon shoulders,'' remembering Franchina. ''Or they could represent the different sizes the manufacturer actually produces, later. We could tie these models to the dimensions we'll eventually use to slope the patterns,'' he continued. ''What do you think?''

''Sounds interesting, Ross. It's just that I have such a hard time visualizing what you're talking about. I've seen demonstrations of some of the graphics stuff used to do television ads, but—''

''I know—next, you have to actually see how this works. And to use it, so you can tell me what's missing, what else ought to be in the program. But not until I get some of the basic functions. I've looked into the existing software, for grading, and cutting, and I plan to include some of their features. But they're all separate—no interfacing.''

''Would it help if I sent you the actual dimensions—the ones we use when we slope the patterns?'' Julia suggested.

''You bet! The sooner the better, but I know you don't have time—''

''Connie could get them together for you. I know she wouldn't mind doing it. I'll ask her, if—''

''No, why don't I call her myself, tomorrow. If that's okay with you?''

A couple of days later, he called with another progress report. ''I ran into a woman in the home ec department, Julie, who teaches fashion design. Maybe you know her.'' He glossed over exactly how he'd ''run into'' the instructor, but Julia guessed it was probably a more deliberate encounter than he was letting on. ''She got all excited when I told her what we're trying to do, and she mentioned that there are a bunch of standard sleeve shapes, for instance, and skirt shapes. She suggested maybe the program could include a sort of dictionary of the standard styles, or whatever you call them. What do you think?''

Somewhere on the edges of her mind Julia time-traveled, and saw herself sitting on a bench in the Parc de Monceau, listening to Ross's hesitant explanation. ''I'm pretty new at this, so I'm probably going to make some awful blunders. Up until twenty-four hours ago, I thought the whole idea of fashion, and everyone even remotely involved, was pretty damn boring." And now he was trying to make it possible for her to design fashions with a computer.

"What about your own work, Ross? It sounds like this is taking an awful lot of your time, working on—"

He broke in before she could finish. "This *is* my work right now, Julia. It's what I want to do. I told you I can follow my nose wherever it leads me, remember? Well, I think we might ultimately change the entire manufacturing process, and open up some new possibilities for designers as well. But I need help—your help. I don't know enough to do it alone. Right now all I want is for you to tell me if you know what kinds of shapes that woman was talking about, and what you think of her idea."

"Well, there are about forty skirt shapes everyone uses at one time or another—the morning glory, the hoop and the harem, peg-top, sarong, yoked, ruffled, tiered, and uh—" she hesitated, trying to remember more. "Then there's the kimono sleeve, the Juliet, lantern, raglan, petal, leg-of-mutton and puff. And the A-line dress, the drop waist or flapper, chemise, sheath, tent, bib, blouson, cocoon, caftan, empire, pagoda, princess, peplum—"

"Hey, hold up, I can't write that fast. Okay, I get the idea. But would you like to be able to pop one of these shapes up on the lighted screen in front of you quicker than you could draw a straight line on paper?"

"Your subtlety overwhelms me, McCutcheon!" she responded with a wry grin, then sobered. "But I have to warn you that I still have lots of reservations about using a computer, not just because it's a computer but because I can't picture anything that's so rigid, and—and geometrical, working for the design process. Fabric is fluid, body movements are fluid, and what pops up on *my* computer screen when I hear you talk about standard shapes, whether it's bodies or clothing parts, is anything but flexible. Yes, I know—I shouldn't prejudge. Maybe I can tell you better if I ever get to actually see it."

That idea grew and began to take definite shape during the few days left before the spring-summer preview. Julia and almost everyone else at Taggart worked straight through the weekend, though by the time Elaine came in on Sunday, it was almost noon. Julia took one look at her face and knew something was wrong.

"What happened?" she asked solicitously.

"It's that obvious, huh?" Elaine answered. "That's the trouble when you reach forty, Julia. Your face is a damned roadmap of everything you do. Or don't do. Tina didn't come home last night, didn't call, didn't anything." Elaine's older daughter was sixteen now, though at times she acted more like a willful two. "Then when she breezed in this morning, she claimed she'd spent the night at her friend Jody's. But she hadn't, cause I called there when I was trying to find her. So we had it round and round. But she won't admit to anything, even to being on the pill. Her grades have been going to the dogs lately, too."

"I thought the girls were spending the weekend with their father."

"Yeah, well, he called Friday night and begged off again. They haven't gone to Walter's for two months now. He says they're nasty to Betty, and he doesn't want her upset right now." Elaine looked away. "She's pregnant, you know."

Elaine's ex-husband was a walking cliché as far as Julia was concerned. He was forty-three, and had recently married his twenty-two-year-old secretary.

"Anyway, he says it's my fault," Elaine continued. "He accused me of letting them go to the dogs, says he doesn't want to see them again until they learn how to behave like 'ladies.' "

Julia shook her head in disbelief. "Really, Elaine! How you ever could have married such a jerk is beyond me! Doesn't he have enough sense in that pea-sized thing he calls a brain to realize Tina and Maggie might feel he's shucking them off and getting himself a new family? Look, why don't you take the girls with you to Atlanta, then come on to the ranch afterward?''

Julia would be flying to Dallas Wednesday night, and then Friday afternoon, she was going to the ranch for the weekend, maybe even longer. She hadn't been home for almost two months now, which was far longer than she liked to be away, and the need became more compelling every day. October was nearly over, and November was the slowest month of the year—the only extended period, really, when she and Ben could get away to recharge their batteries. She'd even been thinking about returning after reporting back to Tony, in order to be where she could spend more time with Beth. Tony was going to have to wait a few days longer for his regional reports, which in any case, she suspected were only some kind of red herring to support his licensing idea.

''You know how much Tina enjoyed riding the horses the last time she was there,'' Julia continued. ''And they could browse around Atlanta, go on a tour of those antebellum homes while you're at the mart. It would get her away for a little while, give her a little breathing space.''

''Yeah, maybe so,'' Elaine sighed. ''If we're still on speaking terms by then. I'd really like to, but I'll have to let you know, Julia, okay?'' She gave Julia a tired smile and went on to her office.

By the time the opening was over, Julia had pretty much decided what she was going to do. She'd thought a lot about what Alex had said that last day in Paris, and about the door he'd accused her of hiding behind, keeping everyone but a few close friends at a distance. After the strain of her two days in Dallas, she was positive.

''McCutcheon.''

The hand holding the telephone to her ear shook slightly. ''Ross?'' Julia's voice cracked without warning, and she had to clear her throat before she could go on. ''It's Julia.''

''I know—what's wrong?'' His voice rose with alarm.

It was the first time *she* had called him since the day after she returned from Paris. Besides that, it was only eight-thirty on a Saturday morning. No wonder he'd assumed the worst. She laughed quietly into the phone, to reassure him. "Nothing. I, uh—how do you feel about barbecue?"

His response was silence. For once she'd thrown him, instead of the other way around. "I don't understand what you—" He stopped, suspicion blossoming, then asked warily, "Where are you?"

"At the ranch. I thought maybe you'd like to come out—that is, if you don't already have plans for the day."

"Just say when," he shot back instantly.

"Anytime. As soon as you can!" There was no hesitation in her reply either, now that she heard the eagerness in his voice.

"How do I get there?"

Her father's ranch was nearly fifty miles west of Austin, but only the last few miles were off the highway, on unmarked ranch roads, which required directions. He wrote down everything, just to be sure, then mumbled, "I'm leaving in five minutes." Julia thought he was going to hang up, but instead he paused, then almost as an afterthought added, "Don't change your mind about anything before I get there, okay?"

"Okay," she assured him laughingly. "And Ross," she caught his attention once more, then paused, adding a tiny bit of suspense at the very last minute, "perhaps you should wear your armor." If it sounded a bit cryptic, she didn't care—it would give him something to think about while he was driving. "And bring your toothbrush and razor this time."

The fifty miles felt more like two hundred. There was only one stop light, ten miles out, near Lake Travis, and then two small towns in the next forty miles. Austin sat along a geologic fault line, with the land to the west rising up to become the Texas Hill Country and the Edwards Plateau, while the land to the east dropped and flattened toward the coastal plain. The Hill Country alternated between areas that were pitifully barren, supporting nothing but prickly pear cactus, cedar and mesquite—because their roots were able to go clear down to hell in search of water—and fields lush with native grasses and wildflowers. The fields were cut by meandering creeks, where fat Herefords grazed their fill and black, white and brown Spanish goats kept the lower branches of live oak trees neatly trimmed to a uniform height. It would be another two months before the first freeze turned the grass brown, and with the rain and cooler temperatures of fall, it was greener out here now than it had been in the middle of summer.

As the miles rolled by, Ross traveled mentally through every minute he'd spent with Julia, since his first glimpse of her sitting on the bank of the Seine, and ending with that stupid telephone call to Paris. And there was simply no way to wipe that out, much as he would like to. When he'd heard Alex's voice on that damn phone, all he could think about was the two of them together, in the same hotel and the same room, making love in the same bed where she'd made love with him. And how in holy hell he could ever have conjured up that crazy picture was the mystery of all time!

Living those few minutes over and over a thousand times since, remembering the rage in his gut and in his head, had shaken his faith in himself more deeply than he'd realized at first. Had it emerged without warning out of some need he didn't even know he had—to believe, for God's sake, that she'd been celibate for the past fifteen years! That, except for three months in her entire life, a sensuous woman like Julia had acted the virgin, that her wonderful sexuality simply hadn't existed until he'd come along to release it?

No matter what her relationship with Alex had been in the past—and he had little doubt they'd been intimately involved at some time or other, whether briefly or for an extended time he couldn't even guess—Julia was neither devious nor dishonest. And she must have resented like hell the implication that she wasn't to be trusted, that he didn't have faith in her. At least he understood that much! What he couldn't fathom, though, was how that mindless macho response had sneaked up on *him*, of all people. Wasn't he the great one to be casting stones at Julia for some goddamned imagined infidelity! How well he still remembered that he and Marilyn had somehow gotten involved a few times in group scenes—back during that living hell, when he didn't think he'd ever care about anything again—when everyone was too stoned to even notice who they were fucking! But that was long after he'd discovered Marilyn was sleeping around, and by then he didn't much care, one way or the other! She'd gotten bored with being alone, of waiting until all hours of the night for him to come home from the lab, if he did. And when he did come home, lots of nights he was too tired, too drained, to even talk to her. And who wanted to talk, or do anything else, with a drunk? Later, when he'd finally managed to drag himself up out of that pit of despair, he'd resolved to never again bury his head in the sand and ignore what was going on around him. The need to know, to learn, had become almost a compulsion, whether it was people or paintings—or the fashion business.

By the time Ross drove through Marble Falls and realized he had only a few miles to go, his hands were sweaty on the steering wheel, even with the air conditioning. The little town had become the center of a resort area in recent years, thanks to Lyndon Johnson's rural electrification and flood control dams on the Colorado and Pedernales rivers. The Pedernales—which Ross had been in Texas long enough to know was pronounced Perdanalez by the locals—was the Colorado's largest tributary and drained a good part of the Hill Country. Pork barrel legislation may have put the dams there, but the flooding was real enough, even now, and two people had drowned in Austin only last year when creeks running through the city flooded several busy traffic intersections.

Five miles beyond Marble Falls he slowed a little to watch for the small wooden sign pointing to Oatmeal, and found it just about where she'd said it would be. He turned right onto the narrow black-topped road, pulled the directions out of his shirt pocket and flattened the paper out on the seat beside him, holding it down with the palm of his right hand. He glanced at the odometer, watching it intermittently until he'd gone a mile and a half. At the section road, he turned right again, this time onto caliche and gravel. A quarter of a mile further along, he slowed down to turn left and cross the first cattle guard she'd mentioned. A half mile past that, the road forked and there were three signs nailed to a cedar post—Blanton, Lester and Hemphill. He veered to the left, following as the road wound back and forth until he wasn't sure what direction he was going in anymore. Judging by the sun and the time, it had to be more or less east. Then he came to the second cattle guard—the steel pipes causing a deep, fast rumbling sound as his tires set them vibrating—and he headed through open pasture high with grass, at least a foot higher than it was just a few miles back, where cattle were taking a late-morning siesta under the shade of a clump of live oaks.

Almost a mile farther along, the land began to drop and the cedars and live oaks looked taller, which must mean he was approaching the river. And then he passed the Hemphill gate. A mile on this road took longer than he'd expected, but now there was only one more to go. He wiped his hands on his pants, then slowed for another cattle guard, continuing to glance at the odometer from time to time. Then he saw it. BLANTON RANCH. The big sign was suspended between two tall posts on either side of a wide cattle guard. No ornate gate, no steer skulls or cattle brands, no lazy B or rocking R.

There was still another mile to go, however, before he spotted a big clump of tall trees, sort of like an island in a sea of grass, and the tip of a peaked roof topping a big stone two-story house. The ranch road widened to a large circle in the midst of house, pens and barns, and he pulled up next to four other cars already parked in the shade, wondering if they belonged to family or guests. He turned off the motor and just sat there for a minute, looking around.

The red, white and blue flags of three "countries" fluttered gently from a tall flagpole in the front yard—the United States, Texas and France—serving as a reminder to one and all that the state not only had once belonged to France, but at one time had been an independent nation, the Republic of Texas.

Both the size and style of the Blanton "ranch house" came as something of a surprise. The two-story center section had the ageless look of a French farmhouse, though the rock it was built of bore the mark and color of the limestone lying little more than a foot below the surface of the ground, all across this huge geologic uplift. Different in both style and materials from the original, the single-story wings appeared to have been added later, though the diagonal cedar siding had been bleached to blend with the natural buff color of the rock.

Ross was just getting out of his car when the front door opened, and a tall man with gray-blond hair appeared. He was wearing dark brown cords and cowboy boots, and a western-style shirt open at the neck. He waved at Ross.

"Get out, come in," he called, even as he hurried toward the car, eating up the distance with a few purposeful strides. "Glad you could come, boy!" In spite of Ross's white hair, the word didn't seem incongruous on his lips, and he obviously knew who Ross was.

"I'm Carey Blanton, Julia's father." Carey stuck out his hand to grasp Ross's in a quick firm shake. "We've all been looking forward to having you. The girls are down in the river pasture, feeding a couple of newborn kids that lost their mama last night. But they'll do all right with Julia here. Come in, come in. Bring along whatever you have there." He was as voluble and homey as the Texas stereotype, but his speech was disarmingly straight to the point. He was a damned handsome man, Ross realized, with a body every bit as firm as Ross's own, though he must have at least twenty-five years on Ross.

Carey only nodded when Ross mumbled something about the "beautiful place here." He ambled ahead of Ross, up the wide flagstone walk toward the front door. "Make yourself at home, look around all you want. We're pretty informal around here. But come along in here first and let me fix you a cool drink after that long drive. The fire's been going in the pit all night, and we're about ready to lay the meat on. The girls'll be up shortly." He pulled up abruptly and turned toward Ross with a broad smile creasing his face.

"Unless you'd rather go hunt them?" He didn't wait for Ross to answer. "Right straight down there—about a half mile." He pointed off to the east, across the land sloping toward the river. "Can't miss 'em, but if you do, just holler out. They'll hear you."

Ross matched him smile for smile, nodded and agreed, "Yeah, I think I'll do that. Thanks." He handed his attaché case, which contained nothing more than a change of shirt and his razor and toothbrush, to Carey Blanton. "If you don't mind."

Before he'd gone a quarter of a mile his forehead was wet with perspiration, and he was rolling up his shirt sleeves, but that didn't slow him down as he picked his way across the field among clumps of buffalo grass and fossil rock. All he could think about was seeing Julia again. Not that that kept him from noticing the openness, the sense of having plenty of room, that came as he walked across the land, open and unfenced as far as he could see in any direction he chose to look.

Off in the distance, he saw a small shed that looked to be some sort of animal shelter, and headed directly for it. When he got closer, he saw that it was inside a small fenced enclosure, in which there were a dozen or so baby goats, along with a half-dozen adults. The shed was open on one side, and two people seemed to be working at something there in the shade of the corrugated tin roof.

Ross slowed his walk to come up quietly. They looked like nearly identical young boys from the back, both of them wearing faded blue jeans, workshirts, and dusty boots. For a minute, he thought he might be in the wrong place—until he spied two pigtails hanging down under their scruffy-looking western hats, one dark and the other blond, whipping around as they wrestled a spindly legged black and white kid. One used both hands to hold on to a nippled bottle of milk, while the other one grasped the little animal by the shoulders, trying to restrain the eager baby. He stood outside the fence for two or three minutes, watching the proceedings with a smile on his face.

Then Julia looked up and turned, as if she'd at last sensed someone was there. "Ross!" She let go of the tiny goat and, with an unexpected burst of excitement, tossed her hat high into the air as she sprinted toward him.

"Oh, *Mother!*" The exclamation was one of mingled dismay and exasperation, and claimed all of Ross's attention—just in time for him to see the slim young girl knocked flat on her rear by the little goat's eager nudging at the bottle. She sat sprawled there for a moment, her face flushed with both heat and embarrassment, before she pushed her straw hat up and back off her forehead.

And that was when Ross got his first good look. It was a face he'd seen before, or at least one very much like it, in the photograph of a young man on a horse—in the extra bedroom in Julia's apartment.

Chapter 12

JULIA LEANED ACROSS the fence and threw her arms around Ross's neck, laughing and talking at the same time. He just stood there, petrified by what he'd just heard and seen, to say nothing of her unexpectedly warm welcome.

"I didn't expect you so soon. You must have driven a hundred miles an hour! Oh God, I bet I look awful. Why do my best-laid plans always go awry with you? I must smell like the goatpen! What time is it, anyway?" She jumped from one conclusion to another, thinking out loud.

Ross pulled his stunned thoughts together, then held her away from him, filling his eyes. "You look good to me," he told her quietly, "but maybe you ought to introduce me to your friend there." He nodded toward the blond girl still sitting in the dirt, watching them—then pulled open the gate far enough to inch his way inside the pen.

"Oh!" Julia seemed to suddenly remember their audience. "Beth. Ross, this is my da—"

"Yeah, I know. Your daughter," he finished for her, then strode quickly to where Beth sat, leaned toward her and extended a hand. "Hi."

The young girl grabbed his offered hand and let him pull her to her feet, almost absently dusting off the seat of her pants as she gave him the once-over. "Hi," she answered, then looked at her mother with one eyebrow lifted.

Ross couldn't help the grin that lit his face at the familiar expression.

Beth grinned back. "She sprung me on you, didn't she?" He nodded. "I guess she's ashamed of me. Or something." Her teasing tone left no doubt that she knew better.

"Something," Ross agreed.

"These little bottomless pits should have enough in their stomachs to hold them for a couple of hours," Julia broke in, to change the subject. "Why don't we head back up to the house for a shower, Beth—get rid of the goatpen?" She wrinkled her nose to emphasize what she wanted to do.

"Maybe you'd like to take a swim?" Beth asked quickly, turning to Ross as they walked back across the pasture. "How about if Mom and I take a shower and then we all—which would you like better, the pool or the river? The river's a little low right now, but—?"

"Sorry, but I didn't bring my suit—didn't even think about it, to tell you the truth. Guess I had other things on my mind." He glanced at Julia and smiled, then wrapped an arm around her shoulder. She didn't pull away, and even reciprocated by slipping an arm around his waist, which came as another surprise to Ross. Was it her unsubtle way of telling Beth something about their relationship?

"No problem," Beth responded on an expelled breath. "Carey keeps a bunch of suits around, for friends who drop in unprepared. He says you can learn a lot about people just from the way they behave with most of their clothes off. Of course, not many of his buddies are in as good shape as you are," she conceded, assessing his body before glancing at her mother with a conspiratorial smile, "but I'm sure you can find one to fit." Then with only the slightest hesitation to warn him, she blurted, "Your hair's white but you're not really old, are you?"

Ross only shook his head, agreeing, and tried not to laugh. He had the distinct impression that this was just the beginning—that she was feeling him out, trying to decide whether to like him or not.

Beth chattered on unperturbed as they walked across the pasture. "Carey put the hands to digging the pit yesterday. They started the fire last night, stayed up all night feeding it. Look, you can see the smoke." She pointed off toward the river. "The beef went on about eight o'clock this morning, and they're going to put the *cabrito* on pretty soon now. That's goat. It's really going to be something! We haven't had a party like this for a long time, have we, Mom?" Ross caught a kind of understanding look pass between her and Julia. "Of course, we have to wait for all the others to get here, so we're just having a make-do lunch." She paused briefly, but apparently it was only to organize her questions, then she began to interrogate him about his work and where he lived in Austin.

"I go to St. Michael's—it's in the hills about ten miles west of Austin. You've never heard of it?" He shook his head. "You don't have any kids?" Again he shook his head, not minding her direct and quite unsubtle approach to finding out what she wanted to know about him. "It takes kids from all over the country, plus day students from Austin. I'm a boarding student—that means I live there." He nodded solemnly to indicate that he understood, keeping a straight face. "I'm in the eleventh grade." She paused again, then turned toward him. "I'll be sixteen next month."

He nodded but still didn't say anything, and again he caught a glimpse of that same little satisfied smile as she cast a quick glance at her mother.

They came up at the back of the house, passing through a gate in a tall cedar fence that enclosed a lush expanse of deep green carpet grass surrounded by tall poplars and live oaks, and headed toward a big rectangular pool set into the U formed by the main house and its wings. Delicate mimosa trees dripped with feathery pink blossoms and there were flowers everywhere—in beds edging the rock walkways, spilling out of huge earthenware pots placed around the pool area, and climbing up trellises set against rock walls.

"See you back here in a few minutes," Beth tossed over her shoulder as she peeled off toward one wing of the house, leaving Ross and Julia standing near the edge of the pool.

"She just got her braces off," Julia commented as they watched her walk away, "and suddenly she's smiling and talking all the time—like she's been let out of school, or jail, or something. I can't get over the change." She felt Ross's hand on the back of her neck, turning her to face him.

"I knew you were big on surprises, girl," he chided, a big smile creasing his face, "but, well, don't you think—" He checked himself, stymied, unable to find words to express exactly how he felt.

"I'll understand if you decide this heavy dose of family is more than you bargained for, Ross," she ventured. "I'm not the carefree single girl you probably imagined. I have a lot of awfully mundane responsibilities, which certainly are anything but conducive to romantic fantasies!"

"I'm not one to be intimidated by beautiful young girls—or smart ones, either. I take it she's sort of precocious, right?"

Julia nodded. "The word is 'gifted' now, but yes. I used to worry because she was so quiet—and now she hardly ever stops. I hope she doesn't get on your nerves."

"I like her style. In fact, I think I prefer it to the secretive types! Why didn't you tell me, Julia?"

Her eyes refused to meet his and instead seemed fascinated by his chin. "I don't know," she mumbled.

He took her face between his hands, then drew a deep breath and plunged ahead. "She's beautiful, Julia—and I don't see how you can ever forget what he looked like with her around."

"She looks that much like him? You really think so?"

He laughed, breaking the tension. "Well, you could hardly say I was anticipating a daughter, right? That's how I knew instantly who she was, before you said a word. Except for those eyebrows—they're all you. One even flies up the same way yours does."

Julia laughed softly, thanking him with her eyes, then lifted one hand to his cheek and leaned forward to place a light kiss at the base of his throat.

"Alex says I expect too much of people," she explained, deliberately taking the risk of mentioning his name to Ross, though she couldn't bring herself to repeat his exact words. "I've thought about that a lot in the last couple of weeks. And I decided he's probably right. Maybe I wasn't keeping the doors open with you, like you asked, Ross—doors that go both ways. I guess I'm scared, and I've sort of been keeping you at a distance." Her slight smile was almost apologetic. "I suppose that sounds trite—a cliché."

Ross's eyes never left her face, taking in not only each word but every nuance of expression there as she spoke.

"I don't want to lose what I feel with you, but I've got to take that chance. And if this, this weekend, scares you off—I guess I'll have to learn to live with that, too."

It was so much more than Ross had allowed himself to hope for from her that he couldn't speak for a minute. Instead, he wrapped his arms around her and held on tight. "I don't scare easily, Julie love," he whispered into her hair finally, blinking back the burning behind his eyelids. "I haven't even been able to figure out how or why it happened myself, but I do know I made a mistake. That—and that the last three weeks have been pure hell."

He held her away from him then, and she saw the sparkle come back into his eyes. "We'll have time to talk, but right now you smell like goat! And Beth's going to be back out here in about thirty seconds, ready to challenge me to God only knows what." He brushed her lips lightly with his own, trying to keep his hands off her this time. "So how about telling me where the suits are and then you can go shower."

"You're sure you can stand it without me for a few min—"

"She's a bad one for teasing, son—or have you already learned that?" Carey Blanton called out while he was still at least thirty feet away, probably to warn them he was there. "Beth says Ross needs a suit, Julia, so I came out to see to it. I told Lupe to fix lunch and serve it out here. Just a little something to hold us." He stopped and glanced at his wrist. "Annie will be finished in about half an hour. So you go on and quit pestering this boy."

Julia laughed and made a face, then surrendered Ross to him and walked toward the same sliding glass door Beth had gone through a few minutes earlier.

"That's Julia's—that wing of the house," Carey explained to Ross as he led him around a half-dozen reclining lounge chairs, into a sort of small cabaña built out from the opposite wing. He headed toward the mirrored closet doors lining one wall of the generous-sized dressing room, continuing to talk all the while. "We added her wing after Tom died. Fixed it so she could have privacy whenever she wanted, but close enough so she didn't feel alone."

The room was simply furnished, with two padded boudoir chairs and a dressing table, and through the door standing open off to his right, Ross caught a glimpse of still another room, almost as big as the one they were in, where big pots of lacy green ferns and pink bougainvillea vines hung above the cedar ledge of a hot, bubbling Jacuzzi with blue and yellow Mexican tiles.

"She came back here to live, you know, after she had Beth," Carey continued, while he pulled open the closet doors to reveal a tall built-in chest of drawers, then turned suddenly and looked directly at Ross. "I suspect she hasn't told you much about that time, has she?"

"No. In fact, I didn't even know about Beth until just a few minutes ago," Ross admitted with a grin, wondering somewhere on the edge of his mind why Carey Blanton's face seemed so familiar. Julia didn't really look much like him, except for the tall slim body and the way they both moved.

"Yeah, she's kind of private that way." Carey peered at him rather intently, Ross thought. "Even around us, but I guess we just have to try to be understanding about that. She's never learned to live with what happened. I always kind of wished she could feel closer to her mother. Maybe it would have helped. But my Annie was away a lot when Julia was a girl, you know. Julia and I've always been close, but somehow they never, she—'' He either didn't know what to say or how to say it. ''Well, anyway,'' he breathed, ''Julia went to France when Beth was about a year old. Did she tell you that?''

Ross nodded. ''That she spent a year in France, yes, apprenticing with Balmain. That's all.''

''Yeah, an old friend of Annie's. Anyway, Annie and me, we kept Beth while she was gone, so she's sort of like another daughter and granddaughter all rolled into one. Just thought you might like to know that.'' He hesitated again, which made Ross wish he could figure out how to help the man. Was he struggling with some question, or simply trying to tell him something?

''Have you ever seen a computer chip up close, Carey?'' Ross asked, putting two and two together and taking a stab in the dark. ''They carry an electronic circuit that's complex as hell and microscopic to boot. You have to be meticulous beyond belief and have the patience of Job to work out all the intricate details—especially when it comes to fabricating them. In the process, you make a lot of mistakes, but you learn a lot, and fast. You even get to where you can sort of anticipate where the problem areas are going to be.'' He paused momentarily. ''I spent about five years of my life designing chips. Since then, I've been working on software for computers, trying to figure out how to give some pretty complex instructions to a machine that has a vocabulary of only two words—yes and no. So I guess I must be the tenacious type—when I think the result is going to be worth the effort,'' he explained slowly, hoping Julia's father would understand the metaphor, if that's what he was fishing for. If not, well, he'd probably think Ross was way out in left field, or maybe just obtuse.

Carey Blanton's face broke into a slow grin as he realized what Ross was saying—and then he whooped with laughter, gesturing toward the drawers in front of him. ''Take whatever you want, Ross. And if there's anything else you need, anything at all, just holler." He was still chuckling and shaking his head. "I sure do like the way you put things, Ross. You ever consider going into politics?"

Ross was standing near the edge of the pool with Beth when Julia came out. He took just one look and clapped a hand to his forehead in mock dismay, moaning, "Oh my God, the temptation test!"

Beth giggled, first at him and then at the look on her mother's face, covering her mouth with one hand out of habit. Julia was wearing a turquoise blue maillot with a bright green zipper running down the front, between her breasts, which was open halfway to her navel. She started to walk around the pool toward them, but then reversed direction when she heard a car honk twice out front. It was common custom in the country to let the people you were visiting know you'd arrived, since they might be in the barn or animal pens, or even farther away from the house. By the time she got to the French doors at the back of the main house, Alex was already pushing his way through them.

"Hi there, babe," he yelled, waving wildly at Beth, then grabbed Julia in his usual bear hug, hoisting her off her feet. "You finally saw the light, huh, Julia baby?" he whispered just before setting her back down, then rushed toward Beth and grabbed her up, too, swinging her around and around. "Little girl, you get more damn gorgeous every time I see you. Ross." Alex grinned hugely, one arm still around Beth while the other shot out in friendly greeting, his exuberant enthusiasm including everyone.

"Alex," Ross intoned, clasping the outthrust hand and smiling to cover the jolt he'd felt at Alex's unexpected appearance, "you got here just in time—to even up the odds, I mean. These two are—"

"Yeah, I know what you mean. They'll gang up on you every time."

Thirty minutes later, they were all sitting on the edge of the pool, talking and dangling their legs in the water, when Beth suddenly shouted, *"Maman!"* and jumped up to run to the woman who was coming toward them. "Come and meet Ross—and Alex is here, too. Can I go tell Lupe to serve lunch? We're starving, aren't we?" She turned to appeal to the rest of them.

Julia watched Ross rise slowly to his feet and turn, then go completely still as her mother came closer.

For one startling instant, Ross thought he must be losing his grip on reality. The way she walked, the aura that seemed to move with this woman, everything about the way she held her body seemed familiar. He could almost swear he'd seen her before. She wore a simple beige and white striped dress, alternately gauzy and textured, that hung loose and straight except for the sash tied around her hips. And low-heeled woven-leather shoes. Was that why she seemed shorter than he remembered? Even her hair was shorter, and a slightly different color, but the slow smile—oh, that suggestive, mysterious smile! And then she was standing next to Julia, and he was seeing them together for the first time.

"Maman, this is Ross McCutcheon," Julia told the woman who looked very much like a slightly older version of herself, except her eyes were dark brown instead of blue, and her curly hair was streaked with gray.

"Ross, I am so happy to meet you," Julia's mother murmured. Her voice was unmistakable. Ross looked from one to the other and then back again, staring, unable at first to fully comprehend the reality of what he was seeing, then down at the warm hand he held in his own.

"Ross is a long-time admirer of yours, Maman," Julia continued, to give him some time to recover from the shock. "He took me to hear the Delius concerto in Paris, and afterward, at dinner—it's almost too much of a coincidence to believe—he told me about the first time he heard you, when he was eleven years old, in Chicago. But then Ross believes in the hand of destiny."

Julia gave him an indulgent smile, but Ross continued to stare at Julia's mother, trying desperately to get control of conflicting memories. Beth and Alex watched and listened, spellbound by a story neither had heard before.

"You made a truly indelible impression, Maman," Julia went on, breaking the almost holy silence. "He called you unique, beautiful—and brave. 'She spoke to me in a language I never even knew existed before,' I think were his exact words."

Anne-Marie Lacombe's lips curved into a gentle smile. "For a young boy to hear so much, to understand so much, is the highest compliment, my dear Ross. Julia does not intend to be cruel, I think, so you must forgive her this small indiscretion—to tell me this confidence." The glance she sent toward Julia was unmistakably disapproving, however. "It is what one wishes for most, to touch one life, to bring awake something that is there, but only slumbers before. So you see, she would indulge me, because she knows how much I will cherish what you have told her." She had only a slight accent and most of that was noticeable only on certain words, like her daughter's name.

"Madame Lacombe," Ross murmured at last, finding his tongue enough to at least recognize the introduction.

"Please. Anne, or at least Anne-Marie," she requested.

Ross shook his head slightly, disbelievingly. "I'll try." He smiled at last, and his face lit up with the pure joy of meeting this woman he'd thought about for so many years.

Without warning, and surprising even Julia, Anne-Marie reached up on tiptoe to kiss Ross's cheek. "We must talk together, you and I. Later. After these rascals," she waved a hand lazily toward Alex and Beth, "have something to eat, *n'est-ce pas?*"

Carey Blanton seemed to appear out of nowhere to rest one hand on Anne-Marie's shoulder. She covered it with her own, and when she turned to look at him it was as if the very air came alive. It was always like that when these two were together, only Ross had never seen it before. On her lips Carey's name became "*Cara*" and even at times "*Cara mia.*" Ross watched them surreptitiously, fascinated, all through lunch—

a Tex-Mex feast of tacos, enchiladas, chili con queso, guacamole salad and the hottest picante sauce he'd ever tasted.

The afternoon passed slowly, or at least that's how it felt to Julia, maybe because she was feeling a little guilty. Ross responded when someone spoke to him directly, and even smiled at the right times, but seemed terribly distracted. Then, about three o'clock, Elaine and her two girls arrived, and with them, to Julia's surprise, was Max Starke.

Elaine waved gaily as she came out onto the terrace. "God, I always forget how hot it can be down here at this time of year," she breathed as she hugged Julia. "All I could think about driving all the way out here was that pool!" She walked straight to the edge of it, slipped off one shoe and stuck her toes down into the water. "Ahh boy, does that feel good!" she breathed, before answering the question on Julia's face. "Max decided to come with us to Atlanta, Julia. He took the girls around while I was at market. They had a ball—even went to a rock concert one night."

"Hello, Julia," he greeted her quietly, smiling. "I'm afraid I let Elaine twist my arm because she told me about this place and I really wanted to see it. But I'll be going back to Austin tonight, so not to worry."

"I'd like it if you stayed, Max, unless you'd really rather go back to town, of course. We've got plenty of room. Come and meet Ross, and my mother and father. And Beth. I have an almost-sixteen-year-old, too. Did Elaine tell you?"

"No, she didn't." He sounded somewhat taken aback, and glanced at Elaine with some consternation. "I must be intruding on a family get-together, Julia, I—"

"No one ever intrudes around here, Max. You'll see what I mean before the evening is over. My father—well, he's sort of the gregarious type, you might say."

Elaine burst out laughing at that. "That's the understatement of the year. Come on, Max, let's greet the folks before the thundering herds come stomping through and we never get another chance."

Beth took Tina and Maggie off toward the horse barn, while

Julia joined Elaine for another swim, at the same time keeping a close eye on Ross. Within minutes, however, he was completely engrossed in some animated conversation with Alex and Max, and she breathed a sigh of relief.

"Here I get myself all decked out in the sexiest suit I could dig up," Elaine complained, "and he doesn't even glance this way. How the hell can you seduce a man who isn't looking!" She was wearing a tiny black crocheted bikini—and she didn't expect an answer. They pulled two lounge chairs out of the shade and stretched out. It had already cooled off some, since the sun was no longer directly overhead. "God, you can pick them, I have to give you that! Those light blue eyes of his just slam into you, don't they?"

Julia nodded absently, watching Ross. "He hasn't said a word to me since Maman. He's either still in shock, or angry. Maybe I should have warned him a little bit." She told Elaine about Ross's first encounter with Beth, and then with her mother. "I doubt he's recognized Carey yet, either, but when those bozos from Austin light here for barbecue tonight, well— I have to keep suppressing this awful urge to drag him away, bodily if I have to, before anything else falls on him. I'm afraid the next one might just crush him."

"Listen, honey, from what you've told me, he's one of the few men in the world whose ego doesn't depend on putting somebody else down. I'll bet he can take you, and Carey, and all this, too," she waved an arm to indicate not only the place but everything associated with it, "and still have plenty left over." She looked thoughtful for a minute. "Him, and your father. God, can you imagine what it must have been like for Carey, thirty-five years ago, amongst all these Texas rednecks, with a little woman who wouldn't stay home?" She hesitated, looking off toward where Max was sitting.

"And what about Max?" Julia asked, catching the direction of her glance.

"Yeah, well, maybe it's just wishful thinking, because you're always telling me I fall for the wrong kind of guys. But he's different, Julia, not at all like we thought."

"I'm so glad you discovered that for yourself." Julia's remark got Elaine's full attention. She described how Max had used subtle questions at the textile mill to coax new ideas from almost everyone involved in their discussions. "He never trumpeted his own ideas, or even took credit when we finished, even though it wouldn't have happened the way it did without him. I couldn't help comparing that with the way Tony would have handled it. I knew that I'd been wrong about him," she confessed. "My fault, not his. He didn't make a lot of noise, so I didn't pay much attention. I guess a lot of women make that mistake on a personal level, too—they don't even notice a man as a sexual person unless he makes a lot of noise about it. Apparently Max doesn't feel the need to beat his chest—at least not in public."

"Not in private either," Elaine confessed, "but who needs it when he makes you feel so damn good you wake up believing you were born yesterday, and there's still hope, and faith, and everything isn't all tarnished!"

Three red-faced and sweaty girls came pounding through the main terrace door just then, their excited voices and clumping boots too loud to ignore.

"Wow," Beth exploded, "have you seen that red Mercedes convertible out front, Mom? A 560 SL! Can't be one of Carey's mossbacks—they wouldn't have the guts, would they?"

Ross strolled over and somewhat sheepishly owned up to the red Mercedes, then asked Beth if she could drive.

"I'm taking driver's ed at school right now, so I can get my license as soon as I'm sixteen. But I learned how a long time ago. Carey taught me. By the way, Mom, we fed the bottomless pits again, so they should be okay for a while."

"So how about driving me around—show me the ranch before it gets dark," he suggested, "if your mother says it's okay. Anybody else want to go?" He looked at Julia, but she shook her head. Tina and Maggie opted for a swim with Elaine and Max instead, and Carey and Anne-Marie had already gone off hand in hand to see to arrangements for the evening.

"Okay if we're back in about an hour, then?" Ross asked Julia as she walked out to the car with them.

"I guess I ought to warn you, Ross. Some of my father's political friends are coming from Austin for barbecue this evening."

"Why?" he asked with a wry smile.

"I don't know. Just for fun and games, I guess, or maybe he needs to talk to them about something."

"I meant, why start warning me now?"

Julia had the grace to at least look a bit chagrined, but he beamed at her and then reached inside the car to fold back the canvas top.

Beth was as expert as she claimed, Ross decided, as he watched her guide the Mercedes over the rough ranch road, seeming to anticipate every pothole and deftly moving out of the well-worn track whenever she hit a section of washboard. They settled into a comfortable silence at first, but then she gradually began telling him about the ranch. "Carey runs about a thousand head of cattle, mostly Herefords—those Longhorns up near the gate are just for show. He's got seven miles of riverfront, probably more than anybody else around here."

"And goats?"

"Yeah, and sheep. But he pretty much keeps the sheep rotating in the south pastures. They ruin the grass if you leave 'em too long in one place, you know. Chew it right down to the ground. The lambs are cute, but they grow up dumb. Sheep and chickens are about the dumbest animals on the face of the earth! Hey, would you like to go down to see how the meat's coming in the pit? I can smell it way up here, can't you?"

He nodded. "Sure, wherever you say. You're the driver."

A little farther along, she turned the car off the road and headed straight out across the pasture, steering carefully to avoid the animals, rocks and clustered live oaks. Faint tracks indicated they weren't the first vehicle to come this way recently, and Ross felt perfectly at ease in her hands. As they crested a small ridge, she slowed the car and then stopped, giving him time to take in the scene spread out below them.

It was nearly dusk now, and the setting sun reflected off the meandering surface of the Pedernales, turning the ribbon of water a pale pink-orange, stretching as far as they could see. On the near bank, perhaps fifty feet up from the river, a long narrow trench had been dug in the ground, and it was alive with hot glowing coals and thick gray smoke. Perhaps a half-dozen men mingled around the edge of the pit in the dusky half-light, talking and laughing. Blended by distance, the sound floated up to them like a lonely song, cast adrift in the otherwise silent dusk. From time to time one of the men would reach across the trench with a long-handled fork to turn the meat, which hovered over the flickering coals as if floating on magic carpets. Another ranch hand, carrying a bucket and mop, constantly circled the pit, dipping and dabbing at it.

"You prefer this to living with your mother in New York?" Ross asked finally.

"Not particularly. Besides, I spend summers there, and long vacations—whenever I'm not in school." She didn't say any more, but glanced at Ross from time to time, trying not to be obvious about it. Then, after a few minutes, without any warning, she blurted a sudden question. "You're sleeping with my mother, aren't you?"

He felt sure the initial shock showed in his face, and for the first time, he wasn't sure what to say to her—neither denial nor confession seemed right.

She took pity on him. "You don't have to answer. I know you are. She's different." She looked away, and he sensed she already regretted asking.

"You subscribe to the notion that it makes people look different, I take it? Sex, I mean," he explained.

She shook her head. "That's not what I meant. She acts different with you. Besides, she's never brought a man to the ranch before, except Alex."

"I care about her, Beth—a lot."

"Dr. Ruth says sex is for people who can take care of themselves and take care of each other. Is that what you think?"

"Dr. Ruth?" he asked, puzzled and increasingly uncomfortable with the subject. He knew she was testing him again.

"Yeah, the one who writes that column in the newspaper. Don't you ever read her?"

"Oh yeah, her. Sure, sometimes. Doesn't everybody?" He smiled, beginning to relax when he realized she'd asked out of a natural curiosity, rather than out of jealousy or resentment. It was simply a subject she'd thrown out for discussion. "Yeah, I do agree with her, Beth. I expect my birth parents couldn't take care of themselves, let alone each other, and that's the reason they had to put me out for adoption. I don't know for sure, of course, but—"

"You're an adopted kid?" She sounded amazed. "And you don't know who your biological parents are? I thought you could look for them, find out about them, once you got old enough. Couldn't you find them?"

"I've never tried. Don't feel the need, I guess. Or maybe I'm afraid of what I might find out. Anyway, I already had a mother who loved me—she died a few years ago—and a grandmother who's a lot like yours. So I feel pretty lucky. The only thing I ever missed was not having any brothers or sisters." He looked at her. "Don't you?"

"How can you miss something you've never had?" she answered curtly, putting an end to that subject. They sat and watched the smoking pit in companionable silence. "I'm different from ninety-five percent of the other kids, did she tell you that?"

He shook his head and waited.

"Because I'm gifted. My mother explained it to me when I was seven, because she didn't want me to get any wrong ideas. She said some kids feel bad about themselves because they're different. Or I might begin to think other kids were dumb and be nasty to them, which wouldn't exactly make me everybody's sweetheart. We talk about it sometimes. She also sent me to St. Michael's when I started seventh grade, so I'd have lots of competition, and not get a big head. Maman says it only means I have a bigger responsibility, to use the gift I was given. But I tell you, Ross," she turned toward him, her face growing even more animated than usual, "it's just not fair!"

"How come?" he asked quickly, worried by her tone of angry protest.

"Well, take Evan Hoover, for instance. He's in my chemistry class, and he has a photographic memory. He was born with it, he didn't have to learn it. I think the only way to make it fair would be to let the rest of us use the textbook during exams! Don't you?"

"What does your chemistry teacher say to that? Did you try the idea out on him?"

"*He* says everybody's born with something someone else doesn't have, and we just have to learn to live with it. It all averages out in the end, he claims. But only a man would believe that! There's not a female alive—at least one who's awake up here," she put an index finger to her temple, "who doesn't know that's a lot of *bull!*"

The word reverberated in his head for one brief instant, and then the last piece of the puzzle fell into place as Ross realized why Carey had looked vaguely familiar when he first met him earlier in the day. Julia's father was the state's controversial agriculture commissioner—Carey "No More Bull" Blanton!

Chapter 13

ROSS STROLLED AROUND the edge of the crowd, sipping at his margarita from time to time, watching Carey Blanton circulate among the two dozen or more men and women milling around on the grassy area beyond the pool terrace. Tall oil-fed torches illuminated the yard, throwing flickering shadows onto the big round tables scattered across the lawn, each one clothed in white and lit by a glass-chimneyed hurricane lamp. A long banquet table set up along the edge of the rock terrace served as bar, and white-coated waiters carried an array of relishes, condiments and salads toward another table, just a few feet away. It wouldn't be long, from the look of things, until the smoked meat would be coming as well.

He spotted Max and Elaine, talking to a couple of men and a plump blond woman wearing a white western hat with what looked to him like a square-dance costume. One of the men kept clapping Max on the shoulder whenever he laughed, revealing a gold wristwatch shaped like the state of Texas, outlined in diamonds that reflected quick glints of light from one of the torches. The other man sported a western-style tweed sport coat with gray elephant hide patches on the elbows, to match his boots.

Most of the crowd from Austin who'd come for Carey's little get-together fitted the glitzy nouveau riche Texas myth, the one pictured in the society pages of the state's biggest newspapers, and in *Ultra,* that slick bit of puffery published out of Houston, which should have embarrassed everyone pictured in its pages. The only reason Ross knew about the magazine was because it came regularly in his mail—a way of padding their high-income "subscriber" list and "conning" advertisers.

Anne-Marie appeared perfectly at ease as she passed among these "foreigners" in her long loose-fitting galabia of tawny striped cotton that alternately revealed and then hid the contours of her small body as she moved. Her only jewelry was a delicate, thin rope of silver and turquoise hishi that undulated gently in the valley between her breasts. Put up next to her, most of the other women looked gauche to Ross, and he couldn't help wondering, not for the first time, how this unique Frenchwoman had ever come to be the wife of a Texas rancher in the first place.

She glanced up at that moment, caught him watching her and hurried toward him. "Ross, you are alone," she began, reaching for his hand to touch him, a natural expression of her concern. "Where is Julie? Is she not here?"

"You don't need to worry about me, Anne-Marie. I'm not shy." He could listen to the way she pronounced her daughter's name all night long—the sensuous, caressing slide before lifting a little at the end in an almost-question mark.

"Last time I looked, she was over there, with Beth." He glanced toward the food table. They were still there, but now Beth was holding a bowl of tortilla chips, and both of them were gesturing with their hands as they talked. "It sort of looked like she might be getting after Beth about something, and I didn't want to interfere," he explained.

"Mais, non," Anne-Marie protested, laughing. "They speak in French, that is all. A bad habit, I'm afraid—a way

to be private in a crowd." She turned back to him. "I'm very happy she has brought you here, Ross, though I would wish not to have this—these others here."

"I've waited all these years," he confessed, laughing at himself, "certainly I can wait a little longer to ask about your 'Poems.' "

"You know of them?" she asked, surprised.

"Julie sent me a copy of her tape, just a few weeks ago. Until then, no, except the one you played in Chicago. Have you written more?"

"Oui, many things in the years since, but no more of such poems. I never recorded them. Only for Julie, because she says she must have them with her in New York. But they are somewhat personal for me, so I don't like to have someone else play them." She looked at him appraisingly. "I played a few times, when I was on tour, when to be alone became almost too much to bear. Julie was only a little girl when I wrote them, and I had to be away from her so much. And from my husband. What I felt then, I began to write in my music. In my poems."

"I'm sorry. I'll give the tape back to her. I didn't mean to—" he began, but she quickly held up a hand to stop him.

"No, no. I did not say so for you to think you intrude—how is it Julie says?—that you have invaded my privacy. Never before did she do this, and if she wanted you to have them, Ross, that is enough." She smiled again, and released his hand. "Now I must speak to others, so you will excuse me?"

Anne-Marie's smile could be as enigmatic as her daughter's, Ross realized, intrigued anew each time he caught a flash of Julie in one of Anne-Marie's expressions or mannerisms. She had to be at least in her midfifties, perhaps older, yet she moved like a young woman and—very much like what he sensed in Julia—there was about her an unmistakable aura of physical sexuality.

Even out here among his political cronies, Carey Blanton's eyes constantly sought out Anne-Marie, and hers didn't stray long from him, either. In his own way, Carey was as much an anomaly as his wife, Ross decided. He'd run for state agriculture commissioner almost four years ago on a pledge to transform the economic climate for Texas farmers—so they could "eat the whole hog, not just the hooves and chitlings." He seemed possessed of a natural wit, and reporters were quick to repeat his pithy comments, delivered in his Texas "good old boy" vernacular.

When the city of Austin announced it was going to buy electric power generated from West Texas feedlot residue, Carey Blanton had commented, "For the first time in history, BS is going to flow from the countryside into the state capitol." His political opponents tried smearing him as a liberal agitator, but he'd simply turned their label to his own advantage. "I like being called an agitator," he'd told huge crowds all over the state. "That's the part of the washing machine that gets the dirt out!"

Beneath the jokes, however, Carey Blanton was both smart and deadly serious, and as agriculture commissioner, he was bent on doing a whole lot more than fighting fire ants and toadying to the ultraconservative Texas Farm Bureau. He began negotiating directly for foreign trade agreements, selling Texas cattle and sheep to Mexico and Texas wheat to China, then set up local farmers' markets all over the state, and co-ops, so small farmers could sell to volume buyers like Safeway. And he was constantly exhorting the state's farmers to become their own "middlemen" by building or buying processing plants for their produce. Cambodian refugees were engaged in a pilot project to grow Oriental vegetables on idle state land near Houston, a group of New Zealanders was growing kiwis in West Texas, and an exchange program with Israel was in place to develop grapes and cotton that required less water.

Ross knew Carey was running for re-election, and with the chemical industry and conservative farmers' organizations lined up against him, largely because of his pesticide regulations, he was facing a tough fight. They sounded pretty minimal to Ross, and he had a hard time understanding how anyone could possibly be opposed, except out of pure greed—and there was plenty of that. The legislature had been lobbied into excluding farm workers from unemployment compensation benefits, even though they were subjected to more hazardous working conditions than almost any other group of workers in the state, until the courts stepped in and ruled their exclusion unconstitutional.

Ross glanced around and found Beth, Tina and Maggie, along with two other teenage girls and a boy he'd never seen before, sitting at one of the tables, coke cans in hand, snacking on crisp tortilla chips and salsa. He ambled over, but as he got close enough to overhear a few words, he realized they were embroiled in a heated discussion, and decided not to intrude.

"I really couldn't care less, Beth," Tina responded in a lofty and somewhat bored tone. "Our maid throws most of my clothes in the laundry at home, anyway. So it's no big deal to me." The hair on top of her head was short and stood straight up, like the topknot of some rare tropical bird, while the rest hung to her shoulders in a frizzy cloud that dwarfed her delicate features. Her bright pink sleeveless knit blouse was pulled up slightly in the front and pinned in haphazard gathers between her breasts, revealing and directing attention to her navel—which sported a huge fake ruby.

"Jesus! I don't see how you can be so dense!" Beth exploded, giving full vent to the exasperation Tina provoked. "You think paying three dollars and a quarter to get your shirt laundered, while Matt here only has to pay a dollar and a quarter, is irrelevant? Do you expect your mother to support you all your life? How are you going to feel when you go after some job, and Matt," again she pointed a finger at the boy sitting between them, who was looking more and more uncomfortable all the time, "is offered five thousand dollars more than you are?" She paused to give everyone time to make the connection. "The point, Tina, is discrimination—*not* whether you happen to take your dirty clothes to the laundry!"

"Maybe," Tina admitted grudgingly. "So—?"

Ross continued to keep his face and eyes directed elsewhere, hoping they wouldn't notice that he was eavesdropping.

"So—what we've got to do is figure out some way to convince them we're tired of being taken to the cleaners, and that we're not going to keep quiet about it. There's this woman attorney in California who's planning to bring suit against the cleaners and laundries there. Well, if we got a protest going here at the same time, something noisy enough to get the attention of the news media, and you and Maggie did the same thing in New York, or New Jersey, or wherever, it might spread and look like it was becoming a nationwide thing," Beth explained, as persuasively as she knew how. "And that would get the attention of the networks—we'd get on national television!"

Ross was so engrossed in what he was hearing that it gave him a start when Julia sidled up and quietly eased an arm around his waist. "You finally recognized my father?" she asked, reaching her lips toward his ear to whisper. It was the first chance they'd had to talk alone since lunch.

"And your mother," he acknowledged with a wry smile, unconsciously bending his head toward her slightly. Without warning, her tongue darted out, sending a wave of hot-cold sensations down his back. He shivered slightly, but his response was lightning quick. "I'm warning you, Julie love," he threatened menacingly, one arm holding her tightly against him, "I've had just about all I can take today. You try that just one more time and I'm going to drag you off to the nearest bed—kicking and screaming if I have to!"

Julia gave a low throaty laugh, delighted with his response. "What have I ever done to make you think you'd have to drag me?" she murmured, nibbling at the tip of his earlobe this time.

He set her away from him, but he was grinning. "Watch it! You're setting a bad example for the young innocents there." He dipped his head slightly toward the table where

Beth and her friends were sitting, then almost choked on a laugh. "Innocents, hell! I've been standing here listening to them plot a damned rebellion! And guess who's behind the whole thing?"

"I don't want to hear! If you were a parent, you'd realize the real meaning of ignorance is bliss. It's better not to know everything that goes on inside their devious heads." All expression suddenly disappeared from Ross's face, and a flood of confusion hit Julia. Had she hit on some hidden sore spot, something to do with why he didn't have any children after eight years of marriage? Maybe he couldn't! Now that she really thought about it, she realized her inane comment was inexcusably insensitive.

"You and your mother are a sight for sore eyes amongst all these cowgirls, you know that?" Ross commented, a smile replacing the rigid mask as he changed the subject completely. Julia wore a simple red and white narrow-striped shirt, unbuttoned low to reveal unadorned smooth skin, a calf-length white skirt and flat white sandals on bare feet. Her hair was loose tonight, and delightfully tangled, and long Mexican silver earrings swung freely as she moved her head.

"One of these days, McCutcheon," she drawled, only halfway teasing, "you're going to get brave enough to come out from behind that humor."

He was about to ask her what she meant just as Carey's hand came down on his shoulder. "Time to eat. How about joining us, you and Julia?" He pointed toward one of the tables. "We're having a little powwow, and Julia's the best idea man we've got, did you know that?" He ducked his head playfully as if dodging a blow. "Sorry about that, little girl. She ought to be in politics instead of that fashion stuff! She's the one thought up our 'Taste of Texas' day in Boston—country music and the whole damn show. Two hundred New England grocery store buyers came for a taste of barbecue, picante sauce and tacos. Course that's all it takes to get 'em hooked. Now they're buying Tex-Mex like crazy up there."

* * *

An hour later, Ross rose from the table, compelled by the urge to stretch his legs, and to get away alone for a few minutes. Julia looked up, questioning, but he shook his head. He moved across the grass, away from the noisy party, not knowing exactly where he was going, then on impulse opened the gate and wandered out into the dark empty pasture beyond.

It was peaceful out here, and once you got far enough away from the lights, the sky was just about like it said in the song. Most people thought of "Texas big" in terms either of exaggerated egos or the open range, but to Ross it was the night sky, where you could see a million bright stars, uninterrupted from horizon to horizon in any direction you wanted to look. They seemed so close tonight, in fact, that it felt like the sky was pressing against the earth.

It was hard to believe that Julia's phone call had come only this morning, and after a day filled with one surprise after another, he felt the need to get away to himself for a few minutes, to try to put everything into perspective. Looking back now, it seemed perfectly obvious that the "guest" bedroom in Julia's apartment was Beth's, and he couldn't figure out why it had never occurred to him that Julia might have a child. Because he knew she'd been married only three months before her husband left for Vietnam, and she was so young back then? God, what an experience that must have been! Losing a husband she loved and having a child, before she'd even had a chance to finish school, when she was only twenty years old!

He came to a big broad outcropping of water-worn rock, and eased down onto one contoured edge, his eyes roaming the sky as he remembered telling Julia about Anne-Marie Lacombe. Even in his wildest dreams, he'd never put the two of them together, and could hardly believe it even now, after seeing them side by side and the resemblance. Anne-Marie hovered in his mind, somewhere between the artist on her pedestal and a Texas rancher's wife—"Maman" to Julia and her daughter!

He heard cautious steps crunching the dry grass behind him, and turned to see who it was.

"Ross? Mind if I join you?" Alex asked quietly as he came into sight.

"Have a seat," Ross invited, forcing himself to friendliness while moving over to make room. "I just hope the scorpions and snakes in these rocks are in for the night," he jested, trying to make conversation.

"I saw you leave," Alex confessed, "and decided maybe it was a good time to talk." He paused for a second, then continued. "Julia hasn't told you anything about us, about our relationship, has she?"

"She doesn't need to," Ross protested.

"Maybe not now," Alex observed, "but there was a time, wasn't there? Julia, she's a great believer in privacy, you know. Thinks it's an invasion of *my* privacy to tell you or anyone else about me."

"I don't know what you're talking about, and I don't want to know," Ross insisted, wishing he would shut up.

"And I don't give a shit whether you do or not!" Alex exploded suddenly, then turned to look straight at Ross. "I want her happy, Ross, and from what I've seen today, maybe you're the one who might be able to bring that off. So I'm telling you what she won't."

Alex looked away again, staring off into the distance as if he could actually see something out there in the dark. "I'll never forget the first time I laid eyes on her, in the weight room behind the gym. She was trying to bench-press fifty pounds. Hell, I bet she never even told you we went to the same school Beth goes to! She was pretty scrawny back then—Julia, I mean—but so was I!" He laughed, as if at a private joke. "I'd never seen any girls trying to lift weights before, but she was serious, wasn't just playing around to tease the guys. Told me she was trying to strengthen her legs, improve their shape. But trying to bench-press fifty pounds isn't going to do much for your legs! She wasn't very well 'endowed'!" He chuckled softly again.

"Most of the guys at school, well, I'm not sure how they knew. Intuition, maybe. I was always sketching, whenever an idea struck me, and I didn't mind letting everybody know that I was going to be a big fashion designer one day." He shrugged one shoulder, making it plain enough what he thought of that now. "But the old cliché that kids have a real talent for cruelty is true, you know.The first time Julia heard them throwing jibes at me she really laid into them about being tolerant, then named a fault each one of them had which she'd had to learn to 'live with.' "

"Boy, I bet they loved her for that," Ross commented, trying to imagine the scene, still wondering where Alex was headed.

"It's different at that school, Ross, or at least it used to be. The social environment, I mean. Nobody felt like they had to be girlfriends or boyfriends. They didn't even have to have a date to show up at the prom—boys or girls. It was okay to be different, but not as different as me. But then, that was twenty years ago! Julia was always one of the most popular kids, the way I suspect Beth is." He fell silent again for a few seconds. "She used to ask me all kinds of questions, trying to understand something she couldn't, I suspect, at least not at the time. We had some pretty crazy conversations. Argued, too. But she never laughed at me and never passed judgment. She was just a good friend. And she let everyone know it, even after Tom showed up. That's where they met, you know. Anyway, over the years she's been kind of a touchstone for me—always there, no matter what. The voice of reason in my life."

Alex met Ross's inquiring expression head on. "Sure I love her. Maybe like the sister I never had, or the parents I wanted mine to be—they never gave a shit about me, especially after they discovered what I was. I'm gay, Ross—have been from the first time I can remember even thinking about sex, when I was about eight."

A cold front had come through during the night, and it was cooler today, though still clear and sunny. The tension inside the car was almost palpable as Julia and Ross drove in silence over the narrow, winding blacktop roads of West Lake Hills. Julia's flight to New York was due to leave in two hours. There were so many questions she wanted to ask, so much she wanted to talk about, but she was waiting for some cue or sign from him. Julia had a nagging sense of time running out, and she shifted uneasily in her seat as she looked out the window, catching an occasional glimpse of a rooftop, or a quick ribbon of rock wall. More often than not, the only evidence of the residents living somewhere behind the thickets of cedars, live oaks, redbuds and scrub brush was a rural mailbox, set out on a post at the edge of the road.

The small incorporated city of about three thousand people was located in the hilly area west of the Colorado River and Lake Austin, and was considered one of the most exclusive and expensive in the Austin area. None of its citizens could own less than an acre of ground, and most of the older houses had been designed to fit the particular sloping, rocky pieces of terrain they occupied—whether to capture a view of Austin itself, spread out along the far bend of the Colorado River, or a lush green inner valley. In the past few years of rapid growth, however, and especially with the influx of several high-tech companies—IBM, Motorola, Advanced Micro Devices, Carbomedics and a host of others—real estate developers had discovered the western hills. And with them had come the tasteless, characterless ranch-style houses so typical of speculative development. Velvety slopes were gouged out to pour flat concrete slabs, leaving huge yellow caliche and limestone scars, and instead of hiding the flatland misfits with natural vegetation—cedar, Spanish oak, yaupon, redbuds and mountain laurel—yards were scraped clean and replaced with city lawns. Now, rather than the majestic blooms of the hardy white yucca and the brilliant yellow of native coreopsis, there were little rectangular beds of petunias, impatiens and roses that had to be constantly watered from May through October.

Ross must have sensed how she felt, because at that moment he reached out and covered one of her hands with his, glanced over at her and then grinned. "Do you remember before bucket seats?"

Julia burst out laughing at the picture his question brought to mind, knowing it was his way of telling her he wished she could sit closer. The tension disappeared and she nodded understandingly. "But fire-engine red? You?" she chided, shaking her head in disbelief.

"Yeah, I guess it was something I had to get out of my system. Beth likes it, though!" He gave her hand a squeeze and then returned it to the wheel, slowing as he turned into the wide mouth of a pebble-concrete driveway and then stopped the car before a hefty gray steel pipe barring their way. His window purred open and he reached out to the small box mounted on a post just at the edge of the drive and punched several numbers on what looked like a push-button telephone. Almost instantly, the barricade swung back out of the way and he drove on through.

The driveway continued on for a couple of hundred yards, around a curve and past a fenced tennis court on their right, then down a gentle slope to cross a clear shallow creek. Off to their left, the water widened and darkened into a fairly deep long pool, with concrete edges wide enough to walk on. Ross drove slowly up the opposite bank to where the drive split to encircle a stand of tall oaks and pecans, then pulled to a stop and turned off the motor. Dead ahead, inside the circle of lush grass and stately trees, a family of dark rusty-red pigs, all made of weathered boxcar steel, grazed contentedly.

"Oh, I love them," Julia exclaimed as she threw open her door and scrambled out of the car, laughing and muttering to herself as she circled the little family, viewing them from different angles. Ross grinned as he got out and joined her, enjoying her almost childlike glee.

The house—all rough rock and diagonal cypress siding, weathered to a natural gray and halfway hidden by the trees—stood a little to the left and parallel to the creek-pool. Up beyond the curving drive, above the house, she could see what looked like a Japanese gazebo, and behind that a small greenhouse. She hung back, waiting for Ross to lead the way.

"Here. You can have the run of the place, Julia," he told her laughingly as he left her and walked just a few feet away to another boxed-in control panel similar to the one at the gate, and this time punched out an electronic tune. "Everything's open now—go wherever you want."

"Where should I look first?" she asked, torn between exploring outside some more, or going inside first.

"Up to you." He waited for her to decide, then followed her to the creek-pool, watching her walk along the edge to look down into the water, which she quickly discovered was stocked with fish. She grabbed his hand and swung it playfully, glancing at him from time to time with what he thought was a quizzical expression. But she didn't question him. When they reached the dam at the far end of the pool she turned at a right angle, toward the house, leading him past his deer-proofed hillside garden, across the rock terrace just outside the kitchen, and at last up the small hill to the flower-ringed gazebo. And once inside, she eased down onto the edge of a wooden bench with a sigh and pulled him with her, keeping him close.

"I can hardly believe it. It's so serene." She glanced around slowly, taking it all in. "So quiet, but alive. It feels Japanese and Texas at the same time." She couldn't begin to describe the unique duality of the place—dynamic yet serene—though her mind sought parallels in order to find some way to express what she felt. A sense of harmony and fit enveloped her, like a kind of homecoming—to a place she'd lost while still a young girl and thought never to find again. A place that nourished the spirit.

"You had it built, didn't you?" she asked hesitantly after a minute. "It feels like you."

He nodded and smiled, then pulled her close and began nuzzling the curve of her neck, trailing quick kisses along the edge of her jaw as he began working his way toward her lips.

"How much land do you have?"

"Sixteen acres," he mumbled into the corner of her mouth. "The taxes shot up just about the time I arrived in town, and the former owner said he couldn't afford to keep all this 'useless' land."

Julia laughed, then remembered something. "Where's this swimming pool you've been trying to entice me with? I didn't see a sign of it."

He pulled her up. "Come on."

She stopped just inside the door to look around, trying to take it all in at one glance. The entire space was white and natural wood, from the polished floor to the high mansard-shaped ceiling. A long hallway stretching straight ahead of her appeared to cut through the center of the house, like a catwalk where it was two or three steps above the room opening off to the left. Track lights illuminated two big paintings on the only solid spaces in the far wall of the big living room, and she was drawn to one of them instantly—a big square of pale billowing clouds, or mist, all smoky yet emanating an eerie sort of light, as if the sun were trying to break through.

She stood staring at it for a few minutes, then slowly walked closer, watching the subtly changing colors as she moved. Unconscious of anything else for a few minutes, she hardly noticed when Ross put a glass of white wine and Perrier in her hand.

"It's wonderful," she concluded finally. "Sort of Turner-esque. Who did it?"

The thing she'd noticed first was exactly what Ross had mentally predicted she would. "John Guerin," he answered. "From UT. I asked him to do a New Mexico landscape for me, and this is what he came up with."

"Nothing about it says landscape, except the sense of the horizontal—and even that's suppressed by the square shape," Julia commented, then began to look around her again, through one of the wood-framed glass doors opening out onto a shaded terrace, this one looking off to the creek-pond down a gentle grass-covered slope. It was so quiet she could hear frogs croaking softly. Then she turned away and spied a larger-than-life fountain pen, one of the old refillable kind, carved out of richly grained walnut—about six feet tall and mounted on the wall with the exposed tip pointing up. She laughed delightedly, then explored the rest of the room, with Ross following quietly behind, watching her. There were only open archways from one space to another, not doorways. She turned to him in silent question, unsure where to go next.

"I've imagined you here so many times, Julia, I'm afraid you might turn out to be more of my wishful thinking."

She came to him then, slipping her arms around his waist. "Would it help to touch?" she asked invitingly.

He accepted her invitation gladly, wrapping her in a fierce hug. But it wasn't enough. His lips sought hers and she felt his hands exploring her back, beginning to massage the muscles in the same rhythm his tongue used to smooth the edges of her slightly parted lips, starting a wave of heat rushing through her limbs. She leaned into him, urging him closer with hands pressed flat against his back, and the kiss deepened, quickly becoming an expression of urgent mutual need as his tongue turned firm and seeking, and she opened to receive him.

Ross moved his hands in circles over the slippery fabric of her blouse, slowly descending to her hips to press her tightly against him, then bringing one hand around to work its way between their bodies, making space to cup first one breast and then the other, finally coming to rest around her throat as he slowed their kiss and gradually pulled away from her lips. Julia opened her eyes to look directly into his, so icy blue yet so warm and deep.

"Just don't go away from me like that again, Julie," he pleaded, his voice barely audible. "Tell me I'm behaving like an ass, yell at me, or anything else you want to. But don't shut the door on me. Don't close me out, so we can't talk, can't try to—"

"I won't," she promised, brushing her lips against his as she shook her head slowly from side to side, whispering between short soft caresses, "never—ever." Her hands shaped his face and stroked through his hair. "Next time I'll scream at you like a fishwife"—one hand cupped the back of his head, relearning the shape of it before sliding down to his nape—"and stamp my foot and throw crockery." She had an urge to feel the shape and texture of him everywhere, over the curve between his neck and shoulder, down across his chest, around his rib cage to the small of his back—

Julia's eyes flew open with the shock of being pushed away, at the same time hearing a near-moan of indrawn breath.

"Julie—stop that, we don't have time!"

"Why not?" She looked at him with a puzzled expression.

"Your flight leaves in an hour! And you came to see how the program works, remember?" He had to force his breathing to slow, to try to ignore the pounding in his chest that was shaking his whole body—and then to try to smile, instead of shouting in protest.

"I'm not going anywhere, Ross." Julia smiled lazily. "Not today. And the computer can wait—I can't!"

Chapter 14

LATER SHE COULDN'T even recall where his bedroom was, or how they got there. Time stretched out endlessly as Ross caressed the heartbeat in her throat with his lips and tongue, quickening its pace before moving down to her breast. Once again, he gentled his lips to trace the smooth white line of scar tissue, moving slowly, inexorably, as her body strained to meet him. He suckled strongly yet tenderly, even as his tongue continued to fan the glowing coals of her pleasure. By the time his mouth began blazing a path down across the concave slope under her ribs, Julia was hardly capable of any conscious thought at all. And when at last, the exquisite softness of his lips found her, and his tongue slid home, a long sigh of satisfaction escaped her very soul, even as an icy-hot flame flared up to engulf her in long waves of wanting.

Ross gave her time then, to learn to breathe again, for her heart to slow as she came back down. "And that, Julie honey," he whispered against her lips, "has been one of *my* fantasies since I first began to love you, in the garden at Giverny."

Then he was filling her, slowly, persuading her to want

more, and more, and then still more. He stilled to let her feel the throbbing beat of his heart deep within her, then withdrew just as slowly, only to inch still higher before sliding down the valley to fill her again. She rose to meet him, and a cloudburst of sensation exploded in one blinding flash, before mushrooming into a great, warm, overwhelming sensation of loving, and of being loved.

At last they lay quietly, in a cocoon of contentment, Julia on her side with her body sort of halfway over his, one breast pressing against his chest and her head nestled in the curve between his shoulder and neck. Ross's left arm circled at an angle across her back to slide slowly down into the valley of her waist, up the slope of her hip, then back down again. Neither of them spoke, but they didn't sleep, either.

"Have you ever thought about starting your own business, Julie?" Ross asked after a few minutes, straight out of the blue. "Put *your* name on your designs instead of Ben's, and give the marketing ideas you've been talking about a try at the same time? Why do you keep using your talent and energies to fight guys like Tony? You could work here, in Texas, have more time with Beth. Keep your New York apartment, be there whenever you needed to. How about it? I could be your first investor!"

Julia laughed, surprised to hear so neatly put the very idea, and all the reasons for it, that had been hovering in the back of her mind for almost two years.She raised up on her elbow to look down at him. "You're serious?"

He raised his head just enough to brush a quick kiss across her lips, before letting it fall back on the pillow again. "You bet your socks I am! I'd like to see you doing what you really want to, giving your ideas a try—and I don't see that happening at Taggart any time in the near future. But I also want you with me, Julie! All the time, or anyway most of the time. Not a weekend every couple of months. Come back to Texas. Marry me."

She watched his eyes as he spoke, and had to fight back the tears that rose without warning, unable to speak herself for a minute after he finished. "Something started for me, too, Ross, back on that bench in Giverny," she agreed finally. "At first I thought it was just a physical thing." One eyebrow lifted slightly and her lips hinted at a smile. "Because I love the way you look, Ross, did you know that? The blue of your eyes, your white hair and the wonderful warm browns of your skin. Here"—she touched a finger to the crinkles at the edge of one eye—"and here"—caressing fingers smoothed the hair back from his temple. "And the way you feel." Her hand dropped to stroke his, back against back. "I love the way you walk. Your sudden smile when you're talking, the unconscious touch on my arm, my shoulder, my hand. The way your hand fits itself around the back of my neck. And I can't seem to separate any of that anymore, from—from so much more that I haven't even begun to put into words inside my head. And I need to be able to do that."

She rolled away to lie on her back, staring up at the ceiling. "I'm not an inexperienced teenager, Ross, and neither are you. Both of us are carrying around a lot of emotional baggage. Just look at what you ran into today—a child you didn't even know existed! We're like minefields, with all the hurts and hang-ups we've accumulated over the years lying just under the surface somewhere, waiting to blow up in our faces when we're least expecting it. We need a little more time, to learn to know and understand each other better."

"Maybe," he murmured, knowing exactly what she meant. But he didn't plan to admit it. "If that's what you want. I guess I just don't see that happening very fast, with you in New York and me here. And I hate seeing you going up against a stacked deck."

"But that's another reason why I can't just cut out right now, though you probably wouldn't even believe how many times I've thought about it. I have this awful feeling that time is running out. Beth is changing so fast. More and more she seems to have a life of her own now, and in another year she'll be going off to college. I try to spend as much time with her as I can, either here or in New York, but—well, starting a new business would take a lot of time, too." She paused, reflecting.

"I've invested a lot more than money in Taggart, Ross. I can't just walk away and leave Ben now, not yet, because Tony would eat him alive, squeeze whatever he could out of the company and then sell out, leaving Ben with nothing but a gutted shell."

"You really believe Ben is that vulnerable?" Ross asked, astounded, "a man who built a three-million-dollar business, with hardly any capital outlay, in just three years?"

Julia let a long sigh of resignation escape from between her teeth, trying to resist the urge to run from it, to seek safer ground by changing the subject. But it was time to stop hiding what she really thought and felt, if they were ever going to have any chance at all. She sat up suddenly, reaching for her clothes, which she was somewhat surprised to find neatly draped across a nearby chair.

Ross never took his eyes off her, sensing her sudden withdrawal. "What's the matter, Julie?" he asked, finally, rising to sit on the edge of the bed and began pulling on his pants as he became painfully aware that something was.

"What's the matter!" She spun around, spitting out the words in angry disbelief, stepped into her panties and then fastened her bra. But she was too consumed by frustration and a building anger, and instead left off dressing to pace back and forth at the foot of the bed.

"You can ask that after you've just gone macho on me again, patronizing, or whatever the hell you want to call it? Dammit, Ross! Why is it that every man in the world has to jump to the conclusion that only a male could build a business like Taggart?"

He wanted to smile at the picture she presented, her hair curling wildly about her face and neck, her wonderful long-legged body covered by nothing but two brief strips of lace. But he didn't. Instead, he waited and listened.

"I built that company as much as Ben! No—more! He's an intuitive designer, and a sweet man, but he's tentative about almost everything else. And often not very well informed. The truth is that our success has been mostly the result of *my* assessment of what's been happening with women. Of who and where our customers were going to be. What they needed and wanted, and why! *My* market analysis, and *my* sense of timing!" Her eyes were flashing and her face was flushed. "And it was my idea to stay away from big equipment outlays, to contract out almost everything. That's one of the reasons we were able to show the big profit gains we did in such a short time—and that was part of *my* long-range strategy, because I knew we'd have to go public if we wanted to attract enough capital to make it big. Me—a mere woman!"

She stopped pacing finally and stared at him, daring him to dispute her claim. "What's so damned irritating—and unfair—is that if I act ladylike and keep my mouth shut, everyone assumes I'm unimaginative, a follower who needs a leader. A man, of course. But if I take the lead—come out with good ideas and the data to back them up—I'm a bitch! And if I even try to take credit for what I do, I'm acting the prima donna!"

"Come here!" Ross commanded, startling her, and, without thinking, she went to him, letting him circle her waist with one arm to pull her down onto his thighs. "And I suppose when you went public, it was your idea not to hoard a majority of the stock, like most young owners do because they're afraid of losing control. You planned to use it as a tool for growth, right?"

His lips began butterflying across her face as he spoke. "I don't have a bit of trouble believing you, you spitting hellcat! But did you ever stop to think that I might occasionally jump to the wrong conclusion because you're so goddamned close-mouthed? You put me in the position of having to pry everything out of you, and then act like I'm invading your privacy if I ask questions. You're wily as hell when it comes to holding out, I'll give you that—and don't try to deny it. Not after yesterday, dammit!"

"I'm not," she answered, suddenly meek, which took all the wind out of his sails. "That's why I just told you all that.

My skeletons are out of the closet, Ross. But what about you—you're as bad, or worse—I know almost nothing about you! And no matter how much I might want to, I'm afraid of walking across that minefield."

"Shoot—I'll tell you anything you want to know," he urged, anxious to resolve all their problems right here and now.

"Oh, so now you want to put *me* in the position of having to pry information out of you? You want to play games—twenty questions, you've got a secret—and I'm the one who has to guess what it is? No thanks, Ross," she chided. "The ball's in your court. How you decide to hit it back is up to you."

He frowned for a second, then nodded. "Okay," he agreed, beginning to smile. "I'll work on it. So what now? Computer, food—?"

"Nope. I'm calling your bluff, McCutcheon. First we swim—if you even have a pool, which I doubt at this point!"

They circled down a stairway and into a semidark cavern lined with native rock and rough-sawn cedar surrounding a long rectangle of glassy water. Illuminated by a single light recessed into the ceiling at the far end of the pool, a smaller round pool cut across the corner of the larger one, its surface all bubbly and steaming.

"It's a little cool today, but just to show you—" As he spoke, he reached over to a small control panel, and almost instantly she heard a low rumbling sound as the ceiling at the far end of the cavern began to move, smoothly rolling back on itself to expose the open sky, letting the late afternoon sun flood the grotto and transform it from a place of mystery to one that felt open and light. He punched at the control box again, and then the floor-to-ceiling glass panels forming the outside wall also slid back, like the curtain of a stage, exposing the flower-edged patio beyond. And then the almost whispery words and melody of "Yesterday" flooded the cavern.

Julia seemed to hesitate for only a second, then before he realized what she intended, her body curved into a graceful arc that broke the smooth surface of the water with hardly a splash. He watched, waiting for her to surface, but she was almost at the other end of the pool when she came up for a breath. She continued to the far edge of the pool, made a turn and started back toward him.

"Could you please turn that off?" The words burst from the water as soon as her head appeared, taking him by surprise.

"Sure," he agreed, stepping back to the control panel on the wall. "Don't care for that one, huh," he asked, puzzled by her response, "or was that one of those mines you mentioned?"

Julia crossed her arms on the edge of the pool and rested her chin on them. "I guess so," she admitted. "Sorry."

"Maybe you better tell me right now if there are others—music, I mean. So I can stay away from them."

She thought a minute. "Only John Lennon's 'Imagine.' It's a wonderful song—I just can't bear to listen to it." With that she turned and swam away from him again, putting an end to any more questions.

"Looks more like a computer shop, not that I've been in many of them," Julia commented, glancing around the big square room Ross referred to as his lab. Shelves lined the walls and, along with counter- and tabletops, were loaded with all manner of electronic equipment—computers, monitors, keyboards and printers, amplifiers, an elaborate tape deck and record player, speakers and some she couldn't even put a name to.

"I work here most of the time, actually," he explained as he walked around, flipping a switch here and there on one piece of equipment after another. "The company offices are out on Loop 360—that's where most of the others work." He glanced back at her and grinned. "But since I'm the boss, I get to choose where and when I work."

"How many 'others' are there?" Julia asked, walking around the square island in the middle of the room, noting labels—IBM, Tektronix, Compaq, Amiga, Sony, Hewlett-

Packard, Mitsubishi, AED, Summagraphics. A few pieces of equipment had no labels to identify them, but she recognized the multicolored Apple logo, from watching Dick Cavett ads on television. Obviously, this was the "brains" and heart of the house, the master control center for everything from the entrance gate to the retractable roof over the pool. Two chrome chairs with padded seats, backs and arms were the only furniture in the room.

"Roll a chair over here," Ross instructed as he pulled the other one toward one of the computer terminals lined up along one edge of the island of tables, where monitor screens now glowed luminescent green, amber and even a light gray. "All I want you to do for a couple of minutes is listen and watch, okay?" he asked, one hand reaching out to touch her arm, then, as if he couldn't resist, he suddenly pulled her closer for a swift kiss. "I can see you're going to be quite a distraction," he mumbled, before turning back to the computer.

"I'm going to start you out on the most user-friendly machine there is—you know what that means?" he asked.

"Who doesn't?" was all she said, but he could read her dislike of the jargon in the shrug of one shoulder and lifted brow.

"The idea is to show you what kinds of things the machine can do, and as painlessly as possible, Julie. So just listen and watch for a few minutes, okay? But as we go along, I want you to be thinking about what you know has to be done in order to produce a garment, from the moment you first get an idea through the whole process, to production. About what your sketcher, or assistant, or whatever you call her, does, how the patternmaker goes about getting out that first pattern, what the sample hands do to it, and when they do it. I can manipulate the machines, Julie, but you know more about all this than I do, and I need your help. Got it?"

She nodded and rolled her chair forward to watch, determined to concentrate—and to learn.

"You're going to have two ways to input," he explained, "besides the keyboard, I mean. The mouse and this—it's called a graphics or digitizing pad—with a light pen." He indicated a flat box about twelve inches long sitting on the desk off to the left of the gray screen in front of him. "I'll show you that later. This is the cursor—think of it as a pointer—and the mouse moves the cursor on the screen, see." He hit the return key on the keyboard and the short flashing vertical line moved down the screen. "Look." He turned over the small plastic box he held in his right hand, to show her the rubber ball protruding through a hole in the bottom, then put it back down on the desk and began rolling it around.

"Let's just type in a few words." His fingers moved swiftly over the keyboard. "Now we'll use the mouse to point to some instruction you want the machine to carry out. Suppose I don't like what I just wrote." He rolled the mouse again, holding down the button on the back of it, and the cursor moved down the screen again, blackening what he'd just written there. Then he rolled the mouse again and an arrow suddenly appeared, pointing at the word "Edit," one of several lined up across the top of the screen—File, Search, Format, Font and Style.

"Now I'm going to hold the mouse button down while I drag the pointer down this menu of instructions, to the one I want it to do." When the arrow reached "Cut," he released the mouse button and the words on the screen simply disappeared. "But, wait. Suppose I change my mind. That's not what I want after all, or maybe I think it should be in a different place—I just paste it all back, wherever I want it. Move the cursor to where you want it, press the button, roll it up to 'Edit' again, hold the mouse button down while dragging the cursor down to 'Paste' and then release it." The words he'd written earlier jumped back up on the screen.

"Got the idea?" he asked, glancing at her briefly. "There's a menu under every one of these words, see?" He proceeded to show her, first changing the words on the screen from plain text to italics, then to bold type, and finally changing each line of type to a different size. "You want twelve-point type, you point to '12 point' and release the mouse button." He rolled his chair away, pulling on the arm of hers at the same time to position it in front of the computer. "It's your turn—get the feel of it."

The mouse seemed to have a mind of its own the first few times Julia tried to move the cursor where she wanted it, to say nothing of having to chase it all over the table. Her efforts seemed clumsy and inept at best, a feeling that was foreign indeed to her when it came to using her hands.

"Wait a minute," he ordered, reaching across the table for a rectangle of clear plastic about the size of a standard pad of paper, lifted the mouse and placed it on the plastic. "Keep the mouse on this, don't let it go off. You'll feel the edge with your hand as you move the mouse around, and pretty soon it'll be automatic to just lift it a little and then roll the ball across the same short space on the desk when you want to cover a lot of territory on the screen."

She practiced for a few more minutes, until he announced, "Okay, let's try drawing now." He reached across in front of her and pressed two keys. The text disappeared almost immediately, to be replaced by a white rectangle in the upper left corner of the gray screen. "This is like the table of contents in a book, tells you what's on this disk, including whatever the program is you're using plus anything you add to it." He pointed the arrow at "File," dragged the mouse down the menu to "Eject," and the machine made a soft purring sound as it pushed a small flat square of plastic out of a slot just below the screen. "And this is the disk we store all that information on."

He continued instructing her, explaining everything as he went along in the same straightforward way, until Julia couldn't help wondering why everything to do with computers had always seemed so damned complicated and foggy before. All she had to do was choose whatever she wanted to do from one of the "menus" listed across the top of the screen. And she understood now that her choices changed with each "program." With the one she was using, for instance, the "Edit" menu included not only cut and paste, but invert, fill, trace edges, flip horizontal, flip vertical and rotate. There were little cartoons along the edges of the screen, too—a lasso, a hand, a paintbrush, a pencil and an eraser—which indicated still more things she could choose to do to the images on the screen. She could vary the width of the line in an instant, to say nothing of filling in spaces with a whole array of shadings and patterns, and stretch out any image—a circle into an oval, for instance—simply by moving the mouse around on the plastic tablet.

And all kinds of ideas and possibilities were starting to jump into her head while she worked, as the reality of what Ross had been telling her began to hit home. But there was still so much more to learn! And now, with Ross to teach her, she not only could but very much wanted to. He was constantly encouraging, always ready to explain, no matter how silly or stupid her questions must sound to him.

"You're a wonderful teacher, Ross," she said, without taking her eyes from the screen. "It seems a shame you gave it up."

He grinned, watching her manipulate the image on the screen. "Yeah, well, maybe having you for a pupil inspires me."

Julia shook her head to disagree, glanced at him briefly and was distracted enough to lean over and plant a quick kiss on his surprised lips. "Thank you for that, but I suspect your 'technique' comes naturally—I've never heard you talk down to anyone, even Beth or Elaine's girls. Why did you dislike it so much? Teaching, I mean."

"Most of the students I ran into didn't want to work seriously. Everything had to be fun. The kids coming out of public school today can't cut the mustard when it comes to college-level work, but if we flunk them out, a lot of universities would go out of business. One of the best guys in my department at UT didn't get tenure, mostly because he refused to compromise when it came to grading. Failed too many students. They're in the catbird seat and they know it, so why hesitate to spout off about what you're doing wrong—even if it's just the way you hold your mouth. At the same time, they feel threatened by a system that says you have to have a college degree or you're nobody—so the faculty is the primary enemy! Who the hell needs that kind of shit? Maybe if I'd run into some kids from St. Michael's I'd feel different about it, I don't know."

"Maybe," she agreed, too involved in manipulating the image she'd drawn with the mouse to say more at the moment.

"Beth is—" He stopped, as if losing track of what he'd started to say, then simply watched her, showing her what to do when she got into trouble.

"What about Beth?" Julia asked finally, still distracted.

"I like her. A lot. She reminds me of—she's—" He stopped again and ran his hand through his hair in the classic gesture of frustration, somehow unable to find the right words.

Julia sensed more than heard the effort he was making, and glanced quickly at his face, realizing instantly that he was trying to tell her something special. She took her hands off the mouse and keyboard, laid them in her lap and waited, watching his face.

"She reminds me of my own daughter. I don't mean in looks, but what I always think she might have been like. Bright, feisty, right up front about everything, curious, and absolutely fearless. Maria, her name was." He pronounced it with a long "i," like in the song "They Call the Wind Maria." "She was always investigating, exploring—it gets you sort of excited, doesn't it, watching one like that?"

Julia nodded mutely, dreading what she sensed was coming.

Ross read the silent question in her eyes. "She drowned in our swimming pool. When she was three."

"Oh, my poor Ross," Julia cried, her heart breaking for him. Without thinking, she turned to enclose him in her arms, overwhelmed with the need to comfort and share his pain. His arms came around her, too, and they simply held each other. Tears flooded Julia's eyes and rolled silently down her cheeks, until finally Ross felt them on his neck.

"Hey," he reprimanded gently, reaching into his hip pocket

for a handkerchief. "Here." He dabbed at her eyes, then down her cheeks to the corners of her mouth.

"How did it happen?" she asked, sniffling, then looked up quickly, almost apologetically. "I'm sorry, I shouldn't have asked. I know how painful it must be."

"Yeah, well, it used to be, but after eight years I guess—" He met her eyes at last. "I could have prevented—I didn't—" He paused, then began again, his face expressionless now. "I hired a full-time housekeeper, thought that would be enough, gave her instructions never to leave Maria alone with Marilyn—my wife. But Marilyn went through dry spells, and hadn't had a drink in over two weeks. The housekeeper got a call. Her daughter had gone into labor and couldn't reach her husband, needed to get to the hospital. So she went. Marilyn must have started hitting the stuff about noon, and just kept on until she passed out. Maybe Maria got on her nerves, I don't know. Guess I'll never know."

Julia put her fingers across his lips to stop him. "But you couldn't have foreseen that, Ross, so it wasn't your—"

"Maybe not. And maybe Marilyn would never have started in the first place if I hadn't left her alone so much. I didn't even think about it until it was too late—got caught up in the anything-can-happen excitement, sort of a compulsion, too, I suppose. It didn't leave you with time or energy for anything else. I bought her a big house in Los Altos, cars, clothes, whatever it took to keep the guilt at bay, telling myself that was all she really wanted anyway. After Maria came, I tried to spend more time at home." He smiled wryly for the first time. "Couldn't help myself, I guess. That kid knew how to get what she wanted right from the start. So I have lots of good memories, too, Julie." His mouth broke in a full smile, and he stroked her cheek lightly with one hand. "Just wanted to get one of those mines out of the way."

"Why didn't you tell me before, Ross?"

Ross thought a moment. "I know the past can influence what we are, Julie. But with you and me—well, I don't know about you, but I care more about what's going on with us now. I've had my hands full, just figuring out what you think about Monet or Manet, and the poems of Anne-Marie Lacombe—and don't think we've settled the score on that one yet, my love—and figuring out that you're after a lot more than just designing and selling clothes to women, aren't you? You're plotting revolution, too, just like Beth!"

He'd taken her by surprise again, and it showed on her face. He was moving too fast for her, but before she could ask exactly what he meant, he was rolling his chair away from her, over to another computer, to flip another switch and then enter a command and wait until the screen lit in a beautiful shade of violet. "Now come on over here with me—the pièce de résistance is yet to come!"

Obviously, he didn't want to talk about it anymore, or perhaps just not right now, but at least he'd finally volunteered one piece of personal history, and she'd just have to be content with that for now.

"What do you think, Julie? See anything interesting so far?" he asked, reaching out one hand to massage the back of her neck as she moved her chair next to his and sat down again.

Julia turned away from the screen with a quizzical expression already in place. "Interesting? Oh! Yes, of course, but down the line from—from the way I think, or do my first rough sketches. It's so—too rigid, maybe. How can I explain?" She stopped to think, unconsciously nibbling on her lip. "Maybe I could show you better—if you have a piece of paper! Or does everything have to go through a machine around here?"

She felt his hand tighten around her neck. "You're damned cool about inflicting a fatal wound to the ego, Julie love. If you didn't get any messages this afternoon, maybe we'd better give it another try." He started to rise, reaching over to pull her up with him.

"Not now, Ross," she protested playfully, waving a hand at the monitor. "I need to find out more about this."

"You're changing into a computer nerd before my very eyes," he joked, shrugging his shoulders helplessly.

Julia laughed and really relaxed, recognizing that she'd held on to some apprehension right up to this very moment—fearing he might still somehow turn into a Mr. Hacker-Hyde the minute he got in the same room with a computer. "Paper," she repeated insistently, "and a pencil, if that's not asking for too much high-tech."

He shook his head, but got up and went into his study, then came back with a pad and pencil. Now it was his turn to watch in awe, as she freely sketched first one figure and then another, the lines all loose and flowing, only detailed enough to suggest what she was thinking about, drawings that carried that special flair that was her personal signature.

"I'm not sure I can get the same feel for what I'm doing any other way, Ross. Feel—I don't know how else to explain. But that's important, I think. Maybe I'm just not familiar enough with the computer yet, though I'm impressed with what I've seen it do so far—"

"But I never meant you couldn't use that, too!" Ross interrupted. "We can put these, or anything else you do on paper, into the computer and then continue with all this other stuff—stretch it or rotate it, shade one area. That's exactly how I've been constructing the image data base I mentioned to you. The body types and various kinds of garment shapes—remember?" He jumped up again and went back to his study, this time returning with a couple of fiber-tipped pens. "Here, do one in color, and I'll show you."

She drew quickly, caught up in his enthusiasm, tore the sheet from the pad and handed it to him, then followed him around to another side of the island table.

"We can put this image into the computer—kind of like Xeroxing onto a screen, with either a video camera or this flatbed scanner." He raised the cover of a rectangular flat box, laid her sketch face down on the glass plate underneath it, and then adjusted the controls. "There's one other way, but it's too slow. Go back and watch the monitor—it only takes a few seconds."

Amazed, Julie saw her sketch appear on the screen almost

immediately, exactly as she'd drawn it, even to the color tone of the felt pen. Then Ross began showing her what this machine could do, changing the colors at will, or filling in shapes with both patterns and colors. Now the curving lines on the screen were perfectly smooth, instead of slightly jagged, and when she commented about that, Ross told her it was because the program contained an anti-aliasing feature. "And don't get your hackles up about computer jargon, Julia. You need to learn what to call some of these features so you'll be able to tell me, or anyone else, exactly what you need and don't need to do the job, okay?"

Julia nodded eagerly, and without the least hesitation. "Tell me about the other features."

That was all the encouragement he needed, and he talked quickly, demonstrating what the program he'd been working on almost constantly for the past month could do. First, he showed her how to enter her drawing into the computer's memory, then began calling up the line drawings of different body types that were part of what he called the image data base he was building into the program for her.

"You can create transparent effects, so you can see the body shape through the clothes you draw, or you can simply cover up the body underneath," he explained. "You can go 3-D, too, or leave it as is. To do shading or patterns, you simply impose a 2-D image on a 3-D object, see?" It wasn't long until he had her in front of the monitor, showing her how to call up a figure, then overlay it with whatever style feature she selected from a "dictionary" of styles.

"Wait, Ross," she protested when he started to go on to something else. "I need to practice this a little first, so I don't forget how."

"Okay, I'll go put on some music. Any special requests?" He waited, then realized she was too engrossed to even hear him.

Julia only remotely heard the music when it started, already lost in what she was doing. Ross retreated to his study, leaving her free to concentrate, though he came back whenever she called for help. Once, she completely lost the image on the screen, and almost broke down in tears of frustration, only to have Ross come to her rescue. She lost track of time completely, until he appeared in the doorway and asked if she wanted something to eat, or drink. The interruption annoyed her, and she brushed it away with one hand. At one point, she looked down and noticed a glass of wine next to her keyboard, and sort of wondered how long it had been there.

She had no idea what time it was when he came back again, and this time placed his hands on her shoulders to get her attention. "Come to bed, Julie. It's late. The computer will still be here in the morning. You can save everything, start where you left off."

"Not yet, Ross—please?" She twisted around in her chair just enough to glance up at him. "A few more minutes?"

Ross nodded indulgently, then gave in and turned to leave. "My God, I've created a monster!" he muttered, almost under his breath. But Julia heard him and let out a whoop of laughter, then jumped up and ran to catch up with him.

Chapter 15

THEY TALKED ABOUT Ross's computer program for hours the next day, even while they were soaking in the steamy hot tub. Most of the time, however, they talked while Julia was "practicing" on one computer or another, discovering what it and she could do together. About the only time they stopped talking, in fact, was when they were in the cool, refreshing water of the big pool, stretching out their bodies to get rid of the physical malaise that came with hours of sitting in front of a screen and keyboard. And when they were making love.

The more Julia learned, the more questions she asked—and the more questions Ross asked her. She was at last beginning to understand just what he envisioned for this "software," and the more she understood, the more excited she got. He was after a lot more than simply automating specific tasks, such as grading patterns or creating the markers, which some of the big manufacturers were already doing. What he wanted to do ultimately was integrate every operation along the way, from initial design through production. And to do that would take not only the graphic design program she was learning to use, but also an "engineering package" and a way to "interface" between the two.

On the flight back to New York Tuesday morning Julia tried to concentrate on the paperback Ross had given her just as they were leaving his house—to pass the time on the plane, he said—but fascinating as she found it, *The Soul of a New Machine* was no competition for the ideas churning inside her head. And by the time she arrived at Ben Taggart a little after one that afternoon, she had a plan worked out. As luck would have it, Tony was the first person she ran into, guiding Claire Kennamer toward the elevator with a proprietary arm slung over her shoulder.

"I can't talk right now, Julia," he greeted her, "and I've got appointments all afternoon. But be in my office first thing in the morning, nine sharp, with all the figures from Dallas." He started into the elevator, then threw back at her, "Nice of you to decide to show up at last."

"Yes. Well, I'll tell you about that in the morning then, too," she responded breezily, then continued on to her office without giving him the opportunity to add anything more.

"Ah, there you are!" Connie jumped up from behind her desk to take Julia's bag, then followed her into the office. "I wondered if you were going home first or coming here direct. When those arrived about an hour ago, I knew you'd be along soon," she explained, without waiting for Julia to notice the flowers. A salt-glazed stoneware "basket" stuffed with lilacs sat on her desk, their delicate, subtle aroma already pervading the big room.

Julia dropped her shoulder bag and picked up the small white envelope from her desk, curious as to what he could possibly have to say—she glanced quickly at her watch—only four hours after she'd left him standing at the boarding gate in Austin! "Sure seems quiet around here. I miss you." The "miss" had been crossed through, and above it was written "need."

Julia spent the next couple of hours reading her mail and making phone calls, then talked in turn with Elaine, Max and Alex, getting her plan in place for the next morning. And finally she went to Ben's studio to talk with him, too.

Her head was still racing in high gear when she went to bed that night, so she grabbed up Ross's paperback to try to slow down. Instead, she was even more revved up and wide awake by the time she'd finished it. Had it really been like that, for Ross and all the others? Trying to create a machine that was in fact an extension of themselves, with a special kind of intelligence, something no one had ever done before, and under the pressure of a race against time? Suddenly she reached over to her bedside table and picked up the phone. He answered on the first ring.

"McCutcheon."

"Was that the way you worked, too? Was it really like that?" she asked him right off, without any preliminaries.

"Julie! Whoa, back up and tell me what's going on. Where the hell are you?"

"At home, in bed. I just finished Tracy Kidder's book. Oh," she stopped, realizing what time it was. But it would be an hour earlier there, and judging by how quickly he'd answered the phone, he must be at his desk. "I didn't wake you, did I? Are you still working—or partying?"

"No, yes, and no," he laughed. "And yeah, I suppose it was like that sometimes. You mean it didn't put you to sleep?"

"No. Are there others? Books I could read, I mean, about computer stuff."

"Sure. Take your pick next time you're here. The history, and the people associated with it, are pretty interesting. Better than fiction—I guess nobody's imagination is wild enough to invent some of those characters!"

"You're spoiling me, you know."

"How's that?" he asked, amused, but having a hard time keeping up with her.

"The flowers. I love them, but—"

"Oh." He sounded relieved. "Guess you're just going to have to get used to it then, right?"

"I already am—that's what I'm worried about."

"You worry too much, Julie love—anybody ever tell you that? You don't want any more flowers?" he teased, already knowing her answer.

"Well, no—that's not what I meant, either, damn you!" He was still chuckling when she hung up.

"One buyer told me she made only five appointments this time. She prefers to walk the aisles, look for something that 'really bowls me over,' was the way she put it," Julia was telling Tony when Elaine and Max arrived. She quickly explained to him that she'd asked them to come, and also Ben and Alex, because she wanted to discuss something that would interest everyone, after she reported on the Dallas market.

"That's the kind of buyer we do well with. It's the department stores where we're down," she continued as they sat down.

"Yeah—our biggest accounts," Tony pointed out, his voice heavy with sarcasm.

"We could expand the number of smaller accounts we handle to make up for that, though I suppose higher bookkeeping costs might offset some of that gain." She glanced briefly at Max, only to see him shake his head.

"Not really, at least not when we get the system fully integrated, so our production orders are tied in with our new inventory and shipping system," Max injected.

"We could also go after the specialty store chains a lot more aggressively than we have been," Elaine added. "Julia and Claire and I have been talking on and off for the past month about how to target our promotions more—fine-tune our pitch for different markets."

Julia nodded. "It's the department stores who get burned the worst when 'unseasonable' weather hits, since they've got the big inventories. That's just one more reason for the increasingly conservative response we're seeing from them. They buy based on what sold best last season, and also select only the most conservative numbers when we do come out with a really new line. The result is that they're constantly losing customers to the more innovative smaller shops, which don't risk as much because they buy so much less of any one style or fabric. The big stores resist change, rather than embrace it and promote it, which I think says something about both their management style and their customers."

"You mean the housewives in the boonies, I presume, the last ones to adopt a new style," Tony commented.

"What I'm trying to say is that we're seeing too much homogeneity, Tony, in style and seasonal variation. Women are more and more eclectic, not less. Playing more roles, not fewer. And we can't afford to see them as 'housewives' *or* 'careerwomen,' as I've pointed out before. Most of them are both, and we've got to stop thinking in stereotypes."

"Don't try to tell me the customers with the really big bucks to spend on fashion are 'careerwomen,' Julia. Look who's buying couture, for God's sake—the women with sugar daddies!"

Ben and Alex had come in while she was talking, and Tony waved them forward. "Join us, Ben," he invited magnanimously, "if you can stand to listen to Julia's favorite diatribe still one more time."

Julia refused to be put off by his sarcasm. "And I intend to keep saying it, Tony. We should diversify our collection more, not for different customers, but to satisfy the same woman. We've got to give more attention in our designs to all the different ways women want to *feel!*"

"Ah boy, now we're in the never-never land of your female psychographics again, right?" Tony laughed disparagingly, jumping up to begin pacing behind his desk. He seemed so hyper this morning he couldn't sit still for very long. "I thought you wanted less seasonal variation, Julia, not more! Can't make up your mind which way to jump?"

"There's a lot of interest in the spring-summer collections in Dallas because buyers consider it a preview of what's coming for fall. But most of the buyers I talked to don't want delivery of fall styles before June 30, and would prefer them even later," Julia pointed out, ignoring his dig. "They said they intend to start fall buying pretty light this year. We're promising delivery no later than April 30 for the spring-summer line, while they'd rather have it earlier—not later than the end of March. Remember, it can go to 90 in April there. Spring-summer buying is big in the Southwest because summer is so long and strong. Spring arrives early, but it's so short it's just a lead-in to summer, so orders are only fill-ins. Our summer line ought to be delivered and on the floor ready for customers when the weather begins to change—when they're eager for a wardrobe change and bored with what they've been wearing all winter. And if we don't complete deliveries until June, the fervor for hot-weather clothes has already cooled off considerably, at least in that part of the country."

"We could take a look at our shipping schedules in light of what she's saying, Tony," Max commented, "to see if we can't make some adjustments."

"Okay," Tony nodded curtly. "But most other houses seem to be moving toward more seasonless apparel, though as I've told you all before, I can't see it. I take it from what you're saying that you've finally decided to come over to my side, huh, Julia?"

"No. Perhaps it's too subtle for you, but I see a difference between seasonless and bridging the seasons, Tony—just as there's a difference between seasonless apparel and providing more options when it comes to colors and fabrics, for delivery between seasonal showings. But the point is, we've just seen a higher percentage of walk-ins than ever before, in Dallas, and in Atlanta, too, from what Elaine tells me—at the same time that we're seeing an increase in open-to-buy. Pat Pace opened a second outlet in Austin, for instance, so her open-to-buy for The Finale stores is up 20 percent. And if we had more diversity in our collections, we might get more of that increase than we're getting now."

"Well, it's going to take me a while to put all the market week data together, so I suggest we simply cool it for now, until the final count is in on the spring-summer collection." He didn't even look at her, but glanced instead at his watch as he plumped back down into his high-backed chair with a huge sigh. "Now, what's this other thing you've dragged everyone in here for, Julia? I can only give you a few more minutes."

"I got a small taste of designing with a computer this weekend, and I think it's something that might turn out to be important. It could mean streamlining every operation we do, cutting costs and time while improving quality control, maybe in the end even doing the same for production as well. A friend of mine is working on software that's probably going to revolutionize the entire fashion industry—and it's going to so dramatically change the way designing is done that what we're doing now isn't going to be commercially viable. At the very least, the process will be automated and integrated from design to patternmaking, grading and marking. Of course, the markers won't actually be paper anymore. That information will be in the computer that controls the cutting machines. It's not a question of whether—only when—it's going to be available." She had to pause just to get her breath, and she glanced over at Max. He was wearing a slight smile, which she read as either encouragement or agreement.

"There'll be direct spillover into advertising and publicity, of course, and we should be able to use the same equipment to both design and produce all our own camera-ready visuals as well as some actual printing, for advertising and other promotions, and even our own videos." She glanced at Elaine, and caught her brief nod of understanding. "And we here at Taggart have the unique opportunity to get in on the ground floor, to explore and influence what can be done, how to do it, and for how much—at no cost and with no strings attached."

Ben was already shaking his head before she finished, and the objection he raised came as no surprise. "I'm sorry, Julia, but the creative process is simply incompatible with the kind of inflexibility inherent in machines. I don't know much about computers, of course, and it may work okay for pattern grading and the markers, but it offers me nothing but constraints and rigidity. The designer must have complete freedom." He smiled, then chided her. "I have to confess I'm more than a little surprised that you'd get so carried away by this kind of thing. Must have been a pretty persuasive salesman!"

"I've never seen a sketcher with a freer line than Julia's," Alex interrupted. "And I doubt Julia has fallen for anything here, Ben. Let's see what she has to show us before we pass sentence," Alex suggested.

"You're making a good point, Ben," Julia continued enthusiastically, "and I thought the same thing at first. But it doesn't take away your freedom at all—just the opposite, in fact, once you learn how to use it. Here, let me show you what I mean." She opened the folder under the stack of papers she'd brought with her, and began handing illustrations to Ben one at a time.

"This is my first sketch, Ben, which you can see was done directly on paper with a fiber-tipped pen. The loosest kind of scrawl, the kind we do by the hundreds sometimes, before we eventually get what we're looking for. But Ross fed this one into a computer, and my sketch appeared on the screen exactly as I'd drawn it. Look, here are just some of the things I tried with it." The more she talked, the more enthusiastic she became, showing him one black and white printout after another, made at various stages as she worked on her design.

"Then I decided I needed to show how this particular style might look on different body types, because the computer program gave me that option—it already has the three basic body types built into it. It takes only seconds to call them up on the screen." She interrupted herself to select three more printouts to show him. "After that, I superimposed the sketch over the figure, and also could change the dimensions to fit this particular body type. And I could look at it as a transparency on the figure or let it go opaque." She stopped, waiting while the sketches were being passed around to the others.

"These were printed with a computer?" Ben asked, an unmistakable whisper of disbelief in his voice.

"Yes," she answered quickly, warming to her subject. "You would just love it, Ben, I guarantee you. You can feed anything you draw into the computer and then do all kinds of things to it. Or you can work directly, using the image data base built into the program." She began describing how she could pop a mannequin onto the screen and manipulate it into any position she chose. And the more she talked, the more her hands took part in the conversation. "Sitting, running, kneeling, or simply bending over. You can rotate the figure on the screen like a three-dimensional object, Ben, viewing it from any perspective, even above or below it. Stretch or compress it. Drape it with any stylistic feature you can select from a vast 'dictionary' of stylistic shapes. Overlay sections with different patterns or shading, or with colors—hundreds of colors—or draw your own fabric pattern and then apply it."

She stopped again, then handed him several color printouts. "You also can do freehand drawing, like this, with a mouse or with a light pen directly on a sort of drawing tablet called a graphics pad."

"What's your opinion about all this, Max?" Tony asked finally, sliding his wristwatch up and down impatiently.

As usual, Julia thought, he had to feel out the others before risking an opinion himself. Was Max going to go public with his support this time, she wondered, or would he stay safe in neutral territory as usual?

"Well, of course some of the big producers are using computer-aided cutting techniques already, and we contract with them whenever we can. For the workhorse styles in our collections, the ones where we know we're going to have big numbers. Some of them are doing the pattern grading that way, too. The problem is that it's too expensive for the small guys, so just having it available isn't going to help us much unless the cost comes down to where the small outfits can afford it. On the other hand, if everything could be integrated into one package, it's worth looking into. Of course I can't commit on the design process, Tony—not in my ball park."

"I think we should let someone else do the experimenting," Ben injected again. "We'll hear about it soon enough if it's any good. This isn't something we have to be first on, certainly. The company's forte is design. And of course marketing, Julia."

Ben's response didn't particularly surprise her, but Julia was more than a little disappointed in Max's half-a-dozen-of-one, six-of-another response.

"Hell, what have we got to lose, Ben?" Alex exclaimed, exasperated with their conservative, unadventurous attitude. "This is our slowest time of year. Spring market week is over, and you're taking off for the Caribbean in a few days. Max is getting spring production started, and still tidying up loose ends from fall and Julia's resort collection. Elaine's probably going to take some time off, too, but there's nothing going on right now that Claire or one of her other assistants can't handle. And Nat and I are leaving Monday for the south of France." He paused long enough to toss a quick grin at Julia. "My new sketcher, Julia. Come by later and meet him, okay?"

It was the first Julia had heard anything about a new assistant, though she had to admit she'd been more than a little preoccupied during the past few weeks.

"The point is," Alex continued, "if Julia's willing to do it, why look a gift horse in the mouth? How much time do you need, babe?"

"Two or three weeks," Julia answered quickly.

In the end, Ben deferred to Tony's "better business judgment," in spite of Alex's seemingly persuasive argument, and Max said no more. Tony kept glancing at his watch, then said he'd "take it under advisement" and let her know. As they all walked out of Tony's office, Julia was muttering to herself under her breath.

"What's that you're saying?" Elaine asked, though she knew very well that Julia was angry—and disappointed.

"I said I may have to suddenly get very sick, so I won't be able to come in for the next couple of weeks! And I resent like hell being pushed to behaving like a child! It's ludicrous—what a bunch of Neanderthals!" They continued walking down the hall together.

"Julia," Elaine began, just as they reached the door to Julia's office. "I know you think I can't tell which way is up when it comes to men, but in the last couple of weeks I've discovered that Max doesn't usually do anything, even the little things, without a reason. I've also learned, from watching him deal with Tina, that sometimes pushing straight ahead—the only way you and I seem to know to go—doesn't always get the job done. Talk to Max, Julia, before you jump to any more conclusions, okay?"

"Sure," Julia agreed. "I just wish he'd given me a little more support in there."

"I think he did, support you I mean, the way he thinks works best with Tony. He just has a different strategy in mind, for making sure you get to do what you want. I know he's gung ho on the software thing—he told me he talked with Ross about it Saturday, at the ranch."

Julia wasn't able to find the time to seek out Max until Friday afternoon, and by then she was beginning to despair that Tony would even mention it again. She was sure he was just going to let the whole thing die through indecision. But Max advised her to lay low and wait a little longer.

"Have you got a minute, Julia?" he asked quietly, indicating the chair beside his desk. "I'd like to, uh, try to explain something." He sounded uncharacteristically unsure of himself, almost as if he were trying to get up the nerve to say something personal. Then he smiled apologetically. "I don't like to indulge in amateur psychoanalysis, but when it comes to Tony, it's sort of hard to resist, isn't it?"

Julia laughed, relaxing as she sat down.

"You've watched him operate long enough to see how insecure he is, right?" In fact, Julia had never thought about it in that way at all, but now that Max put it into words, she could see he was probably right. "He's the kind of guy who needs to massage a new idea around until it comes back out sounding like his own, Julia. Either that or he has to find some self-serving reason for supporting someone else. I've talked to him a couple of times this week, and I think he's coming around. But I didn't realize until this morning—you don't want to hear why, but—"

"No, go ahead. Maybe I *should* know," she assured him.

"Yes, that's what I thought. Tony resents your influence with Ben, and I think he's come to the conclusion this would be a chance to get you out of the way for a while. I doubt he cares about the program itself, one way or the other, but if Ben doesn't like it, or sees this thing as some kind of threat to him personally, it may serve to drive a wedge between you." He waited, hoping she would understand that Tony wanted to undermine not only her relationship with Ben, but her position at Taggart.

"Aside from that, though, Ben will be back here before you are, so Tony'll have a clear field to work on him about this licensing thing without any interference from you. But I'll be here to help balance the scales." He looked down at his hands. "I also wanted you to know for sure, in case you still had any doubts, that I'm with you all the way, Julia—about the licensing, and on this fashion CAD-CAM idea of Ross's. And if I can help in any way, well—" he stopped, shrugging a shoulder as if the rest didn't need saying.

Julia shook her head, reflecting on how wrong she'd been about Max, again. Why hadn't she sought him out before now, to talk and to really listen—especially after her experience at the mill? Instead, she'd fallen back on the same old superficial impressions and assumptions, even after she knew better. She'd done to him exactly what she'd accused Ross of doing to her. And how many other erroneous assumptions, she wondered, was she still operating on, without even stopping to really think?

Saturday morning she tried to call Beth, but got no answer, then resisted the urge to call Ross, too, because she really didn't have anything to report yet. But she felt so restless that she decided to go shopping in spite of the cold blustery rain coming down outside. Her first stop was a fairly new bookstore on West Broadway she'd been meaning to try out, where she browsed the shelves and picked up a small paperback titled *Silicon Valley* that promised to be "riveting"—which was just what she needed if she was going to make it through this weekend. The back-cover blurb hyped the "cutthroat world of high-tech and high finance, and a maverick scientist whose brilliant idea skyrockets him into a multimillion-dollar corporation—putting him on a fast track of power and prestige by day, endless cocaine and lavish parties by night, until his affair with a beautiful journalist blazes too hot for his jealous wife." But she also wanted some elementary information about computers, and she was amazed to discover how many choices there were. In the end, she bought Joel Shurkin's *Engines of the Mind,* a history of the computer, "beginning with the mad genius of Charles Babbage and the remarkable Countess of Lovelace"—who, Julia learned, was the daughter of the poet Byron—and Everett Rogers and Judith Larsen's *Silicon Valley Fever.* She started to pass up John Shore's *The Sachertorte Algorithm and Other Antidotes to Computer Anxiety* because it sounded so cutesy, with the author using his Aunt Martl's pastry recipe as a metaphor to explain the nature of programming, but in the end, she said "what the heck" and included it with the others. She drew the line at artificial intelligence this early in the game, even though she was quite intrigued by one author's assertion that "human psychology is now in its flat-earth state of development. Learning, memory, perception, muscular control, thinking, reasoning, sleeping and dreaming are still more or less total enigmas."

After that, she went next door to Artwear, one of her favorite galleries, which showed the work of some of the most talented accessory designers in the country—thinking that she might get some good ideas for the designs that were still only halfway formed inside her head.

She had decided on the theme, and the color palette, and now it was a matter of working out the basic shapes, or silhouettes. What she really wanted to do, she realized with a sudden flash of insight, was to bring them to life on Ross's computer. That would be the ultimate test, at least for her, of the design aspect of the program. She looked over the display of Doug Ferguson's painted metallic scarves that could be molded onto the body, but knew without even consciously thinking about it that they weren't even remotely compatible with her theme. Her attention was really captured by Ted Muehling's oriental scarf clips, and in the end she couldn't resist purchasing one—a matte gold hummingbird, shown attached to a long sweep of iridescent silk.

She stopped next at Untitled, the little shop around the corner on Prince Street with thousands of art postcards, and then at Dean and DeLuca's. By the time she got back to her apartment, it was nearly five o'clock—and she was exhausted. She indulged in a long hot bath, put water on to make tea, and finally dialed Ross's number. The books were her crutch.

"Hello." The female voice took her by surprise. It sounded breathless and loud at the same time—and young.

"Is this 327-2121?" she asked, forcing down the panic that rose in her throat, and the sudden urge to slam down the receiver.

"Just a minute."

She was left holding what sounded like a dead line, and in the silence that followed, she could hear her water boiling on the stove.

"McCutcheon."

She could also hear the smile on his face. "I—I'm sure you must be busy, Ross. I shouldn't have—uh, perhaps we can talk Monday inst—"

"Dammit! Don't you dare hang up, Julie!" he shouted quickly, raising his voice to stop her. "We tried calling you earlier, but you were out. Hold on a minute." Then he, too, was gone.

"Mom! Is that you?"

A wave of relief engulfed Julia, and she let out a long-held breath. The muscles in her legs suddenly felt weak, and she had to sit down. "Beth?" She spoke hesitantly, not sure whether to really believe what her ears were telling her. "What are you doing there?"

"We've been out to the North Campus and MCC, on a field trip from school. Ross took us. Me and four others. It's so hot, he suggested we stop here on the way back for a swim. Hey, have you seen his pigs! Fantastic, huh? He has a collection of swimsuits like Carey's, only for girls they're all bikinis—you should see us! On second thought, maybe you shouldn't. Ross says you're going to be here again pretty soon. Can you stay for Parents' Day this year? I think it's the fourteenth."

"I'll be there, I promise. I'm taking some time off—soon, but please don't say anything to Ross yet. I'll call you. In the meantime, take it easy on him, okay? Now how about putting him back on?"

"Okay, talk to you soon. Ross, she wants you."

"Is that true?" he asked, laughing.

"Yes, it's true," she replied, not laughing. "How did you ever get roped into this? Sounds to me like she's taking advantage, Ross."

"Sure wish you were here, Julie. They're fixing to cook hamburgers next—if you hurry, you might get here before they're all gone." She could hear his smile again. "We're all missing you."

Afterward, she felt even more lonely and left out than she had earlier, but at least she recognized her restlessness for what it was. What she didn't understand was why that old sense of things being not quite right, of not feeling "at home" anywhere, should come back to disturb her now, of all times. Just when she was beginning to let herself believe that what she had with Ross wasn't going to collapse under the weight of anger or injured ego, or waft quietly away with distance, or time.

Sunday morning she got up early and began packing, her mind firmly made up now. She hauled most of her plants next door to the neighbor who usually took care of them when she was gone, then cleaned her apartment before taking a quick shower.

She was supposed to meet Alex and Nat Thorne, his new sketcher, uptown at Zabar's at eleven. The shop had grown from a small kosher-style deli to one of Manhattan's most popular "ethnic" markets, offering smoked fish and Scotch salmon and more kinds of cheeses than anyone could ever dream of, as well as the aroma of freshly roasted coffee beans and croissants, among other things. And on Sundays, it turned into an absolute madhouse. But Julia loved going there, not only for the closest thing she'd ever found to true French croissants, but because the place was overcrowded and cluttered, and exuded the essence of the city she'd grown to love. And people-watching at Zabar's was an "experience." Alex was having about twenty people for brunch, one of his typical "little" parties, as a bon voyage for himself and Nat, and she'd agreed to help him shop for and prepare it.

It was obvious to Julia within minutes of meeting Nat Thorne that he was more to Alex than just a design assistant, for they'd already developed an affectionate camaraderie. Tall and thin, Nat was a sensitive-featured blond with a quiet voice and unselfconscious air of confidence. She liked him instantly. And though they had little chance to talk after the others began arriving, Nat came to the door with Alex when she was about to leave, later that afternoon.

"Alex talks about you a lot," he told her softly, and somewhat shyly, "and I guess I thought he was overdoing it a bit—but he wasn't." He smiled then, a smile that lit his face with a natural beauty she'd only fleetingly glimpsed before.

She smiled to acknowledge his compliment. "You two have a good time while you're 'working' on the beaches. And don't expect to hear even a squeak from me, at least not before the first of the month," she told them. "I'm gone from this place!"

"You mean Tony's finally come around?" Alex asked, almost leering.

"Nope. Maybe he will, maybe he won't. Doesn't matter to me. I'm going anyway." She gave Alex a hug, then on impulse treated Nat to the same. "See you alligators later."

Chapter 16

THE NEXT TWO weeks were the happiest Julia could remember in years, and she didn't waste much time worrying about what might be going on at Taggart while she was gone, or about Tony Gianni. She reveled in the freedom to concentrate on just one thing for however long she liked, rather than having a hundred different demands on her attention. And she felt a deepening sense of satisfaction with that one thing—the collection she was designing with Ross's computer program. In addition, she discovered that he really did need her ideas and experience as much as she needed his, and the give and take between them gave her a new confidence with the computer.

In the beginning she insisted on going back to the Westgate every night, near the Capitol, where her father kept an apartment. She'd planned to rent a car or borrow one of Carey's so she could come and go at will, but when Ross picked her up at the airport in a new emerald green Mercedes sedan, he mumbled something about needing a bigger car now and told her the red convertible was already waiting for her in the parking garage at the Westgate.

There were times when she simply had to abandon the computer to seek relief in the Jacuzzi for her aching neck and shoulders, and Ross learned very quickly where to look for her when she wasn't at her terminal. A few minutes of complete relaxation in the turbulent heat, followed by several bracing laps in the big pool, left her physically renewed, but also often stimulated a rush of new ideas, and she would barely dry off before hurrying back to put the idea down on paper before it escaped her.

And that's the way Ross happened on her late one afternoon, too wrapped up in her sketches to realize she was shivering in the stream of cool air from the air-conditioning vent.

"Save it and then quit, Julie," he ordered.

She looked up to see him holding his own thick terry cloth robe, and she stood up while he wrapped it around her, pushing her arms through the sleeves as if she were a child, realizing that her mind was still miles away. "Talk about computer nuts! You're going back into the hot tub to warm up." This time he went with her, though he let her sink into the steamy water in silence, respecting her need to finish what she'd been thinking about.

Julia let her body go limp while the hot bubbling water rose to her chin. After a few minutes, she asked, "Are you angry with me?" though she kept her eyes closed.

"Nope. Just waiting for you to finish whatever's cooking in your head. Chad Holloway called, asked us to dinner Saturday night. I told him I'd have to check first—you want to go or not?"

"Your patent attorney?" she asked. Ross had mentioned his name before.

"Yeah. He said it would be small, informal. You might enjoy meeting some different types for a change."

"You still down on fashion people, McCutcheon?"

"You still jumping to conclusions, Bonner? I meant you need a break—from computers and me. Besides, it'll give you a chance to ply him with your questions about how to stop the knockoffs."

They'd talked more than once about the eternal security

problem in a business that was rank with copying, adaptations and translations, even outright piracy—though no one ever called it stealing. Copying was so widespread, in fact, that most houses simply hoped for at least one season's head start before the thundering herds came rushing in to make a killing on a fast-selling style. Because when that happened—making a hot new design available at lower prices—it soon became a "ford," a common, mass-produced item that quickly lost appeal to consumers. Fashion designs weren't covered by copyright laws, but computer software was, and Julia wondered if a collection stored in the memory of a computer could be made less vulnerable to knockoffs.

"Okay, if you want to. God, does your body hurt like this all the time, Ross? Even my eyes are killing me! I've read about CRT emissions. Could it be that? Or maybe I need glasses. My neck aches all the way down to my toes."

He slid toward her, turned her around to massage the muscles just below and up the back of her neck. "You've been staring at the screen too long without blinking, so your eyes get dry. You've got to learn to blink. Same thing when you read, but most of us have forgotten that we had to learn to blink when we do that, too. Take more breaks, work out on the Nautilus stuff or whack some tennis balls. And we should try raising the monitor to see if that helps."

"Ahhh. You can't imagine how good that feels."

"As much time as you spend in this tub and the pool, I was beginning to think maybe you preferred them to me."

"And exactly what do you mean by that?" she asked, startled into turning around so she could see his face.

"You don't know why you're so addicted to this? I'd say it's because you're touch-starved. Same reason you go for the soft, slinky fabrics you wear. To satisfy your haptic needs. To put it to you straight, Julie love, you obviously need a hell of a lot more touching than you're getting."

"Oh, is that so?" she shot back, taking quick offense. "And you're the expert on what females need, huh? Don't go macho on me again, McCutcheon. You're a great one to talk about touching—that's about all you do, so you must have some grand passion for it, too!"

"I don't remember hearing you complain. And don't *you* go getting your feminist hackles up. Most women need and get a lot more pleasure from haptic stimulation than men. And I'm not talking about the obvious places. Maybe because of the estrogen in your skin. Whatever the reason, though, I aim to see to it you don't go short, starting right now."

Julia didn't go back to the Westgate at all that night, and the next day she moved her things, throwing caution to the winds and giving in at last to what they both really wanted. It suddenly seemed ridiculous not to, not to mention dishonest.

Ross worked at home most of the time, largely because she was there, she suspected, but he didn't hover. Instead, he left her alone in his "lab" while he worked at the computer in his study, sending information via modem to his office from time to time. He seemed to sense when not to interrupt her, and didn't, unless it was really necessary, but he was available whenever she ran into a problem and needed help, and they fell into a natural routine that worked well for both of them. Music flooded every room in the house, "programmed" for hours at a time from the master control system in the lab, where one entire wall was covered with shelves filled with audio tapes, both reel-to-reel and cassettes.

On the days Ross's housekeeper came, they ate outside in the airy gazebo where Julia loved to sit in the late afternoons, sipping a frosty wine spritzer. Ross asked her to make quesadillas, and chalupas with chicken and guacamole, two of Julia's favorites. Other nights they went out to eat, to the Kyoto or the China Palace, or to the Brick Oven for stromboli and pizza. And when Julia felt like cooking, they raided Ross's vegetable garden, which now was guarded by a black French Scare Cat with green marble eyes, a gift she'd brought with her from New York.

Julia talked to Beth almost every day, and some evenings she and Ross went out to the school and picked her up for supper, delivering her back to her dormitory in time to do her homework before lights out. It was Beth who insisted that Ross come to school with Julia on Parents' Day, where they visited classes together and then watched the girls' B soccer team, the one Beth played on, beat the A team. Then late in the afternoon, while Beth went to shower and change for dinner, they walked back up the hill from the playing field to the headmaster's house for a wine and cheese reception. Ross listened to Julia greet some of the other parents whom she'd met before, but he was lost in his thoughts of the past and the public school he'd attended. This school was a completely different world, both inside the classroom and out, and he couldn't help feeling slightly envious of what he'd missed.

The first thing Julia heard from Mr. Steinbrenner, the headmaster, was that Beth was refusing to accept the French prize, one of the academic awards given each year to outstanding students. "We will of course respect her wishes, Julia, though I tried to persuade her to change her mind," he explained with a slight smile, obviously unsure how Julia might take the news. "But she was quite adamant. Swore me to secrecy, though I thought at least *you* should know."

"Did she explain why?" Julia asked, since Beth hadn't even mentioned it.

"Yes, she was very, uh, forthcoming, in fact. Said she intended to see justice done! That she had an unfair advantage over the others because she'd learned French as a child from her grandmother, with no effort at all, while the girl who stood second for the prize had—uh, she'd worked her tail off, were Beth's exact words."

Out of the corner of her eye, Julia caught the self-satisfied grin spreading all over Ross's face, but had to wait until Mr. Steinbrenner had moved on to other parents before she could confront him. "You knew, didn't you?" she accused, trying to look serious. Instead, a pleased smile broke through and then mirrored his. "Did she swear you to secrecy, too?"

"Nope, she only mentioned it once, wanted to know what I thought. That's the last I heard of it. I told her it was her decision, that she had to do what *she* thought was right. You've done a fantastic job with her, Julie—doesn't it make you want to have another one like her? Don't you feel good, knowing you've got a daughter who stands behind her convictions?" He repeated what Beth had said in the car that day they'd driven around Carey's ranch, about the student with the "photographic" memory, and unfair competition. But while he was talking, it suddenly occurred to him that she might think he was usurping her position as parent. "Maybe I shouldn't have—I'm sorry, Julie, I just didn't think! I should have suggested she talk with you first."

"No, she's the one who has to live with the decision." She took his hand and rubbed it slowly between both of hers, wishing she could feel the touch of his fingers on her neck, or just anywhere. "And she probably was testing you, to see if you'd tell her what to do. Because I suspect she's wondering about us. I've been away from her too much these past few months. She's not a child anymore."

Ross left the house a little after eleven the following morning, telling Julia he was "going to the office" and would be back later in the afternoon. In fact, he was meeting Carey Blanton for lunch at the Foothills, at the top of the Hyatt-Regency Hotel. Carey had called earlier in the week and suggested they "get together and talk a little. Nothing special." But Ross thought he was trying too hard to sound nonchalant, and he hadn't mentioned Julia, though Carey had to know by now that she wasn't staying at the Westgate anymore. With some other father, it might be a ploy to feel him out about his "intentions" in regard to his daughter, but Ross didn't think that fitted Carey at all. So he was more than a little curious by the time he spotted Carey, already seated at a table, staring out the window at the city spread out before him, across on the other side of the Colorado River.

Carey rose slightly to grasp Ross's hand, then stretched his long legs out straight under the table as he glanced out the window again. "It's a damn shame, isn't it? The Capitol's disappeared. Can't see anything but office buildings now, all up and down the avenue." Ross knew he was referring to the view of the Capitol dome, which until just a few years ago could be seen from almost any point in town because the city hadn't allowed any buildings over six stories to be built along Congress Avenue, the wide boulevard that ran from the grounds of the Capitol south to the Colorado River, cutting right through the heart of the downtown business district.

"Big developers from Houston and Dallas bought off the council, and now it's too late. I never have been able to understand why the hell we have to crowd up as if we've got no more land than Manhattan, and build the same damned concrete canyons! It's un-Texan—and just plain stupid. Wouldn't you think we could learn from the mistakes other folks have made?" He heaved a sigh and waited while the waitress set a tall frosted glass and sweating can of Tecate in front of him.

Ross made no attempt to answer Carey's rhetorical question, but instead broached the subject he thought was the reason for Carey's call. "Julia's doing a great job with the computer, Carey. Don't know what I'd do without her help on the program, in fact. Her designs look absolutely fantastic to me—though I'm not exactly unbiased, I suppose." He allowed a self-deprecating smile to curve his lips, but only for a second. "I suggested that she go into business on her own—"

"What'd she say to that?" Carey shot back anxiously, very interested indeed in what Ross was saying.

"Time's not right, or something to that effect. She's worried about leaving Ben in the jaws of the barracuda—Tony Gianni. You know about him?"

"Yep," he grinned. "He keeps her on her toes." He chuckled softly. "Gives her a chance to sharpen her skills, you might say, which are considerable. Julia's got a good head on her for business, and politics. My associates, well, some of 'em hate it when she shows up 'cause all they know to do is bullshit. She cuts right to the bone, makes 'em look bad." He laughed shortly. "Maybe it's because of all the times I dragged her with me when she was little. Her mother was away a lot, you know. Julia would sit real quiet off in a corner somewhere, drawing. Always drawing. But she was listening, too, though I didn't discover that until later, when she was about eleven and started asking the damnedest questions. Yeah," he sighed again, "she could have done almost anything she wanted to. Was a fine painter, too. Maybe you noticed the watercolors in the living room out at the ranch. Fields of wildflowers. She did those the spring Tom left. She'd just walk off by herself across the pasture. Be gone for hours. But she's never painted a lick since the day he died."

He turned to stare out the window again. "I never did understand why she went into that fashion stuff, though. Guess I always thought she'd do something more important." He turned back and smiled to soften the criticism, and Ross guessed it might be the first time he'd ever spoken the sentiment aloud. "Most kids are like that, I suppose—going a different way than you expect them to."

"I think maybe we've both been way out in left field on that one, Carey. I've come to the conclusion from watching your daughter, and your wife, and your granddaughter, that Julia makes you and me look like flyweights. You want a better deal for Texas farmers and farmworkers, right?" He waited for Carey to nod, though he already had his full attention. "That's great, but it's just a small splash in the grand scheme of things. And me—I think computers are the answer to a lot of our labor problems, which amount to a waste of human potential. That also is nothing more than a minor fluctuation in the stream of human history. But Julia? Uh, uh—no small potatoes for her. She's off on a crusade to change the whole damned world!

"I don't know if I can explain it to you, because I'm only just beginning to get a glimmer of what she's got in mind myself. Your Anne-Marie, and my Julia, are going for a lot more than equality. That's too simple. They're out to explode the whole damned myth of what society *thinks* about women—what they're like, what we've expected them to be for centuries. And to accomplish that, all women are going to have to learn to know themselves a helluva lot better than they do now. Develop some kind of unique feminine consciousness, I suppose Julia might call it." He shook his head, more in dissatisfaction with his explanation than the idea. "Anne-Marie has been going about it one way and Julia another, but in the end, I think, they're both after the same thing. Beth's off and running in the same direction—she's hell bent on justice and everything being fair—and I'll give you odds she'll probably end up a lawyer."

"You ever say any of that to Julia, Ross?" Carey asked, watching his face.

"No. I guess you set me off, with your wishing Julia had gone into something more important."

Carey nodded, and a satisfied expression spread over his face. "Anne-Marie says Julia's really happy for the first time in a lot of years, Ross. Deep down happy. My guess is you're the reason." He touched Ross's arm for one brief instant, then swerved toward his can of beer and upended it over his glass.

"You know, I've always thought something must have happened back then, when Tom died, that she never told us, though I can't figure out what the hell it could possibly be. Maybe just my imagination."

Ross had begun to think he'd been wrong about Carey, that he'd arranged this little meeting to size him up after all—to decide whether Ross was good enough for his little girl—but now he realized that once again Carey had been trying to tell him something.

"Parents tend to worry too much I suppose. But Annie always said Julia was strong." He grinned hugely, breaking the intensity of the moment. "Whenever I'd get to going on about Julia—what a fine mind she had and how much she was like me—Annie would shoot me down with just a few short words. 'Remember, Cara, she also flies with the birds,' she'd say." He laughed quietly, savoring the memory. "It got to be sort of a private joke between us. Annie was usually home during the summers, and when Julie was about eight—she was just beginning to get long-legged and awkward about then—Annie found her lying flat on her back way out from the house in the tall grass—looking up at the sky with her legs sort of drawn up and crossed and her gangly arms flailing all over the place. Annie asked her what she was doing, and Julia answered, 'Flying with the birds.' "

Julia twisted and turned for what seemed like hours, before finally opening one eye. A dim light was coming down the hallway from Ross's study, and she knew he often got up to work for a while when he couldn't sleep. She had trouble staying asleep herself at times, and would wake in the middle of the night, her head churning with ideas, impatient for morning to come so she could try them out on the computer. Now, she got up and felt for her robe in the dark, then slipped into her slides before going to join him. But she couldn't find him—in the lab or his study, the kitchen or even down in the pool—and she was just beginning to get worried when she saw a light on out in the yard.

She stepped outside to look, then finally spied him prowling around, aimlessly it appeared, down along the bank of the creek-pond, so preoccupied that he didn't hear or see her. "Ross?" she spoke softly, not wanting to startle him.

"Yeah, I'm over here," he answered. "Sorry if I disturbed you." He stopped, peering down into the water for a second, then turned to watch her come toward him.

"I guess my mind was working overtime. You too?"

"Not really." He was quiet for some time then, so she waited, not speaking again, either. "Sometimes I can't get her out of my mind," he explained slowly at last. "Maria, I mean. I keep seeing her face." The words stopped suddenly, as if choked off by a rush of emotion.

She felt helpless, unable to think of anything to say. "Sometimes I wonder if the hurting will ever stop, don't you? Maybe if we were—what? Less intelligent? Then we'd be less aware, wouldn't feel so much!"

Ross put one arm around her and drew her close, then the other one, too. "You don't really believe that, do you? Everyone hurts, Julia. We just have different ways of dealing with it—of expressing it, or not expressing it. Some people can't put it into words, so they find another way. Like your mother, in her music."

"Maman?" she questioned, as if considering the idea for the first time. "I suppose she might have a few unpleasant memories, from when she was a young girl during the war. Was that what you meant in Paris, when you called her brave?"

"No! You really don't understand?" He leaned back to look at her, surprised, then thought about Anne-Marie for a moment, remembering. "I think I was almost embarrassed, in my youthful ignorance, first for her and then for myself. Because she was revealing what I thought we weren't supposed to—I don't know how to describe it—there was something naked about her music, painfully honest. That's where her genius lies, I suppose. She was putting herself on the line, sort of baring her soul, letting us know not only what was in her mind and her fingers, but also way inside someplace—what she felt." He straightened suddenly. "Personally, I think that takes a hell of a lot of guts, and it's always stuck with me, that vision of inner strength. Most of us aren't brave enough to expose ourselves like that. We have to keep up a façade, for protection."

"Well, it seems to me she's pretty much had everything she wanted all her life. What does she know about losing—about really hurting?"

Ross pushed himself farther away from her, even more astonished at that. "You mean you've never talked with her about things like that, or really listened to her?"

"She never says much to me about how she feels—too busy, I suppose. First with her concert tours and now with her master classes and recording sessions."

Ross turned his back on her, shaking his head in disbelief tinged with disappointment while he stared into the water. "Maybe she's respecting your precious damned privacy. And maybe it's time you listened to her 'Poems' with the ears of a woman and a mother—instead of a child." He sounded impatient with her in a way she'd never sensed before. "See if you can't hear the pain as well as the joy she put into them. How she really felt during those years when she had to be away from you, and from Carey. They must have been very much in love. All you have to do is see them together today to know that! Do you have any idea at all what it must have cost her to miss watching you grow up? To be constantly at war with herself! Dammit, Julia, how could you miss it? You of all people!"

The more he thought about it, the angrier he became. "She did what she had to, not just what she wanted to. And you—you're still punishing her for it! You haven't thought about *her* for a minute, have you—only yourself! You've had both of them, Carey included, tiptoeing around you for years! Shit!" He turned and stalked toward the house, as if he couldn't stand being with her any longer.

Julia stood in shocked silence on the bank of the creek, holding her breath until he'd disappeared inside the house. Then a sudden wave of confused anguish engulfed her, triggering the tears she hadn't realized were waiting. She sank down into the grass, right where she stood, clasping her knees to her chest and rocking back and forth, giving in to the little girl inside her, sobbing her heart out. Crying in the dark one last time for the mother she loved so much—and had missed so terribly.

"Julieeeee." The name was torn from his throat—a shout that ended in pure terror, jerking her into a waking nightmare of pounding footsteps. She pushed herself into a sitting position, feeling cold and stiff, the grass under the palm of her hand the only tangible sensation in a world of dark confusion.

"Julie," Ross shouted again, this time with relief, and slid to his knees to gather her into his arms and bury his face in her hair, muttering incoherently as he hugged her to him.

She could feel the pounding of his heart, in his chest and his neck and his throat. "I must have dozed off," she tried to explain, as much for her own benefit as his.

"I thought you might have fallen into—I was afraid you'd—oh my God, Julie, I couldn't stand to lose you, too." He was squeezing her so hard she could barely breathe, smoothing her hair, feeling her face, then up and down her arms and her back, as if to make sure she was real.

"I may be so in love with you I'm a little crazy sometimes, but if you think I'm going to throw myself in the creek just because you get angry with me—!" Her voice got stronger at the very idea, which, irrational though it might be, she found insulting. "If I were ever going to do something that stupid, Ross, I would have done it a long time ago, believe me."

Ross shook his head, but kept his face hidden in her hair, unable to force himself to let go of her yet. "I didn't have time to think. Lost track of time. You didn't come in. Then I couldn't find you when I came out to see why. It's so dark out here. You don't know the place very well, and I went off and left you alone. I love you so much I'd die if anything happened to you, Julie."

He heard her sniffle, and when he lifted his head, he couldn't help noticing that her eyelids were puffy, even in the shadows cast by the yard light. "God, I'm sorry, Julia," he mumbled, gently brushing his lips across her cheeks and then her hot, swollen eyes. "Can you forgive me? What I said about you and your mother, well, that's between you and her, and I shouldn't have tried to, to—" His eyes were swimming with tears.

Julia shook her head to deny what he was saying, then laid her fingers across his lips to stop him, and finally leaned forward to kiss them quickly. "No more. Not now. Lord, I must look terrible. Let me up from here so I can go hide. I don't want you to see—"

He helped her up then and put an arm around her waist as they started back toward the house. "You just said you loved me, do you realize that?" he asked, his voice almost normal again.

Julia nodded, happily. "Did I?" she teased, then relented. "It's not exactly the kind of thing I go tossing around lightly, in case you haven't noticed."

At that he smiled a little, too, and she felt hugely rewarded for her efforts. "I've noticed."

Chapter 17

THERE WERE EIGHT at the Holloways' Saturday night, and it was informal only because they all knew each other too well to be formal. When it came to dress, however, Ross's friends could easily have passed as New Yorkers, or perhaps Californians, which one couple was. If the women were colorful, the men seemed perfectly at home in dark business suits, which Julia suspected was their normal office attire—except for Ross, who wore navy gabardine trousers and a gray and white houndstooth cardigan. His one concession to the occasion was a dress shirt and tie—the first time she'd seen him wear one since Paris.

The others were already there when she and Ross arrived, standing around in the kitchen talking while Chad fixed drinks. Even curiosity about Julia didn't stop Stan Lunsford's wife, Bonnie, from regaling them all with interminable tales about their six-month-old son's latest accomplishments, including how many disposable diapers he went through in a day's time. Stan gave her a few more minutes to get the baby out of her system and then cut her off.

"Discovered any more little high-tech companies about to put the skids under Big Blue, Ross?" he inquired, laughing.

Ross shook his head, answering in kind. "Not this week, anyway. Guess Julia's keeping me too busy." He draped an arm over her shoulder and pulled her closer. "Stan's one of those I-told-you-so's. Why I put up with him I don't know. He's my broker, in case you hadn't guessed," he explained loud enough for all to hear.

"Did he tell you about that?" Stan asked Julia, but she could only shake her head, unable to even follow what he was asking. "Ross is convinced it's the small companies, working on what everyone else might think is a harebrained idea, who are going to pull the fat out of the fire for the semiconductor industry. A classic case of oversupply—too many companies doing the same thing have just about ruined the business, that and the foreigners. But he insisted, against my advice I might add, on investing in one that's been sitting right on the edge of bankruptcy for months, just because they were building some really far-out machine. He wanted them to have a chance—let his emotions rule his head."

"They got raided at the wrong time, that's all. Lost a couple of their best engineers," Ross explained, defending himself, but with good humor.

"Now Tim, here—he's really an expert on oversupply." Stan turned toward Tim Ragsdale, who up to now had stayed quiet, except for a few words when Ross introduced her.

"I read where Jerry was in town, reading the riot act to that meeting of semiconductor equipment manufacturers," Ross commented to Tim. "Said their stuff works only about 40 percent of the time, and they might as well be working for the Japanese." He laughed, then added, "Sounds like Jerry." Julia didn't have the slightest idea what they were talking about, but Ross quickly explained. "Jerry Sanders is the head of Advanced Micro Devices. Tim here is in charge of the Austin AMD group. They're designing a bunch of new chips, tailor-made for their customers."

Julia looked at Tim with new interest. AMD was one of the

Silicon Valley companies she'd read about, and she recognized the name of its flamboyant CEO.

"Yeah, Jerry promised we'd put out a chip a week this year, you know." Tim's smile was slow, while the others laughed out loud. "But things are beginning to look up, though our engineers are still working overtime without extra pay to stay on schedule. He said he tried to get in touch with you, Ross, but apparently you were out of town at the time."

"Jerry's the one who thought up the austerity program at AMD, after the bottom fell out," Stan jumped in to explain to Julia. "STAUNCH! Come on, Tim, tell her what that means."

Tim smiled bravely. "Stress Those Actions Urgently Needed to Check Hemorrhaging." Everyone laughed again, including Tim this time.

"You got out at the right time, Ross. Even dropping a mil on that little fiasco—"

"You know, Stan," Ross cut him off abruptly, "I hear, no matter how good his advice might be, what you really want in a broker is confidentiality."

Stan heeded the warning without blinking an eyelid and smoothly switched direction midstream. "Did you see where Alliant went up two points this week? Looks like you were right about that one, anyway. Their midrange supermini is going to sell for a little under a half-mil, and it's four times faster than a comparable Digital VAX. Data General's is too slow, and too high-priced, too. And the CRAY is going for six mil. So I predict it's going on up."

Digital Equipment Corporation and Data General were the companies involved in the story Ross had given her to read on the plane, and Julia now knew what a supermini was from her reading, and also that CRAY was the company that had built the first supercomputer. At least she no longer felt inadequate when people talked about things like that—only bored.

Gretchen Holloway's table was set with white china bordered with a delicate wreath of pink flowers, on dusty rose handwoven linen place mats, and a greenish Mexican glass vase in the center held three short branches cut from a pink crepe-myrtle bush, probably from the Holloways' yard. The table itself was the only source of light in the room, with three tall white candles placed so that no one had to peer around them to see the person across the way. Heavy cut-glass water tumblers didn't match the green-stemmed wineglasses, but the total effect was at the same time elegant, comfortable and intimate.

"I understand you've got a big security problem in the fashion business, Julia," Chad commented just after they sat down. "Ross says you have some questions I might be able to help with."

Julia suddenly felt embarrassed about asking his professional opinion in a social situation. After all, his expertise, the information she wanted, was the way he made his living. "Oh, I wouldn't want to—" she began, only to be cut short by his engaging smile, and then his own apology.

"I haven't had much reason to consider the kind of problems you're up against, so I don't know if I can help. I remember reading a newspaper account—oh, a year or so ago I guess it must have been—about a decision by some French court. One of their big name designers had copied a particular 'creation' from another one. The thief was ordered to pay damages, something like $10,000 as I recall, plus an additional fee for every time he claimed it as his own."

"Yes, I remember the case," Julia confirmed. "It was Yves Saint Laurent. If he really did steal the design and the court decision was justified—$10,000 is not a deterrent! Unless the judgment alone were to hurt his reputation, which it hasn't. I'm sure he made much, much more than that on it, though it took five years in the courts."

"I doubt that decision could have come down in an American court," Chad volunteered. "But tell me what you're after."

"Well, Ross mentioned that software can be copyrighted. I know fashion designs can't, but I thought perhaps there might be some way to at least improve security if the designs could somehow be tied to the software. Would that be infringement of copyright? Or could the program be varied only slightly by each user, and each version copyrighted?" She moved her shoulders in a dismissive shrug. "I'm afraid my ideas must sound terribly naive. I'm too much the beginner." She saw Chad glance at Ross with a slight smile.

"That's an interesting idea, but once a design's down on paper, or you show it, you'd still have the same problem. The copies could be made from pictures, couldn't they?"

"Yes, of course, but that's not usually the way it's done. It's too much work, and takes too long. Generally a knockoff manufacturer, or maybe even a store, buys a garment and then uses it as a pattern to make the copies. After-the-fact copying is probably impossible to stop. All anyone would have to do is modify it a little and then claim it's not the same garment. The worst disaster of all, though, is to have a design stolen before it's been shown—that's where I thought the software might offer some protection. But perhaps that's a pipe dream."

"Maybe we could talk a little more before you go back to New York—pool our knowledge, you might say—with a little help from Ross on the software possibilities. You've raised an interesting question."

When Ross asked Mary Alice Ragsdale about her job, Julia was surprised to learn that Tim's wife was the governor's speech writer. "It's harder than any kind of writing I've ever tried to do before," she confessed. "I used to be a reporter for the *Houston Post,*" she explained to Julia, "in the capitol bureau. It's especially hard, trying to work in the humor he likes, though he's right—the best way in the world to reach an audience and get them on your side is to share a joke, or poke fun at something together. Unfortunately, he doesn't have a natural wit, like Carey Blanton does. God, how I do love to listen to that man."

Ross's eyes sparked with quick humor, and he shot a glance in Julia's direction, then turned his attention back to Mary Alice.

"He doesn't need a speech writer—that one—it just seems to flow naturally. What the world needs is more politicians like him, witty and smart at the same time. What charisma that man has! I attended his fund-raiser last week at the French Legation, billed as *Une Soirée du Cochon Entier*—an evening of the whole hog!"

Julia was beginning to feel uncomfortable. She was afraid Mary Alice would be embarrassed when, or if, she discovered Carey was Julia's father, and tried to think of a way to change the subject. But Ross spoke first.

"I'd probably better warn you, Mary Alice, before you get too carried away about Carey Blanton"—his hand reached out while he spoke, touching Mary Alice lightly on one arm—"that Julia's a fan of his, too. In fact, I suppose you might say they have a very special relationship. She's a member of his brain trust, the best idea man he's got—or so he says." He paused, smiling at Julia. "He's also her father!"

Julia could hear the bemused shock at his unexpected revelation in the few seconds of absolute silence that followed it. Then everyone at the table began bombarding her with questions—was she really from Texas, why didn't she sound like it, and all the others she'd long ago come to expect. She explained that her mother was French, but didn't mention her name, and as soon as possible steered the conversation back to Mary Alice.

"Tell me how you go about writing the governor's speeches. Do you spend a lot of time with him talking about the issues? How do you know what he wants to say?"

"Well, first I contact the group he's going to speak to, find out what they want him to talk about. Then I get with the governor—which is the hard part, because of his busy schedule—and we go over his position on those issues. Sometimes he tells me what to soft-pedal and what he wants to emphasize. I'm already familiar with his record, of course, and I sit in on staff meetings. It's just a matter of researching the information I need, and then putting it together in a 'creative' way."

Julia laughed, understanding better than Mary Alice probably realized.

"I'm having great fun right now, for instance, on one for the state NOW organization—they've just voted him man of the year, you know. So I get to use some of my favorite quotes, like Phyllis Schlafly's 'I'm a Christian, and I believe all good Christians believe that God made man to take care of women, to protect them, to go to war for them, to help them with their jackets and make sure nobody messes with them.' "

Julia laughed until tears came to her eyes. "She really said that? You didn't make it up?" she asked, disbelievingly. "Wherever do you find material like that?"

Mary Alice nodded and grinned. "I'm always looking. My friends, too. Even Ross sends me little bits and pieces in the mail from time to time, from all sorts of places. I've gotten to where I read everything for good quotes and jokes. Tim complains bitterly, says he'll never again marry a woman who clips his *Wall Street Journal* before he gets to it." She smiled indulgently at Tim, and Julia was fascinated by the subtle and very intimate smile he gave his wife.

"When we got married, Tim was horrified to discover that I kept everything on index cards—boxes and boxes full of them filed by subject or name. Water problems, New Right, John Kennedy, Phyllis. But now, all that's in my handy-dandy PC, filed and cross-filed by three, sometimes four, key words. I can cull any subject in just seconds."

"You ought to come out and take a look at what Julia's doing, Mary Alice," Ross injected, his enthusiasm growing as he explained how Julia was helping him with a software program for designing fashions with a computer. "And her designs—well, they make everything else look out of style. Dull." He reached for Julia's hand across the table. "Wait until you see them in the flesh—you'll see what I mean."

"Ross, you know they'll never be anything but illusive electrical impulses inside your machine," she admonished gently, though she loved hearing his praise. "And maybe a few pretty pictures on paper, thanks to still another machine, to demonstrate the possibilities with your software. That's why I let my imagination go about the options I think women would really like to have. I believe they may behave, and feel, one way when they're playing mother, or schoolteacher, or medical doctor—but that doesn't mean they don't turn into the sexy temptress in the evening, or—" She suddenly laughed a little, slightly embarrassed by what she might be revealing about herself.

"I'm with you on that," Gretchen agreed. "Ross says you're also in the marketing end of the business, so you must be saying that a lot of other women agree with you, too. So how come what you're designing isn't for real?"

"Well, partly because I'm also trying to do things that recognize seasonal differences in various parts of the country, and most of my colleagues think the only option we have is to all do things at the same time—show and deliver, I mean—so it's difficult to try something new in that sense. Besides that, they don't really believe customers will buy anything that's adapted to regional needs, that they want exactly what's *in* in New York, or Paris."

"Pooh! I think they're the sheep!" Bonnie burst out, surprising everyone. "I'll bet they think instant folksy when you even mention it, don't they, Julia? After all, we're just a bunch of urban cowboys down here in the oil boonies, right?" She hardly paused for breath. "Those New York navel watchers think the sun rises *and* sets on the east coast! Like the weathermen on the Today show and Good Morning America! Stand right in front of the middle of the map and yak, yak, yak about New York, then turn around and wave an arm in the direction of California—like they're not even sure where it is. The rest of the country doesn't even exist! Talk about provincial!"

"Now don't go getting yourself all upset, Bonnie honey," Stan muttered, trying to calm the rising tide of disdain. "Julia lives in New York, remember? You're not being—"

"Most of 'em wouldn't dare show their faces in public without an 'obvious' Adolfo, or Mackie or whatever," Bonnie continued indignantly, waving a dismissing hand in his direction. "I was reading the other day about Pat Buckley showing up at some charity style show in New York in a black and white wool suit by Bill Blass—along with five other people in one version or another of the same suit!"

"What do you mean by regional designing, Julie?" Gretchen interposed. "I've always thought it was a problem with fabrics more that anything else. Wools, for instance—certainly that's why cotton sweaters have gone over so big down here, summer and winter."

"Sure," Julie agreed, "but Bonnie's on the right track. I see it sort of like what architects call the 'regional imperative' in building design—which draws inspiration from place. But that means how the availability of certain materials, skilled craftsmen or conditioned air influence what buildings look like, not folk architecture, or the local vernacular in any form."

"Right," Bonnie jumped in again. "Why don't we have lunch one day next week, Julia, and I'll show you what some of the local designers are doing? Have you heard about the Austin Fashion Network—a group of designers who get together for showings, and exchange information and stuff. I buy mostly from them, so I don't meet myself every time I go out."

Julia was very interested, indeed, and readily agreed when Bonnie suggested they go the following Tuesday, and then asked the other two women to join them, too.

Ross listened with a half-smile on his face, inordinately pleased at Julia's show of interest in the local scene, even if she was only being polite.

"What company is she with, Ross?" Stan asked while the women were concluding their arrangements. "With ideas like Julia's, it might be worth looking at—the stock could be about to take off. Or is it privately held?"

"Ben Taggart," Ross answered, "and it was Julia's idea for the company to go public, about two years ago."

Stan raised both eyebrows. "Yeah? Sure, I know the company. It's been a damned good performer, though it was beginning to level off. Until just recently.'' He turned directly to Julia, really interested in her for the first time. ''Maybe you can tell me what's really going on, then, Julia. All we're hearing are rumors.''

''Rumors?'' Julia asked, puzzled, thinking she must have missed something he'd said earlier.

''Yeah, that Taggart is about to conclude a big license deal.''

''Where'd you hear that?'' Julia asked as calmly as she could manage.

''It's in all the trade papers. Your stock is up two points just in the last week—and looks like it may keep right on going, even higher.''

When the restless depression hit her so unexpectedly the following Wednesday, Julia tried to lose herself in work. But by midafternoon, she was finding it impossible to concentrate, or to escape the sense of dread that was beginning to engulf her at the thought of what might happen after Sunday, when she was going back to New York. Only four more days. Less than that alone, since they were due at the ranch to spend the Thanksgiving holiday there with Beth, and her mother and father. But she hadn't fooled Ross with her quick ''I'm going out to sketch awhile,'' and a few minutes later he joined her, bringing with him two glasses of her usual white wine and Perrier. She sipped. He waited.

''I really do love this place, Ross,'' she blurted at last. Tears were brimming in her eyes, but then he already knew something was bothering her. ''The creek, and the rock cliffs down below the dam. Your hillside vegetable garden, the oaks and yaupon, with their red berries at this time of year, the yucca and prickly pears. The wildflowers, from early spring to late fall—even that cloud of late yellow moths you can see out there. Things I've known all my life. And the house. Life feels more intense here than anywhere else—the colors, the smells, the sounds. I'm more alive, somehow, yet more at peace, too. I suppose because they're the sights and sounds and smells of my childhood, without any of the sad associations. When I'm here, my cup runneth over." She turned toward him with a quivering smile, just as the tears spilled over and began to run down her cheeks. "And I can hardly bear the thought of leaving." Her voice broke on the last word, and she covered her face with her hands as she gave in to her conflicting emotions.

"Then don't," he replied immediately, pulling her into his arms.

Her throat closed up so she couldn't speak, and instead rolled her head from side to side against his neck. He reached for his handkerchief and dabbed gently at her face, but she took it from him and dried his neck instead, laughing and crying at the same time.

"Why?" he asked. "Because you don't want to leave New York either?"

"In a way," she admitted, sitting up to wipe her eyes, feeling better already. "I could no more completely give up New York now, I suppose, than I've ever really been able to give up Texas. It's an absolutely maddening place in lots of ways, crowded and noisy and rude and irritating. But there's a—oh I don't know—a vitality that comes through, like no other place in the world. Paris has it, too, but in a different way."

"I'm not asking you to give up everything to come here, Julie. Or to come here at all if you really don't want to. I just want us to be together. I don't have to stay here, if that's what you want. I can do what I'm doing just about anywhere. It might take a little while to arrange it, but—"

"You'd give up this place for me?" she asked, waving a hand toward the pool and the creek and the family of rusty red pigs. "But that's one of the things that bothers me, the thought of leaving this! And I'd *never* get rid of the guilt if you gave it up because of me. It's an extension of—it's who you are. And I don't know anymore if I can stand being away from you. Something has to give! I just don't know what." She was on the verge of tears again.

"Sit on it for now, then. Let it simmer, as you like to call it. We'll work it out somehow—you know that, don't you?" She didn't even attempt an answer, and after a couple of minutes he shook her gently. "I said you *know* that, don't you? I love you, Julie, and nothing's going to change that. Not time and not distance." Then he grinned mischievously. "Anyway, I'm going to be in New York next week on business—or did I forget to mention that?"

The noise of Manhattan traffic hit Julia like a blast of heat from an oven the instant she stepped out of her apartment building. Were her ears suddenly supersensitive or had the decibel level in the city doubled in the short time she'd been gone? Visions of that day fourteen years ago when she'd stepped off the boat from France into the unceasing din of screaming tires and blaring horns flooded her memory, reminding her again of what she *hadn't* been hearing while she was gone. The noise had an oppressive effect, provoking in her an almost uncontrollable urge to run, to turn around and go right back to Austin. But that was probably as much a subconscious desire to run to, as it was to run from.

It took several days before Julia began to fully appreciate how much Tony had managed to set into motion in just three weeks. Everyone from the sample hands in the workroom to assistant sketchers were gearing up early for the fall-winter collection, resulting in an atmosphere that was almost as frenetic as the traffic outside.

Taggart was moving into the big time, Ben told her excitedly. They were going to scoop the big names, who wouldn't be showing until the end of April, with a splashy opening in the Atrium of the Trump Tower—an opening no one could ignore—scheduled a week prior to the Paris collections and almost two months ahead of most other American designers.

"Let the rest of them use the March regional marts to preview what's coming in the fall," Ben argued persuasively. "We'll have the prestige of a New York opening behind us when we go to market week. That's what you wanted, wasn't it, Julia? A change in timing—in our schedule?" He'd either misunderstood what she'd been plugging for at their last meeting, or Tony had managed to twist it all out of shape. Whatever the case, it seemed useless to try to correct it now. Ben wore a distracted expression and his eyes wandered, as if his attention was always somewhere else. He couldn't focus for long on anything except the problem he was having with a fabric, or getting the accessories he wanted. He'd already made most of his fabric decisions, and all he really wanted from Julia was confirmation that he'd made the right ones. Several numbers had already gone from the patternmaker to the sample hands, so the die was cast, and Julia felt completely helpless to change the direction of what was going on.

She saw little of Alex or Nat Thorne, since they were so involved in preparations for the World Menswear Congress in January, and fast on the heels of that, the New York Designers' Collective. She lunched with them one day shortly after she got back, and Nat was full of questions about the design software. Though she was glad Alex's relationship with Nat had survived the Riviera and, at least on the surface, seemed comfortably stable, it was a part of his life she rarely questioned him about. When he found the time he'd undoubtedly tell her about it anyway, whether she asked or not.

Tony also had moved in on Elaine's department in Julia's absence, and she discovered that the advertising and promotion campaign for the Taggart collection was already in place. Two of Elaine's copywriters were already drafting a series of timed releases that were to go to all the major fashion publications, each one calculated not only to hint that changes were under way at Taggart, but also to generate a lot of speculation and anticipation, which in turn would enhance press coverage—before, during and after the opening.

"The key word here is 'suggest,' " Elaine pointed out the next day while she, Julia and Max were having lunch together. "We aren't really saying what we're going to do, but we're about as suggestive as you can get, beginning with a little tease in the first release to hook them, then building up a little more each time—what you might call a crescendo of innuendo. Tony plans to feed out the line a little bit at a time. We're all under strict orders not to even go into the same ladies' room with a member of the press unless we clear it first with him. It's a damned dangerous game, if you ask me, unless he's already got the license deal in the bag."

"You heard about the stock?" Max injected, giving Elaine's hand a quick affectionate squeeze by way of apology for interrupting.

Julia nodded. "And the rumors. Sounds like someone has already started feeding out the line, wouldn't you say? What's it at now? I haven't looked in the past couple of days."

"Close to twenty. Up a whole point yesterday."

Julia continued eating, her only acknowledgment a raised eyebrow.

"Over the next couple of months," Elaine went on, "we're going to be sending out a real snowstorm. I warned Tony it could backfire. We might get even less coverage if we commit overkill, but he's running so fast these days he can't stop to listen to anybody." She paused, about to take a bite of her tuna sandwich. "Said if I couldn't 'think big'—his favorite slogan now—he'd get someone who could."

"That bastard! He wouldn't dare!" Julia burst out, unable to control her burgeoning anger any longer. "My God, Elaine, why in hell didn't you call me?"

"Why? And ruin your time with Ross? To tell you the shit was hitting the fan, and you should come flying back here and try to stop something that wasn't stoppable? Get into a big hassle with Tony when he already had Ben in his hip pocket before he even made his first move? I doubt it would have made much difference, Julia, even if you'd never gone in the first place, so don't go taking off on a guilt trip."

"It's not guilt—I was so damned naive! So sure he'd go to the board first. That we had time."

"Join the crowd," Max put in. "He was ahead of all of us, Julia. But he was mad as hell himself—when it first came out in WWD about a license deal in the offing, I mean. Said he'd find out who leaked it if it was the last thing he did, sounded worried that it might throw a monkey wrench into negotiations. So I guess he must be talking licensing with somebody. He probably was more worried the board might step in if they got wind of it. Things were pretty tense for a few days, and then his witch hunt just seemed to run out of steam." He took a sip of coffee. "This thing at the Trump Tower is a step in the direction he wants the company to take, but not so far that he has to go to the board first. You notice it's scheduled just two weeks before the next board meeting? My guess is if it's a big success he'll have the entire board on his team within minutes, with Ben leading the cheering section. If it's not—well, Tony will deny the rumors, say they were just that. All he'll need to do is go in there and justify the cost of the Tower. I can just hear him, can't you? 'Gentlemen, we just gave this tired company a publicity shot in the arm like it's never had before! And we'll be seeing the results in our orders over the next twelve months.' Ben will go along with him, either way. He's in too deep to do anything else."

"So how did it go?" Elaine wanted to know, jumping in the first chance she could find. "With Ross, I mean."

Julia nodded. "Fine, I think—at least Ross sounded pretty satisfied with progress on the program." They'd done so well the last week, in fact, that the design portion of what would ultimately be an integrated package was almost complete. "And I did a whole collection, if you can believe it. I'm kind of excited, in fact. Maybe the designs were in the back of my mind all along, waiting for the chance to get out. It was fun, not having to worry about what to carry over from last season, or what Blass and Beene or anybody else might be doing. No one standing over my shoulder, second-guessing me. I let out all the stops—wait until you see the color printouts I brought back with me. They'll give you some idea how we could use the program in your area, too, Elaine."

"Sure, that's great, Julia, but what I want to know is what happens next with you two? Are you leaving Taggart?"

"No! I mean probably not. Oh damn, Elaine, I don't know

what I mean. Not right now at least, I guess. One minute, I think about all the sweat and tears I've put into this company, and know I can't just stand by and let Tony ruin us. And the next, I'm wondering if I can take being away from Ross even one more day!"

"You're going to marry him?"

"Lainey, honey, maybe—" Max mumbled, obviously embarrassed by Elaine's continued probing.

"A real bulldog, isn't she?" Julia commented with a wry smile for Max's benefit, to let him know that she and Elaine were too close for Julia to take offense. But Julia hadn't missed the affectionate way he'd tried to corral Elaine's curiosity, which said more than he probably realized about how far their relationship had progressed while she was gone.

"I don't know how it's going to work out, Elaine," she explained honestly. "It's on hold—simmering—for now." The word seemed to flip a switch in her head, and a picture of Ross's Japanese gazebo flashed in front of her mind's eye. "I've decided not to make any decisions for now." She had to pull herself back from the edge of a mental precipice, and she began telling Elaine and Max about the merchandising strategies she'd encountered on her trek through Austin's specialty fashion shops with Bonnie and Mary Alice.

"At one called Morgan's, which is run by a very interesting-looking young man with short, curly red hair, the door is always kept locked. His customers have to knock to be let in, an exclusivity ploy that seems to be catching on. He's on a first-name basis with most of his customers—knows what kind of thing they like and what to show them—who's daring and who's not, what kind of jobs they have. And they always feel comfortable there, even if all they really want to do is look or talk, because he never puts any pressure on them. He's a friend, or consultant, not a sales clerk." She paused, thoughtful for a minute.

"But he doesn't buy at the Dallas market. Never even goes there. Only to New York, where he scouts designs by 'interesting new designers.' He sells *Details* in the shop—it's the only fashion magazine in the place, in fact." She smiled and sort of chuckled. "And he also offers the services of an intimate little beauty salon located in the rear of the building, accessible only through his showroom. I'll bet you anything it's next to impossible for a woman to go straight to or from getting her hair done without stopping to look at the latest arrivals. He gets new stuff all the time. Those are the kinds of specialty shops I've been talking about, Elaine, the ones that appeal to the same customers we design for. They're popping up right and left down there, not just in Austin—and I don't mean another chain outlet."

Later, in her office, Julia was flipping through the pages of *W*, skimming an article about the late Christian Dior, when a quotation caught her eye. "You can never alter a woman's style unless you alter the man in her life." Was that really true, she wondered, absentmindedly reaching for a yellow highlighter and marking the designer's remark before clipping the whole piece. Then she picked up a small "stick-it" pad and dashed off a few words—"Now you've got me doing it"—stuck the slip to the article, and addressed an envelope to Mary Alice Ragsdale.

Chapter 18

TIME PASSED MORE quickly than Julia had anticipated, partly because of the moved-up fall showing, now scheduled for the first week in March rather than the last of April. The shorter lead time overlapped the seasons even more tightly than usual, which meant preparing the fall collection at the same time they were getting ready for the January presentation of summer apparel. And that meant most of the staff would be putting in extra hours from now till Christmas, as well as during January and February. She talked to Ben and Tony about hiring temporary sample hands to lighten the work load on their regular staff, but Tony nixed the suggestion as an unnecessary cost. By mid-December Max's assistants began costing out the samples.

Ross came to New York twice during the first two weeks she was back in New York, but when she asked about his "business" he brushed off her question with the comment that he was just "consulting" for a company that was developing new CAD-CAM manufacturing equipment. Actually, she didn't care whether he was simply using that as an excuse or coming out of real need—so long as they could be together.

In spite of the increasingly chaotic atmosphere at the office, Julia rarely stayed late or took work home anymore. Somehow the almost compulsive drive to pour all her time and energy into developing Ben Taggart, Inc., simply wasn't there anymore, and on occasion she wondered whether that could mean she was making an unconscious decision about her future with the company. Then again, perhaps she just wasn't ready to call it quits on her new designs—the collection that existed only in the memory of a computer and in a few printouts. She felt a compulsion to go ahead with the promotional materials, to carry the project through to its natural conclusion whether it was only an exercise or not. If nothing else, perhaps Ross could use them to demonstrate the features of his software.

Most evenings, she listened to music while sketching ad layouts or writing copy for press releases and handouts. The color printouts needed word descriptions because she wanted people to know what she was trying to do—wedding style not only to fabric and function but to climate and region as well. The key words were variability and adaptation, but the right way to say what she wanted to didn't come as easily as the visual images.

She was doing the rough drafts by hand, planning to keyboard them into the computer when she got a chance, and to format them for the printer then, too. How much easier it would be if only she had her own computer, here and now, and could try out her ideas, both words and layouts, with no more trouble than the roll of a ball and the click of a button! And her ballooning frustration at not having access to one just spilled out naturally one night when Ross phoned.

"I never dreamed I could miss a damned machine so much!" Julia exploded. "Was that part of your plan—for me to get so addicted I'd go crazy with this typewriter, to say nothing of a pencil?"

He laughed at her. "You're just now learning that you can never go home again? It's pretty tough going back to the old way once you know how much faster and better it can be done, right?" He lowered his voice until she could barely hear him. "First, you get addicted to my house. And now, my computer. What about me?"

"I just hadn't gotten around to that part yet, that's all." Her voice changed, too, slowing to a seductive purr. "Maybe that's why I'm having so much trouble writing this copy!"

She moved on quickly. "I've been baking cookies, and made a batch of fudge. I can hardly wait. Have you talked with Beth? When are you getting in?" He was bringing Beth to New York for a couple of days before they all went to Chicago for Christmas with his grandmother.

"Wednesday. Around four by the time we get there. But we both have keys, so don't worry about getting home early just for us."

She could hear the grin in his voice, and she was smiling now, too. "I'm not even going in on Wednesday, so I'll be here. Whenever."

"How's it going otherwise?"

She knew what he meant. "Well—I've been thinking, Ross," she began, then hesitated. He waited for her to continue. "Taggart stock is still up, though it does seem to have leveled off for the moment. Maybe I should sell at least some of mine."

He waited for her to explain why, but she didn't. "You need the money?"

"Not particularly, but maybe this is a good time to get out. While it's up."

"Does that mean you think it's going down?"

"No, or at least not much. Unless this whole thing bombs. But it won't, not so bad that we can't recover."

"Then why sell now?" he persisted.

"Well, Tony's doing a pretty good job of taking over my role in the company, of making me superfluous. Maybe it's time for me to just bow out—"

"You're willing to throw in the towel, give him a clear field, make it easy for him?" Ross chided.

"No, not really, but—"

"Isn't that what you'd be doing?"

"But I thought you wanted me to—"

"I never put any strings on what I want, Julia. Don't lay anything on me—and don't use me for a crutch. I know it's hard for you right now, but it has to be right for you, or you'll regret it later. Maybe you should give it a little more time, think about it."

He obviously had no intention of even helping her to decide, let alone advising her what she ought to do, but she gained confidence just from hearing him say what she already knew—that it had to be right for her. No matter how much she might wish she could lay it off on someone else at times, the decision was hers alone to make. She could never live with it any other way—and for some reason, the very inescapability of the dilemma she faced made her think of her mother.

When they finished talking Julia tried to go back to her writing, but it was late and she felt burned out. It came to her then that there really was something else she wanted to do—for the first time since that awful night when Ross had been angry with her. So she put water on to heat and started a fire in the fireplace, then inserted the cassette into her tape player while she waited for her spiced tea to steep. At last she curled up on the couch, determined to give her full attention to the music—to "try to hear it with the ears of a woman and a mother, instead of a child."

Julia's mind drifted to other times, to remembered fragments of conversations and exuberant hugs, brief telephone calls and interminable waits at the airport. And to the quiet times, when words had seemed unnecessary, then to the silently shared grief and understanding at the hospital in San Antonio, when everyone else was asking the question she could never answer.

Gradually, Julia's recollections grew more recent. Ross had gone off with Anne-Marie to her studio, a separate building set off about a hundred feet from the house, to hear her latest recording, of Lukas Foss's *Capriccio*. Julia and Carey were watching Beth show two friends from school how to saddle their horses. For some reason, Julia was reminded of Elaine's comment about Carey, that weekend she'd come to the ranch with Max and the girls—"Can you imagine what is must have been like for him back then, with all his redneck buddies chiding him about his woman running off all the time, leaving him at home to take care of the kid?"

"Daddy?" Julia began hesitantly as they'd stood outside the horse pen, leaning their elbows on the fence, suddenly feeling shy and unable to phrase the question the way she wanted to.

He'd turned to look at her, probably because she hadn't called him that in years. "What's on your mind, honey?"

"It must have been as hard for you as it was for me. For Maman to be gone so much, I mean. To make it work between you. How did you stand it?"

Carey understood perfectly well what she was asking, but he took his time before answering, staring off across the corral at the cattle grazing way off in the pasture. "Didn't have any choice," he said finally.

"Why not?"

"Why?" He looked at her, surprised. "You have to ask that? Because I loved her, and it was the only way there was!"

She remembered straightening her shoulders, physically working up her nerve. "I meant, why couldn't she stay home with us? Teach—or, or do something else."

This time, his eyes stayed on hers when he spoke, and refused to let her look away. "I heard what you meant all right, Julia! If she loved us as much as we love her, how come she went off and left us so much, isn't that it?" Carey shook his head in disbelief. "Didn't you ever wonder how it was for her, Julia, being pulled two ways at once? Burdened with the sacrifices her mother and father, even her grandparents, had made during the war so she could continue her lessons. Knowing up here," he paused to put a finger to his head, "that she had an obligation to use the chance they gave her. But it was more than that, too. Music is like food to her, and I doubt she could do without it, could have ever in this world been happy if she hadn't tried to go all the way with it. To be as good as it was in her to be. You know something about that, don't you, Julia? So why is it so hard for you to accept the same thing in her?'' He seemed unable to go on for a minute, though Julia couldn't ever remember seeing him at a loss for words.

''She was good at not letting you know,'' he continued, ''not letting you hear the tears in her voice whenever she called home. But I heard them.'' He sighed deeply, remembering, and then he turned away from her. ''It was knowing how much Annie was hurting, Julia, and trying *not* to tell her flat out to quit and come home that was so damned hard!''

She remembered how she'd had to look away from him then to hide the tears in her own eyes, tears that streamed down her cheeks now, as elusive glimpses of what she'd never been able to see or hear before began to come together. Listening to her mother play the ''Poems'' she'd written twenty-five years ago. Until at last Julia understood why they'd always left her feeling slightly uncomfortable, with the vague sense that something was incomplete, unfinished, or perhaps simply beyond her reach.

Until at last she knew that what was unresolved had been inside herself, rather than in her mother's music.

The phone rang just as Julia was putting the last stubby white candle in the little glass holders scattered all around the living room, and she cast a last quick glance back at them as she hurried to answer it. At least the place would look a little bit Christmasy when they were lit, and the scent of the pine boughs stuffed into the basket next to the fireplace helped, too.

''Bonner.'' The word came out more abruptly than she intended, maybe because her mind was reviewing all the other things she still needed to do before Ross and Beth arrived.

''Perez,'' Connie responded, equally abruptly.

''Sorry, Connie, my mind was somewhere else, I guess.'' Indeed, she thought somewhat sheepishly, just because Ross was constantly on her mind didn't mean she had to ape the way he answered the phone.

"Well, do you think you could locate it and haul it up here? I hate to ask you, Julia, but I'm afraid you're the only one who can straighten this thing out. Alex and Elaine didn't want me to call you, but we just got the proofs back from the printer on Alex's stuff, and—well, I guess you'll have to come see for yourself."

Julia knew Connie wouldn't call her today unless they really did need her, so she didn't even consider arguing, but glanced at her watch and made a quick calculation. "It'll take me about forty-five minutes. But don't expect me to stay, Connie. Ross and Beth are due about four, and I intend to be back here long before that."

"Right. I'll tell Elaine. See you. Bye."

The sky had turned a uniform gray by the time Julia climbed out of the taxi in front of the Taggart building an hour later, and wisps of what looked like white cotton candy were skittering along the streets and sidewalks, blown by gusts of frigid wind. She flipped up the wide collar of her navy pea jacket to protect her ears and hurried inside. The weather forecasters were predicting two to three inches of snow by nightfall, and she was beginning to worry about whether Ross and Beth would get in ahead of it. She stepped off the elevator and headed straight for her office, resolved to finish and get back home as quickly as possible, only vaguely noting that a strange odor seemed to pervade the entire place. Perhaps it was something the sample hands were cooking in the microwave they'd just had installed in the workroom. Peeling off her coat as she hurried through Connie's office, Julia paused only long enough to instruct her secretary to let Alex and Elaine know she was there, and then pushed through the door into her own.

The lights were already on, and Ross was sitting in the chair behind the desk, but pushed back away from it. A multitude of images and sounds and scents suddenly began colliding in her head. The soft strains of an old French Christmas carol, one of her favorites. A long table covered in white with a low-spreading arrangement of cut poinsettias and gardenias, the creamy white blooms adding their exotic scent to something else that was the aroma of Christmas itself, all pungent and spicy. A big cut-glass punch bowl at one end of the table was filled with eggnog, a tall aluminum coffee urn stood at the other, and in between was a silver chafing dish, a huge platter of sliced turkey and ham, baskets filled with baguettes and croissants, a big wooden cutting board holding several kinds of cheeses, plates of cookies, and—

"Merry Christmas, Mom! Surprise!" Beth yelled at that moment.

Julia's attention swung to the other end of the room, where her daughter sat in front of the lighted screen of a computer monitor. Next to it was another monitor, with its screen split into windows displaying three different color variations of one of Julia's new designs. And next to that was a laser printer and video camera, already mounted on a stand ready to use.

Beth ran to Julia and squeezed her around the waist while planting a big kiss on her cheek. But Julia was too stunned to speak, and could only stand there and look helplessly from Ross to Beth and then back to Ross again. "Look at her! We really pulled it off, Ross." Beth laughed with pleased delight.

He came toward them finally, and also gave her a quick hug, followed by an equally quick kiss. "Santa arrived a little early, but—well, Merry Christmas, Julie."

"You brought them for me to use over the holidays?" she stammered, still not sure she understood what was going on. Connie hovered in the doorway, watching with a Cheshire cat grin.

"No, they're keepers—yours. You may want to arrange them differently, or maybe even take one home, but you can decide about that later."

Alex stepped around Connie just then, with Elaine and Max right behind him. "Has the party started yet? You sure took your time getting here, Julia baby." He gave her shoulders a squeeze, then went immediately to the coffee urn, and came back with a cup for her. "My special recipe, guaranteed to thaw you out, though I doubt you need it with him around." He rolled his eyes toward Ross.

She knew from the wonderful spicy aroma as well as the deep red color that it was hot mulled wine, her favorite cold-winter-night drink. Ross obviously had had more than a little inside help with his surprise party, but when she turned to search out Connie, Ben and Nat Thorne were just coming through the door and Connie had disappeared. Julia couldn't help smiling at the thought of all the secret phone conversations that must have gone on between them—and without her getting even the slightest inkling that something was afoot.

Her office filled rapidly after that, with people milling around between the computers and the refreshment table, peering curiously at the screen that displayed her work. Beth was back at the other terminal, having great fun explaining exactly how it worked to anyone who asked or wanted to try it. At the moment that was Nat Thorne.

Julia stayed close to Ross, not saying much, feeling like some ghostly spirit able to see and hear everything that was going on around her without anyone knowing she was there. Except Ross, who kept bringing her back down to earth with an occasional touch of his long fingers wrapped affectionately around the back of her neck, or with the mention of her name mixed in with what he was telling Max. She listened to the two of them with one ear, and to bits and pieces of other conversations going on around them with the other.

"The most sophisticated video program available today? Probably Cubicomp's PictureMaker," Ross responded to Max's question. "But so far, there's no engineering package to go with it—you can't go to the machine shop with it—though I hear they're working on one. The Mac's bit-mapped, high-resolution screen is perfect for what your design people need, though. Besides that, the mouse-menu-windows concepts are easy and fast to learn. Once the user gets the idea, it's easy to step from there right into the 3-D video program on the other machine, which uses the same access system, though it offers a lot more options and features. Not only solid modeling and texture mapping, but anti-aliasing, metamorphosis, transparency, and multiple or single light sources."

He turned to glance at Julia. "After Julia came to Austin, I added phong shading so she could get reflective surfaces, to get the look of shiny fabrics. We're using an AED 767 monitor, which can display up to 256 colors simultaneously. It has eight video memory planes, which allows us to fine-tune the shading, and it also supports thirty-five millimeter slide generation as well as videotape production."

Julia let a sort of secret, self-satisfied smile steal across her face as she listened, no longer feeling shut out by the "foreign" language he was speaking. After a few minutes more, she excused herself and went in search of Consuelo, finally spotting her hidden away in a corner near the computer table, taking with Billie and Arlette.

"You will keep this man, no?" Arlette suggested, laughing as she vigorously nodded her head for emphasis.

Julia nodded once, slowly, and answered her in French, then turned to Connie. "And you—" She gave Connie a fond hug before kissing her on the cheek and whispering "Thank you" at the same time. Connie nodded her head slightly, too, and they exchanged a long understanding look. Suddenly overcome by the nearly overwhelming emotion of the moment, Julia felt a rush of heat flood her cheeks and throat. She turned and walked away, afraid she might spoil the party by crying.

It was almost dark outside, she noticed, as she stared out through one of the big floor-to-ceiling windows at the swirling snow, coming down in big flakes now, and then at the images of people behind her reflected in the glass. Two of Ben's assistants and the seamstresses from the workroom. Elaine in flamboyant red and orange, next to Claire's more conservative and somber taupe with touches of yellow. Ross completely at ease in brown corduroy trousers and a tan fisherman's sweater—looking so very different from the stranger who'd obviously felt uncomfortable among all the "fashion types" at the Hotel Angleterre, just four months ago. Alex in soft black kid pants topped by a brilliant blue cut-velvet sweat shirt, and Nat in his pencil-slim trousers and bulky hand-knit sweater—the picture of avant-garde menswear, which at the moment demanded a rather extreme inverted triangle silhouette. And Ben, in a natty wool knit pretending to be a classic navy suit, complete with diplomat tie and tasseled slip-ons. All three of them leaning toward the refreshing natural beauty of a young girl, her daughter, who held them in thrall with the secrets of her computer!

"Computer-aided design software is to designers what word processors are to writers, you see," Beth was explaining patiently. "You put in lines and shapes and shadings instead of words. Rather than changing the size of the print you can change the size of the picture, or move one piece of it somewhere else, just like you can move a paragraph of writing from one place to another. Or do this—" she depressed the mouse button and rolled it across the desktop, stretching the image on the screen first to the right and then the left.

It was at that moment that Julia saw Tony appear in the window-mirror, hesitating at the door as if he were undecided about joining the party. She turned and hurried to greet him, determined to try to make him feel a part of the happy-family atmosphere that had reappeared among the Taggart staff as if by magic with Ross's little surprise party. Urging Tony toward the refreshment table, Julia chattered about safe subjects—the snow and what his plans might be for the holidays. Ross joined them and she introduced him to Tony, who surprised her by launching immediately into questions about their progress on the design program, with apparently genuine interest.

"A picture's still worth a thousand words, Tony," Ross responded, "so how about if Julia gives you a little demonstration?" He watched silently for the next half hour, except when Julia turned to him with a question, and in fact looked away only once—to catch Consuelo's eye and give her an almost imperceptible nod, which she returned with a small satisfied smile.

The fun and excitement of being together for Christmas, to say nothing of the buoyant effect of Ross's surprise party, stayed with them through the next two days. They ate and laughed and wrapped presents, after trudging through the snow to look at the store windows filled with scenes of Christmases past—from Lord and Taylor's historic New York mansions to Saks Fifth Avenue's Victorian townhouse in the midst of preparing for a holiday celebration back in those days of ornate elegance. Beth and Julia split off from Ross to shop, before meeting for lunch at a tiny Italian café where they had calzone Siciliano, the stuffed crusty Neapolitan cousin to pizza. Then it was Julia's turn to go it alone, while Ross and Beth went off on some "secret mission." She spent the time searching for an appropriate gift for Ross's grandmother. In the end, nothing seemed quite right, and she settled for a big box of Belgian chocolates made from antique molds at Le Chocolatier Manon, though it was far too impersonal a gift.

Ross's grandmother was an imposing-looking woman, standing tall and straight in spite of her eighty-four years as she waited for them at the half-open front door of her big two-story frame house. Arlington Heights had been just one of several small farming-commuter villages strung out along the Chicago and Northwestern railroad tracks when she'd first come here sixty years ago as a young bride. But the fields had long since sprouted housing developments and shopping centers instead of corn, and now it was nearly impossible to tell where one town ended and another began. And Chicago's O'Hare Field, which Ross said had been "plunked down right in the middle of what used to be Klehm's peony farm," was only a few miles away.

A small brown terrier suddenly bounded across the porch and leaped clear of the steps, to race straight as a bullet toward Ross, who was just lifting a bag out of the trunk of their rental car. For a minute, it looked as if he would collide head on with Ross's legs, but swerved at the last second, not even slowing his speed while he circled wide to come back and do the same thing all over again. His mouth was stretched in a wide smile, and Beth stopped to watch, laughing delightedly at the little dog's uninhibited display of happiness at seeing Ross.

"Brown Dog!" Ross's grandmother admonished, just as Ross yelled, "Come here, Brownie," and grabbed for him. It was apparently a well-practiced game they played, and though the little dog came perilously close, he always managed to escape Ross's clutches at the last minute. Ross grinned, shaking his head at Beth as if to say, "Isn't he something?"

Emily Maguire stepped forward to greet Julia with a warm smile lighting her deep blue eyes. "Ignore that silly dog and come in and get warm," she invited, taking Julia's shoulders in her outstretched hands to give her a brief embrace. Her hair was completely white but plentiful, and she wore it twisted into a loose knot pinned at the back of her head. Still a beautiful woman at eighty-four, Julia thought, as she watched Emily turn toward Ross, just coming through the door. They exchanged one long loving look—eye to eye, since Emily was every bit as tall as he was—before he wrapped his arms around her and kissed her cheek. Then both of them were laughing and talking at the same time.

Later, when they went upstairs, Ross deposited Beth's bag in a room that was all jonquil yellow and cheery in spite of the gray winter day, and then Julia's and his own in the larger room across the hall. Julia started to protest, sure that Emily would disapprove, but Ross was adamant. "There's only one moral standard in this house, Julie love—honesty. What else would you expect from someone who would name that mutt Brown Dog!"

Julia wanted to point out that he might be confusing honesty with a lack of imagination, then decided to simply follow his lead.

Ross picked up on her hesitancy. "Have you got something to hide, Julie? Okay, okay, I know that's a question I shouldn't be asking on Christmas Eve! But she already knows how I feel about you, so she'd probably be worried if we *didn't* sleep together!"

"I didn't realize you were so devious, Ross. Talking about

me behind my back, and surprise parties, and who knows what else,'' she retorted almost petulantly, thinking about Beth's revelation two nights ago in her apartment, when it had come time to go to bed. ''I'm taking my own room if it's okay with you, Mom. Ross and I talked about it a long time ago, so there's no need for you to get all up tight and pretend you don't sleep together when I'm not here.''

''Don't talk to me about devious, girl. I've been taking lessons from you,'' Ross chided playfully, rocking her inside his arms. She made a face at him and pulled away, then took her cosmetic bag and disappeared into the bathroom.

Emily was waiting for them in the kitchen with a pot of hot tea. Beth was there ahead of them, and was at work on the plate of Christmas cookies set out on the kitchen table. ''I hope you don't mind that I looked around some, Mrs. Maguire,'' she was saying. ''You've got some fantastic stuff in this house.''

''Old-fashioned, I suspect you mean,'' Emily replied.

''Maybe. My mom lives in an apartment in New York, and I live there with her part of the time, when I'm not in school. But her place is, well, like her, sort of all mixed up.'' She tossed Julia an impish grin to let her know she was teasing, at the same time reaching for another cookie. ''And Maman—she's one of my grandmothers—has lots of things from France. Different from what most people have—but maybe that's because she's just different, period.''

''And your other grandmother?'' Emily asked, ignoring Julia and Ross.

Beth bit the leg off a camel wearing a green sugar saddle blanket and chewed it slowly, thinking. ''She lives up in the Panhandle, and her house is pretty boring. She likes plastic flowers and she paints china.'' She grimaced to show what she thought of that. ''But she means well. Spends hours at the hospital as a volunteer, and cooking for Meals-on-Wheels.''

Julia was somewhat amazed at her daughter's perceptiveness. Talk turned to questions about Beth's school, with Ross adding some impressions of his own, then to Julia's work, and finally to Ross's surprise party at her office. At last, Ross got up to go cut wood for the fireplace, making a special point of reminding "all you girls that tonight is Christmas Eve—and it's time to get on with it." Beth and Brownie decided to go with him.

There was a tradition in this house at Christmas, Ross had explained to Julia, and on Christmas Eve the menu was always the same—baked ham with cherry preserves made from the tree in Emily's yard, baked acorn squash halves with butter and brown sugar in the center, and a salad—and it was served late because Emily went out early in the evening to deliver gifts and cookies to friends. Only the dessert varied from year to year, and Ross had asked Julia if she'd like to do that part. She suspected it was his way of making her feel a part of his family. While Ross and Beth were gone Julia and Emily worked together in companionable silence in the kitchen, Emily cutting the squash in half and scooping out the seeds while Julia prepared pastry for pie.

"You don't mind, Julia?" Emily asked at length. "A computer for a Christmas present? It's not what most women would want, I should think."

"Mind?" The word fairly jumped out of her mouth, and then she had to laugh. "Oh, I see what you mean. No. I've been going crazy without one, in fact. I thought I'd have to wait until he got everything worked out. I never dreamed he'd do this. I have to confess that I even sort of suspected him of using the computer to make me dependent on him," she admitted, cutting the shortening into the flour mixture. "It's so hard not to put people into neatly labeled little niches, isn't it? I know better, and I hate it when people do it to me. Still, I can't seem to stop myself at times."

Emily turned away from the sink to look at Julia then. "You've brought the light back into his eyes, Julia, that's enough. The sparkle, the devilment, is there again—you know what I mean?"

Julia nodded and smiled, knowing exactly what she meant.

"It was gone, for such a long time. As if a light had gone out somewhere inside. Since Maria. You know about her?"

"Yes," Julia whispered. "I can hardly bear to think what it must have been like for him. It's so sad."

"Yes, to lose a child is perhaps the worst. But to be the one to find her like that, her eyes still open."

"Oh, my God, no," Julia breathed. Emily's words brought a flash of insight as Julia suddenly realized what Ross had really been trying to tell her that night at his house, out by the pond, before he'd turned and lashed out at her about her mother. "Sometimes, I can't seem to get her out of my head," he'd mumbled.

It was the picture in his head—the reason there were times when he couldn't sleep—the picture of his small daughter's body floating in a swimming pool, her eyes open, staring up at him!

Chapter 19

"WHY DON'T I load the stuff in the car while you get your coat, Gran, and then we'll get started," Ross suggested as he came back into the house. "The sooner we leave, the quicker we get to unwrap the stuff under the tree. I'm getting awfully anxious, aren't you?" He looked to Beth for confirmation. "Julia can be doing her pie, and Beth will put your ham and squash in the oven whenever you say, so it'll all be ready when we get back."

"I intend to drive myself, Ross, right up until it's time to go to the happy hunting ground," his grandmother stated emphatically, giving him a no-nonsense look. "But if you wish to ride along while Beth and I make a few deliveries I'll be glad to have your company. However, we do not require a chaperone, so you may wish to reconsider. You could prepare the fire for this evening, instead, and even have it going for us when we get back. Julia might even enjoy a little time alone with you for a change. It's Christmas Eve—have you no romance in your soul, boy?"

Even before she finished, Beth was grinning and glancing back and forth from Ross to Emily. It was apparent even to her that Ross had met his match in this white-haired woman more than twice his age. Julia washed up a few dishes while Ross carried the packages to Emily's car without further argument.

"I have the feeling I missed something—or was all that really just so we could be alone?" she asked as he came in the back door.

He shrugged. "I've been bugging her about not driving at night anymore. She knows that's why I volunteered to take her this time, but she also knows how much I hate going there at Christmas. It was just her way of letting me off the hook."

"Where? How can you hate delivering a few gifts?"

"She's taking cookies and gifts to a home for kids who are up for adoption." He picked up a towel and one of the bowls she'd put into the drying rack, his mind obviously somewhere else, and Julia sensed that he'd just stepped out onto thin ice and was feeling his way very carefully. For the next few seconds, there was no sound in the kitchen except the clink of dishes and pans.

"It's where my mother found me. One of the unadoptables, I was. At the grand old age of five," he told her quietly, continuing to wipe the outside of the bowl, as if it wasn't already dry.

"Have you ever lost a dog, and gone to the pound to look for him? All those poor eternally hopeful animals! All colors, shapes and sizes, long-haired and short, purebreds and mongrels. As soon as someone shows up, every one of them starts barking and jumping against the cage to attract attention, so pathetically eager for the touch of a hand or the sound of a voice."

Julia watched his face as he struggled with his metaphorical tale, wanting to reach out and touch the little boy he was telling her about, to somehow comfort him.

"Most puppies are cute, no matter the breed, so they're the most likely to catch the eye of some kid who comes there to pick out a pet. But the older ones, well—" His voice broke. "They aren't so cute anymore, and they're old enough to know it. To know they're going to get passed over again. But they keep on hoping, anyway."

He suddenly set the bowl down on the kitchen counter and dropped the towel into it, then jerked open the door to the back yard and disappeared, slamming the door behind him.

"You're in the wrong business, Julie," Ross commented, rising from the table. "I've never tasted anything like that rhubarb pie before—must be French!" He walked around behind her chair and planted a kiss on the top of her head.

"It's my mother's, but I think she got the recipe from my father's mother, and I suppose we've both added a touch or two of our own."

"See what I told you about her being all mixed up," Beth injected.

"Okay now, girls, it's time. Leave the dishes where they are. We can all pitch in later," Ross urged, sounding as eager as a child, "but right now I'm heading for the Christmas tree, and I'm not waiting another minute to start."

The only lights in the high-ceilinged living room came from the tall Scotch pine occupying the alcove formed by a large bay window and from the fire in the fireplace. "Why don't you turn on the radio, Ross?" his grandmother suggested as she eased down into an overstuffed chair near the fireplace. "It's almost time for the Christmas Carols from Kings College in Cambridge."

Julia slipped off her shoes and curled her legs up on the couch beside her, massaging her toes with one hand to try to warm them. Ross had insisted she and Beth dress comfortably—like they would at home, he said—so she was wearing flannel-lined jeans and a Shaker-knit wool sweater, which were warm enough. But her feet were always cold in the winter except when she wore lined boots.

"How about playing Santa, Beth?" Ross suggested, since she was already on her knees next to the tree, anxiously waiting for someone to give the magic word.

"Sure," she agreed readily. "Here, Mom. One for you."

She handed Julia a tiny package which, as it turned out, was from Beth herself. Then while Julia was opening it, she looked back under the tree and discovered a brilliant red envelope with her own name on it. "Hey, I didn't see that before," she exclaimed. "A check, I'll bet!"

Ross's face didn't give away even the hint of an answer. "Why don't you open it and see?"

Beth tore open the flap and pulled out a small plastic card. Julia watched curiously as her face lit in a pleased smile. "Hey, thanks. I didn't really think you'd be able to pull it off." She handed it over for Julia to see. "A proxy card for the Perry-Castañeda library at the university. That means I can check out books for a whole semester at a time." She suddenly felt something bumpy down in one corner of the envelope, and dug a couple of fingers in again to investigate. This time, there was wonder on her face as she realized what it was—a flexible gold ring with two keys on it!

"Mom!" she yelled, then immediately looked at Ross. "She really said it was okay? I don't believe it!" She began to giggle and then jumped up, too excited to stay sitting on the floor. Julia laughed as Beth came over and hugged first her, and then Ross, at the same time explaining their "arrangement" to Emily.

Ross was "leasing" his red Mercedes convertible to Beth for the rest of the school year, and next year, too, if she wanted it. They'd talked a "deal"—Ross would maintain the car and pay for the insurance, if Beth would take care of the gas, oil and regular servicing out of her monthly allowance—but only if her mother approved. A strong urge to list all the conditions she wanted to put on the "deal" tugged at Julia's peace of mind, but she didn't want to spoil Beth's pleasure by anticipating and voicing all the things that might go wrong. It was time to let go, to have faith in Beth's good sense—and in Ross's ability to handle any problems that did come up.

Inside the little package from Beth, Julia discovered a Victorian picture button, one of the ornate creations that had been all the rage back in the late 1880s, when it simply wasn't fashionable to own clothing that didn't sport decorative buttons. She'd seen a few in museums, usually with scenes from fables or mythology on them, but this one was far more exotic—about an inch and a half in diameter, it was a miniature scene in what appeared to be the garden of a harem.

"It's beautiful, Beth. I love it. But where in heaven's name did you ever find it?"

"Ross pointed it out to me, but I knew right away it was for you, Mom," Beth replied. "She likes that sort of stuff," she explained to Emily. "Has an old rug from Turkey on her living room floor, with some of the same colors." She turned back to the tree then, picked up another package and handed it to Emily. The long fat cylinder was wrapped in glossy royal blue paper and tied with natural angora yarn.

"I've got to admit I'm really curious about that one," Ross commented.

"Yeah, whoever it's from wishes to remain anonymous," Beth teased, though she'd recognized Julia's handwriting on the card, which had only one name on it—Emily's.

Emily slipped off the yarn, pulled the paper free at each end and peeled it off. Inside was a loosely rolled piece of textured paper, thick but flexible, which she carefully unrolled. Emily glanced quickly at Julia, then back at the paper. All eyes were on Emily as a slow smile of pleasure spread from her lips to her eyes. "Yes," she murmured, "I can understand." She paused for a moment. "How much you feel what you see! I will keep it near, treasure it always, my dear."

Ross walked around behind Emily's chair, overcome with curiosity. He looked down at the big sheet of paper she held open between her hands—an unframed watercolor painting. The colors had a luminous intensity that was rare to the medium, especially the blues and greens, he thought, as he continued to stare, trying to puzzle out why it seemed vaguely familiar. It was loose, and flowing, with no recognizable forms, though he supposed it could be construed as a landscape.

And then, all at once, everything fell into place. The creek that ran through his property, the chalky limestone bluff below the dam, and the wildflowers—the reds and yellows blended together into a mass of orange in the distance. He bent closer, searching for a signature as he held his breath, suspicion building into hope. And then he saw the two tiny red initials, drawn back to back and almost hidden against the orange—JB—and hope blossomed into certainty. She was painting again!

Ross moved to the couch, beside Julia, and simply took her hand between his and held it, stroking lightly, still thoughtful and silent. He smiled indulgently as Beth tried to blow up her ten-foot-long alligator pool float by mouth, knowing all the while that it was impossible. At last, he let himself get caught up again in the contagious excitement of Christmas when he opened the package from Julia to find a hand-knit light blue cardigan sweater—"the color of your eyes," she explained. The modified shawl collar, side pockets and braided leather toggles down the front made it into a casual jacket. He liked it so much he jumped up to model it, aping the way he'd seen Julia model.

While he was up, Ross bent down to swoop an arm under the tree and lift up another package, this one about the size of a shoe box, and carry it back to Julia. "Try this, and if they're still cold after that, I'll get you a blanket."

"Oh, Ross, not more!" she exclaimed quietly. "You're making me feel—"

"Shh," he admonished lovingly as he sat down, "just open it," then turned and laid a bent knee on the cushion between them so he could watch her. Julia suspected he might be playing a trick, that he'd put something small in a bigger box in order to mislead her, but when she spread open the tissue paper inside, she found a pair of slippers—a soft, rich vanilla-colored leather, lined and edged with dark brown fur—that were absolutely delicious to the touch.

"Deerskin?" she asked softly, stroking first the fur and then the leather.

Ross nodded, smiling. "Slip them on," he suggested, "see if they fit."

She tried, but found the toes stuffed with tissue, so had to stop and pull that out first. "They feel wonderful," she breathed with a suspiciously sensual sigh, "and fit perfectly." She started to get up, and when she did one of the wads of tissue dropped to the carpet with a thud. Surprised, she bent over and picked it up.

She was right the first time, she thought, slowly unwinding the crinkled paper, feeling the small box inside. A ring? He wouldn't! She wasn't ready for this. Then a wave of certainty hit. How dare he, without even consulting her? And in front of Beth and Emily! Perhaps that was intentional, to put pressure on her, make it harder for her to say no! Her face flushed as she caught sight of the little velvet box, but she didn't hesitate a second before pushing up the spring-loaded lid.

At first, all she could do was gape—at the pavé set diamond and cabochon ruby butterfly brooch—as expectation and reality collided in confusion, before joy and pleasure washed away everything else.

It wasn't until later that Ross discovered still another gift from Julia, because, appropriately enough, she'd hidden it under his pillow—a Japanese pillow book. He'd never seen one before, or so he claimed, though they were a tradition of long standing in the Middle East and Japan, where they were a common and acceptable form of sexual stimulation. This one was very old, and the ends of the wide strap of leather holding it closed were fastened at one edge with a tiny silver padlock.

"To help me get your mind off your computer," she whispered seductively as she offered him the key to the lock.

Ross began turning the pages, looking at the erotic pictures with an almost clinical eye, instantly fascinated by the variety he found there, in both pictorial composition and sexual positions. After only a few minutes, though, he closed the book with a quiet laugh and reached up to switch off the lamp beside the bed.

"Only when you're around, Julie love! I doubt I could stand

the torture, otherwise,'' he murmured, sliding down under the covers and pulling her into his arms. ''You sure as hell haven't needed any help so far—but I'll keep it handy, just in case!''

Julie snuggled to fit herself against him. ''You've given me too much, Ross, but it was a wonderful Christmas. The computers, and—oh, I love my slippers. And my brooch makes me feel—I don't think I should tell you how! I love it—and I love you,'' she murmured contentedly.

He tipped her chin up, wishing he could see her face better, then whispered, ''I love you, too, Julie. Merry Christmas,'' just before his lips came down on hers. Their loving was long and slow at first, which perhaps was why the end, when it did come, was so exquisitely intense. And Ross held her where she was, cushioning her body with his own, long after their breathing slowed, reluctant to let her move even a few inches away.

''My slippers are a good fit, don't you think?'' Julia murmured into the curve of his neck, as she rolled off him to lay on her side.

Her innocent-sounding question was somehow so incongruent and unexpected that all kinds of warning flags went up inside Ross's head. He suddenly had a strong sense of déjà vu, which caused him to remember other times when she'd ''set him up.''

''If you say so,'' he ventured conditionally, grinning and waiting.

She made a pretense of surprise, lifting her head to glance down at his face, though she couldn't really see him very well in the dark. ''You don't know? About Cinderella?'' Disbelief was evident in the tone of her voice. ''Honest?''

''Honest,'' he agreed. ''So put me out of my misery, Julie.''

''Weeellll,'' she began reluctantly, drawing out the word. ''Charles Perrault, who wrote the original version of Cinderella back in the late sixteen hundreds sometime, called it *pantoufle en vair*—a slipper of fur.'' She spelled the French word for him so he'd understand. "But texts were hand-copied back then, and somehow it came out *pantoufle en verre*—glass—and never got corrected." This time she spelled the French word for glass.

"Un, huh, that's interesting," he commented, somehow doubting that was all there was to it.

"Fur has always been associated with eroticism, and in the Cinderella story, the fur-trimmed slipper that fit perfectly was symbolic of the perfect vagina to please the prince! So you see, when I saw the slippers tonight, I thought you wanted to know—" She felt the growl begin in his throat even before she heard it.

Then he was rolling her over onto her back, his knee pushing her thighs apart, all in one fluid motion. In less than a second, he was home, and breathing the words into her ear, again and again, with each thrust. "It fits, Julie, my love. It fits."

A few of the New York fashion houses, such as Liz Claiborne, showed their fall-winter collections in February, but most American designers waited until the end of April or early May. Scheduling their press preview for the first week in March, just prior to regional market week, meant that Taggart was coming out somewhere in between, but it also meant long days and frazzled tempers.

For Julia, the compressed calendar meant planning for the fall-winter New York and regional marts while also working with Max to coordinate the delivery of promotional materials and sample garments in time for summer market week the last of January. And working with Elaine to complete all the fall-winter press materials earlier than usual, selecting the models, and even the right music. It also meant that decisions made one day were unmade the next, as Ben gyrated wildly between not caring a fig about who or what, and acting like an impossible-to-satisfy prima donna. Working with Elaine and Max was easy. Acting as go-between with Tony Gianni was not.

In spite of the almost constant crises and hassles, however, time suddenly seemed to slow down for Julia. And as January progressed, a kind of lethargy began to take possession of her, subdued but ever-present, like background music. At times she felt as if her entire life had been put on hold, as if she'd traveled past some unmarked point of no return—making it as impossible to go back as she now found it to go forward. She was waiting, but she didn't know what for—nor was she even sure she'd recognize whatever it was when, or if, it did arrive.

Even the cold light of the January sky felt heavy, and the gray stone buildings across the way seemed to press in, as if both were conspiring to hold her prisoner at Taggart. A dull sameness pervaded everything, morning turning unnoticeably into afternoon, both inside her office and out. At times she saw herself as a big snowflake, like the ones coming down outside her window right now. Wafted aimlessly from place to place by the unpredictable winds of someone else's need. Carried along, helpless, toward an unknown destination. She stood by the window, watching the flakes float by, trying to focus on one of them long enough to track its destiny. Would her life, too, end alone, in the cold, arrested without warning by the ledge of some high window? Or might she continue falling, until she no longer had any recognizable identity?

She carried on odd bits and pieces of silent dialogue with herself, and began to agonize over every decision, even the little ones—what to wear today or what to eat. Ross came and went, brightening the gray days with his oh-so-light blue eyes, warm smile and caressing hands, and they talked almost daily on the phone. At times some long-submerged worry would pop out, shocking them both, as it had this morning when she'd called him just to talk, then surprised even herself by asking if he would like to have another child.

"You're pregnant?" he'd shot back immediately. He may have tried to sound calm, but concern was heavy in his voice. "I thought you were taking the pill."

"No. Yes. I mean I'm not pregnant. But—well, you must want another child of your own. And time is running out for me, though it doesn't really feel like I'm—oh, I know it's not too late yet, but—" The frustration of being unable to decide anything, big or little, threatened to overwhelm her. "The trouble is—I—I don't think, uh, I'm not sure I want to have a—"

"For God's sake, Julia, with all you have to do right now, how in hell can you find time to dream up still another problem?" he asked, his voice heavy with exasperation as he interrupted her stammering attempt to bring what had been preying on her mind out into the open. "Is it something we have to decide right this minute?"

"No, of course not. *We* don't have to decide anything! I'm sorry I bothered you with my inconsequential concerns. But *I* don't want to have any more children, and I just thought maybe you ought to know—so you can go find yourself another woman. One who does!" And with that she'd slammed the receiver back down on its cradle, where it wobbled precariously for a few seconds before she covered her face with her hands and burst into tears.

She was staring at the silent dark screen of her computer terminal, longing for the solitude and time to lose herself in designing again, as she had during those few weeks in Austin, when her office door flew open without warning and bounced off the wall with a loud bang—so sudden and violent that it brought Julia right up out of her chair. Impossible images flashed before her eyes, and for one frozen instant she thought she was hallucinating. She glanced frantically at her watch, trying to make the world right itself again. And then she heard him speak.

"Get your coat and boots on! Now!" Ross ordered from the doorway, one hand propped belligerently on his hip while he waited for her. His face was flushed and he was breathing hard. Either he'd been running—or he was very angry. Julia struggled to get her arms into her coat, without a word of protest, and then followed meekly when he took her by the hand and dragged her through Connie's office.

"Julie's going home, Consuelo. And she won't be in tomorrow, either. Call if you really need her, but try not to, okay?" Connie nodded, but looked too concerned for him to leave it at that. "Just a small emergency, nothing I can't handle."

He spoke only a few words in the taxi on the way to her apartment—"Where the hell are your gloves?"—which didn't make her feel any better, but at least he continued to hold her hand, enclosing it between both of his from time to time, trying to warm it. As soon as they got inside the door, he stripped off his coat, then hers, throwing them over the back of a chair as he guided her to the bedroom and left her standing near the bed. "Get those clothes off while I run your bath water."

Julia began smiling, right where she stood, as an absolutely wonderful sense of relief washed over her. All the awful, nagging decisions either didn't exist anymore or were being made by someone else, freeing her from some heavy burden she hadn't even realized she was carrying. The water was hot, just the way she liked it, and birch-scented steam rose from the bubbly surface as she sank into it, then slowly leaned back and closed her eyes.

Did she doze for a few minutes? Ross was holding a glass of white wine to her lips, tipping it up as she took one sip, then another. Then he was searching the linen closet for a washcloth, spreading it over his big hand to soap it. He began to wash her, all over, as if she were a baby, and Julia closed her eyes again, shutting out everything except the mental images created by the touch of his smooth-slick soapy hand, followed by the slightly rough cloth. Sliding up and down her arms, across her chest and down the valley between her breasts, only to rise and come back around again, in ever smaller circles, yet denying her now-aching nipples. A sigh escaped her lips without conscious volition as his hand began a new assault, this time traveling down over her stomach. His fingers followed a natural pathway through wet curls, finding her already moist and sensitive, caressing for one brief second before descending again, then withdrawing and continuing on down and around her thighs. Lifting her legs out of the water one at a time to soap them all the way to her toes, sliding his fingers between them, tickling and arousing her at the same time. Then she felt the edge of the cold wineglass against her lips again, and without even opening her eyes, accepted another sip.

Engulfed now in the sensual haze wrought by the loving ministrations of his wonderful hands, Julia at last felt strong arms under hers, lifting her to stand, but only long enough to enclose her in a big rough bath towel. Then he lifted her off her feet and carried her to the bed—where the covers had been pulled back ready to receive her—and began to make slow, gorgeously gentle love to her body and soul. Rubbing his hands through the towel to dry her, then gradually exposing her throat—drying, licking, then drying again—before exposing the swell of one breast and doing the same to it. At last allowing one straining nipple his unhurried attention, then covering it carefully before going to the other, working his way downward with all the maddening constraint he could muster.

Her body waged war with itself, fighting to prolong the nearly unbearable agony of pleasure while at the same time seeking its ecstatic end. All the forces within gathered and focused on one spot, like the sun through a magnifying glass, and when finally he entered her, slowly but fully, she burst into a white-hot flame, burning brightly for unmeasured minutes before dying into a glowing ember—warm, quiet, constant, and content.

Ross had planned to call out for dinner, but after raiding Julia's refrigerator and freezer, he decided he could fix it himself. So while she slept, he put potatoes in the oven to bake, defrosted steaks in her microwave and prepared a simple salad of lettuce and tomatoes. Then he built a fire in the fireplace and set the table, rummaging through drawers, cabinets and closets until he found everything he wanted—including candles for the table—and put an audio cassette into her player. When the stage was finally set to his liking, he put the steaks under the broiler and went in to wake her. It was nearly ten o'clock and dark outside, but she needed to eat.

The next thing Julia knew, the bed felt like it was tilting, and something warm and heavy pushed against her hip, nudging her over. Gentle fingers stroked her cheek and smoothed back her hair, then slowly massaged her neck. "Julie." The voice was so low she barely heard it—wondered if she was dreaming. "Julie love. Time to wake up, dinner's ready." She opened one eye, cautiously, and then the other, to an orange-yellow glow, coming from another room, trying to make sense of both time and place. Then she felt herself being lifted to a sitting position she wasn't quite prepared for, and wrapped in something warm—enclosed inside his arms. "Are you awake yet?"

She nodded, her words muffled against his shoulder. "I'm so glad you came, Ross."

"I know." He gave her a quick squeeze, then pushed her upright. "Go wash your face. Brush your teeth. Dinner is waiting, madam, and I want you wide awake so you can really appreciate the chef's efforts. No need to dress. Come as your delectable self, but with robe, please—or you might get more service than you're ready for!"

They ate in front of the fire, which was the only light in the room besides the candles, sitting on the floor on cushions placed between the couch and Julia's glass coffee table. Ross kept up a constant lighthearted conversation to entertain and distract, finally allowing a peaceful silence to fall while he leaned back against the front edge of the couch to watch the flickering light play over her face and hair.

Julia joined him with a sigh of obvious contentment. "I doubt I'll be able to waddle back to bed. You'll probably have to carry me again—if I'm not too heavy after all that." She waved a hand at her empty plate, giggled at the thought, then fell silent as Ross enclosed her hand in his, staring into the fire.

"What I said on the phone, Ross—I don't know what got into me. You're not still angry?"

"At myself, yes. I should have figured out that you needed help sooner."

"Is that what it was?" she mumbled wonderingly, turning the idea this way and that, considering the possibility.

"I should've seen it sooner. Or you should've said something. I'm sorry."

"But why now? I don't remember ever needing help before." She stopped, knowing that was simply not true—and that it was time to stop lying to herself, and to him.

"I doubt that. It doesn't mean you're weak or can't take it. You're a super woman, Julie love, but not superwoman. She's a cartoon character. You're real. And all us real people need someone to lean on sometimes. When things get to be too much and we just sort of cave in. There's no shame in admitting it, or in asking for help. I wonder why the hell it takes most of us so long to see that! Maybe you're just not used to the idea—that you're not alone now, I mean—that I can be here, or anywhere else, any time you need me, even when you just sort of would like to have me around." He smiled engagingly, trying to entice her to do the same.

She nodded, tentatively, still trying out the idea, then whispered, "Yes, maybe."

He leaned forward to turn a log, then settled back again, reaching out an arm to pull her closer. "Anyway, the world's not going to come to an end if you take a day off to catch your breath. And you'll be able to handle things a lot better if you do. So right now, all that's allowed on your schedule is sleeping, eating, and—" He grinned with self-satisfaction, then began feathering quick kisses all along the edge of her forehead, eye and ear.

"Ross? What I said on the phone this morning?" She paused, reflecting. "I didn't really mean it."

"Sure you did. Oh, maybe not all of it. You don't want me out hunting another woman, do you?" He bent around to see the expression on her face, grinning to let her know he was only teasing. "It came out because it was there, inside some place. Going macho—isn't that what you've accused me of doing a couple of times? Do you think I have to impregnate you in order to prove, to you or anyone else, that I'm a man? Or that having my child is a way to prove you love me?" He blew a breath out between his lips. "I thought maybe you and I—well, that we might have managed to get ourselves disentangled from that kind of adolescent garbage, Julia. But I guess sometimes the old stuff comes back to haunt us, doesn't it?"

"It wasn't that, Ross. I—was thinking about Maria, how you lost her, how much you miss her, that you should—" The tears were welling again, and she blinked furiously, frustrated anew by her inability to control them.

"Shh," he whispered against her temple. "We have Beth, Julie. You and Anne-Marie and Carey have raised a wonderful girl, but now she's mine, too—or at least that's the way it feels to me. But most important of all is us, and I meant what I said this morning. *We* will decide about this together. It's your body, so it's a very personal kind of decision for you to make, and I'm not going to let you carry around a load of guilt if you decide you don't want to. I guess I'll miss Maria, think about her, wonder about what she might have been like, as long as I live. But I don't want a child because I need to feel immortal, either—out of fear that my genes are going to die out if I don't reproduce myself. There are already lots of kids in this world, and too many without parents or anyone else to give them the kind of care and love they need. The point is, I have some pretty strong feelings when it comes to children, Julie, as you've probably surmised by now. And we need to talk about that, talk to each other—not have you putting words in my mouth, or imagining what I do and don't want."

Chapter 20

DURING THE NEXT two weeks, that night and the following day with Ross began to seem like only an instant in time to Julia, a moment when all the worries, questions and decisions simply didn't exist—only leisurely loving, and sleeping, and eating, and then loving again.

A few days before Julia was due to go to Chicago for January market week, another reported "rumor" about Ben Taggart, Inc., appeared in the *Wall Street Journal*. The result was another flurry of speculation, about not only a big license deal but also a chain of boutiques, both at home and abroad, which in turn sparked another round of trading that sent the price of Taggart shares up three more points. Julia was wealthier on paper by about a half-million dollars than she'd been just three months ago. Under the circumstances, however, she didn't find that news particularly reassuring. Who or what was the source of all the rumors? Someone at the meeting when Tony talked about licensing and boutiques? Or had that information simply been passed on to others down the line? Certainly Tony's highly "suggestive" press releases didn't help dampen the rumors. The question was still on her mind when she went to get Ben's final approval on the press materials, which were due to go to the printers before she left town.

"Taggart's going higher than we ever imagined back in the old days, isn't it, Julia?" Ben observed happily. He claimed complete ignorance about the source of the rumors, then blithely wondered if perhaps the boutique idea wasn't a good one.

"I'm worried about what's going to happen if or when we don't go through with a license deal, Ben. And if we don't open the boutiques. Have you thought about that? Our shares are liable to take a really big tumble then, maybe go lower than they were before all this started." She hoped to at least bring him down to earth, so he'd be prepared for what could be coming next, but his enthusiasm was at too high a pitch to be dampened by anything she said.

"Oh, I doubt that, Julia. I'd be willing to wager, in fact, that when the press gets a look at our Trump Tower show next month, the price of a share of Taggart will go up still a couple of more points. Listen, that reminds me, I want your opinion on something else." He rummaged through a stack of sketches on the table next to his drawing board. "Ah, here they are. Take a look at these, tell me what you think."

She flipped through the sheets of drawing paper, recognizing instantly that they weren't Ben's. "A new sketcher?" She wondered if he was interviewing for another assistant and hadn't mentioned it to her.

"No. A junior designer is what I've got in mind, with the possibility of giving him his own name, starting a new line, if he works out. It's about time, don't you think? Just look at those, Julia—the originality, the sensitivity to line, the fluidity. He could be another Vionnet. Do you recognize the work?"

That sounded a warning bell somewhere on the edges of her mind. "Should I?" she responded noncommittally, not even looking up.

"Nat Thorne!" He laughed, anticipating her surprise. "He's wasted in menswear, Julia. You can see that for yourself. This is where his talent lies. I've been watching him. We talk from time to time—he brings his ideas, asks my opinion, looks at what I'm doing."

Yeah, Julia thought, and apparently also massages your ego. "I don't know, Ben. Let's go slow on this. Alex needs Nat, relies on him. And we've got too much going right now to even consider anything more at the moment, right?" She deftly changed the subject, showing him the promotion materials he needed to review.

Julia spent two hectic days at the Chicago Apparel Center—a twenty-five-floor building housing eight hundred showrooms that carried three thousand lines year-round, plus another thousand during market weeks. But late in the afternoon on the second day, she checked out of the Holiday Inn topping the Center, took a cab to the Chicago and Northwestern station and caught a commuter train to Arlington Heights. She'd talked briefly with Emily on the phone, so she was expecting her. They fixed dinner together, talking all the while, about nothing particularly taxing or personal. Emily described the Edvard Munch retrospective at the Chicago Art Institute she'd gone to the previous week.

"They say he was fixated on women, sex and death, but I don't see it—the fixation, I mean. If you look at them all together, it's apparent that he was developing his ideas. Oh, there was one woodcut of a woman's head, a portrait of ecstasy, I suppose you might call it. A dreamy, flowing sexual sort of thing with a green border—with sperm floating in it."

Julia laughed, entranced and entertained by Emily's perceptive and pithy comments—with the result that she felt rested and ready to go again by the time she arrived back at work the following day.

The next two weeks were filled with last-minute decisions about the numbers scheduled for the Trump Tower, final fittings and accessorizing. By mid-February it looked like they were coming in slightly ahead of schedule, which at least meant a little breathing space for last-minute hitches.

The press kits had just gone out, and Julia was relaxing at

her desk with the new issue of WWD when the world suddenly came crashing down, almost crushing her for a few seconds—a sensation that was quickly followed by shocked disbelief. Angry protestations screamed silently inside her head, as she reached out and flipped the intercom button. "Consuelo. Would you come in here, right away?"

The door to her office opened almost immediately. "What's wrong? Are you sick?" Connie almost ran toward Julia, who sat with one elbow on her desk, leaning her forehead into the palm of her hand. Something was very, very wrong, and Connie hadn't liked the sound of Julia's voice at all.

"I want to be sure I'm not imagining this. Come take a look. Tell me what you see," Julia instructed in a quiet voice.

It took only a second for the shock to register on Connie's face, which told Julia everything she needed to know. So it was true! There were knockoffs, and then there were knockoffs—and this was the worst possible kind!

"Dear Lord, what happens now?" Connie whispered.

"Find Tony—and Max and Elaine, too. And, uh, Alex. Ask them to drop whatever they're doing. Emergency. Tell Elaine to bring her copy of WWD. Did I mention Ben? Get him. Ah damn, I've got to think up some way to soften the blow. This is going to kill him. Him? What about the rest of us?" She looked up, surprised to see Connie still standing in the doorway. "Go on—I'm just thinking out loud!"

Julia pored over the pages again, analyzing, counting and waiting.

"Have you read that?" she asked, answering Elaine's quizzical expression as she came through the door, pointing to the copy of WWD she carried in one hand. "Take a look, page eleven. Quick, before the others get here."

Tony exploded through the door. "What the hell's got your bowels in an uproar this time, Julia?"

During the past month, Julia thought she'd become inured to his snide, patronizing comments where she was concerned, or at least had learned to live with them—but this time his words sent her into "overload," and she just turned away without speaking.

Elaine poked her copy of WWD at him, open to page eleven.

"Holy shit!" It seemed to burst out involuntarily, and he darted a frantic glance at Julia, then at Elaine, as if to confirm what he was seeing.

"What's all the brouhaha about, Julia baby?" Alex queried jovially, though he looked as if he hadn't slept for a week, worse than Julia could remember in a long, long time. The Designers' Collective was only two days from now.

"Looks like we may be in big trouble." She showed him.

"Jesus Christ!" was all he could think to say as he looked down at the pages she held out to him.

Max and Ben came in together at that moment, and there was nothing she could do to soften the blow for Ben. He took one look, then dropped like a stone into the chair next to Julia's desk, his face suddenly drained of all color, too stunned to utter even an angry exclamation. It was as quiet as a church for a few minutes, with everyone but Ben gathered around the two copies of the trade tabloid, trying to determine the extent of the damage.

Knoblock was a moderate-priced apparel manufacturer, one of several well-known knockoff houses which produced less expensive copies of last season's designer best sellers. A few years ago, under the guidance of a new vice president, the company had shifted from polyester to updated styles in natural and blended fabrics, tripling its sales within five years. For the last couple of years, far from trying to hide the fact that it was a knockoff house, Knoblock had shown a collection twice a year, usually at some fancy restaurant, at which they proudly pointed out and identified their copies to the fashion press—an Anne Klein jacket in pink tweed, shown by the designer last year in red herringbone tweed, going for $90 instead of $380, or a Gloria Sachs sweater offered at $36 instead of $180. The reason they could sell for less was, quite simply, volume. While Ralph Lauren might sell five hundred sweaters with a knitted-in farm scene at $400, Knoblock would produce twenty-five thousand and sell them for $60.

Up until now, the company had always copied individual styles—one or two from Perry Ellis, another from Laura Ashley, one from Anne Klein, and a few from Liz Claiborne and Ben Taggart. The big news, according to WWD, was that this year the company was doing a coherent collection. What the WWD piece didn't say, however, was that this time Knoblock has ripped off designer originals that hadn't even been shown—Ben's fall-winter collection!

The first thing Julia thought was, There's a rat somewhere in the house of Taggart! But then two other "facts of life" also quickly became crystal clear to her. One was that Taggart couldn't possibly keep it quiet because the press kits were already out, and it wouldn't take the fashion press very long to put two and two together. The other was that Knoblock had been able to make a reasonably safe prediction about the likely best sellers in the collection, reducing the risks inherent in knocking off originals that hadn't been shown and had no sales record, because Ben's designs were largely derivative from the previous season. And that was one of the dangers inherent in sticking with a fashion cycle that was in the decline stage.

Max was the first to speak. "I suppose in a way this just confirms some of the points Julie's been trying to make—the high-volume producers are the ones who can afford computerized manufacturing technologies, so now they're able to produce knockoffs faster than they used to."

"Shove your fucking computers and high-tech crap," Tony exploded. "What I want to know is who the shit's responsible for this? And what do we do now!" He turned to Max. "You call this security?"

Connie poked her head around the door and mimed to Julia that she had a phone call. "Tell whoever it is I'll call back," Julia said. "I don't know when."

"You know as well as I do there's no way we can keep what's inside somebody's head from going out, Tony," Max responded to Tony's criticism. "But we can talk about our security measures later. Right now, I suggest we try to figure out just how bad off we really are. What we can't tell from this," he put a finger to the tabloid, "is how much of the collection they're using. So somebody ought to get over to Knoblock and take a look. Now!"

"Yeah, and you can be the somebody," Tony growled, then looked over at Julia. "And take her with you—she knows Ben's stuff from A to Z. His face is too well-known. Keep a low profile, and your mouths shut, understand?" He turned and stomped toward the door, looking at his watch. "It's two o'clock now. Be back here by three, three-thirty at the latest. In my office. Jesus, can't you see what the press is going to do with this one!"

They looked at each other after he'd gone, each one silently puzzling over the same questions. Except for Ben, who still seemed in a daze as he got up and walked slowly out the door.

"Anybody got any ideas about who the creep is who's responsible for this?" Alex asked in a low voice, almost a mumble.

Max shook his head. "Are you ready to go, Julia?" He walked behind Elaine's chair, gave her shoulder a squeeze and then went to help Julia with her coat. "We'll see you in Tony's office, but probably closer to four."

Julia so disliked sitting in judgment that she always tried to get excused from jury duty, but this time there was simply no way she could avoid it. Knoblock had literally, and deliberately, gutted the Taggart fall-winter collection. The very heart of it was gone, the workhorses they were counting on to be big sellers, the styles they'd costed out in the most popular price range to give Taggart the largest margin of profit. Because there was no need to wait until orders came in on those styles, production was scheduled to start well ahead of the opening, which meant that thousands of yards of cloth had already been cut. All that was left were a few glitzy evening dresses and the more experimental numbers, and most of those hadn't moved beyond first pattern. No samples and no costing had been done on them. Another problem was sheer numbers—there simply were not enough left to make a major presentation.

Ben was silent as he listened to Max and Julia report what they'd found at Knoblock. The group in Tony's office was larger than it had been earlier, and included Jon Bloom, Ben's senior assistant, Arlette Kovacs and Katie Dupré from the atelier, as well as Claire Kennamer. Julia wondered where Nat was as she listened to Tony state the obvious.

"We can scratch the Trump Tower—and believe me, it's going to cost us a fucking bundle to back out so goddamned late!" He paced back and forth behind his desk, angry, yet at the same time seeming to relish the challenge of taking charge during a crisis. He certainly wasn't interested in listening to Julia's opinion, or Max's, or anyone else's, for that matter.

"The way I see it, we'll just have to cut our losses and go with what we can salvage from our spring-summer line. That means resurrect the best sellers, run the sample hands twenty-four hours a day, in shifts—hire a few extras to help out—and make them up in whatever fall fabrics we've got left in the warehouse. Add a few of those glitzy gowns and do enough samples to show in Chicago, Dallas, Atlanta and LA, which at least gives us a few extra days."

Ben had come in clutching a sheaf of sketches in one hand, and now he broke his long silence. "I think we're going too fast, Tony. Before we decide about the Tower, maybe we should look at these." He thrust forward the bundle of sketches. "Julia's already seen some of them. They're really awfully good, aren't they, Julia?" He was seeking support wherever he could get it. "If we included some of these, we'd have enough for a presentation—a good one." It had finally hit home with Ben that, for the first time in its short history, the company wasn't going to have a new collection for the most important season of the year, and he was willing to try anything to keep that from happening.

"Lemme see those!" Alex lunged from his chair and grabbed at the sheets Ben held out to Tony, then quickly flipped through them. "Where the shit did you get these?"

"Don't tell me you don't recognize his style, Alex," Ben chided innocently, "even if you've never seen these particular sketches. They're Nat Thorne's, of course. We've already talked, Julia and I, about moving him over to our side of the house, making him a junior designer, maybe give him a new line with his own name after a couple of seasons. He's that good, you know."

Alex glanced at Julia, not wanting to believe what Ben was saying, yet unable to hide the questioning appraisal she saw in his eyes. What could she say?

"Yeah, I guess I'm just beginning to realize how good!" Alex mumbled, subsiding back into his chair. His entire body seemed to sag and slump, and he stared fixedly at his hands, avoiding Julia's eyes.

She noticed Connie crack open the door to Tony's office and peer around the edge again, but was too concerned about Alex to wonder why. Julia was, in fact, torn between what she suspected Alex was thinking, and trying to decide whether it was even possible to use Nat's designs.

"The problem is, Ben, we'd still have to do the patterns, to say nothing of the samples and costing. It would simply take too much time to do that many. We've got exactly two weeks! We'd have a hard time even doing the press stuff in time. Probably couldn't use any photographs, only sketches. What do you think, Elaine?" She felt a light touch on her shoulder, and looked around to find Connie standing half-hidden behind her chair.

"You have a call, Julia," Connie whispered. As Julia almost automatically shook her head, shaking off the interruption, Connie became insistent. "He says I'm to drag you to the phone if necessary. He wants to talk to you now! Says it's important."

Julia jumped up from her chair immediately and followed Connie to the door. "Excuse me a minute. I've got a call," she explained over her shoulder, then dropped her voice to a whisper. "Is it Beth—did he say what's wrong?"

Connie shook her head. "No, it's not about Beth. Line four."

Julia grabbed the phone off Tony's secretary's desk, stabbing at the line of buttons at the same time. "Ross? What's wrong?"

"Take it easy, Julia! Nothing's wrong here. Consuelo told me what happened. Have you decided what you're going to do yet?"

"No. It looks like there's not a lot we can do—except cancel the Tower presentation and see what we can salvage ftom last season's collection. We're talking about it right now, and I need to go. I'll call you later. Tonight, after I get home, okay?"

"Wait a minute, Julie! Don't hang up yet. There's something you need to know. That's why I called. I didn't mention it before—it was going to be a surprise. You remember I've been working with Frank Ellinger, at Ellinger and Renkin, when I'm in New York? Hell, it didn't take much convincing. Ellinger's got a sharp nose for where the big bucks are, and he's going to make a pile off this thing."

"Ross, I really don't understand what you're talking about, so can we talk about whatever it is later? They're waiting for me in there, probably deciding without me! I've got to get back."

"What I'm trying to tell you is we've got the interface between your designs and the computer-controlled cutting machines, Julia. We've spent the last month debugging the program, in fact. I was going to show you, give you a demonstration next time I came up. That means we can feed your designs into the engineering package. We've finally got integration, Julia, from design to cut cloth. We can produce the master patterns from your designs, grade them, and then send that information to the marker program, which controls the cutting machines." He paused for a second. "Do you understand what I'm telling you?" He waited again.

"I'm not—say it for me again, please? Straight and clear so I can be sure." Her voice was barely a whisper.

"Just think of it, Julie! You tell me you've already written the ad copy for the color printouts, the stuff for the press packages. Taggart's got the hall—and you've got an entirely new collection sitting on the drawing board, ready to go! You've even done the costing, with a bunch of new, innovative fabrics. This is your chance to set the world on fire, Julia baby!" He laughed at his own use of Alex's flip endearment, giving vent to the excitement that built as the scenario he was painting took on vivid coloration.

"Frank Ellinger can cut at least fifty different garments for you in the next two or three days—or however many you might want to do," he continued. "More maybe, if Taggart's willing to pay people to work straight through. Go talk to Arlette, see what she thinks the atelier can manage to put together in two weeks' time. Max will back you up, Julie—he knows about everything we've been doing. Refer any technical questions to him. You can do it, Julie girl. Go sell it to them!"

"You're saying present my own collection? At the Trump Tower?" she asked, too stunned to believe what he was suggesting.

Ross let her words reverberate across the distance between them, until Julia found her own answer.

"Yes, of course! Wait a minute, let me think, get used to the idea! But how?"

"I can be there by noon tomorrow, start right away, once you decide which numbers you're going to use, unless you do all of them."

Her mind was racing now—way ahead of him, to possibilities so engaging, and so suddenly *right*, that she began to smile without even knowing it. A bright light illuminated all the dark, fuzzy corners of her mind, putting a quick end to the agonizing over decisions that had plagued her for the past two months. "I'll let you know what they decide—if not tonight, first thing in the morning," she told him, then quickly hung up.

It took Ross only a few seconds to decide that he needed to be with her, whether she succeeded in selling the idea to Ben and Tony or not. He punched in his secretary's home number and listened to it ring, sitting forward on the edge of his chair, the sense of urgency he felt making it seem much longer than it actually was before her husband answered.

"Let me speak to Nita, Gary."

"Sure, I'll get her." Ross tapped the eraser end of a pencil against his knee, waiting impatiently. "Hi, what's up?"

"I need out of here on the next flight to New York. Into any airport, I don't care. Make it for two. I'm taking Jake Sibley with me. Can you see to that while I make a couple of other calls? I'll get back with you in a few minutes." He depressed the disconnect and then punched in another number. "I'm on the next flight to New York, Jake, and I'd like you to go along. We may be going ahead at Ellinger and Renkin with more than a test run. I know, don't remind me. That's why I want you along. And if this deal doesn't work out, we might as well finish it up, anyway. Just pack your bag. Nita will give you the particulars in a few minutes, and I'll be by your place thirty minutes before whenever our flight leaves."

His next call was long distance. "Frank? Ross McCutcheon here. Something's come up, and I think we may have our first chance to run the program for real—your first paying customer. I'll know for sure tomorrow, but I wanted to give you a little warning. I told them we could deliver in two, say three days at most. What do you think?"

"Jesus Christ, Mac! You must be dreaming! You know we've still got some bugs in this thing! How many would we have to cut in two days?"

"Fifty, seventy-five different numbers. I don't know for sure yet. A whole collection, Frank, whatever that is. But only a few of each one. Not for production at this stage. That'll come later. I should be at your place by ten or eleven in the morning, maybe earlier. Could you talk to your people first thing—feel them out, see if they'd stick with it until the job's done, work out shifts? Try sweet-talking them with overtime, tell them they'd be pioneers, whatever it would take if we get the green light?"

"Okay, if you say so. But you better bring along whatever that stuff is you're on—sounds to me like we're going to need it. See you."

Ross was grinning when he hung up. Frank was right, he *was* on a kind of high, but it was self-generated, maybe the result of a sudden surge of adrenaline through his bloodstream, but mostly it was mental—like girding up to do battle. He thought about Julia, doing battle on two fronts, at this very moment. Trying to convince Tony and Ben that it was possible to do the job in the time they had left—and at the same time to go along with a whole bunch of new designs that bucked predicted trends.

Whether it was the adrenaline or just focusing his attention on Taggart, a sort of misty, shifting fog suddenly lifted and a new picture began to emerge. And once glimpsed, it was a possibility he couldn't sit by and ignore. He almost leaped from his chair to grab for the phone again, waiting even more impatiently this time as he continued to consider one name after another, sparing no one. He skipped the preliminaries and began talking as soon as he heard Stan Lunsford's voice on the other end of the line. "Mac here. Don't talk, just listen. I'm leaving for New York tonight, and I want you to do two things for me—top priority, understand? As soon as the New York exchange opens in the morning, start buying Ben Taggart. And get quotes for me at least midday and at closing, starting tomorrow."

"You know something I don't, Mac?"

"Call it a wild guess, worst-case scenario, insurance, whatever you want. Maybe nothing, but I want a daily report, either way." He gave Stan three phone numbers in New York. "You ought to be able to catch me at one of them, but if not, leave word with Julia's secretary, Consuelo Perez. She's okay."

"You've got some pretty obvious connections there, Mac," Stan warned, "which could mean trouble down the line if the SEC gets wind of this. You realize that? Since Gary Lynch took over enforcement, they've really been coming down hard on insider trading."

"That's not what's going on, but it's a chance I'll have to take. And I won't be selling, taking any profits, if that's what's got you worried."

"Okay. Let's say it starts down. How much do you want, and at what price?"

"It's been hovering at close to twenty-three, but I can't see far enough ahead, don't know how much it may fall, or how fast, which is why I want to keep a close watch for a while. Buy whatever you can get your hands on in the next few days, but be prepared to go as high as two hundred and fifty thousand shares, if we can get that much. Sell anything you have to in order to do it, except the young guys—leave them alone. I don't care about the other stuff."

"Wow! I wish to hell you'd tell me what's going on."

"And one more thing, Stan. Find out who's been selling Taggart shares in the past three months—by name, no matter how small the transaction. As fast as you can."

It took Julia only a few seconds to plan her moves after she finished talking with Ross. "Get the color printouts from my office, would you, Connie? On the double! And those samples of my new fabrics from Monarch. Get help to carry them if you need to, but bring them in right away." The "samples" were three-yard lengths of cloth, and there were about fifty of them.

Ben was still pushing the idea of using Nat Thorne's designs when she walked back into Tony's office.

"So you're willing to ignore the fact that the little weasel went behind my back, huh, Ben?" Alex snarled. "You do realize that he never peeped to me about any of this?" He waved one hand toward the sheets of paper spread out on Tony's desk. "Too chicken to face the music, probably." He paused for effect. "Oh yeah, I forgot, you two are cut off the same bolt of cloth, aren't you? You didn't peep, either, did you, Ben?" Julia couldn't remember ever seeing Alex so angry before. "You were planning to just snap him up, take him under your benevolent wing—all without even a hint of a word to me, let alone my approval!"

Ben didn't even attempt to answer Alex, though he had the good grace to at least look embarrassed at what everyone knew Alex was saying. Tony seemed oddly detached, watching silently as he continued to pace back and forth like a caged cat.

"You've got a valid point, Alex," Max injected. "We all need to be more straightforward with each other, though I suspect that when we're not it's more a matter of oversight than intent, of being so damned busy that we let things slide we shouldn't. Right now, we're faced with making a decision of major importance to this company, though, and we're going to have to be as objective as we can. Look at it from every angle, consider every possibility."

What was Max up to now, Julia wondered, confident that his motives were never as simple as they appeared on the surface. Ross had said Max knew about Ellinger and Renkin, and that he'd support her, so he'd also probably guessed who her call was from, and was setting the stage for her to bring it up. She watched his face, knowing as sure as anything that she was right when he looked over at her as he finished speaking.

"There *is* one other option that we haven't considered," Julia began, pausing only long enough to be sure she had everyone's attention, then started describing the one thing they hadn't considered—the new collection she'd designed in Austin. Most important of all, she told them, Ross's integrated software made it possible to go directly to the cutting machines with these designs, tomorrow. If they mobilized every hand available, maybe even hired a few extra seamstresses, they could produce enough samples for the Trump Tower and the New York showroom, plus the four major regional marts—Chicago, Dallas, Atlanta and Los Angeles.

Ben and Tony began shooting questions at her immediately, almost before she'd finished explaining how Ross's software worked, but Max interrupted, deflecting the questions, at least momentarily. "Let's hold our questions until Julia's finished, then ask her to fill in any gaps."

Connie brought in the color printouts and Julia passed them around, explaining that some were variations of the same style, and that these printouts, as well as copies of her original sketches, were the kind of illustrations that were available in almost unlimited numbers for release to the press. And the copy to go with them was already written, too. It only needed polishing, which Elaine's staff could easily handle in the time remaining.

"Even if news of the knockoff hits the press tomorrow—and we might have a few days of grace if they don't catch on to it right away—we could be ready with a press release, complete with illustrations, before the end of the week. They'll assume we're out of the picture for fall, but we can cut that off before it mushrooms out of control by giving them something new to talk about," she continued, then unfolded her fabrics from the Monarch mill, which were perhaps the biggest surprise of all, especially to Ben. He held on to two of the pieces, running his fingers back and forth over the surface while he listened to her, a rapt expression on his face.

"Well, it's an appealing idea, Julia," Tony allowed finally, considering. "But I for one am not ready to make a decision based on three or four designs. You *say* you've got a collection in your computer, but—well, I'd have to see more than you've got here, I'm afraid."

Ben nodded, agreeing with Tony. "I hope you won't take this personally, Julia—I guess I just can't get very excited about all this computer stuff. It pretty much turns me off, in fact, and I don't mind admitting it. I've fallen in love with your fabrics, they're wonderful. But frankly, I don't understand why you've gotten so carried away with this, this software or whatever you call it. Apparel designed with a machine is always going to look exactly that—as if it were designed by a machine!"

"I understand how you feel, Ben, because I thought the same thing at first," Julia responded quietly, persuasively, trying to help him see beyond this stumbling block. "But is that how these really look to you? Use your wonderful imagination. Can't you forget that I used a computer?"

"Yeah, Ben, who gives a shit who the designer is, right—you, or Nat, or a machine?" Alex interrupted. "Just take whatever you can get, wherever you can get it." He stopped, suddenly realizing how that must sound to Julia.

"Sorry about that, babe, I know they're yours. And if the others on that disk are anything like these—well, the truth is, we'd have the best damn collection to come out of this house in one fucking long time." Julia knew his slap at Ben was only a sign of how deeply he'd been hurt, by Ben as well as by Nat.

It was Max who forced them all back on track. "Even if you and Tony wanted to, Ben, using your own designs and/or Nat's, I doubt you could put enough numbers together for a collection, because it would take too long to do the patterns and cut them the old way."

"Time *is* the problem," Julia agreed. "You can settle for a repeat of last spring, which I think would be a terrible mistake. We'd be better off not showing at all, at least not right now. And that's our one other realistic choice—to postpone for a couple of months. But won't you at least let me show you the rest of my designs?" She glanced at her wrist. It was nearly eight o'clock—no wonder tempers were getting short. "I can print them all out, have them ready to look at first thing in the morning. This could be our one chance to show a new fall-winter collection—and keep our reputation and credibility from falling into the basement!"

"What do you say to sleeping on this, Ben?" Tony suggested. "Are you willing to look at what else she's got in the morning? We don't want to rush into a decision as big as this one, right?"

"Sure, that's probably a good idea." Ben got up slowly, folded one of the fabric samples and then laid it on top of the others on Tony's desk. "We're all getting weary. Not the best time for decisions, anyway."

Alex watched Ben for a moment, his eyes narrowing. "There's one other thing you and Tony might want to sleep on, Ben. I've got a pretty good hunch who sold you down the river." He kept his voice low, but every person in the room heard him and stopped—like a frozen frame of film.

"You were right about Nat, I'll give you that," Alex continued. "Everything he does has a creative touch. He's great—sensitive, innovative. But he doesn't know his ass from a hole in the ground when it comes to producing the samples. Doesn't have even an inkling of what's involved along the way, or how long it takes. All he cares about is the vision in his head, and getting it down on paper. I can remember when I was like that, too, can't you?" He paused, reflecting on a naïveté long gone, coaxing Ben along with him.

"What made you think your own back was safe, Ben?" he asked softly. "I figure Nat had to be the one to leak your designs—so you'd have to use his! It was probably his way of forcing your hand. He set you up." He waited again, letting the idea sit amongst them like an unexploded bomb. "He's just big-headed enough to figure that once he got his big chance, you'd have to offer him a helluva lot more than junior designer. And if *you* didn't, someone else would!"

Tony was grinning by now, apparently relishing the vicious exchange. "Sounds to me like maybe the green devil's riding your back, Alex! What do you say to calling Nat in here? See what he has to say for himself?"

"Sure, Tony, you do that," Alex agreed, his voice dripping sarcasm. "And when you find him, let me know, will you? Cause the bastard hasn't shown his face around here for the past three days. No word, no nothing. I called around, but he seems to have magically disappeared into thin air!"

Now it was Alex's turn to grin, and just as maliciously, as he glanced from Tony to Ben and back again. "You a big believer in coincidence, Tony?"

Chapter 21

"I'M BEAT, AREN'T you?" Julia sighed, picking at her fruit salad. She really wasn't hungry, but had suggested to Alex that they get something to eat, after the fiasco in Tony's office. He needed someone to talk to, even if there was little else she could do at this late date.

"Yeah, I suppose," Alex mumbled. "I'm too numb to tell anymore. Sometimes I wonder if the Collective is worth the hassle. It's like an inside joke. All we're doing is playing the game, keeping up with the rest of the boys. And the press coverage is really hit and miss—they're fickle as hell."

Both of them had been skirting the real issue, Nat Thorne, for the past thirty minutes, but Julia decided there was little point in putting it off any longer. "Ben showed me those sketches only a few days ago, Alex. I didn't have any idea what was going on until then. Took me completely by surprise, though I'd seen the two of them together several times, talking. But that's the way Nat was, Alex. Remember at Ross's Christmas party, he was really interested in what we were doing, asked a lot of questions, seemed to want to learn about everything?"

"Yep, that's our boy. Now I guess we know why." He rubbed a tired hand across his forehead.

"I told Ben I knew Nat was good and you needed him. I wish he hadn't sprung it on you like that, and I'm sure he wouldn't have, if not for this—this crazy thing."

"Maybe. I'm not so sure, Julia. But then, I'm not too sure about anything at this point. Just when you think things are going okay, that maybe there's a chance for—oh, hell, it all just blows up in your face! You want to know what I thought—why he took off like that? It'll give you a good laugh!" He chuckled mirthlessly. "I had lunch last week with Larry Goodenough—you remember him?" Julia had assumed that his affair with Larry was long over. "I swear it was strictly business. Nothing more. But Nat knew about us—I told him one night when I was in my cups. Shouldn't have, I guess. Shit, don't know why I'm still thinking like that now."

He straightened, as if physically shaking free of something. "Nat happened into the restaurant, saw Larry and me together. I saw him going out the door, but hoped he hadn't noticed us. I haven't seen him since. Thought he cut out because, well, because he thought Larry—that we had something going again." He scrubbed his fingers through his hair, shaking his head in disbelief. "I really let him get to me, didn't I? Jesus, can you believe I could still be that naïve?"

Julia tried to reassure him. "It's not being naïve to believe in someone, Alex. It's more like an investment that carries risks, the kind of risks we have to take, because the alternative is too—too barren, too sterile, too lonely."

He watched her face while she groped to find the right words. Then he nodded, understanding better than she realized what she'd just admitted. "That's my line, remember? Seems to me that's what I've been trying to tell you all these years!" His smile was rueful. "But I'm glad something good has come out of all this for you, Julia." He reached in his pocket for his wallet. "I've got things to do. Let's get out of here."

Julia went back to her office and spread the fabric samples on the floor where she could see them easily from her terminal, then opened the first "document," laughing to herself as she thought about how she would have reacted to hearing a fashion design called a "document" four months ago. Then, glancing back and forth between the screen and the fabrics on the floor, she made a color choice, and the image on the screen flashed and changed. After a few more color and shading changes, she sent the first command to the printer and got up to put a tape in her player while she waited for the printout.

It was a routine that occupied her for the next four hours, and by the time she finished, the big rectangular table in the conference room was completely covered with eleven-by-fourteen-inch color printouts of the forty designs she'd chosen from the more than seventy stored on file disks. Across the bottom of each sheet of paper she attached swatches of the fabrics to be used for that particular design, providing two to three different choices. She'd also planned to print out her copy and the ad layout, but decided to go home and get a few hours' sleep rather than risk feeling dull-headed in the morning.

When she opened the door to her apartment, one of the lamps in the living room was already on, and she hesitated for a minute, remembering all the warnings she'd read about going into a—

"Julia?" She heard his voice before she saw him, rising slowly from the couch where he'd been resting. "My God, woman, I was really beginning to get worried about you." Ross was on his feet, coming toward her, so her imagination hadn't conjured him up out of thin air.

"Oh, McCutcheon, am I ever glad to see you!" She dropped her shoulder bag on the floor with a thump and rushed to meet him, throwing her arms around his neck and hugging him cheek to cheek. "Ouch! And am I ever a wreck. My neck!" She massaged it ruefully with one hand as she drew away and grinned impishly, feeling too pleased to keep it to herself.

"I just finished printing them out. Forty different designs, in color, complete with fabric swatches. You should see them—they're absolutely, positively *magnificent!*" Her voice rose on the "magnificent," and then she was laughing happily.

Ross picked up on her lighthearted playful mood and laughed, too, then gave her another quick squeeze. "Tell me what happened."

"They decided to 'sleep' on it—Tony and Ben. They need to see more." She lowered her chin and her voice. " 'We can't afford to make such an important decision on just a few drawings—drawings made by a computer at that.' " She grabbed his hand while she talked, pulled him into the kitchen with her, flipped on the light and got a bottle out of the refrigerator. "So I said I'd have more ready to look at first thing in the morning."

He watched her fill two stemmed glasses with her favorite wine. "Yeah, I know that much. I talked to Elaine on the phone—otherwise I would have had the police out looking for you before now. She said you were going back to the office, that you'd gone out to eat with Alex, and they had put off the decision until tomorrow." He accepted the glass she handed him. "You really think it was Nat? How's Alex taking it?"

"Maybe. Could have been, I suppose—who knows? Alex is pretty bitter, angry. No telling what he's liable to do in the state he was in tonight. I think he feels like hitting out at someone, needs something to help salve the hurt."

"What *can* he do? With Nat gone and no proof?"

"Find him. Said he had some ideas about where to look—gay bars, I'll bet. It's so sad. He seemed so—oh, settled maybe, quietly happy, with Nat. I thought maybe this time—" She paused, sipping thoughtfully at her wine. "What a screwy business! Everyone talks about knockoffs, adaptations and translations, even pirating, but no one's willing to name what happened to us what it really is—just plain criminal theft!"

Ross watched her face for a moment. "And what if Ben and Tony decide no, Julie, what happens then?" That eventuality was the real reason he'd come to New York, instead of waiting to see if she'd get the go-ahead. But to his utter amazement, he saw her face light up with an excitement she simply couldn't restrain. She raised her glass to mime a toast.

"Like I said, one way or another, McCutcheon, that collection is going on the market! I guess all that simmering on the back burner paid off. Whatever was in the stewpot finally got done!"

He started to grin as he listened, infected by her bubbling enthusiasm.

"I know it sounds terribly egotistical for me to be the one to say it, but those designs—and the options they offer all kinds of women, in different parts of the country, the new fabrics—are just too damned good to file away on a floppy disk!" She led him back into the living room and Ross followed willingly, dropping down beside her on the couch.

"I didn't design them for one kind of woman, the way Bill Blass and Oscar de la Renta do, or for a particular body, like Galanos—a flat front, a flat behind and no waist." Just the thought of the "Galanos body" seemed to instantly transform her enthusiasm. "Sometimes I wonder if women are ever going to cry 'enough'! Just how much longer are we going to be willing victims—letting some goddamned man define what's 'feminine,' letting them destroy what we are, out of their own weakness?" One thought tumbled quickly on top of another to feed the fire of a slumbering anger.

"It's not the Galanos woman, or the Blass woman, who's going to change that, you know. Fashion is already too serious for them, which means they no longer have the freedom, or the will, to be themselves, to explore and take chances. It's the unruly masses, the women who are struggling to find themselves, like me, that I'm designing for—women who are proud of what's inside here, and here." She laid a hand flat across her chest, then put three fingers to her temple and smiled wryly. "And when I really looked at what I'd done, tonight—all at once for the first time—it just sort of came together for me. I'm proud of my work, and I don't mind saying so." She tossed Ross a self-conscious glance. "I suppose all that sounds silly to you."

"Come here." He reached out a hand and pulled her over to him, then wrapped his arms around her. "We made a deal, in case you've forgotten—no putting words in each other's mouths, and no pushing each other into neatly-labeled pockets. The only time I think you're silly is when you forget to eat! So tell me what you've got in mind."

She reached over to the coffee table to get her glass and took a sip before she answered. "I'm also thoroughly convinced that what I'm saying about marketing, about merchandising, is going to sweep the business eventually. So why should I stand around and wait for someone else to come up with the same idea and start the ball rolling? If Taggart wants in, that's okay with me—I'm willing to give them first dibs. If they don't, well, I'm going to do this collection, even if I have to bankroll it myself, and I'm going to market it the way I think it ought to be done. You coaxed me over my hang-ups and gave me the tools I needed—opened doors for me I never dreamed even existed."

Her voice softened as she spoke, and then she turned to look directly into his eyes. "And doors I thought were closed to me forever." She kissed him then, putting all the love she couldn't find words for into one tender caress. When it ended, she reached for her glass again, clinking the rim lightly against his before they both drank, smiling at each other until Julia spoke again.

"So you'd better get your machines oiled up and ready to go first thing in the morning, McCutcheon!"

Ross shook his head, bemused. "Is this the same woman I had to put to bed a couple of weeks ago? The one who couldn't even figure out whether she was hungry or tired, let alone what to wear?" he teased.

"One and the same. And I've got to warn you, Ross. That wimp of a girl could come back anytime, or at least I can't guarantee that she won't."

Ross took her face between his hands, slowly and deliberately loving her with his eyes. "It's true, Julie. I did think you were a schoolgirl when I first saw you at Giverny, from a distance.'' He stroked her lips with a gentle thumb, before brushing them with his own. ''I remember thinking to myself—what is it about French females, even the little girls, where do they get that special something? Look at that one there, with the unruly curls coming loose from her pigtail, and her funny pants and dusty shoes laced halfway up her legs, even *she* has it—that indefinable 'flair'!''

He smiled ruefully, caressing her lips with his thumb over and over again. ''That's why I was so surprised when you spoke to me in English. But from the moment I sat down on that bench, I knew you for a woman, Julie love. The most enticing, fascinating woman in the world. And I want to be around when you need me to bathe you, make love to you, feed you or put you to bed—and the next time you come home shouting 'absolutely, positively magnificent!' ''

By seven the next morning, Julia had already been awake for an hour, thinking out strategies, trying ideas on for size, but lying as still as possible so she wouldn't wake Ross. She hadn't asked him, and he hadn't volunteered, to help her convince anybody of anything, and Julia suspected he understood that she wanted to do this alone. All he asked before they parted after breakfast was that she call him at Ellinger and Renkin as soon as she knew, whichever way the decision went.

Elaine and Max had moved the chairs back, away from the big conference table, and lined them up along the wall. Now they were sitting together talking, waiting like everyone else. Arlette had looked over the display much earlier, after Julia had asked her to come so she could answer questions about what her seamstresses and tailors could or couldn't do in two weeks. Tony stood back from one end of the table, expelling smoke from his lungs with a great show of impatience as he watched Ben—who was still deliberating over her sketches and printouts—then grabbed up the pages of Julia's ad copy and began glancing over the top sheet again, only because it was something to do while he waited. Ben was on his third or fourth time around the table, obviously in no hurry. Julia watched him reach out occasionally to touch a swatch of fabric, then nod as if carrying on a silent dialogue.

"The question is, can we get away with bucking the color forecasts. The last Tobe Report—didn't you see it?" Ben asked finally.

It wasn't a question Julia was expecting. The Tobe group was an international fashion forecasting service, and their report went to just about everyone in the business, from fabric mills and designers to manufacturers and retail stores. "Yes, I did, but—well, is it a particular color that's a problem?" She didn't want to jump to any conclusions or put words in his mouth. "We can still incorporate some of the uncut yardages you were going to use, especially the jerseys. They'd be good for the drape and fluidity we need here, and here." She pointed to a couple of her sketches.

"Your fabrics are fantastic, I told you that yesterday. But the American Color Association panel is predicting neutrals for the next two years—black, mocha brown, army khaki, gunmetal gray. You've included a few brights, which everyone will be using to pick them up, but mostly you've got intense, saturated colors. They're almost passionate."

Julia smiled for the first time, agreeing with him. "I know. But do you really think women are in the mood for those protective colors—colors that say, 'Don't notice me, don't touch me'? How many women do you know like that today, Ben? And are they our market? From a marketing standpoint, I see this so-called wave of conservatism everyone is mouthing as a gross oversimplification, and therefore misleading and potentially dangerous."

Ben nodded thoughtfully, taking everything she said under consideration. "You'd want your own name this time, wouldn't you, Julia?" he asked then.

The way he asked was a shock at first, which was rapidly displaced by disappointment and a feeling of a kind of sadness. The credibility and viability of their company was probably at stake, and here Ben was off on an ego trip, probing around to see how far she might be going to invade *his* territory. In the beginning they'd worked together on almost everything, as partners rather than competitors, each of them doing what they did best. It was Julia who'd researched the market, so the resulting split in their roles had occurred naturally, without needing to be negotiated—or so she'd always thought. Everything Julia had designed had gone out as part of the Taggart line, and she'd never asked that it be any other way. But working together, cooperating to build the company, was one thing—letting him take advantage of her, protecting Ben's fragile ego at the expense of her own, was something else.

"That's only fair, Ben, don't you think?" she answered quietly.

"We can settle that later!" Tony interrupted impatiently. "We're wasting time. What's your opinion, Ben? Will it fly? We've got to make a move, and the quicker the better. Charlie Harkins called me last night. He's getting antsy, wants to call an emergency meeting of the Board. I told him I thought we could handle it, but—"

Connie strode across the room, her arm extended toward Tony. "Here," she muttered through terse lips, shoving the newspaper into his hands. "At least now you won't have to worry any longer about when the sky is going to fall. It just did."

Everyone jumped up to gather around as Tony laid the tabloid flat out on the table. The headline was short and to the point—"Knoblock or Knockoff?" It was just below the big WWD logo in the upper left corner, and alongside two color photographs that took up the rest of page one—one from the Taggart press kit and the other from the Knoblock show. Bold white letters, dropped out of a wide black band across the bottom of the page, proclaimed "Knoblock beats Taggart out of the starting gate, pp. 4 and 5." Inside, more photographs illustrated a two-page spread that spelled out the implications of the budget-house "collection" for the garment industry, and ended with an assessment of Taggart's chances of recovering from what was described as a "near-fatal blow." The piece ended with the statement, "A spokesman for Taggart refused to comment, except to say that the company was going ahead with its fall showing."

"You knew this piece was in the works?" Julia questioned Tony, surprised that he hadn't even mentioned that the publication had contacted him.

"Sure, but not when. What could I do but stonewall? And what I told you all earlier still goes—nobody around here talks to the press but me. Not a word, understand? We've got to keep this thing from being blown all out of proportion." He glanced around at each of them, one at a time, waiting for affirmative nods he didn't get.

"The *Times* will have it tomorrow or Friday," Max pointed out, "and so will the *Wall Street Journal*, but with this out, we'll probably start seeing a drop on the exchange by closing today. If we simply postpone, let speculation run rampant for another couple of months, it could take us years to recover." He looked directly at Julia. "So we've got to do what we can to control the damage now. And the best way to do that is to go ahead with the Trump Tower and Julia's collection. How long before you could get a release out to the press, Julia?"

She thought quickly. Today was Wednesday. But the release wasn't the only thing she would need to do, and even with Elaine's help, it would take some thoughtful planning. They couldn't afford to make any mistakes now. And then there were all the decisions to be made so Ross could enter the information into the computer, before Ellinger and Renkin could start cutting.

"Tomorrow afternoon. Friday morning at the latest."

Max understood why it would probably take that long. "That means in the Monday editions at the latest. What do you say Tony? Ben?"

Tony kept his eyes on Ben, expecting some signal, a facial expression, a nod, or even a shake of his head—something to indicate a response one way or the other. And when Ben smiled, it triggered a nearly audible collective sigh of relief in the room.

"Okay, that's it, then. The ball's in your court, Julia," Tony announced. "Let me see the release as soon as you've got it ready to go."

"We're on, McCutcheon!"

"Great! I can get away from here by lunchtime. We'll celebrate, then lay out the schedule."

"I can't afford time for—"

"Listen, Julie, you're not going to make it through the next two weeks if you start off skipping meals."

"Okay, I guess you're right," she admitted without further argument.

"I'll arrange for something to be brought in. Why don't you ask Max and Elaine to join us? And anybody else you need to have in on the planning, about twelve-thirty in your office. And listen, Julie, I'm not telling you what to do, but Connie—well, you can't do everything yourself, you know, and she's—"

"I'm way ahead of you, McCutcheon. I just hired a new assistant to the vice president for marketing, and she's already looking for someone to help her—her replacement. And Ross?"

"Yeah?"

Her words softened and slowed. "In case I get too busy to remember to tell you—I love you."

He was silent for a second. "Well, maybe I can think up a way or two to keep you reminded."

Julia laughed and hung up, then hunted through the minifile on her desk, quickly calculating the time difference between New York and Paris. After that she put in a direct-dial call to Kiki's Boulevard Haussmann showroom, and by the time she finished, it was all beginning to feel real—for the first time. She got up from her desk then and went to close the door to her office, to ensure privacy and no interruptions, because she still had one more call to make. And this one was to Texas.

They were already a smoothly coordinated team, Julia realized, mentally stepping back briefly to listen and watch—

Max and Elaine, Ross, and Connie and herself—while they munched on sandwiches and talked, reviewing what needed to be done in the next two weeks.

"I'm going ahead with some of the models we had scheduled for Ben. Connie and I will go over their portfolios as soon as we finish here, and notify the ones we don't need or want. One of us will let you know, Max, so you can figure what the kill fees come to." She straightened and looked at him. "If we have any hope of getting through this with our sanity still intact, we've got to eliminate unnecessary stress. To put it bluntly, that means bypassing Tony wherever we can. But if that makes you uncomfortable, Max, please be honest and say so. If not, would you keep the books for us? I'll report to him whenever I think it's necessary, so you wouldn't—"

"Sure, but why not let me do the reporting, too," Max suggested. "I'm not sure he wouldn't prefer it that way at this point, though I can't figure why the change. Uncharacteristic as it sounds, he's apparently willing to do just what he said, Julia—he's turning the whole show over to you."

"Okay, that would be a big help. But I don't think there's any mystery, Max. He wants the responsibility to be all mine in case we bomb, so there won't be any doubt about who's to blame!" She shifted mental gears. "Now. I intend to take advantage of what this CAFDAM program—computer-aided fashion design and manufacturing—will do. You'll find a description in my copy, Elaine. Partly because I want to showcase Ross's integrated software, but also because the real theme of the collection I've designed is diversity. The eclectic woman. The multiplicity of roles, moods, emotions, jobs. And not just the differences among women, but the variety of roles and emotions experienced by one woman."

Elaine and Connie were taking notes while Julia talked. She spoke rapidly, sure of herself now, knowing exactly what she wanted, and where she was going.

"Variety, multiplicity, diversity, eclecticism—those are some of the key words. And that concept will be carried through in the models, too, varying color types and sizes, and ages—all of which will be used to suggest climate and other regional variations as well. So there'll be no cadres of models all dressed alike—no clones—even if we had the time to produce that many sample garments, which we don't. We can group models to a certain extent, or we might move them along the runway in waves of three—a blonde, redhead and brunette—but they'll be showing three different numbers. And I intend to spotlight two special models. Which reminds me, Max, I need to talk to you about getting someone for the lighting, which is probably going to make or break this show."

Max nodded to acknowledge that he'd heard her while continuing to eat.

"One of them is Dominique Chapotin," Julia continued. "She'll be arriving from Paris Sunday night—March first. The other one is, well, she'll be in about the same time, probably by noon Monday. That means we can brief everyone Monday afternoon, then have two run-throughs, Monday and Tuesday night, late, after the traffic through the Tower slows down. Can you talk to them about that, Max? Arrange it." Again, he simply nodded his head. "And we'll still have most of Wednesday to patch up whatever is bound to break down. We can expect an early and anxious crowd, and we'll start passing out the press kits by—oh, say about seven—with a crew there ready and waiting." Elaine nodded, understanding that that particular instruction was directed at her. "And the champagne."

Julia moved on to the press release next, the one responding to how Taggart intended to deal with their apparent loss, which they needed to get out as soon as possible. "Can you start on it as soon as we finish here, Elaine? You might look over the copy I've already written, see if you can find anything usable there. I think the way to go is to say nothing about our loss, but to emphasize the big news—take the offensive. We're announcing an entirely new concept we've had under development for some time, which we believe is going to set the industry standard for years to come. A bold new concept in design *and* production *and* the merchandising of apparel. Make some pretty sensational claims, but not too much detail. Whet their appetites.''

Ross listened, the corners of his mouth tucked into a slight smile as he watched Julia, the astute businesswoman he'd never seen in action before, and was reminded of Carey's remark that ''Julia's a good one to have around when you're plotting strategies.''

She began to nod her head as she thought about what to say. ''Yes, I think that's it. Because it's so new, so revolutionary, we don't want to take the chance that some maverick might jump publication date. So Taggart is keeping the whole thing under wraps until the opening. Press kits will be available at the Trump Tower presentation, March 4. What do you think?''

''Sounds interesting. Let me play with it awhile. I'll get back to you as soon as I have a draft,'' Elaine agreed.

Max leaned toward Ross. ''My bet is that Ben and Tony haven't got the foggiest about what they've really turned loose here,'' he murmured with a big grin and a slight tilt of his head toward Julia. ''She makes Tony's big license deal look timid as hell—and the chain of boutiques, too.''

''Use your own name as contact, not Tony's,'' Julia instructed Elaine, ignoring them. ''I'll explain why to him, or Max can—that since we're the ones who have worked this out, we have all the pat answers, know what to say and what not to—which takes the monkey off his back, so he'll probably go for that. Oh, and one other thing. I want a special invitation printed up, to go not only to the fashion press, but to all the major newspaper fashion editors around the country. And every one of our accounts, not just those in New York. Even if they don't all come, it won't hurt to let them know ahead of time, get their curiosity up. The newspapers will be expectant, pick up stories off the wire and from news services. But do the release first, then lift whatever you can use from that and from my copy for the invitation. I want them fancy, but elegant.'' She waited until Elaine stopped writing.

"Okay, what next?" she asked, as if she'd mentally been going through a list and now was ready to attack the next item. "Ross, tell me exactly what you need, and how soon."

"In a nutshell—the style numbers you want us to cut and in what fabrics. What size and how many of each number. Do you know for sure which ones you're going to use yet?"

Julia shook her head. "No. And Max, as soon as we finish here, I need to see yardages of Ben's fabrics, whatever we have left in the warehouse, for color and drape. The jerseys especially."

"Sure. I'll go make a call right now, have them delivered here for you within the hour. And I'll get inventory numbers on your Monarch samples right away too, so you can key-board that information into your documents." He seemed to be thinking out loud. "I'll see that a master fabric key is available for Ellinger and Renkin, matching numbers and fabric swatches." He turned to Ross. "I suggest you assign someone over there to do a visual check with the key before you cut, just to be sure. We can't afford many errors at this stage."

Ross nodded, understanding immediately. "Sure. And I'll be back here later in the afternoon to help out. I can't make her decisions—but I can input the fabric numbers or anything else, and make copies of her disks to take over to Frank Ellinger's. His men have agreed to work in shifts, starting tomorrow, and go straight through until we're done."

Thursday morning both the *New York Times* and the *Wall Street Journal* carried stories about the "Knoblock knockoff" of Ben Taggart, Inc., and also reported increased trading in Taggart stock the day before, closing two points off.

Julia didn't see Ross all day, though he called at four that afternoon to tell her they'd run into a "minor snag," so he probably wouldn't be leaving until late. "Be sure to eat—and don't wait up. Orders from headquarters, hear me?"

She didn't get home herself until almost nine, but it was well after two A.M. and she was still reading in bed, waiting and worrying, when she heard his key in the lock and leaped out of bed, not even bothering with a robe. The unusual slump of his body spelled exhaustion, and just one glimpse of his tired face was enough to give her stomach a wrench, but she greeted him with a smile and a hug.

Ross held on to her, effectively stopping her from moving away, savoring the feel of her, and the closeness.

"A 'minor snag,' huh?" she whispered into his neck. "I'll bet you're the one who didn't eat."

"Don't remember," he mumbled into her temple. "But no more snags."

"Come on, take off your shoes. How about a hot shower? You can tell me about it later, while you eat." She took his hand and led him into the bedroom. "Get comfortable while I go fix. Orders from headquarters."

When she returned fifteen minutes later, she found him sound asleep, and didn't have the heart to wake him. He was lying crosswise on the bed with his feet still touching the floor, one shoe on and one off, as if he'd just sat down and then leaned back to stretch out for a second.

Chapter 22

THAT DAY WAS only a harbinger of all the days—and nights—to come for the next two weeks. The press announcement went out as planned, but at market closing on Friday, Taggart shares were down almost ten points, to thirteen and an eighth.

Julia hired three temporary seamstresses, and spent the afternoon consulting with Arlette about construction details, buttons, accessories, and a seemingly endless stream of other petty matters—which Julia knew only too well could make a big difference in the final appearance of a garment. Ross worked along with the men at Ellinger and Renkin, and was gone from early in the morning until late at night. In the end, it took four twenty-four-hour days, in around-the-clock shifts through Monday night, to cut all the numbers, though the first finished bundles of cut cloth began arriving at the Taggart offices in Frank Ellinger's small van late Friday night.

Arlette's atelier hands came in Saturday morning, ready to start assembling sample garments, and worked straight through the weekend, as did Julia, Max, Elaine and Connie. Ross called whenever the van left Ellinger and Renkin, and the four of them would go down to help unload, sorting and trundling the bundles into the elevator and then to the conference room, where they were being stored temporarily. It was up to Julia to set workroom priorities, to assure that the numbers she considered crucial to the collection were completed first. Because no one was ready to say with complete assurance exactly how many garments *could* be put together in the time remaining.

Julia didn't even hear Ross come in late Monday night, so when she awoke the next day she slipped carefully from under the covers. In the kitchen, she made a pot of coffee, put an English muffin in her toaster-oven, and then peeled a fresh mango. Thirty minutes later, with breakfast finished and a roaring fire going in the fireplace, she was on the couch with her feet propped against the coffee table, knees bent to support a big drawing pad. At first, her lines were hesitant and tentative, as she tried out ideas, feeling her way among the fuzzy pictures in her mind's eye. Over the next hour, however, her drawing became more and more detailed, until finally she got up to stretch her legs and refill her coffee cup, then moved everything to the worktable. Still tiptoeing around in her robe and slippers, she returned to the kitchen once more to fill a big jar with water, got out her watercolors, and then settled down to really serious work, sure of what she wanted now.

Two hours later, she was still so engrossed in her work that she didn't hear the shower, or even hear Ross when he came into the living room. "What are you doing still here, Julie?" he asked quietly, coming up behind her. "Are you feeling okay?" The unexpected sound surprised her, and she jumped up from her stool, looking around almost guiltily—or so it seemed to Ross.

"Oh, you startled me! I hope I didn't wake you. I'm working at home—thought I'd stay here so I could fix you a well-earned breakfast. Did you get enough sleep?"

He opened his arms in invitation and she walked into them without hesitation. "That's why you're not dressed?"

She nodded. "There's coffee in the pot, but let me go start your br—"

He didn't let her go. "In a minute. What did I catch you hatching up now?" He was looking over her shoulder, at the sheets of paper scattered all across the top of the long table.

"Stage sets. For the opening. Here, let me show you. You have to see them from the beginning, from Act I, I suppose you might say. I want the environment in the Atrium to change as we move through the presentation." She showed him one watercolor after another, with sharply drawn images superimposed in black ink on the pure color washes—each one only slightly different from the one preceding it, like a series of animation drawings. The total effect, from beginning to end, was one of metamorphosis—a visual transformation over time, using color and lighting to change the mood, the look, the very atmosphere.

"You're good, Julia," Ross concluded finally. It was a simple statement of fact. "Do you realize how good?"

"Nope, but I do love hearing you tell me." She came to him again, and snuggled close, slipping her arms around his waist. "Even if it turns out that no one else thinks so."

Ross pushed her away a little so he could see her face. She was smiling, not worried at all, as he thought she might be, and he let his mouth break into a foolish grin. "My big job's done—so I'm yours to command, love of my life. Make me your slave," he commanded melodramatically.

She giggled at him. "You'll have to talk to my head henchman—Max the Ax. He's coordinating the slave labor." But she quickly sobered, remembering that there *was* something else she needed from him. "Could you look at what Elaine's put together so far about your program, Ross? We've described how it was used to produce this collection, and the saving in cost and time. I've already pointed out the wonderful features, the flexibility you've built into the design software, and I also want to mention any capabilities we didn't use, for whatever reason."

"Hold it a minute, Julie," he protested. "In the first place, it's *our* program! It wouldn't be what it is today without the input I got from you. I'll be glad to help Elaine, but this is your show. Why bore people with a lot of computer stuff? Don't do it for my ego—"

"You hold it, McCutcheon." She wasn't quite used to playing this role yet, so she started off by adding a dash of bravado. "I'm not worried about your ego, though I believe credit should go where it belongs. But this is the perfect opportunity to show the fashion world, especially all the artsy types, that their hang-ups about computers are just that—hang-ups. Think of my collection as the sugar-coated pill. When they see the results, not on paper, not in preachy words, but in the flesh, I predict they're going to find the whole idea pretty damned palatable!"

"Maybe, but why stretch your luck with a lot of detail at this point?"

Julia took a deep breath, firm in her resolve. "Because I don't agree that what you're calling too much detail *is* too much. A good readable description of your software, what it can do, and the potential significance of integrated software, from design to production, for the entire fashion industry—all of that is going into our press kits as a separate and very special document. It's important information, but it's also you and I working together. The computer nerd and the fashion fluff-head—and that's going to knock their socks off!"

He smiled lazily, watching her left eyebrow and the quirky corner of her mouth, which just wouldn't stay still, betraying the excitement she felt just thinking about it.

"So I don't want any misleading or inaccurate statements in our copy, which is the reason I'd like you to check every word. I'd also like it if you'd add something about the future. Integration's not complete yet, so what's the next step, where do we go from here? But that's up to you. The copy is in my MacPlus, in Elaine's office. Max has initiated her, by the way, and she loves it. Now she's even got Claire on the machine." She smiled, thoughtful for a minute. "Sometimes I feel like a kid just beginning to grow up. Do you ever wonder how you could have been so wrong, so stupid or insensitive, or whatever? And for so long?" she asked, bemused at her own thoughts. "We used to call him Mr. Vanilla, Elaine and I."

The Monday editions of *Women's Wear Daily,* the *New York Times* and the *Wall Street Journal* all carried articles about the Taggart announcement, making it a sure thing that other major newspapers across the country would pick up wire- and news-service stories on Tuesday or soon after. And Elaine had already gotten calls from *Time* and *Newsweek,* as well.

The newspaper reports were loaded with speculation about whether or not Taggart could deliver on its claim—a collection that anticipated a whole new fashion cycle *plus* a bold new marketing concept. The long front-page piece in the *Times* pointed out, "The fashion industry is on the verge of choking itself to death with outmoded production practices and equipment, in spite of the fact that it is one of the biggest manufacturing industries in the country today, with one out of every sixteen dollars being spent on apparel and textiles." In addition, several "industry sources" were quoted as expressing interest in the technological advances Taggart was claiming, especially if they affected production time and cost, which in turn might ultimately enhance the industry's ability to compete with foreign imports.

On Tuesday, the price of Taggart shares began inching up again.

Julia's days were filled with constant visits to the workroom—where she sometimes helped work out a construction problem, giving silent thanks to the seamstresses at Balmain, from whom she'd learned so much—and with consultations with Ross and Max, who now were working together on preparations at the Trump Tower. Max had enlisted Claire's help with the ten-year-olds, a class from an elementary school in the small Connecticut town where Elaine lived. They were to be part of the garden scene, the show's grand finale. The only time Julia went to the Tower herself was late at night, to check on lighting effects or some other question about the staging, before going home to fall into bed for a few hours.

A great deal of her time was spent in working out the runway strategy and developing the script for the presentation. She tried to keep Ben involved, too, and often consulted him about a problem with one sample or another, until he finally seemed to feel at ease, and came to ask what she needed him to do next. And when he did that, she gave him what she billed as "an assignment *exceptionnel.*" His face lightened visibly, and as he left her office, she noticed the usual bounce was back in his walk.

Tony appeared from time to time, floating in and out of her office or Max's or the atelier, as nervous as a reluctant groom, unsettling everyone with his cryptic warnings about "how much we all have at stake here," usually followed by a mumbled assurance that he was only "checking in" to see that everything was "going according to schedule."

Julia knew without being told that Ross was responsible for the constant flow of lunches and other "surprises" that helped make the long hours bearable for the entire Taggart staff. One afternoon, it was tea and scones at four o'clock, and the next, baskets of fresh apples and pears and grapes, complete with stubby little fruit knives for everyone to keep. A big box of Godiva chocolates sat open on one corner of Connie's desk, for anyone who might need a "fix." At first, Ross was noticed mostly because of his distinctive white hair. But it wasn't long before he was accepted as part of the Taggart team, by sample hands, assistants and secretaries alike. He shuttled back and forth between the Tower and the Taggart offices, where he sometimes worked at a computer in Julia's office, or sorted bundles of cut cloth in the conference room, or delivered cartons of notions and trimmings to the atelier. He was behaving like a good French waiter, she decided, staying out of the way, yet always there when he was needed, helping with a hundred little tasks, yet never doing it in a way that demanded attention or even thanks.

And that was difficult *not* to notice, probably because it

went against every preconceived notion Julia held about men in general. She was very much aware that most people, both men and women, operated on the assumption that the male ego was to be satisfied, no matter the cost to females. And she abhorred the arrangement that generally accorded women less of the important things—justice, respect, pay and even physical space—than men, and then assumed they were by nature satisfied with less. It was simply impossible for her to understand how any reasonably intelligent woman who had ever tried firsthand to make a decent living could accept such outrageous garbage! Certainly her own experiences in that regard had only served to feed the fires of an anger that blazed hotter with every passing year.

Alex was one of the few exceptions to the rule, at least in Julia's experience—or that's what she'd thought until recently. But now she was beginning to wonder if perhaps that was due to her own expectations. Ross didn't fit that preconceived mold, either, she knew now, no matter how hard she'd tried to make him. And then there was Max Starke—and Carey Blanton. Carey was special, simply because he was her father, but she was finally awaking to the realization that what a man *didn't* do—in her father's case, try to run her mother's life, even when he knew she was hurting and he was dying to help her—could be more important than what he *did* do. Carey had respected Anne-Marie's right to make her own decisions, no matter how unsatisfactory the end result might have been for him personally.

Julia remembered how Carey had always insisted on taking her along with him when she was a child, even when Lupe or someone else was available to stay with her. And now she realized that had been his way of making it possible for Anne-Marie to do what she needed to in that other part of her life, that her mother would never have agreed to leave her daughter with a succession of nameless strangers. Rather than just a personal idiosyncrasy, it had been a part of her father's commitment to the woman he loved—to share the responsibility of caring for their child.

As the days went on, Julia asked around from time to time, but no one had heard from or about Alex, and she felt a growing sense of unease. She began calling his apartment at least once a day, at first late in the morning, then at different times, but he was never there, no matter what time of day or night she tried. And when she managed to locate Nat Thorne's telephone number, she discovered it was "no longer in service."

The second weekend passed without notice, except for a minor crisis on Sunday afternoon.

"Oh, nooo," Claire wailed, staring at the screen of the Macintosh monitor. "But I didn't *do* anything!" She was in the process of proofing the copy describing Ross's integrated software, and it had simply disappeared. "God, how I hate this shit!" she exploded, then frustration won out, and she dissolved in tears.

"Here, maybe I can figure out what happened. Let me give it a try," Elaine suggested, trying to soothe her with a pat on her shoulder. "You didn't notice any kind of electrical surge, no flashes on the screen? Didn't hear anything funny?" She was tempted to join Claire in a good cry herself, just to get rid of the tension, but the thought of trying to reconstruct all the carefully thought-out sentences they'd worked so hard on, and from scratch, kept her from it. Claire was too upset to speak, so Elaine played with the edit and search menus, tried "looking" into the scrapbook and notebook and every other possibility she could think of, even closing the document so she could see if it had somehow been dumped into the "trash." But nothing turned up the missing material. "Shit!" she muttered herself, giving up.

"Look, why don't you go get a Pepsi or something?" Elaine suggested to Claire. "Wash your face and take a few deep breaths, then come back here and sit down at the machine, calm and collected as you can manage. Write down every word you can remember, don't worry about the order, just get it down. Then go home and get some sleep. I'll do the rest. Okay?"

Just the thought of staying late again tonight conjured up

the mental image of a woman—herself—running "amuck" through the halls, screaming and cursing and bashing everything in sight with a huge stick, a "sight" that gave her great pleasure. It even occurred to Elaine to wonder how she'd ever managed to live for nearly forty years before learning to indulge in the flights of fantasy on which her sanity now seemed to depend. Then she remembered that Tina and Maggie were alone tonight, and she jumped up to go call home.

"Does that diabolical smile portend something interesting for tonight?"

Elaine's smile broadened as she whirled around at Max's first intimate word. "You're out of luck." She told him what had happened, while he slowly ran a hand up the entire length of her arm from waist to shoulder, stopping along the side of her neck to lightly caress the lobe of her ear with his thumb. "I'm afraid there'll be nothing left over by the time I get home tonight, for you or anyone else. Sorry!"

"But I copied everything off your working disk earlier this afternoon. Thought you were already finished with it. If Claire hasn't added or changed too much, it shouldn't take her too long to redo it."

Elaine sighed with relief, and something else—adoration perhaps? "Ah, Max, you're just plain indispensable around here, you know that?"

"Only around here, huh?" He pretended grave hurt, but then gave her a quick kiss. "How about if I call Tina, tell her we might be a few minutes later than we thought? She could call out for a pizza and salad, and then everything will be ready when we get there."

Julia was in her office Monday afternoon when Alex called. He was all right, he told her, and yes, he'd finally located Nat—in a hospital over in Jersey City. "That's where I am now. Feels like I've been here for months, but I guess it's actually only been about five days. The doctors thought he wasn't going to make it at first. He's still unconscious, but they're saying he could wake up any time now, because the swelling in his brain is going down."

"My God, what happened—do they know?"

"Not exactly. Just that some bastard beat the shit out of him! The police think whoever it was—probably more than one person from the look of him when they brought him in—dumped him out of a car. A bum stumbled over him in a vacant lot near the mouth of the Lincoln Tunnel. No wallet, no identification, no money." He sounded both depressed and exhausted. And bitter.

"That's awful!"

"Yeah, well, I guess Nat's just one of those guys who's unlucky in love!"

"Oh Alex, you can't know—"

"Yeah, I can. They had him in surgery for three hours, trying to repair the damage!"

"Oh—" She couldn't think of anything to say to that.

"So how's everything going? Sorry about walking out on you, Julia baby."

"It doesn't matter, but I was so worried about you."

"Yeah, well—sorry about that, too. Guess I'll stay here for a while. At least until he wakes up. I called his mother in Poughkeepsie. She's coming down sometime today. But—" He paused for a few seconds, and Julia guessed he probably didn't know what he was going to do after that.

"Why don't you wait until you can talk to him, Alex? In spite of what you may think happened. Give him the benefit of the doubt, listen to what he has to say first? We don't really know for sure it was Nat."

"Before, when I was still looking for him, a couple of guys at a place down in SoHo remembered seeing him. Said he was flashing a big roll of green. Buying drinks. Full of himself, according to them."

"But that doesn't sound like Nat, Alex! He's always so quiet, so low-key."

"Yeah, he is—was," he agreed, considering the idea. "I

don't know. But if he didn't leak Ben's stuff, where the hell did he get the money?"

"Wait, Alex, talk to him first, for both of you. Please?"

He thought about it a minute. "Yeah, sure. Why not?"

She made him promise to call again the next day, and if she wasn't there, to at least leave a message with Connie. When she hung up, she felt sad but at the same time relieved. At least she knew where he was, and could put aside all the awful scenarios her imagination had kept dreaming up.

Kiki arrived as planned on Sunday evening, but it wasn't until the following afternoon that Ross discovered the identity of the second special model Julia had mentioned—and the first time Ross saw the two of them together, he knew Julia's idea was absolutely inspired.

Kiki's face was all sculpted planes, shadows and highlights, and her caramel blond hair was straight and glossy. Tall and willowy, her every move, whether body or facial expression, was fluid yet measured—dramatic, cool, and elegant. A delight to the eye, yet a bit unapproachable. Anne-Marie Lacombe, on the other hand, was all warm tones, relatively short as fashion models go, with curling hair and a ready smile, all of which contrasted with the aura of dignity, stature and power that seemed to envelop her. She exhibited a "presence" that drew the eye and inspired the imagination—yet there was also an elusive imp somewhere inside the body of the woman, glimpsed only occasionally in the flash of her bright eyes. As different as the two were in physical appearance, they both seemed at the same time knowable *and* mysterious—and for the first time, Ross thought he was beginning to understand what Julia was trying to say about the women for whom she'd designed her collection.

The Monday-night rehearsal was barely short of utter chaos, and the fact that Claire didn't even show up was no help. Max had rounded up about eight men from the warehouse to act as stand-ins for the ten-year-olds, who were to appear as butterflies and bees in the garden tableau. Because of their age and the late hour, their rehearsal was set for the following afternoon, and the stand-ins were there strictly to test placement and lighting. Ben had come along to watch over the brightly colored costumes he'd designed—his assignment exceptionnel—to see to it they weren't damaged. And he was livid.

"This is absolutely the last straw, Julia!" He began unloading his frustration on both Julia and Elaine, venting his exasperation with Claire. "All week long, it's been something like this, every damned day. She's either late, or sick, or something. Even when she does come in, the kids seem to pick up on her depression, or whatever the hell it is, and the next thing you know, they're dragging themselves around as if they're about to expire. Can't you find someone else, with a little fire in the eye, somebody we can depend on to carry through here?"

Julia tried to think who might be available to take over Claire's place, but couldn't on the spur of the moment. "I'll see if I can get someone else tomorrow, Ben. Would you mind filling in, just for tonight? Perhaps if you'd go out there—here, take this walkie-talkie—tell us where to place them, and we can direct the lights from up here. With the kids here tomorrow, it will be bedlam if we don't get their positions worked out tonight." She turned to Max for affirmation and for help in mollifying Ben.

"Yeah, Ben, you've got a far better eye for this sort of thing than she does anyway. We just hated to pile any more work on you, but the costumes are fantastic, and you're the one we really need to tell us where they should be. You know the effect Julia's trying for."

Julia glanced at Max, a bemused little smile lifting the corners of her mouth. What a gift he had for saying the right thing to massage the old ego—to make everyone feel important, to make them want to help!

Max turned to her as soon as Ben left. "Don't worry, Julia, I think I know who we can get to handle everything tomorrow night. She's good with kids this age, and we can depend on her. Ben's the one to spot and locate them anyway, and I'll get one of the crew to make a floor sketch—a map."

Later, when they were almost done for the night, Elaine and Ross sat together at a table near the edge of the runway waiting for Max, Ben and Julia to make a few last-minute changes in the lighting for the garden scene. Ross listened with one ear while Elaine prattled nervously about Claire.

"She used to be so on top of everything, so full of energy! But the last few weeks—well, I can't figure out what's happening with her. She's constantly late, and then comes in absolutely washed out. Maybe too many late nights with Tony," she mused worriedly, "though what she sees in him—oh hell, I should talk, I guess. And now, just when we need her most, she caves in."

Something about the picture Elaine painted sounded a familiar chord. Ross had seen the same pattern too many times to ignore it. "Sounds like she's on coke to me." Elaine looked shocked, though whether by the idea or by the bluntness of his words he couldn't tell.

"Sure, why not? It makes you feel great, until you do too much of it. The greater the stress, the more you need it. After that, it's downhill all the way—and not only physically. Motivation falls off, nothing seems very important. The last couple of weeks have been pretty hard on everybody. She may have gone on a binge, which disrupts sleep. That could explain what you've been seeing, Elaine. You say she's always tired, depressed, makes a lot of mistakes, comes in late or not at all."

Elaine nodded, considering the possibility, then let the thought mushroom. "I wonder that she can afford it, on her salary. Not that she's exactly underpaid."

"Come on, Elaine," Ross chided. "The stuff is selling for as little as seventy-five dollars a gram in New York these days—smaller amounts for as little as ten dollars, and I'm not talking about crack."

Elaine turned her full attention on Ross now. "You sound like you know a lot about it." It wasn't a question.

"Yeah, both first- and second-hand. It's the drug of choice, the badge of success and status, and not only in Silicon Valley. From what I hear, Wall Street and the Garment District are riddled with the stuff. All I'm saying is maybe you should at least consider the possibility. Talk to her. She may need help."

Both Kiki and Anne-Marie were staying at the Pierre, and on Tuesday, Ross and Julia met them there for lunch. It was Ross's idea, and though Julia was reluctant to take the time, she realized that an hour away from Taggart would be good for her—away from even thinking about tomorrow night.

"Julie," Anne-Marie began as soon as the waiter had taken their order, "Carey is coming from Washington. He's testifying before a Senate committee today, and it may run over into tomorrow. But he said to tell you he'll be here sometime in the afternoon, may have to come straight to the Tower, but isn't going to miss this, no matter what—even if Texas should decide to secede from the Union, or the whole damn cotton crop gets flooded out." She laughed quietly. "His exact words."

"I can imagine," Julia laughed with her. "But I'm glad he wants to come, Maman. I can't wait until he sees you in those green pajamas!" She smiled to herself, thinking about the way her mother looked in the clothes she'd designed for her. "I just wish I'd thought to arrange for Beth—"

"She'll be here late this afternoon," Ross interrupted. "I'm picking her up at the airport, so you don't have to worry." He was enjoying her somewhat confused reaction. "Anne-Marie and Carey have a two-bedroom suite here and she'll be staying with them—your Maman arranged it all with Mr. Steinbrenner." He tossed a conspiratorial glance at Anne-Marie, who was smiling at both of them. "Beth's going to be Tina's assistant tonight, so you can catch her act at the Tower."

He was moving too fast for Julia. "Tina?"

"Yeah, she's Max's recruit—he put her in charge of the birds and the bees, taking Claire's place." Julia stared at him, trying to make sense of what he was suggesting. "Not to worry, he said—no rubies in the navel!" He gave her time to digest the news, and Kiki and Anne-Marie stayed silent, too.

"It all suddenly seems like such a big deal, Ross," Julia mused worriedly. "If I fall on my face, everyone is going to be there to see it, even Beth, and—"

"You really want to do this, right?" Ross asked, then waited until she nodded. "You've got complete artistic control, so you're doing it exactly the way you see it?" She nodded slightly again. "You've okayed every move, every word, when it comes to the publicity?" Again her head moved up and down, slowly, as if she were adding up everything he said. "Then as I see it, no matter what happens, Julie love, there's no way you can lose! You're no amateur, so why so little faith in yourself at this late date?" He grinned at her, and she finally grinned back, once again relieved of her fears.

Just as they finished dessert, the waiter came to the table to tell Julia she had a call. The interruption reminded Anne-Marie that she had an appointment with a reporter from the *New York Times*, so she left at the same time, which left Ross and Kiki alone at the table. Ross ordered more coffee, mentally searching for something to talk about until Julia returned. He still found himself slightly uncomfortable around Kiki, though he couldn't put his finger on exactly why. Perhaps it was just her all-seeing eyes.

"So, Ross," Kiki breathed. Her smile seemed doubtful for a second, then tilted toward decision. "You are the one, yes?"

He saw no reason to pretend he didn't know what she meant. "Yes. I'm the one." He waited, more than a little curious about what else she might say.

"At first, in Paris, I think she is only—how you say—swept away? By the look of you."

"Not my brilliant mind?" he teased, both her and himself.

"*Non!* By the color of you—what else? I fear that she will see only the color, and not the man behind it. I worry for her, that she will be hurt too much by such a man." Ross realized then that she was being quite serious, in spite of his attempt at levity. "But I never see her like this before, how she is today. And I know her well. You have taken something from her, *n'est-ce pas?*" He was about to protest her accusation, but she didn't give him time. "The sadness in her eyes you take away, I think."

He wondered if he'd heard her right as he tried to understand her odd way of putting the English words together. "You think so?" he asked, almost holding his breath and still in some doubt about what she really meant.

"Oui." She breathed out the word in that unique way he'd noticed the first time he met her. "It is difficult for me to say. It was better, my English, with Julie, when she make me speak it so I will be prepared for when I have my own business. But I do not speak of fashion now, so I do not know the words so well."

"Say it any way you want and I'll figure it out, if it's about Julia," he urged, leaning forward, eager to hear what she was trying to tell him. "Tell me about her, the way you knew her back then, that year she was in Paris after Tom died."

"Yes, perhaps that is it. That she has finally let him go—or that he has let her go."

"Maybe. The guilt. Is that what you mean? Because they argued, disagreed about Vietnam? She seems to think it was partly her fault. That she should have tried harder to persuade him not to go, but I've tried to tell—"

"Yes, of course she had the guilt, but she can speak of that. No, it is more than that, I think. Something so terrible for her—I do not know what it can be." Kiki shook her head, and her hair followed in fluid waves. "She find no way to escape, and at times it drive her, as if by a demon. Then she would wake at night, get up from bed and go outside. At first I think, ah, it is the Texas in her—she must have the wide open space, it is in her blood. But no, it was only to move the body, to exhaust it, so she will sleep again. I worry, I tell her it is dangerous to go so in the street at night. But she say to me it is no matter, because she will go crazy if she does not, so—"

"And she never told you what was bothering her?" He was remembering Carey's comment about how hard Julia had taken

Tom's death, wondering if there'd been something she never told him and Anne-Marie.

"Mais non, though we talk much to each other of what is in here." Kiki swept one hand toward the valley between her small breasts. "I think perhaps she can never tell anyone." She lifted both shoulders and her eyebrows went up at the same time, while the lids dropped and fluttered once or twice in the typically Gallic "who knows" gesture.

"Julie and me, we learn early that we are different. How we see. Sometimes shapes, and—and, how you say—relations?" Ross only nodded. "But always the color is more intense, so perhaps we are more aware. We *feel* color." She shook her head, dissatisfied with her attempt to explain. "I am so sorry that I do not say it well. But I make the guess. What bothers Julie is to do with what she sees—here." This time the tips of her fingers touched her temple.

Ross blinked his eyelids, trying to stem the burning sensation. His throat was so tight he could only nod to Kiki, because he was nearly overcome by a burgeoning sense of pity, empathy, and finally, a deep sadness. He didn't need to know exactly what Julie saw in her head to understand what Kiki meant.

The final run-through at the Trump Tower took until midnight, but even so, Julia insisted on going back to her office. "I've got to make some changes in the schedule for tomorrow, for Connie. If I don't do it now, I'll just worry all night that I might forget something," she explained to Ross. "I couldn't sleep yet anyway—I've got to find some way to climb down off the ceiling." She laughed, somewhat self-consciously. "It's finally beginning to come together, don't you think?"

Ross nodded. "You're going to knock their socks off, Julie love." He took her hand and raised it to his lips. "But I know a better way to relax."

She smiled apologetically and shook her head slightly. "I'm afraid I couldn't—my mind is too—"

"Yeah, I was afraid of that. You've turned into a real nerd, you know that? No time for anything but work. Anyway, the work is more interesting, right?" He was teasing, and she knew it. "The truth is, anyone who sits at a terminal ten hours at a go is in love with her computer—she's not interested in fooling around!"

"But you, my love, are the one who got me started on this nasty habit of working night and day," Julie teased as they got off the elevator at the third floor.

"Go do whatever you have to, Julie—I'm off in search of food. Connie must have something around here besides chocolate." A few minutes later, he brought her a glass of wine, put a cassette in her tape player and then stood hesitantly beside her desk, not wanting to interrupt her. But she noticed and looked up.

"I suppose this isn't the time or place, but—" It was simply too much on his mind, after the conversation with Kiki at lunch. "I need to tell you something. Have wanted to for a long time." He paced a short path along the far side of her desk, threading the fingers of his right hand through his hair and down to cup his neck. "That night in Austin, out by the pond, when I couldn't sleep and you came out looking for me? Sometimes it wakes me up—seeing her. Maria, I mean.

"I got home from work about six that evening. I used to try to get home early, so I could play with her, then go back again after she went to bed. Marilyn was stretched out on the deck chair, passed out, no more than six feet from the edge of the pool." He stared fixedly, and Julia knew he was seeing the scene exactly as it had been that day. "Maria was floating, in the pool—her eyes wide open, staring right at me. Startled, she looked—surprised by what had happened." Tears flooded his eyes and then spilled over as he forced himself to remember, living it all over again. And finally he lost his way, forgetting why he had to tell her.

Julia rose and slid her arms around him, rocking him gently while smoothing her hands up and down his back, stroking his hair, sliding down to the back of his neck. "I know—your grandmother told me, Ross. That you were the one who found her, I mean." She sighed tiredly. "Oh, God, the awful pictures we carry in our heads, you and me, my dear, dear love."

He pulled away to look at her, his eyes still shiny with tears. "No, that's what I was trying to tell you. It's still there, and always will be, I suppose. But since you, and Beth, well, it's not so bad anymore, not so vivid. And it comes less often. I don't know why. But I wanted you to know that."

Julia searched his face silently, then nodded. "For me, too. I lied to you, you know, when I told you Tom never came back. His helicopter crashed and burned, and they shipped him home, what was left of him. To San Antonio, to the burn unit at Brooke Army Medical Center. Why anyone would try to salvage—" She stopped and swallowed, again and again, then drew in one long painful breath, determined to get the rest of it out somehow.

"There was—he—he didn't have any feet anymore, no legs, no genitals, no hands, no—" The tears were streaming down her face now, and she had to gulp for air.

"Stop, Julie, for God's sake!" He stood motionless.

A shiver shook her shoulders, and then she made herself go on. "No, I—I've never told anyone before, but I want to. I was the first one there. I watched him die. Willed him to die." She walked away from Ross then, over to one of the tall windows, and stood there for a minute with her back turned toward him.

"And while I stood there looking at him, I decided that no one else was ever going to know, because I didn't want his son or daughter to think of him like that. Or his mother. What mother should have to know that about her child? But she hasn't ever quite forgiven me, because I got to see him before he died—and she didn't."

After a minute she turned, and he saw a soft little smile appear on her lips and in her eyes. "But the picture in my head has begun to fade, too, Ross—since that first day you came to the ranch. You said you recognized Beth immediately because you could see Tom in her face, remember? And now, after all this time, because of you I think, I can see him again, too, as he was before that awful day—healthy and whole, smiling and loving. I no longer have to dread my memories of him." She came back into his arms then, and they stood locked together in silence as the seconds stretched into minutes.

"Now, let me hurry up and get finished so we can go home," Julia urged, pushing herself away from him finally. He was reluctant to let her go, but acquiesced, watching her for a few minutes to make sure she was all right. He sat down at the computer on the far side of the room, trying to regain a sense of the ordinariness of where they were and what they were doing.

It was at least fifteen minutes before Julia spoke again, and what she said almost knocked him off his chair.

"How do you feel about getting married this weekend?"

Chapter 23

Ross swiveled around, trying to assess whether she was just joking.

"Or have you changed your mind?" Julia suggested when he didn't answer right away, though she was smiling.

He shook his head, more to clear it than in response. "I didn't know you were even thinking about it, especially in the middle of all this. Why don't you come over here so we can talk," he suggested, patting one thigh.

She rose, detoured to flip the wall switch for the overhead lights, then came toward him with a slow smile. Sliding one arm around his neck, she eased down onto his lap. He reached up to meet her lips, settling her close against him. "Now. What have you got in mind?"

"I've made a decision. No—a decision and a half."

"Just now, tonight? What happened to bring that on?"

"No, a while back, but I thought you were too busy to even talk about it at the time."

"Me?" He sounded both exasperated and impatient. "So tell me about the one and a half decisions."

"Well, first of all, I want us to be together, too—and I don't see why we should wait any longer."

"No? Why not?" he asked, utterly amazed at how simple she could make it sound after months of hesitation and finding excuses.

"Because I love you." She smiled teasingly. "Which I don't think I've mentioned for a day or two. Not just infatuated, though I suppose there's that, too. You give it an awfully good try, McCutcheon, in case you think I haven't noticed, but no one can live in a perpetual state of courtship." She sobered abruptly. "But the real test comes when the caring is pitted against all the distractions—the petty irritations at work, or trying to figure your income tax, and all the stuff children drag into your life whether you want it there or not. We've learned to deal well with each other, you and I. And you've given me the time I needed to learn something I've never had the chance to before—that affection feeds on routine, on hours and days of comfortable companionship. I guess I want to believe that neither one of us will lose track of what holds it all together, the listening and talking, the touching and caring, the attention."

Ross sought her lips again, sealing a pledge. "And the half a decision?" he asked, still butterflying kisses along the edges of her lips, across her cheek, coming to rest just under her jaw.

"That's the how—how we're going to manage it, make it right for both of us. The part I've decided is that I'm going back to Texas. But whether I'll still be working with Taggart or on my own is what I don't know yet. And I probably won't until this show is over and the orders come in, or don't. So maybe you'd rather wait and see, if you're worried that I'll change my mind."

For answer, he brushed his lips back and forth across hers. "You've already made the only decision I care about, Julia love—and I'm not as good at waiting as I've been pretending." And then his lips sought hers in earnest, warming the liquid in her veins as one hand slid up to enclose her breast while the other shaped the back of her head, holding her securely while she melted against him.

"Could we go home now?" she whispered, the words separated by the light touch of her lips—to his temple, just below his ear, at the corner of his lips, the tip of his chin—"or would you rather spend the night with that computer?"

A relative newcomer to the Manhattan skyline, the sixty-eight-story Trump Tower was often cited as a prime example of the new skyscraper architecture of the 1980s, and was already as famous as its older siblings along Fifth Avenue. The glass-sheathed bronze tower was defined by floors forming "steps" back from the street up to the sixth floor, to create both the skylights needed to "open" the atrium inside, and a "window box" look from the outside, complete with the requisite greenery.

Though it housed commercial space as well as condos, it was the atrium, an elegant pink marble shopping emporium with an eighty-foot-high waterfall cascading down one side, that was largely responsible for the Tower's reputation for elegance and glamour. Six floors of famous boutiques ringed the open atrium—cut by brass-trimmed, mirrored escalators moving through open vistas of glass and greenery—offering shoppers everything from designer fashions and handcrafted Italian shoes for children, to diamonds and Belgian chocolates.

The mirrored bronze tower reminded Ross of the gaudy "carnival" glass in the Saturday flea markets he'd visited with his grandmother when he was a child. And the atrium interior was vaguely reminiscent of the Charles de Gaulle air terminal in Paris. But whether Julia liked the building or not, he knew it would never have been her choice for this show, because the open space created almost insurmountable staging problems. But she'd managed. Oh, yes, he thought, watching the crowd that was bunching up at the door now, how she'd managed!

Tony was there, handing out his personal greetings along

with the elegant portfolios containing color printouts of Julia's key designs as well as the promotional information she and Elaine had labored over so long, carefully shaping and honing each phrase. Soft music provided a comfortable background for the quietly bubbling atmosphere of excitement and expectation that pervaded the open space as people milled around, moving toward the long table crowded with white-wine spritzers in tall green-stemmed glasses—pored over a variety of small yellow, salmon and ruby-red flowers—silver trays filled with chocolate-dipped strawberries and tiny cheese cookies. Bougainvillea vines spilled from huge pots at either end of the table, trailing their delicate pink blooms all the way to the floor.

From the beginning Julia had planned to control the open space with lighting, to create the illusion of season, place and temperature through both spots and projected colored light, while hiding in darkness the views of the atrium she didn't want. A big black-and-white-striped tent had been erected to serve as dressing room and to mask the staging area, and a comfortably wide runway extended out from it for about thirty-five feet, widening at the end into a circular turnaround. Audience seating was arranged in groups facing the runway, which was low enough to provide the visibility and feeling of accessibility Julia wanted, leaving wide aisles for easy access.

Julia had left the apartment much earlier than usual this morning, and looked tired in spite of the bright yellow sweat shirt she was wearing with her faded jeans when Ross had last talked with her about four-thirty. He suspected the long hours and nervous tension of the past few days were beginning to catch up with her, and he couldn't help worrying. She seemed to have little awareness of her own physical and psychological limits, or else was unwilling to admit them, even to herself. Instead, she pushed herself mercilessly, operating on the assumption that she could take and take and take—and then seemed utterly amazed when the machine began to break down.

Ross saw Beth coming toward him wearing a worried look,

and waved her over. "Hi, honey!" He gave her a hug as if he hadn't seen her in days, simply because he felt like it, though he'd talked to her in the staging area behind the tent only a few minutes ago, where she was helping Tina get the kids and their costumes organized. "Need help? How's it going back there?"

"No, Tina and Ben don't even have anything for me to do right now, so I came out to watch the show for a while. Carey's still not here?" Beth asked anxiously. She'd been serving as girl friday, messenger, or whatever anybody needed all day.

Ross glanced toward the entrance for about the twentieth time as he shook his head, then looked at his watch. Only five more minutes. "He'll be here, don't worry. How's Julia holding up, can you tell? Think she's going to start on time?" Ross had exited the tent long since, when it got really frantic in there, full of half-dressed models painting their eyes and lips, and twisting up their hair, dressers arranging garments on racks, placing the right shoes underneath each one, and rolling pantyhose to be ready for instant changes.

"Yeah, she was lining up the first models when I saw her last, giving them a final once-over. I think she's beginning to get a little crazy, 'cause she was laughing like she's actually enjoying it. But she's okay."

Ross gave her shoulder a squeeze as he heard the music come up. Vivaldi's "The Seasons" was the opener. The crowd quickly quieted, and then the lights took control, directing all attention toward Elaine, who was standing near the entrance of the tent. Julia wanted more narration than usual, she said, partly because the press kits hadn't gone out ahead of time, but also because she intended to make sure the audience drew the right conclusions about what they were seeing. So Elaine was going to tell them not only the what, but the why.

"The collection we present tonight, ladies and gentlemen, is just a beginning," Elaine began, her low-pitched, somewhat throaty voice sounding too big to be coming from such a tiny body. "A glimpse into the future of computer-aided fashion design—and the beginning of a new era in the marketing and merchandising of fashion as well.

"The new Taggart silhouette fits the body, but gently, providing both flexibility and comfort. And a hint of sensual movement underneath. Taggart is not for the timid, or the brash. As Taggart has pioneered in the field of computer-aided fashion design, so are the fashions we present this fall for pioneering women. Women who are willing and eager to explore themselves—their heads—and imaginations—and feelings. Women of all colors, and all ages. Women who are serious about clothes because they know that symbolism is important in transmitting a sense of power."

The entire runway was flooded with a warm, golden light, and the flap of the tent was folded back to allow two models to emerge, one a black-haired chicana from Houston and the other a strawberry blonde from Minneapolis, "ooching" their way down the runway in the professional walk of models everywhere. Elaine introduced them by name as well as the cities they were from, which was Julia's way of both personalizing her presentation and identifying the region of the country the particular numbers were suited to.

Ross watched and listened, fascinated, since he'd caught only disembodied bits and pieces during rehearsals—and began to understand for the first time some of the messages Julia hadn't put into words.

"For the golden harvest months of October and November, Taggart uses orange as a neutral, because of its matchless versatility in combination with a wide range of other colors," Elaine continued. "Natalie wears a Mediterranean blue cotton Donegal tweed jacket flecked with orange and gold, for instance, over a froth of apricot wool voile—cool wool."

The models turned, posed, then moved back toward the opening of the tent as the applause began. The crowd glittered under the lights as jewelry winked on hands that were making notations with the gold-tasseled pencils provided by Taggart. Then other models began to pour from the tent—from Denver,

Miami, St. Louis and San Diego—and Ross lost track of time, until he felt a hand on his shoulder.

"Have I missed her? Has she been out yet?" Carey's voice was soft as he bent toward Ross.

Ross turned slightly, smiling his relief at the older man's arrival. "Nope. Pretty soon, I think. You run into trouble?"

Carey shook his head in disgust. "The boys at the Energy Department sprung a big one on us today, just as I was getting ready to vamoose out of there," Carey whispered. "A high-level nuclear waste dump, right in the middle of the most productive agricultural area in the whole damned state of Texas, right smack through the Ogallala Aquifer, which runs all the way up to Nebraska!" He grinned suddenly. "Like I've said before, those Republicans are nothing but a bunch of guys wearing hundred-dollar hats on two-bit heads! Leave it to them and they'll put the whole damn Great Plains breadbasket out of business!"

As the insistent beat of Vivaldi faded away, the crowd stilled, sensing something different, expectant, straining to hear the soft, disembodied impressions of Debussy that seemed to issue from another, distant world. Both Ross and Carey turned their full attention to the runway.

A single model emerged from the tent, and this time Elaine spoke only three words by way of introduction—"Kiki Chapotin, Paris."

Kiki's tawny hair and tall willowy body flowed like honey as she moved along the runway in one long sinuous sweep of gold, violet and pale orange. Shock waves seemed to bounce off the glass walls of the atrium, and then the audience broke into wild applause, some of them rising from their seats.

Beth turned to Ross with a grin of self-satisfied excitement on her face, and spied Carey for the first time. "She's pretty good, huh?" she tossed at both Carey and Ross, then swung back to watch Kiki turn and pause, smiling slightly as she made eye contact with various individuals in the audience, before moving back along the runway toward the tent.

Ross had heard a lot of talk about the models during the

past few days, how some merely walked well while others filled the catwalk with their special charisma, but he was unprepared for the effect of this woman, who seemed to fill the entire room with her "presence." Julia obviously had known, and it made him aware again of how much more she seemed to see, in people as well as things, than he did.

The lighting began to change now, subtly cooling from gold to gray as models from Boston, Atlanta and Seattle paraded down the runway, dressed for the colder temperatures of December and January—each in a bulky winter day suit, and then one of Julia's favorites, her slim wool and cotton trousers, topped with a variety of jackets. A few minutes later, the music faded into nothingness again, only to be resurrected in the playful mood of Erik Satie. The audience hushed, instantly expectant, knowing that something special was in the offing again. And they weren't disappointed.

"Ladies and gentlemen," Elaine announced, "one of the outstanding pioneers of our time," pausing a moment, "and the first woman to wear trousers on the famous concert stages of Europe." This time there was no mention of either her name or a city to identify the model.

Loud applause greeted Anne-Marie Lacombe the instant she emerged, unhurried, walking naturally, exactly as Ross remembered seeing her cross the stage of Orchestra Hall in Chicago. Here was no tall, willowy professional model, moving in a practiced, artful walk, but a woman of great magnetism in spite of her diminutive size. The warm sparkle of high humor lit her eyes as a smile of infinite mystery curved the corners of her generous mouth.

Some in the audience seemed to identify her immediately, and a wave of murmured whispers among both the curious and the surprised rose up to compete with the music as she moved along the runway—a vibrant figure in emerald green palazzo pants of whisper-soft wool challis, tucked into tiny flat pleats at the waist, then flowing from her hips to define the entire length of each leg, from thigh to ankle, with each step she took. Her short-cropped cardigan jacket in amber Battenberg lace was very nearly the same color as her short, curling hair, and two big square-cut emeralds set in gold glittered at her ears, while a half dozen or more gold bracelets circled her left wrist, emitting the muted music of tiny bells.

Ross and Beth turned to glance at Carey at just about the same time, then back at each other in silent agreement. There was no doubt in either of their minds that Carey was, at least for this one moment, speechless.

Elaine's commentary moved on as other models appeared, with the music and lighting continuing to change, growing progressively more "casual," until at last Ross recognized one of the tunes he'd heard the night Julia took him to the Greene Street Cafe.

Beth touched Ross's arm. "That's my cue. I'd better be getting back. Keep your fingers crossed." She slipped into the darkened area around the edge of the audience and made her way toward the back of the big canvas tent. Ten minutes later, Ross recognized the shift into the final segment of the show, with Elaine's comment, "Seasons *do* still matter. Whether they're measured in physical or psychological terms, they bring variety into our lives. So to reduce seasonal offerings is to reduce the *variety* of apparel available to consumers." Then she was moving into anecdotes to illustrate the regional variations in climate across the country, even during the same "season."

The lights dimmed while she spoke, subtly shifting tone once again, becoming warmer and warmer, while small bodies moved on silent feet through the shadowy aisles within the audience. "Just this year, for instance, while the Siberia Express and the Alberta Clipper have been freezing toes in the Midwest and Northeast, retailers in the Southwest have been scrambling in vain to satisfy their customers. It's too early to wear the look or the colors of spring—in January. So what does a trial lawyer wear in court—in a city of perhaps two million people, don't forget, not on the beaches of the Caribbean—when the temperature never drops below freezing?

And what does she wear that evening to her ten-year-old daughter's piano recital, or to the theater with her husband?

"And what does the public relations director for, say, Texas Instruments, wear to the office in the middle of February, when the redbud and peach trees are blooming, and it's 97 degrees outside—the kind of temperature we New Yorkers think of strictly in terms of summer vacation. And all the crawly and winged things are beginning to emerge from their winter hiding places?"

The lights over the runway came up to sunny daylight, and another wave of models emerged from the tent, first in daytime answers to Elaine's questions, all in saturated reds and pinks, deep yellows and oranges, and brilliant blues and greens, layered to achieve new effects in both color and style. From the aisles came a soft fluttering sound as small arms were slowly raised and lowered, giving life to spotted and striped butterfly and moth wings, in hues of red, and the palest blue, green and yellow, and even black and white.

"New concepts in regional-seasonal dressing mean new fabrics, which we have been showing you all evening. Fluid matte jerseys that drape like silk, under bulky cotton tweeds. Nappy blends that have bulk without the weight and warmth of heavy wools, because half the threads are 'floated' to allow the fabric to breathe—a new weaving technique developed by Monarch in close cooperation with Taggart designers," Elaine explained as the models continued to flow from the tent.

When the lights and music both dimmed again, she paused, then asked, "And for evening?" The crowd waited silently for the answer. Once again the music changed, this time to "Glitter and Be Gay" from Bernstein's *Candide,* setting the stage for what was to come. Orangy lanterns began to glow in the dim light of evening, and the butterflies of daylight became fireflies at dusk, their bodies pulsing with light when they lifted dark wings.

Ross suspected he wasn't the only one to be intensely affected by the aura of lush sensuality Julia had created with sound and light, which the crowd quickly confirmed with a crescendo of applause.

It was in designing apparel to wear during the hours "after work" that Julia really let her imagination soar, exploring the multiplicity of roles women were called on to play, from their teens to their mature years. But she also was suggesting a few new ones, taken from her private storehouse of fantasies. Her timing was perfect, right up to the end, and when Anne-Marie and Kiki finally appeared together, the crowd exploded in a climax of wild applause. Suddenly Beth was there, tugging on Ross's arm to get his attention.

"Ben says for you to come right away. Quick. He's at the back of the tent."

"What's wrong, did he say?" Ross asked, following her as she threaded her way through the crowd of standing spectators who now filled the space behind the rows of seats. But she only shook her head silently.

The flap at the back of the tent was rolled up and tied in place, and models were spilling out into the open area behind it, lining up for the finale. He spotted Max, helping the kids take off their wings. "You see Ben anywhere?"

"In there," Max mouthed, motioning inside the tent with his head.

"Excuse me, excuse me," Ross muttered as he inched his way around the women, then quickly looked around inside—at a scene that struck him as slightly surrealistic, with the models and dressers, hairdressers and makeup people all in frenetic but silent motion—searching for Julia's yellow sweat shirt. He couldn't spot her anywhere, but did find Ben, with his head bent toward Tina, apparently listening to something she was whispering in his ear.

"Where's Julia? Is she okay?" he asked, keeping his voice low.

"I would say very much so, wouldn't you, Tina?" Ben drawled, raising an eyebrow as he tilted his head a bit to the right. Ross turned to look, and then could only stare.

The first thing he noticed was her hair, pulled back at the

sides before falling in a wildly curling, kinky mass in the back—like it had been that first night in Paris. Curling wisps framed her face, and Louis the sixteenth diamond chandelier earrings swung from her lobes. Her shoulders were bare, and she was not, quite obviously, wearing a bra. A light blue-green halter—so delicate a color it brought to mind the patina of an old copper roof—crossed just above her breasts to wrap around behind her neck, clinging in a way that made his fingertips tingle. He hardly noticed the gently pleated dusky rose skirt that fell almost to her ankles, revealing black velvet pumps with a delicate pink rose over each toe.

Perched low on her left breast, vibrating its wings as if about to take flight, was the diamond and ruby butterfly he'd given her.

Connie pulled back the tent flap and the models began streaming out, matching the fast, excited pace of the music, and Ross heard the audience applause. Then the crowd quieted, waiting along with the models, who stationed themselves at intervals along the runway. Ben moved out first, taking Tina's hand to pull her around in front of him, and then both of them paused long enough for a butterfly-winged young girl to move down the runway ahead of them.

Julia turned and held out her hand to Ross. A big crescendo of applause blossomed, filling the atrium just as he went to her. He waited for the noise to die down so she could hear. "You're next, *ma belle Julie.*" He leaned forward to kiss her on the cheek. "You knocked their socks off, just like you said you would, you fantastic, beautiful woman! Now go take your bow."

"We are going to do this together, McCutcheon, or not at all. I couldn't have done it without you—and your computer." Her smile teased and caressed him at the same time.

Ross heard a shout from outside the tent and knew the crowd was already getting impatient. "Oh no, Julie, I'm not dressed for—" He had on a sky blue–nutmeg brown striped knit turtleneck with chocolate brown corduroys, clothes he'd come to the Tower to work in earlier in the day.

Julie started shaking her head, stopping his protest before he could finish. "You look the way you are inside, Ross—cool of head and warm of heart—for me, now and always, the most beautiful man in the world."

They looked at each other for one long minute, then Julia took his hand in hers and they walked down the runway together.

The Taggart offices were surprisingly quiet when Julia arrived late Monday morning. Connie greeted her with an affectionate hug. "I'll bet it feels like weeks instead of just a few days, doesn't it?"

In fact, Julia could hardly believe it was possible for so much to happen in only four days—especially since she'd spent most of the day after the show sleeping. She smiled to herself, remembering the late supper party Wednesday night, which Ross had arranged. No matter how her collection might be received by the press and public, it had been royally celebrated by the family and friends she loved most—Kiki, Max and Elaine, Tina and Beth, Carey and Anne-Marie, Ben and Lucy, Connie and Arlette. Only Alex was missing, and Emily Maguire. Exhausted as she'd felt, Ross had known she would need time to get used to the idea that the die was cast, for good or ill, and there was nothing more for her to do.

Selling was scheduled to start the day after the show, in Taggart's New York showrooms and at the fashion marts in Chicago, Dallas, Los Angeles and Atlanta, but it would be at least a week before they knew how buyers were responding. Press reports were likely to depend on how important or "hot" they considered what they'd seen Wednesday night, and also in part on regularly scheduled deadlines. Fashion!Dallas, the weekly fashion section of the *Dallas Morning News*, for instance, appeared every Wednesday.

The phone had been ringing when she and Ross got back to her apartment Wednesday night, in spite of the fact that it was after one. And after nearly an hour of one call after another, most of them from reporters and editors wanting statements or to arrange an interview, Ross had simply unplugged both phones and ordered her to bed. And that was all she remembered until he woke her around five that afternoon.

"Have you seen any of the press reports?" Connie asked, knowing that she'd spent the long weekend with her family and Ross.

"The Friday *Times* and *Journal*, that's all." Ross had brought her breakfast in bed Friday morning. "I thought you said we had a lot to do today," she'd protested, starting to get out of bed. "Besides that, you're treating me like you think I'm sick, which I definitely am not. Sometimes I wonder if you're expecting bad news and hope to make up for it ahead of time, to sort of prepare me."

"Your imagination is working overtime again, Julie honey," Ross chided, while fixing the pillows behind her back, smoothing the covers and then setting the tray across her lap. "Now, drink your orange juice, and then I may let you take a look at one of these." With that, he waved a couple of newspapers which he'd been hiding under the tray in front of her face, then waited for her to drink her juice like an obedient child. The *New York Times* carried a photograph of Kiki and Anne-Marie, and the headline "Taggart Fall Collection the Most Innovative Seen in New York in Decades."

> New York—Julia Bonner, the designer responsible for the Ben Taggart fall collection presented at Trump Tower Wednesday night, took less than an hour to prove that she is not only a formidable talent as an artist who is willing to explore new technology in the design process, but that she may well turn out to be the most astute marketer working in the fashion business today.
>
> Rather than targeting a specific woman, Bonner's collection was as diverse as the models who wore them—one of whom was Anne-Marie Lacombe, the internationally acclaimed French cellist.

Julia glanced up at Ross with a happy smile lifting the corners of her mouth, but he was grinning in anticipation so she knew he'd already read it.

"Go ahead, read the rest," he urged. "It gets even better."

> Bonner uses her apparently intuitive understanding of both style and women to transform the casual into the elegant—feminine, unaffected, confident—in a veritable kaleidoscope of color, texture and pattern, yet never overwhelms the wearer. Eschewing black, even for evening, she instead creates drama and intensity, at times even passion, with her unique use of highly saturated colors in combinations most designers wouldn't dare. As if that weren't enough, every piece shows an exquisiteness of cut and fit, the like of which is rarely seen outside Paris. And all at prices millions of American women can afford!
>
> "I'm designing," Bonner told the *Times*, "for the women who believe that 'what is important to me is the way I look to me.' Marketing fashion to women has changed because most women today behave and are motivated by their own satisfaction and gratification. They don't dress just to attract a man. Their self-perception is reflected in how they aspire to look, and they've begun to regard themselves as authorities—and that means they're not so concerned with looking to others for clues on how to behave, or to look."

"Well?" Ross asked at last. "No comment from the formidable talent? The old ego requires still more massaging?"

"Stop teasing, dammit! Let me see that one. Is it that bad?" she laughed.

The piece in the *Wall Street Journal* was front page, top left corner, the best spot in the paper. Julia quickly scanned the headline—"Stylesetter: Ben Taggart Breaks New Ground with Computer-Aided Fashion Design"—and then the first few paragraphs.

New York—The Ben Taggart fall collection, shown Wednesday night to a glittering standing-room-only crowd at the Trump Tower, may instead turn out to be the harbinger of spring, if it breathes new life into the American fashion industry.

The result of a cooperative effort by Taggart designer Julia Bonner and Ross McCutcheon, president of Tekware, a computer-aided design and manufacturing software development company located in Austin, Texas, the collection was created with a computer program developed by McCutcheon, who integrated the entire package from original sketch to patternmaking and grading, marking and cutting the cloth.

The designer's effort to develop new fall-winter fabrics suitable for mild winter climates is further demonstration of her ability to combine her marketing and design talents. "Retail sales in the South have risen 60 percent during the past decade," Bonner said, "yet about half of all fall-winter sales in that part of the country are at half price."

In addition, the designer points out that 77 percent of the financial assets of this country are concentrated in the over-fifty population, which leaves only 23 percent in the hands of Americans under fifty. "Yet young consumers are diligently pursued, while the no-longer-young are largely ignored. We at Taggart believe that is, at best, a dubious marketing strategy."

"Well, I'm glad at least one of them had the sense to mention your part in this up front," Julia commented when she finished reading. "But it looks good so far, don't you think? At least, the door is still open. We've yet to hear what WWD says, of course, and the others. So let's not count any chickens." She smiled beguilingly. "Anyway, right now I've got more important things on my mind."

"Julie, my love?" Connie's expression turned sheepish as soon as the words were out of her mouth. "Sorry about that.

It was the only thing I could think of to get your attention, to bring you back from wherever you were." She sort of laughed by way of apology. "Patti Berkin, from the Tobe Report, will be here for an interview at two-thirty, and Polly Mellen at four. She's bringing a photographer with her. Says she's planning a big spread on *you,* dear girl. You must have hit target dead center with her. By the way, did you know that half of *Vogue*'s readers wear size 12 or larger?"

"Okay. How about getting Elaine and Max for me, see if they're free for lunch. Say I need to talk, and it has to be sometime today. What else?"

"Alex came in about an hour ago."

Julia looked up, surprised. "And?" she asked impatiently.

"He just asked me to let him know when you came in."

"Okay, I'll call him. Anything else?"

"WWD is on your desk. Tony talked to them. Last week, apparently. We got half the front page, jumping to a two-page photo spread inside. Not bad, I'd say. Thought you'd want to see it first thing. There are a couple of others, too—the *Chicago Tribune* and the *Washington Post*. You've got a bunch of calls, but I didn't make any promises about how soon you'd be getting back to them."

Julia took the phone messages from her. "I want to talk to Ben, too. So let me have the rest of the morning. And I need a few minutes to talk over something with you, Connie. Maybe we could do that around five."

She glanced at her watch. "How about if you take these, then, and get on the phone? Schedule in the remainder of the afternoon, either phone or personal interviews, starting at about one-thirty. No longer than thirty minutes if they come here, every fifteen minutes on the phone, if necessary. After today, they'll have to call me in Austin."

She handed the stack of phone messages back to Connie. "But I intend to be back next week—in time for the board meeting on Wednesday."

Chapter 24

JULIA GLANCED AT her watch again—only thirty more minutes. The palms of her hands were moist, and her fingers felt numb with cold. She took a few slow deep breaths, trying to force herself to relax, then leaned back in her desk chair and turned it around to face the wall of windows in her office. She was beginning to wish now that she'd taken the time to eat breakfast instead of just going through the motions. Ross must have noticed, though he didn't say anything. He'd come with her to New York, "on business" he said, but she suspected it was really in case she needed him, for moral support.

The door to her office opened and Connie came in carrying a small tray. She set it on the desk in front of Julia, then picked up a napkin, unfolded and handed it to her.

"You're mothering me again, Connie," Julia observed absently.

"I made hot chocolate for you, instead of coffee," Connie said, ignoring her. "Better for the nerves, and your stomach—even better still if you could get a few bites of this croissant down." She smiled hesitantly. "Sure you're okay?"

Julia returned her smile. "I'll just sit here for a few minutes and get my head organized, I think. Thanks, Connie."

There were still a number of unanswered questions that worried her, but they didn't really affect the decision she'd come to, or what she was going to say to the Taggart board of directors today.

They still didn't know who was responsible for knocking off Ben's collection, and it was beginning to look like they never would. She couldn't help remembering Alex's haggard face and despondent mood when he'd told her about Nat last week. He'd sat with his head down, staring at his hands.

"It turns out he didn't have much faith in me—in my fidelity, I guess I should say. And me, I was too busy to be bothered. Couldn't see any need to reassure him. Figured he would just know." He got up and walked over to the window, apparently lost in his own thoughts. There was nothing she could say he didn't already know, about what he should or shouldn't have done. And anyway, wisdom in hindsight was too easy, too superficial, perhaps too forgiving.

"I laid my suspicions out in black and white, even some that were just wild guesses. But when I asked him how much he made off Ben's stuff, he didn't have the vaguest idea what I was talking about. At first I thought maybe he was still mentally confused, or had some loss of memory. The doctors said that was a possibility with the kind of head injury he had. But he remembers everything else, unfortunately. The sketches he did for Ben. Seeing me with Larry that day. And every damn thing those guys did to him." He stopped, trying to get control of his own painful memories.

"It hurt him—to find out that I didn't have any more faith in him than he did in me. Hearing what I thought he was capable of doing to us. But he denied it, and I know him too well not to recognize when he's being evasive. I asked where all the bills he was flashing came from, then. He said it was savings. Since I—I—that he didn't give a damn anymore. Decided he might as well blow in on a good time." Alex had turned toward her then, almost in supplication. "I believe him,

Julia. I'd swear he didn't do it! But if it wasn't Nat, who the hell *could* it have been?"

Julia spread some apple jelly on a croissant and then took a bite, chewing slowly as she thought about her conversation with Max later that same day.

"Poor Tony's got a love-hate thing with you," Max had commented, hitting the rolled-up copy of WWD he was clutching in one hand against the edge of her desk. "Loves your ideas and your success—what it means for Taggart and for him—but hates that you had anything to do with it, that he has to share the fame and glory with you." He'd laughed, then straightened out the tabloid enough to read from it.

> With the presentation of its fall collection in the Atrium of Trump Tower Wednesday night, the house of Taggart emerged as a *force majeure* in the American fashion industry. And if there were still any doubts remaining as to who was responsible for both the most imaginative collection this city has seen in recent decades *and* the company's foray into new technology, those doubts were dispelled once and for all when Julia Bonner stepped onto the runway—a diamond and ruby butterfly perched on her left breast, echoing the show's final scenario—on the arm of Ross McCutcheon, the computer genius who developed the software Taggart pioneered.

Max had glanced up with a spreading grin. "Has Ross seen this? Hope it doesn't go to his head, don't you?" he'd tossed out, then continued reading.

> Tony Gianni, Taggart's managing director, said after the presentation Wednesday night that the company is simply "staying in character as an innovator, in both design and marketing. That's been our forte from the very beginning, and we expect the new regional-seasonal concepts presented here tonight to quickly become the industry standard."

Julia was shaking her head long before he'd finished. "I'm afraid I wouldn't exactly call the way he's responded to my ideas in the past two years love, Max. He sounds like that only when he can't do anything else but stonewall, as he calls it. I'm still not sure why he ever came around in the first place—to my working with Ross, or doing my collection, for that matter. He couldn't be sure the whole thing wouldn't flop. It still seems out of character."

"Uh-uh, I disagree," Max had countered. "At first he just wanted you out of the way, remember, so he could have a clear field with Ben? And it worked. After Ben's stuff was knocked off, he probably didn't have much choice, with Charlie Harkins breathing down his neck, threatening to call an emergency meeting of the board. He had to do something or lose control. I think that's when he saw your collection as a way to get rid of you once and for all. He figured you'd go down in big bright flames, Julia. Your regional-seasonal marketing idea, even the colors you were using in your collection, were bucking the trends, don't forget! If Ben didn't go for the computer idea, neither would a lot of other designers, and they'd all come down on you like a bunch of vultures. The press could crucify you, just by quoting them. And then with Taggart on the ropes financially, Ben would have to turn to him to save the company. You'd be out on your ass—where all beautiful women are supposed to be, right?" They'd laughed together, then, in perfect understanding.

The intercom on Julia's desk buzzed, bringing her back to the present. "Time, Julia," Connie reminded, even as Julia was rising from her chair. She walked toward the mirrored wall of her office, watching herself, trying to assess whether she would look to Taggart's all-male board of directors the way she wanted them to see her.

There was only one chair still empty when she slipped into the big conference room, trying to be as unobtrusive as possible. Ben was standing at the head of the big rectangular table, where she'd laid out all her printouts that night—how could it possibly have been only three weeks ago?—and he nodded in her direction, recognizing her arrival. But she had no more than sat down when everyone else in the room rose and started clapping. She glanced around hurriedly, wondering why—only to discover that everyone was turned toward her.

Julia smiled, slightly embarrassed at the overt show of appreciation or congratulations, or whatever it was. She looked around at each one—until her eyes came to an abrupt halt when she spotted Ross, standing just behind Ben, a boyish smile lighting his face as he clapped, too.

"We'll be hearing from Julia shortly," Ben began as soon as the applause died down, "but before I turn the meeting over to the chairman of the board to deal with a somewhat less pleasant matter, I want to introduce Mr. Ross McCutcheon, who most of you know has been Taggart's 'computer software genius.' "

Ross rose briefly to acknowledge another round of applause, in which Julia joined enthusiastically, and then sat back down without a word. She wondered why it hadn't occurred to her that Ross might be asked to this meeting, too, so the board could convey their thanks in person for everything he'd done for the company. But it made her feel good to know that he had.

She continued glancing around the room, finally catching a slight nod from Max, who was sitting just a couple of chairs away from Ross. She couldn't help wonder how Tony was taking the accolades directed to her and Ross, but she couldn't locate him before her attention was drawn back to Ben.

"Not only did Ross have a hand in Taggart's recent pioneering 'foray' into high technology, however. As it turns out, he also came to our rescue in a way none of us was even aware of at the time—so it is with pleasure that I also introduce our new majority stockholder." Ben turned to Ross, expecting him to say a few words.

To Julia, the revelation was like a bolt of lightning out of a clear blue sky—unexpected, unbelievable and shocking. Ben held two hundred thousand shares, so Ross had to have more than that, which meant putting somewhere in the neighborhood of four million dollars into the company! Maybe even more. Her mind reeled crazily, then tried to right itself. Her eyes sought his, finding them already watching her, as if he was waiting. But for what?

She'd known he certainly wasn't strapped for money, just from the hints Stan had let drop if nothing else. And from his house. And the jewelry he'd given her. He was completely at ease about money, so he didn't need to talk about it. More than that, though, he hadn't seemed threatened in the least at finding out that she owned stock in Taggart worth more than a million dollars herself. But why keep his buy-in such a deep, dark secret from her? And why drop it on her now, at the very last possible minute? Did he hope to muddy the water—just when she finally knew exactly what she wanted to do? For a second, it felt as if something had been taken away from her, that Ross had invaded her territory, and she wanted to scream in protest! Did he expect her to stay with Taggart now, no matter what, to help protect his investment? How could he expect her to feel that she owed him that, when he hadn't even consulted her first?

Then she simply *knew* why. It was precisely because he wanted to make sure he *didn't* influence the decision she was trying to make—so she could do what *she* thought was right for her at this particular moment in her life! The answer flooded her consciousness, rushing in with the force of an ocean tide, clearing away all the clutter in its path.

She loved him with her eyes, across the room, ignoring everyone else, trying to tell him that she knew he was trying his damnedest to do what Carey called the "hard part"—*not* advising her what to do, not even helping her to decide, even if her decision took away from his own life and what he wanted. She felt an almost-intuitive certainty about that much at least, even if she didn't understand why he'd bought into the company in the first place.

"I really don't have much to say," Ross began, looking away at last, after he saw the understanding dawn in her eyes, the twitch at the corner of her mouth, and then the blazing smile that broke forth in spite of all her efforts to control it. "I don't mind telling you, though, that I consider this company a damned good investment. Probably even more so now than when I decided to buy in. Because after working so closely with your people, and under some pretty stressful conditions, I've got even more reason to have confidence in them than I did then."

He paused as a polite crescendo of applause rose and then quickly subsided. "But I wouldn't even be here today except for Ben's insistence, and I want you to know that I have no intention of trying to influence you in the decisions you're facing about the future of this company. Just the opposite, in fact." He smiled engagingly, glancing around the table. "Because I find myself with a problem—which I hope you will appreciate. What you might call a slight case of conflict of interest. Therefore, I'd consider it a great favor if you'd ignore what you've just learned about my stock holdings, and also try your damnedest to act as if I'm not even here!"

There was a smattering of quiet laughter mixed with applause, and several heads around the table nodded understandingly as Ross sat back down in one of the chairs lining the walls of the room, brought in especially for this meeting. Julia watched Ross and Max exchange a quick, understanding glance.

Charlie Harkins, at the opposite end of the table from Ben, spoke from his seat. "We all appreciate that, Ross—that, as well as everything else you've done for Ben Taggart—and we sympathize with your personal problem." He chuckled as he glanced around at Julia. When he turned back to the men gathered around the table, however, his expression was dead serious.

"I want to move right along with the rest of our agenda, but first we need to take up an emergency item—an unpleasant development that I am sorry to have to inject into our deservedly self-congratulatory mood here today." The chairman of the board paused to peer solemnly at the others, commanding their attention. "The Securities and Exchange Commission apparently has launched an investigation into Tony Gianni's trading in Taggart shares, in an effort to determine whether he manipulated stock to his own purpose and benefit!" The hushed silence was testimony to the stunned disbelief and shock felt by almost everyone in the room.

"Neither I nor any other member of this board had the slightest inkling that Mr. Gianni was engaging in Taggart stock transactions of any kind," Charlie Harkins continued, "until yesterday, when I was approached by the SEC—which is exactly what I told them. Max Starke and I had dinner together last night, and he showed me a copy of a computer printout from the SEC, which indicated that Tony sold off about three-quarters of his holdings—75,000 shares—at different times, but all between last November, when those rumors about a big license deal first started to hit the press, and mid-February, a week before the Knoblock collection was shown!"

Julia looked to Ross for some clue as to what he was thinking, but his face was bland, almost expressionless—no surprise, no disbelief, no anger, no nothing—and at last the missing answer suddenly fell into place for her with an almost audible clunk! He must have put two and two together weeks ago, the rumors plus the knockoff, and suspected a stock manipulation. *That* was why he'd bought into Taggart!

Ross had come to her rescue, she realized, just as literally and effectively as a white-hatted cowboy or a knight in shining armor, to protect her from the bad guys, the villains. If not Tony, then someone else. Someone who planned to sell high, then buy low and perhaps even increase their holdings enough to get control of the company. And if it turned out that was true, it also meant the same person was responsible for both the rumors *and* the theft of Ben's collection. Certainly not Ben. Or Max. Or Elaine. Who else but Tony? Claire? *Tony and Claire?*

"Now I'm not saying that proves Tony did anything wrong at all," Charlie Harkins continued. "We're going to leave that up to the SEC to decide. But I met with him earlier this morning, and he has volunteered his resignation as managing director. And I would like to entertain a motion from this board that we accept his very generous offer."

Julia's attention wandered as the board went through the formal motions of accepting Tony's resignation, because now she was considering another, completely different, idea.

"I can't imagine what this company would be like today if Julia Bonner hadn't been around right from the beginning," Charlie began then, bringing her attention back. "But one thing I sure as hell do know, and that's what my stock is worth today! I don't have to introduce Julia to you, but I'm going to anyway." He paused. "Gentlemen, may I present the butterfly of Seventh Avenue!" Again there was a little flurry of laughter, as everyone began to recover from the shock of learning about the SEC investigation.

Julia took her time, rising from her chair to move closer to the table at an almost leisurely pace, thinking all the while about what she was going to say.

"Your time is as precious as mine, so I'm going to speak right to the point, gentlemen. And the point is the future of this company. I hope you will take what I am going to say in the way I truly intend it—with real affection for this company and the people associated with it, who have become my dear friends over the past six years.

"Taggart has been good to me and for me. We made a good beginning, all of us working together, but now I believe it's time to move on. So I want to give you my very best thinking about where we should be going, and then leave the decision with you." She met Ross's eyes, looking for home base, reassuring herself one last time before she took the plunge.

"It's time to start contracting only with companies ready to go to CIM—computer-integrated-manufacturing systems. Or perhaps even to set up our own production company, fully equipped with the latest technology! I also think it's time to consider expanding the number of lines we produce, at both ends of the scale. Ben may want to experiment at the upper end, but let's not just make guesses, which is what you'll be doing if you continue to use demographics and past sales alone.

"I met two women when I was in Texas working on the computer program with Ross. Bonnie is a young wife and mother, who told me that her husband gives her $3500 a month to run the house. She tries to buy her clothes out of that, she says—about $2000 a month—but rarely manages it. Mary Alice also is a wife and mother, but she works full-time as the governor's speech writer. She spends around $3000 a year on her clothes—about like the typical reader of *Vogue*—and though she's concerned about how she looks, she has neither the time nor the inclination to spend hours and hours constantly informing herself about the very latest ins and outs. And I still believe that there are at least one hundred Mary Alices for every Bonnie out there, so that's where I'm putting my money.

"Elaine Mettlen, our very able director of publicity and public relations, happens to be one of the best market researchers in the business. And she's of the opinion that we might do well with a younger line. You already saw for yourselves, at Trump Tower, how I feel about the possibilities for extending the age range of our merchandise. What I'm suggesting, though, is that we use Elaine's very considerable talent to guide some of our explorations—and hire a new publicity director."

Julia stopped for a second, watching Charlie Harkins scratch a few words on the pad of paper in front of him, waiting for him to finish. "I also think it's time for us to decentralize, in both design and production. So I'd like to see you spin off a regional office and design center, fully computerized, where we could follow up on some of the regional-seasonal marketing ideas I've already put forward in connection with our new fall collection. And open up a pilot production plant, where we could test new equipment, new technology, aimed at further reducing the time and cost of production, perhaps improving quality at the same time." She looked around at their faces while she spoke, trying to gauge reactions, her eyes returning from time to time to Ross, and to Max.

"Taggart already has the best managing director to coordinate the entire operation, should you decide to do this—if you're lucky enough to get him to take the job. Max Starke not only knows the fashion business, but also a lot more than the rest of us about new technological developments—from the latest in computerized shipping systems, to what weaving looms are capable of doing, to what it takes to put together good quality clothes. And what he doesn't know he'll either find out or else get someone who does know, because his ego doesn't get all bent out of shape at the thought that he might not be superman—unlike so many of your fair sex, gentlemen." It just sort of slipped out, and Julia smiled quickly to soften the unintended ad-lib.

"I am proposing that you put me in charge of Taggart's new regional spinoff, and that you locate it in Austin, Texas, which is centrally located between the state's three biggest cities—Dallas, Houston and San Antonio. Austin also happens to be in the heart of a new and growing microelectronics research and manufacturing complex—so I can continue working on CAD-CAM programs for the fashion industry, with my husband!"

A low murmur began and then rose when Julia paused to give them all time to digest what she was saying. Charlie Harkins looked to be rallying his thoughts to respond, and out of the corner of her eye she could see Ross straightening in his chair. But she didn't dare look at him, because she wasn't quite finished yet.

"I realize that you haven't asked for my advice, and that you may feel I'm being presumptive. But I felt I owed it to you—to the company Ben and I started together, the company I've put most of my energy and my hopes into for the past six years—to give you my very best judgment, whatever you may deem that to be worth. Because I've come to a fork in the road, gentlemen, in both my personal life and my work.

"I'm going back to Texas, though I'll keep my apartment

and be here whenever I need or want to be in New York. But I'm going to do exactly what I've just described to you. All of it. It only remains for you to decide whether I do it with you—or without you." She smiled at Charlie, and then around the table at the other members of the board—and last, at Ben, who looked too shocked to marshal a response in kind.

"I'm telling you this not to pressure you, but just so you'll know what your competition will be doing, should you decide not to do what I suggest. The facts of life, as Tony Gianni would say. And in that case, because I hold this company and all of you in such high regard, I will promise not to raid Taggart—though I'd be mightily tempted—for one year. I'll be taking only one person with me when I go, no matter how I go—as director of Taggart's new regional branch, or on my own—my right hand, Consuelo Perez." She looked directly at Ben, one last time.

Charlie Harkins was rising from his chair, but before he could say a word, Julia sent a long look across the room, to Ross.

"Are you ready, McCutcheon?" she asked, almost seductively. "Shall we leave these gentlemen to their deliberations?"

Ross rose and walked straight toward Julia, a wide smile spreading across his face, his icy-blue eyes sparkling with shared mischief.

"Ready—McCutcheon," he murmured, taking her hand as they walked together toward the door.